Dangerous Passions

KAT MARTIN

St. Martin's Paperbacks

DANGEROUS PASSIONS

Copyright © 1998 by Kat Martin.

ISBN: 0-312-96247-9

Printed in the United States of America

St. Martin's Paperbacks edition/ February 1998

10 9 8 7 6 5 4 3 2 1

To the men who have fought in battle through the years and the brave women who have loved them. To peace and an end to war wherever it is waged.

Chapter One

"I have to do it, Mama. I have to do it for Karl—I have to do it for Peter." Slender, blond Elissa Tauber paced in front of the stone hearth in the family cottage on the outskirts of Tenabrook, a small rural village near St. Just.

Across the warm, modestly furnished parlor, her mother sat rocking in a ladder-back chair near the fire, her once-blond hair now graying at the temples, her narrow face lined with worry. Long, slender fingers gripped the nightgown she had been embroidering with small pink roses for her daughter's twenty-first birthday.

"We've been through this before, Elissa. You can't possibly travel to Europe—it's too dangerous. I've lost one child already. I could not bear to lose another." In her youth, Octavia Tauber, Countess von Langen, had been the image of her golden-haired, blue-eyed daughter. She had been an actress of some renown on the London stage, a beauty whose sensuous allure had a dozen men falling at her feet.

The handsome Count von Langen had been among them, and Octavia had fallen in love with him practically the instant she had seen him. Octavia ached just to think of him, so tall and blond and fair. Two years ago, her beloved Maximilian had died in a riding accident and without him she had withered and begun to age. The bright spark of life that had always burned inside her had flickered and died, the fiery, passionate nature so like that of her daughter.

"I'll be careful, Mama. I won't take any unnecessary chances. There is money left over in the trust fund Papa set aside for my schooling—I can use that. As soon as I have the slightest proof against the man who killed Karl, I shall go straight to the authorities."

Octavia fingered her stitchery. "Perhaps we should go to them now."

Elissa stopped pacing and turned. "You know we cannot. We have only the one single letter. Accusing a man of spying against his country is not a matter to be undertaken lightly. The very people whose help we seek might be the ones involved. We have to have more evidence. We have to find out who this man is."

The countess shook her head. "I won't take the risk. I cannot."

Elissa crossed to where her mother sat hunched over her embroidery, rocking faster now, tension making her hands shake where she rested them in her lap.

She knelt beside her mother's chair. "You would do it, Mama, if you could—I know you would. If your health were better, you would go. You wouldn't let the man who killed Karl get away with it. You would find him and see that he paid. You must let me go in your stead."

Her mother shook her head. "You're too young, Elissa, too inexperienced. You know little of the world and even less of men. You could not possibly—"

"I can do this, Mama. Think of the hours we used to spend pretending we were onstage. You taught me to act, to pretend I was a great and beautiful actress just like you. Remember the elaborate plays we put on for Papa? *Lord of Misrule* at Christmas, *A Midnight Summer's Dream,* the comedies and dramas Karl would make up?"

"That is hardly the same."

"You are right—this will be much easier. I shall pretend to be the Countess von Langen—a woman much like you when you were the toast of the stage."

"You are not old enough to be Maximilian's wife."

"I shall pretend to be the count's younger, *second* wife. I'll be a thousand miles from home—who is to know?" When her mother looked skeptical, Elissa rushed on. "Remember when I was a child? You used to laugh and say I could have been an even greater actress than you were. You said that, Mama. Do you remember?"

Her mother sighed. "I remember."

"Let me go to Vienna. Write to your friend the duchess. You can trust her, can you not?"

"Of course. Her husband was your father's best friend."

"Ask her to help us. Beg her to let me stay with her. Explain why this is so important. Tell her I'll travel as a widow just out of mourning, a woman eager to experience the glitter of Vienna. That will give me the freedom I need to mingle with the men we suspect." She clasped her mother's hand. "With the threat of war so near, it's imperative this man be stopped. If he is passing secrets to the French as Karl suspected, such a message could turn the tide of war and Peter's life could be forfeit. Karl saw how important this was—that is why he was murdered. The duchess will see it, too. Help me do this, Mama. Help me do this for Karl and to help keep Peter safe."

The countess chewed her lip. Things had changed so much these past few years. The grand lifestyle she had known, first as an actress then later as a young woman married to a handsome Austrian count, had slowly faded. It hadn't mattered that in the end her husband's money had dwindled to only a modest income. There was enough to educate their three precious children, buy the boys a military commission, and send Elissa to a fashionable finishing school.

Money had never been important, not when they were so happy. Then Maximilian had died, and the boys, fulfilling their father's dream, had enlisted in the Austrian Army. Now her handsome, warm, intelligent eldest son, Karl, was dead, and his younger brother, Peter, might be in danger.

"Help me, Mama," Elissa pleaded softly and Octavia sighed in defeat.

Perhaps her daughter was right. There were things you had to do in life, some of them painful. You had to live life to the fullest, to do your duty, even if it meant putting yourself in danger. Without Maximillian there to stop her, there was every chance her strong-willed daughter might attempt the journey on her own, which would prove far more dangerous. And, as Elissa had said, there was a time when Octavia would have done the same.

"Fetch the quill pen and ink," she said softly. "Then leave me in peace for a while. I must have time to think . . . if I am to write to the duchess."

Elissa started in surprise, then gave her a fierce, desperate hug. "Thank you, Mama." A smile brightened her face, the first real smile Octavia had seen since Karl had died. From the time she was a child, Elissa had worshiped her brother like the hero he had become.

"You won't be sorry, Mama. I know we are doing the right thing." Turning, Elissa dashed away, her slender feet flying up the stairs.

Setting her embroidery aside, Octavia stared into the low-burning flames. There were plans to make if their mission were to prove successful. Thinking of her beautiful, passionate, and headstrong daughter; of her son, barely cold in his grave; of the ominous letter that had been his last words, Octavia prayed that it would be.

Chapter Two

Plump milk-white breasts, an impossibly narrow waist, and lush, womanly hips. Colonel Adrian Kingsland, Baron Wolvermont, thought of the pleasures awaiting him in the villa below and smiled.

Dressed in his scarlet and white cavalry uniform, he had ridden this night with single-minded purpose—an evening of pleasant debauchery buried to the hilt between the pale, creamy thighs of Lady Cecily Kainz. Cecily was the wife of a wealthy viscount, much younger than her ancient, doddering husband, lusty in her appetites and ripe for the attentions he had lavished upon her since his arrival in the country.

Adrian reached the low rise above the resort town of Baden, nestled at the base of the Austrian hills half a day's ride from Vienna, and reined up his big black stallion. The horse danced a little beneath him, sensing they were somewhere near their destination. Looking down on the summer villas and manor houses surrounding the small, elegant city famous for its healing mineral baths, he could see the blue roofs of the huge Murau villa, Blauenhaus, not far away, though only a few solitary lamps remained lit within.

A quick scan of the second-story windows and he found the viscountess's bedchamber, third from the end in a line of more than fifty, saw that the lamp had already been doused.

He was late, he knew. Still, he had hoped that she would be waiting.

Adrian's mouth curved into a wicked half smile. Then again, perhaps awakening her ladyship might prove even more interesting.

He turned to the man who rode beside him, Major Jamison St. Giles, a friend since his childhood days at boarding school. "Well, my friend, I'm afraid this is where we part company, at least until the morrow."

A frown marred the major's lean forehead. "I don't like the look on your face, Adrian. Surely you don't mean to arrive at this hour—you'll wake up the whole damned household."

Adrian simply smiled. "This isn't an official arrival, Jamie. In fact I intend to be very quiet about it."

"Gad, I had forgotten that Cecily was here. I should have known you were up to something the way you were pressing so hard." He sighed. "I don't think this is a good idea. Why don't you come with me? We'll take rooms at that little inn on the square, get a good night's sleep, and arrive at a decent hour in the morning."

Adrian shook his head. "Not a chance, my friend. I've been thinking about this sweet little rendezvous all week. I don't intend to miss it just because our illustrious commanding officer, General Ravenscroft, happened to call one of his damnable meetings."

Jamison rose up in the stirrups of his worn leather saddle, stretching his long legs out full-length, trying to get comfortable after the tiring hours they had spent on the road. Several inches shorter than Adrian, with black hair and light blue eyes, he was built differently as well, lean and wiry, whereas the colonel was heavily muscled through the shoulders, hard and ruggedly honed from his years in the British cavalry.

They were different in temperment as well, Jamison easygoing and soft-spoken most of the time, while Adrian, a decorated war hero and extremely capable officer, could be hot-tempered, arrogant, and far too reckless at times. It was that reckless streak Jamison saw in him now.

"Need I remind you, Colonel Kingsland, you're here on diplomatic assignment? It would hardly improve Austro-British relations to be found with your breeches around your ankles, half-naked in some woman's bed."

Adrian laughed, a slightly rough-textured sound. "I'm afraid I'll have to chance it."

Jamison shifted wearily, the saddle creaking beneath him. "I realize you're my superior, Colonel, but I still think you should—"

"Relax, Major. I'll join you at the inn before dawn. Tomorrow we'll make our very respectable arrival, just as you wish."

Before Jamison could argue, Adrian nudged the stallion into a trot and rode off down the hill. At the rear of the villa, he reined up and swung down from the saddle, tying the animal beneath the branches of a secluded birch tree. Checking to be sure no one was near, he made his way through the formal gardens and crossed the wide brick terrace to a trellis covered with climbing roses that led up to the second-floor balcony.

Testing the strength of his makeshift ladder, satisfied it would hold his not-inconsequential frame, he scaled the distance easily and swung a booted foot over the wrought-iron railing. No lamps were lit. No sounds came from within. He paused outside the French doors leading into the viscountess's bedchamber and even in the darkness he could make out the gleam of her shiny blond hair, the outline of her body in the big four-poster bed.

The door to the terrace was unlocked as he had hoped it would be. He turned the knob and eased it open on silent hinges. Cecily lay curled on her stomach, her face pressed into a deep feather pillow, her lovely features covered by her sleep-tumbled hair.

She was naked, he saw, the sheet pushed down to just above the curve of her bottom. His body stirred. The arousal that had started to build the moment he entered the bedchamber began to strengthen. Soundlessly, he crossed the thick Oriental carpet and sat down on the edge of the bed. Only a sliver of moon lit the night, but a thin ray slanted across the bed, illuminating the pale skin of a long, slender neck.

His blood pumped faster, grew hotter. Adrian bent forward and pressed a soft kiss at her nape and caught the slight fragrance of lavender. He kissed the smooth white skin across her shoulders, and she shifted a little on the bed. His arousal throbbed, crowding hard against the front of his breeches.

He wanted to turn her onto her back, to fondle her lovely breasts and slide himself into her welcoming body. Instead he trailed kisses down the tiny ridges that marked her spine and was rewarded with a sweetly feminine whimper. He slid the sheet down a little farther, kissed the dimple just above the swell of her left buttock, then moved toward the lovely heart-shaped mole marking the spot just above the dimple on the opposite side.

Adrian froze.

He knew Cecily Kainz with the intimate knowledge of the lover he had been these past few weeks. He knew with certainty she bore no such mole.

Bloody hell!

Feeling the woman stir and begin to turn over on the deep feather mattress, he moved quickly, grabbing the sheet with one hand and jerking it over her body at the same time he clamped his palm over her mouth and pinned her against his chest.

"Don't be frightened," he said softly in German, a tongue he was fluent in, since his mother was of Austrian descent, the reason for his current assignment. "I'm not going to hurt you. I thought you were somebody else."

He could feel her trembling, see the fear in her pretty blue eyes as she clawed at his hand. He tightened his hold, stilling her movements, careful not to hurt her.

"Listen to me. I thought you were somebody else—do you understand? I'm not going to hurt you." When she continued to pry at his fingers, he shook her gently. "I said I won't hurt you. I'll let you go if you promise not to scream."

She calmed a little, for the first time appeared to comprehend. She made a faint nod of her head and he eased away his hand.

"I'm sorry. I didn't mean to invade your privacy. As I said, I thought you were somebody else." His gaze ran over her face, the arch of her throat where a pulse beat frantically, and it occurred to him that he wasn't the least bit sorry. The woman, a girl not more than twenty, was even more beautiful than Cecily. Her features were finer, her face heart-shaped instead of round, with a slight indentation in the chin. Her golden hair wasn't long, as he had mistakenly believed, but cropped fashionably short and curling softly around a face that could have belonged to an angel.

"Who are you?" she whispered.

Adrian smiled faintly. "Merely the friend of a friend." He eased himself away from her with no small amount of regret and began to back toward the door. "My apologies for the inconvenience, angel. I promise to make it up to you the next time we meet. I have a feeling that may be very soon."

Her cheeks bloomed with bright, warm color, embarrassment finally overriding her fear. Her head went up, but her hand trembled where she clutched the sheet beneath her chin. "In that, sir, I sorely hope you are mistaken."

He flashed a roguish grin. "Perhaps. I suppose we shall have to wait and see." He touched his forehead in silent farewell, thinking there was no doubt they would meet again. He intended to make a point of it. "Sleep well, sweet angel."

Adrian opened the door and stepped out onto the terrace. The night was cool, the sky dark with just a scattering of stars. Making his way to the trellis, he swung a long leg over the railing and climbed down, thinking of the girl, his body still hard with desire for her. He reached the bottom without mishap, cursing only once when a rose thorn bit into his hand. It was a small price to pay, he thought wryly, for the treasure he had glimpsed this eve—and the prize he meant to win.

Lady Elissa Tauber sank back against the fat down pillows on her bed, still clutching the sheet to her chin. Good sweet

God, she had never been so embarrassed! Her mother had warned her at least a dozen times not to sleep without her nightrail, but she had never listened. She'd always slept too warm, and during the night often discarded the uncomfortable cotton gown her mother insisted she wear.

She was a grown woman now. She could sleep without clothes if she wished—it was no one's business but her own. Or at least so she had believed.

Elissa groaned into the pillow, thinking of the handsome, powerfully built, dark-haired cavalry officer who had stolen into her bedchamber. She didn't doubt his reason for being there—not after she was awake enough for his explanation to make sense. She had only arrived at the villa two days ago, traveling as the Countess von Langen with Her Grace, the Duchess of Murau. The emperor, who had been feeling poorly, had decided to take the waters for his health. His entourage had come with him, Elissa and the duchess along in their wake.

Until yesterday the bedchamber had been occupied by Lady Cecily Kainz, a frequent visitor to the villa, a sensuous bit of fluff with an eye for every man she met. After what had just occurred, it was clear the viscountess was having an affair with the handsome man in the scarlet uniform. It was equally apparent he hadn't known Cecily had departed—albeit grudgingly—to return to her aging husband.

The viscountess was gone, but at the duchess's insistence, Elissa had taken her room overlooking the garden, one of the loveliest in the villa. After attending a musicale in the Ruby Salon, she had fallen quickly asleep and eventually started dreaming.

Dreams of a man's warm mouth on her skin, of his tongue teasing the nape of her neck, of his big hands skimming over her body. She'd felt flushed and overly warm, her skin tingling all over. She'd been glad she had shed her nightrail— and then she had opened her eyes.

Elissa muttered an oath, tossing her head back and forth on the pillow, slamming her fist against the sheets. Dear Lord, she still felt mortified.

She glanced toward the French doors, wondering if indeed, as he predicted, she would be unfortunate enough to encounter the rogue again. Who was he? she wondered. An Englishman, judging by his uniform, though he spoke German with only the slightest trace of an accent.

And sweet God, he was handsome—with bright green eyes, a strong, hard jaw, and a full, sensuous mouth that curved with a hint of wicked promise. When he smiled, he even had dimples. No wonder Lady Cecily had welcomed him into her bed!

Elissa closed her eyes, trying to block the tall man's image, trying to fall asleep. Tomorrow was another important day and she didn't have time for distractions. Though the duchess had been unflagging in her support, there was only so much time and that time was running out.

An image of her brother arose, young and so very handsome. Captain Karl Tauber—less than six months cold in his grave. She thought of the letter she and her mother had received just before Karl had been killed.

Our army is steadily mounting. We are well trained and ready to face the French, but an accident of fate has led me to believe there is a traitor among us. It is imperative I discover his identity though I know this may mean danger. I do not wish you to worry, yet should something happen to me, I implore you not to let this matter end. You must find a way to finish the task I have started. Thousands of lives are at stake. It is imperative this man be stopped at any cost.

Karl had gone on to say the spy was a man who called himself the Falcon. He also believed he could be only one of three men: a general named Franz Steigler; the British ambassador, Sir William Pettigru; or a major named Josef Becker who was serving as aide-de-camp to General Manfred Klammer.

Two months after the letter arrived, Karl was dead.

No other word had come from him. No other evidence against the men was forthcoming.

Elissa vowed again, as she had before, that she would see her brother's death avenged and do whatever it took to insure her younger brother, Peter, would not be a needless casualty of war.

Standing in front of the cheval glass mirror in her bedchamber, Elissa surveyed her carefully groomed and coifed appearance. There was a reception today at Blauenhaus for the diplomats and heads of state who had traveled to Baden with the emperor. It was imperative she play the role she had come for, the role of the Countess von Langen, widow of a little-known but once-wealthy Austrian count. The part she had been playing since her arrival in Vienna.

Elissa smoothed the narrow skirt of her ivory silk gown, the bodice far lower than the dresses she had worn back home. The gown had belonged to her best friend, Gabriella Warrington, daughter of the Duke of Melbourne. They had met in finishing school, and though Gaby was raised in a ducal palace outside London and Elissa brought up in a modest Cornwall cottage, they had become fast friends.

It was Gaby who had helped aid her mission to Vienna, insisting she take the gowns, which were old, she claimed, and would soon have been replaced, having them altered to fit Elissa's more slender figure. Gaby—along with the grudging but vital assistance of her mother.

"Is there anything else, milady?" Her maid, Sophie Hopkins, a slight, dark-haired girl several years younger than Elissa, stood just a few feet away. Elissa had hired her in London to accompany her to Vienna.

"I don't think so, Sophie. Just hand me my reticule and I shall be on my way."

The girl handed over a matching ivory bag fringed with the same gold-shot tulle that trimmed her magnificent gown. "You look beautiful, milady."

"Thank you." She hoped she did. It was imperative she look the part of a sophisticated lady, a role she was hardly familiar with. She wouldn't have had a chance for success if it hadn't been for her mother. Once she had agreed to Elissa's plan, Octavia had roused herself and tutored her daughter in the role she meant to play, knowing each day, as Napoleon came closer to war with Austria, their mission became more urgent.

"Oh dear, I nearly forgot—" Sophie's hand flew up in one of her highly animated gestures. The girl couldn't seem to speak unless her hands were darting through the air. "Ambassador Pettigru sent a footman to tell you he'd be waiting in the Ruby Salon to escort you into the reception."

Elissa simply nodded. Pettigru was waiting. Her plan had been set into motion. She straightened her shoulders and walked out the door.

The extravagant Petit Salon at Blauenhaus—which wasn't petite at all, Adrian Kingsland thought—sparkled like the magnificent gem it was. Beneath lavish rococo ceilings painted with cloud-filled skies and cherubic angels, crystal chandeliers spun a web of golden light over Austria's social elite. Wealthy aristocrats mingled with the commanders of powerful armies, as well as diplomats and heads of state.

Adrian's regiment had arrived in the country over a month ago, there to act in support of English ministers, ambassadors, and delegates who continued to descend on Austria in the hope of forging an Allied Coalition—the fifth such endeavor since the start of the Napoleonic War.

Serving under General Artemis Ravenscroft, Adrian was there as a diplomatic liaison temporarily assigned to the 3rd Dragoons. Sipping a glass of champagne, he surveyed the elegantly dressed ladies in the glittering salon, searching every face for the one he had encountered, rather fortuitously, late last evening.

So far he had not seen her.

"Perhaps the lady has heard of your arrival and decided to take her leave." Jamie St. Giles took a casual sip of champagne. "If your intentions are as transparent as the look on your face, 'twould certainly be her wisest course."

Adrian merely grunted. He had known Jamison St. Giles since the day he had first entered boarding school. Adrian had never forgotten that day, or the loneliness he had felt as a five-year-old boy miles from home. Jamie, another lost soul, had been his salvation, a friend when he needed one most. It had been that way ever since.

The major chuckled softly. "Making love to the wrong woman—I only wish I could have been there."

Unfortunately, Jamie had still been awake when Adrian had arrived last night at the inn—some hours earlier than expected. He had finally pried loose the story of the wrong woman in the right bed, and now his mouth twitched in amusement every time Adrian's searching gaze happened to pass in his direction.

"I mean to have her," Adrian said simply. "Even if she were to run, I would find her. I would search the whole of Europe if I had to."

"That good, is she?"

"Better," Adrian said.

"What if she is married?"

He arched a dark brow. "Yes, well, that would certainly make matters simpler in the final course . . . as long as the husband wasn't around."

Jamie shook his head but said nothing more, and Adrian started his search of the room again. Around them something shifted in the air and a murmur passed through the crowd. A hundred pairs of eyes swung toward the magnificent couple walking through the tall gilded doors. Standing a few feet from Adrian, Robert Blackwood, one of the British diplomats, leaned close to speak in his ear.

"Incredible, isn't she? Half of Vienna is in love with her, though she doesn't appear to notice. Unfortunately, Pettigru is one of the few men she seems to have time for, more's the pity."

Adrian's gaze shifted, fastened on the slender blond woman gowned in ivory silk and gold-shot tulle who had just walked into the salon. Clinging to the arm of Ambassador Pettigru, who was uniformed in white with a gold sash and huge gold epaulettes, she gazed into the man's ruddy face with rapt attention, smiling with undeniable warmth.

"Let me guess," Jamie whispered, his eyes locked on the woman, "you have finally spotted your quarry." He grinned. "The way she is staring at Pettigru, I would say you have taken on quite a task."

Adrian scowled. "Pettigru is old enough to be her father."

"He is handsome in his way," Jamie countered. "He is also rich as Croesus and one of the most powerful men in England."

His friend was right on both counts—the ambassador was an attractive older man in a number of ways and there was no mistaking the woman's interest.

He turned to Robert Blackwood. "Who is she?"

"Believe it or not, she's one of our own."

"British?"

He nodded. "British and Austrian, I gather. Her husband was a count named von Langen, an Austrian nobleman who died several years ago. No one seems to know much about him or his apparently much younger wife. They spent most of their time in the remote Cornwall country. But apparently Lady von Langen is a friend of the duchess's. 'Twas she who invited the countess to Vienna."

Adrian sipped his champagne, watching the lady over the rim of his glass. Gowned as she was and wearing a hint of rouge, her hair tamed into soft waves instead of a riot of tousled curls, she looked older than he had first guessed, but no less desirable.

"Not the best time she could have chosen, with Napoleon on the march and war a possibility any day."

Blackwood scoffed. "Since when does a woman worry about such matters? I'm sure the countess's main concerns are attending the opera, listening to Beethoven, and deciding which gown she will wear."

Perhaps, Adrian thought, watching the woman flash an elegant, seductive smile, a look somehow incongruous with the charming naïveté he had sensed in her last night.

Then again, all women were creatures of deception. And whatever her reasons for the interest she showed in Pettigru, he didn't really care. The only thing he wanted from the luscious little blonde was a tumble in his bed.

He cast a smile at Blackwood. "I gather you know the lady fairly well. Perhaps you would be kind enough to introduce us."

The diplomat's eyes swung to the woman and her escort. "Of course, Colonel Kingsland. It would be my pleasure."

Setting his empty crystal glass on a passing servant's silver tray, Adrian followed Robert Blackwood across the inlaid parquet floor. After their encounter last night, the lady might not be eager to see him, but he was certainly eager to see her.

There was nothing he enjoyed more than a challenge. Especially if that challenge came in the guise of a beautiful woman.

Elissa smiled into the ruddy, slightly puffy countenance of Sir William Pettigru, a man in his early fifties, and listened as he droned on about the diplomatic affairs he had attended earlier in the day. On the surface, she couldn't imagine the kindly, gray-haired gentleman being a spy for the French, yet as the daughter of an actress, she knew exactly the deceptions a person could accomplish if he set his mind to the task.

It took the same expertise she was using to present herself as a sophisticated, worldly woman—pretending, her mother had called it when she was a little girl. In truth, at one and twenty, Elissa knew little of men, had certainly never been to bed with one. And yet she must *pretend* to be the kind of woman who might be interested in taking a lover, or at least having a brief affair. Only by immersing herself in the role the way her mother had taught her could she be believable in the part.

Believable as she had to be now.

Gazing at the silver-haired man from beneath her lashes, she fluttered her painted fan and laughed at one of his slightly naughty jokes, the same one he had told her at least three times before.

"La, Sir William, for shame . . . telling a lady such a story."

He chuckled, then frowned, pulling his bushy white eyebrows together. "I hope I didn't offend you, my dear."

She folded her fan and tapped him playfully on the shoulder. "Don't be silly. You know very well, Sir William, I find you a most amusing man."

"And you, my lady, are the most charming woman in Austria."

She laughed, a sparkling sound made more so by raising her voice an octave higher. "Thank you, kind sir."

The ambassador droned on, then laughed at another of his silly jokes. Elissa joined in, though for a moment she had lost track of what he had been saying. Footfalls interrupted his next sentence. She turned at the sound of Robert Blackwood's familiar voice.

"Excuse me, Sir William." Blackwood, a diplomat and one of the duchess's numerous houseguests, stood next to a tall man dressed in the scarlet and white of a British cavalry officer. Elissa nearly swooned when she glanced up at the man's handsome face.

"Colonel Kingsland arrived just today," Blackwood was saying to Pettigru. "I knew you would be eager to meet him." He smiled. "And I thought he might enjoy meeting a lady from home." Blackwood made a slight inclination of his head toward the colonel. "Ambassador Sir William Pettigru. Countess von Langen. May I present Colonel Kingsland, Baron Wolvermont, recently of the Third Dragoons."

She felt his glittering green gaze even before she lifted her eyes to his face. Sweet God, he was here—just as he had said. Her cheeks went pale, then suffused with warm color. She took a steadying breath, determined to force her embarrassment down.

Pettigru was speaking. "A pleasure, my lord," he said.

"Sir William," said the colonel. She caught the faint click of his boot heels as he reached for her white-gloved hand. "Lady von Langen." He bent forward with casual grace, pressed her fingers against his lips. She could feel the heat of his mouth through the white cotton fabric, and a curl of warmth slid into her stomach.

"My . . . my lord Colonel." It took every ounce of her will, every trick of acting her mother had taught her, to smile into that devastatingly handsome face when she wanted to turn and run. He held her hand several moments longer than he should have. She hoped he couldn't feel the fine tremors racing up her arm.

"It's a pleasure to meet you, my lady, though I'm surprised we haven't met somewhere before." A faint smile curved those sensuous lips. "In London, I mean. Surely you were there with your husband on occasion."

She gave him a brittle little smile. "My husband, I fear, wasn't much inclined toward Society."

"A pity, my lady." Those bold eyes raked her, taking in every curve. "A beautiful woman should never be kept hidden in the country."

Heat filtered through her. A fluttery feeling rose in her chest. Dear God, what was the matter with her? Unconsciously she straightened. The man was presumptuous and too bold by half, yet a few simple words, spoken in that incredibly male, slightly rough-textured voice, and she felt as if her legs were turning to butter.

"There is nothing wrong with the country," she said a bit tartly. "There are times I quite prefer it."

The colonel eyed her with interest, and it occurred to her she shouldn't have made the remark. She was supposed to be a worldly woman bent on self-indulgence, grateful to escape her previously boring existence, not some shy little church mouse better satisfied in the country.

"Since you fancy the out of doors, my lady," he said, "perhaps you would enjoy a carriage ride on the morrow. I am new to Baden. Perhaps you could show me around."

Oh, dear God. She felt those fierce green eyes on her as if they could see right through her sophisticated façade.

"I—I don't think so. I—I mean . . ." She lifted her chin, forcing herself back into her role. "What I meant to say, Colonel Kingsland, is that I'm afraid I've already made plans for the morrow. Perhaps some other time." She flashed a sultry smile and lowered her lashes, a look of invitation that contrasted with the sharpness of her words.

The colonel looked simply amused. "As you say, my lady, perhaps another time." He spoke to the ambassador a few moments more then made his farewells. He left her with a final mocking smile and a slight inclination of his head. Turning, he walked off toward a black-haired officer wearing the same regimental scarlet the colonel wore.

"An interesting man," Sir William said, his gaze still following Wolvermont's broad shoulders as he made his way with casual grace across the drawing room. "He's a war hero, you know. Fought in the Netherlands and Egypt, wounded in India. They say he's quite fearless in battle. His mother was Austrian, so he speaks the language like a native. His record, combined with his title and considerable fortune, made him the perfect candidate to act as liaison between the diplomatic corps and the military here in Austria."

"How long has he been here?" Elissa sipped her champagne, thinking Colonel Kingsland would also be in the perfect position to know a number of valuable diplomatic and military secrets.

"He's been in the country a little over a month, but until tonight I had not yet met him."

Only a month. Not long enough to be the Falcon. Still, a successful spy had to have help. Surely the handsome colonel wasn't involved but there was no way to be certain. Except for her mother, her friend Gabriella, and the Duchess of Murau, no one knew who she really was or why she was there. Elissa trusted no one and she intended to keep it that way.

Chapter Three

Elissa did indeed go for a carriage ride the following day but not with the handsome Colonel Kingsland. Instead she rode in General Steigler's fine black calèche, taking in the sights of Baden and stopping at a quiet inn for luncheon.

The general sat across from her at a table in the corner. "You didn't enjoy the food?" Steigler asked. "Perhaps you would care for something different." He was a tall, spare man, his features harsh, his thin nose sharply pointed. High cheekbones formed steep hills in his face and his slightly sunken eyes were so dark they often looked black. He raised a long-boned hand toward a tavern maid, but Elissa caught his arm.

"No, please. The food was delicious. I'm afraid I wasn't very hungry." She turned on a charming smile, determined to move toward the goal she had set for herself: winning Steigler's confidence. It was difficult. She didn't like Franz Steigler. His touch was too intimate, his eyes too coldly piercing.

Still, if ever there was a man who looked as if he might be the Falcon, Steigler was it.

"You seem tired, my dear. Perhaps we should return to the villa . . . or if you prefer, the tavern owner, Herr Weinberg, is a friend of mine. I am sure he could arrange a place for you to rest . . . upstairs."

It was the first time he had made so obvious an overture.
He wanted to bed her—a notion she found repulsive. But
even should it come to that, a single night with Steigler would
hardly serve her purpose. She needed to win his confidence,
needed time to get to know him without giving in to his
physical demands, to avoid him without putting him off entirely.

She had to discover if he was the Falcon, but uncovering
the truth about a man like Steigler was no easy task.

"I feel quite well, General Steigler. Perhaps we could simply sit here and talk for a while."

"Talk? My dear, what about?" The remark made it sound
as if it were impossible for a woman to have anything of
interest to say.

"Perhaps, as a famous general and a highly trained military
commander, you might allay some of my fears. Staying at
Blauenhaus, one hears the most frightening stories." She
glanced away, hoping she looked somewhat distressed.

"What kind of stories, my dear?"

She glanced around to be certain that no one was near,
then leaned closer. "Just yesterday I heard that Archduke
Charles is increasing the size of his army. They say he intends
to march on Napoleon, that war might break out any day. I
had hoped . . . believed that Austria was through fighting the
French. Surely it is in our best interests to retain our friendship with General Bonaparte. After all, he has beaten us four
times already. The cost in lives seems far too high a price to
pay."

The general chuckled softly. His callused palm reached out
to cover her hand. She stifled an urge to pull her fingers away.

"My dear Countess. A lady shouldn't bother herself with
such matters. It is up to men such as I to make those decisions, to protect our women . . . and of course our country."

"But what do *you* think, General? The British, of course,
want our support, but the French—"

"I have heard that you are part English. I should think you
would be in favor of a British alliance."

"I'm in favor of what is best for Austria. My husband was

Austrian," she said. "My mother had Austrian blood as well. My heart has always lived here, General Steigler. I am grateful to be returned home."

They talked for a little while longer, but the general said nothing that would give her the least indication that he was not loyal to his emperor and the Austrian cause. All the while his eyes kept straying from the swell of her breast to the stairs leading up to the bedchambers above the inn.

"I believe you were right, General Steigler," she finally said. "I am a bit tired. The evening ahead appears to be a long one. I think it would be best to go home."

Steigler frowned but rose from his chair. "As you wish, my lady."

He returned her to Blauenhaus, though he was quartered himself at the emperor's villa, and together they climbed the front steps to the marble-floored entry. Unfortunately, as she walked in, she collided with the tall man striding out. Elissa gasped and stumbled backward, clutching a pair of wide shoulders to keep herself from falling. Big hands clamped around her waist to steady her. She could feel their solid strength and the warmth of his fingers through her gown.

"C-Colonel Kingsland—"

"Beg pardon, my lady." He flashed her a look of amusement, but made no move to back away. Standing as she was, her breasts brushed the buttons of his uniform jacket, and his eyes strayed downward, lingered several moments on the bare expanse of flesh before returning to her face. His mouth curved faintly and her heart did a mad little dance inside her chest.

Finally he moved backward, the greatcoat over his shoulders swirling around his boots. For the first time he glanced at the lean, dark-complexioned man who accompanied her, and stiffened, his eyes growing suddenly dark.

"General Steigler." He straightened even more, his bearing perfectly correct, but she could have sworn there was a tension running through him that hadn't been there before. "It's been quite some years since our last meeting. I trust you are well."

Steigler nodded. "I didn't realize you were here at Blauenhaus, Colonel. Though I had heard you were back in the
country."

"If all goes well, only briefly. Just until the negotiations
are ended."

"I presume you have met Lady von Langen."

He smiled with a hint of amusement. "I've been fortunate
to have had the pleasure . . . on several different occasions."

Elissa felt the warmth creeping into her cheeks. The general frowned at the colonel's words and his hand settled pos-
sessively at her waist.

"You'll have to excuse us, Colonel. Lady von Langen is
feeling a bit tired. I thought perhaps a cup of tea—"

"I appreciate your concern, General," Elissa interrupted,
breaking away. "But I believe I should rather lie down. As
you said, I am a bit tired. Thank you for a pleasant afternoon." She graced the colonel with a slightly brittle smile.
"If you gentlemen will excuse me . . ."

The general bowed extravagantly, while the colonel made
a curt nod of his head. She escaped to her room, and as soon
as the door was closed, collapsed against it. Her heart was
still pounding and she felt overly warm. Her fingertips still
tingled from the rough feel of the colonel's woolen greatcoat.

Thoughts crowded in, images of the night she had awakened to the hot, shivery sensation of the colonel's mouth
pressing kisses against her skin, of his big hands skimming
over her body. Sweet God, why couldn't she stop thinking
about it?

Elissa took a steadying breath and pushed away from the
door. She had just started toward the bellpull to signal for
her maid when a slight knock sounded and Sophie walked
in.

"Excuse me, milady, but the footman just delivered a message. It's from that handsome Colonel Kingsland. He said I
was to bring it to you straightaway."

Wolvermont. Would the man never leave her in peace?
Elissa accepted the note with a hand that was slightly un-

steady. "Thank you." She opened the missive and quickly scanned the words.

Colonel Kingsland, Baron Wolvermont, requests the pleasure of your company at supper. Tonight or any other night. Please say yes, my lady.

A small, warm shiver slid through her. He wanted to see her. It was insane, completely out of the question. The man had a dangerous effect on her. She couldn't think when she was around him. She couldn't talk, she could scarcely breathe. The part of coquette she played flew right out the window the moment the colonel stepped into the room.

But dear, sweet God, in truth, a tiny reckless part of her wanted to see him. She had tried to tell herself she didn't find him the least bit attractive. He was arrogant and far too bold. One look at that wickedly handsome face and she knew the sort of man he was.

It didn't seem to matter. No amount of self-persuasion could dim her growing attraction to him. The encounter in the hallway had clearly proven that.

She glanced once more at the note. They were dining informally for the next few days, a lavish buffet that allowed the duchess's many houseguests to come and go at their leisure. Tonight she had agreed to sup with Sir William, but tomorrow night . . .

Elissa shook her head. Dear God, what was she thinking? She couldn't possibly spend an evening with the colonel. The man unnerved her completely—it was simply too risky.

Elissa read the note one last time, then sighed and crumpled the paper in her hand. "Tell Colonel Kingsland I appreciate his kind invitation, but I'm afraid I already have plans." She didn't look at Sophie, just crossed the bedchamber and sat down on the tapestry stool in front of the mirror on her gilded dresser.

"He asked to see you and you refused?" Sophie's voice held a note of amazement.

"I told you, I'm busy."

The little maid rolled her eyes. "But milady, he is so handsome. They say he is rich and he is a baron. Why do you not—"

"Just tell him, Sophie. I don't have the energy to argue."

The fragile girl straightened, disappointment clear on her face. "As you wish, my lady."

Elissa almost smiled. Traveling as far as they had, she and Sophie had become friends of a sort. It was difficult to play the role of countess all the time, and she was able to shed a bit of her façade around Sophie, a least part of the time.

The door closed softly and Elissa sighed into the silence of the bedchamber, thinking of the handsome colonel with a mixture of regret and relief. She'd only had a couple of suitors, local boys she thought of merely as friends, none her father had approved. He wanted a wealthy aristocrat for his only daughter, but without a suitable dowry, the odds were never good.

Then her father had died, and living with her mother in the country, she had put off the question of marriage. She didn't want to marry a man she didn't love, and the chance of finding someone she did seemed slimmer every year.

Elissa ran her fingers through her hair, dislodging the sophisticated waves, allowing the fine gold strands to fall into the usual riot of curls around her face. Since her arrival in Vienna, her life had certainly changed. She'd been lavished with male attention, but until now none of the men had affected her in the least.

Part of her resented the hold Adrian Kingsland seemed to have over her, the other part was more than a little intrigued. Though complications were the last thing she needed, it was difficult not to want to explore the strange feelings he stirred, to discover where her attraction to him might lead.

Elissa stared at her reflection in the mirror, at the elegant, sophisticated woman who was nothing at all like the naïve young girl who had traveled here from England. The woman in the mirror was fearless and determined. She was there to discover the man who had murdered her brother, to bring the traitor to justice and protect the brother who still lived.

Elissa had left her rural cottage and crossed a continent to put her plan into motion. And nothing—not even a too-bold cavalry officer with a sensuous mouth and glittering green eyes—was going to get in her way.

How an evening in a villa as lavish as the one belonging to the Duchess of Murau could be boring, Elissa couldn't imagine. Yet in the company of the slightly tipsy Sir William, it was.

Since the time she was a child, she had listened to her father's stories of the extravagant life he had lived in Austria before his family's fortune ran low. Excitement filled his voice as he spoke of the fabulous gilded palaces and exquisite balls, the ladies and gentlemen of the Austrian aristocracy. There were times she had yearned for the glittering wealth he had described, for the glamour and the beauty and the gowns.

Now that she found herself in the middle of such lavish surroundings, there were times she yearned for the quiet life back home.

Elissa sighed into the darkness outside the villa, grateful for the brief respite from Sir William, who had joined the gentlemen for a game of cards. Ignoring the faint sound of laughter coming from inside, she wandered farther into the garden.

It was quiet out here, the moon beginning to slip out from behind the clouds, casting a silver glow on the intricate pathways between the blooming roses. A breeze filled the air, cool but not overly cold.

"Good evening, my lady."

She turned at the sound of the voice, her pulse speeding ahead, recognizing the deeply masculine cadence though she desperately wished she did not.

"Good evening, Colonel Kingsland."

He glanced at the thin shawl draped around her shoulders. "The others remain indoors this night. You are not cold?"

"No, I find the evening quite pleasant. I tend to be overly warm at times, I—" She broke off as the memory of lying naked beneath the colonel's warm hands and hot, searching mouth burst full force into her mind. In the glow of the torches lighting the garden paths, she saw his lips curve faintly, as if he were remembering, too.

" 'Tis an asset, I should think, being so warm-natured. A sign of great passion, perhaps."

He was doing it to her again—shaking her composure, making her feel as if the world had begun to tilt. "I—I don't believe the two are connected." But perhaps they were. She certainly felt hot and flushed now that the colonel had arrived.

"Based on our previous encounter, I'm afraid, my lady, I would have to disagree."

Embarrassment shot through her. Had he heard those soft moans she was making in her dream when he kissed her? Sweet God, she prayed that he had not. Her spine went a little bit straighter.

"If you persist, my lord, in bringing up your previous, sordid behavior every time we chance to meet, I shall be happy to announce your abominable conduct to Sir William and your superiors."

A large, darkly tanned finger skimmed down along her cheek. "I do not think you should do that, my lady. Your reputation would suffer along with mine. However, if it bothers you to speak of it, I shall not mention it again."

He smiled roguishly. "Which is not to say I shall forget how beautiful you looked that night . . . or how soft your skin felt beneath my mouth when I kissed you."

Her cheeks flushed crimson. "You are a devil, my lord."

"And you, my lady, are truly exquisite."

The ground seemed to tilt again. "I—I must be going in." She started past him, but he caught her arm.

"Say you will dine with me tomorrow eve."

"I cannot possibly."

"Why not? You've spent time with Ambassador Pettigru. You've luncheoned with General Steigler. Surely there is room in your schedule to share a little time with me."

She only shook her head. "I cannot." She turned to leave, but once again he stopped her.

"I promise I shall be on my best behavior. I won't even touch you, if that is what you are afraid of."

Her head came up. Her eyes swung to his face. "I am not afraid of you, Colonel."

"Are you not?"

"No."

"Then perhaps, Lady von Langen, you are afraid of yourself." Before she could argue, he caught her chin between his fingers, bent his head and captured her lips. It was a soft kiss, merely the brush of his mouth over hers, yet heat shimmered through her. She started to pull away, but the colonel deepened the kiss, fitting their lips perfectly together, tasting her gently. He eased her into his arms and she found herself pressed full length against his long, hard body, his big frame nearly a full head taller.

Through a haze of warm sensations, reason fought to surface. Elissa tried to pull free, but he held her fast, his tongue teasing the corners of her mouth, his kiss oddly gentle and incredibly persuasive. Her body began to tremble and the hands that pressed against his chest slid up around his neck. The colonel deepened the kiss, his warm mouth persistent, softening her trembling lips until she opened for him and his tongue swept deeply inside.

It was wildly sweet and incredibly erotic, but so unexpected Elissa jerked away, stumbling in her haste to be free of him, saved only by the arm he reached out to steady her.

She glanced up to find him staring down at her, a dark frown marring his face.

"I vow you are a mystery, Countess. One would think you had never been kissed."

Alarm raced through her. Sweet God, she didn't dare let him guess the truth! Her shoulders straightened. She forced her chin into the air. "You forget, Colonel Kingsland, I was married for several years."

"Yes . . . A much older man, I am told. Perhaps that is the reason."

She thought of her parents, the true count and countess, and how much in love they had been. "If you are insinuating

Count von Langen was anything other than a virile, passionate man, you are mistaken, my lord. Now, if you will excuse me—''

Once more he blocked her way, a wall of strength fairly seething with male determination. "Say you will see me. Say it and I will let you go."

Elissa's brow arched up. "I could lie to you, Colonel, merely agree to your terms so that you would let me pass."

Wolvermont studied her face, saw the flush of warmth that still stained her cheeks, the obvious attraction she fought to hide. "You could. But if you agreed, I believe you would enjoy yourself. Join me for supper tomorrow eve. Say yes, my lady, I beg you."

She had to say no—she could not possibly agree to see him. It was easy to play the coquette with the others but the colonel unnerved her completely. If he got suspicious, if he somehow uncovered the truth, the game would be ended. There was too much at risk, too many people depending upon her—Karl, Peter, the gallant soldiers soon to go off to war, perhaps the fate of Austria, mayhap even England.

But as she stared into the green of his eyes, a soft yes trembled on her lips. Elissa dragged in a steadying breath and fought the impulse down.

"I'm sorry, Colonel Kingsland. I'm afraid I must refuse. Now if you would be so kind as to let me pass . . ."

He studied her a long moment more, then made a slight inclination of his head and stepped out of her way. "As you wish, my lady."

"Good night, my lord Colonel."

"Sleep well, my lady."

She searched for a hint of mockery in his face but this time found none. As she made her way back to the house, she could feel his fierce green gaze burning into her all the way.

Her Grace, Marie Reichter, Duchess of Murau, a small, robust gray-blond woman in her fifties, sat before the garden window in her private suite of rooms in the west wing of the villa. Furnished in royal blue and gold, with heavy velvet tapestries and carved rosewood furniture, the suite boasted a lovely private terrace and a beautiful marble bathing room. A small fire burned in the marble-manteled hearth, for the day had turned blustery and cold.

"Beg pardon, Your Grace, but Lady von Langen is here as you requested."

The duchess nodded at her aging white-haired butler, a trusted family retainer for more than thirty years. "Thank you, Fritz. Please show her in."

The girl swept in as she always did, a slender blond whirlwind of brightness in an otherwise dismal day, her pretty face wreathed in a smile.

"Good morning, Your Grace." Elissa sank into a curtsy, then rose gracefully to her feet. In a gown of pink muslin embroidered with roses, she was the image of her willowy blond mother, if a bit more voluptuous in the bosom. Marie had met Octavia Tauber only a few times over the years, but she had liked the woman immensely and was pleased that the count, her husband's dearest friend, had taken such a woman to wife.

She motioned for the girl to approach. "Good morning, my dear. I trust you are enjoying your stay here at Blauen-haus."

"Why, yes, Your Grace. The town is quite lovely and your home is beautiful." She sat down on a stool near the foot of Marie's carved tapestry chair. "And the trip to Baden could not have been more advantageous."

Her mother's frantic message, a tale of treachery among the ranks of the Austrian Army that had resulted in the death of her eldest son, had pleaded for Marie to help her. Karl Tauber had been murdered, the countess believed, to silence the identity of a traitor. His untimely death had prevented him from gaining evidence against the spy who had killed him.

It was Lady von Langen's bold notion—or more likely, her daughter's—that a woman, particularly a young and beautiful one, might be able to discover enough information to at least arouse suspicions. The duchess could then intervene, see the right men were given the information.

Another woman would have said no, but the Duchess of Murau wasn't any other woman. She was fiercely independent, believed that a woman was equal to a man in every way. Perhaps more equal in some. If there was a spy in the country, he posed a tremendous threat to the nation's security. Who better than the sister whose brother had been killed to uncover the man who had done it?

Elissa's voice cut into her thoughts. "You cannot know, Your Grace, how much your help in this matter has meant to my mother and me."

The duchess smiled. "Perhaps I can guess. I have children of my own. My heart would be broken should one be taken from me. I would do most anything to see the man responsible pay for what he did. Still, it would be difficult for me to put another of my children in danger to avenge the death of the first."

"I admit at first my mother was against it. But it was Karl's most fervent plea this man be stopped. And there is Peter to consider. He is a dedicated officer. A betrayal of Austrian forces would put his life in danger."

"I gather you have not yet seen him. Does he know that you are here?"

"No. We thought it better to keep my presence as quiet as possible for as long as we could. The fewer who know the better."

"That is so, of course. What progress have you made?"

"Very little, I fear. Still, I have stirred the men's interest. Is that not a good beginning?"

"I would say you have stirred the interest of quite a number of men. Some of them can be quite charming. Be careful you don't embroil yourself in something you can't handle." Marie reached down to pat the golden cap of curls that crowned the young woman's head. "Remember, these are dangerous men . . . especially to an innocent young woman like you. Do not become so enmeshed in your role you are blind to the threat they pose."

"I shall remember, Your Grace."

But still Marie wondered. It occurred to her that perhaps the girl's greatest threat wasn't the man who called himself the Falcon, but the handsome Colonel Kingsland she had seen kissing Elissa in the garden last night.

Chapter *Four*

Adrian spent the following morning in the diplomatic meetings being held at the emperor's summer villa then returned to Blauenhaus. With the day so warm, the sun shining so brightly, he made his way out onto the terrace. Perhaps the countess had also been lured outside by the beautiful weather.

Amusement curved his lips as he recalled their encounter in that night in the garden. She might refuse to see him, but she was attracted to him just the same. There was no mistaking her response to his kisses, or the soft feel of her arms as they slid around his neck. Her lips tasted even sweeter than her lusciously feminine body. Her breasts were fuller than he had thought, deliciously high and firm where they had pressed against his chest.

He'd been hard from the moment he had seen her in the garden, had wanted to undress her and take her right there.

Searching for her now, he glanced across the manicured lawns and spotted a group of women seated on wrought-iron benches, small bright-colored parasols shading their pale, delicate skin from the sun. The countess wasn't among them.

Gentlemen in velvet-collared tailcoats and ladies in fashionable high-waisted gowns strolled the narrow gravel paths but still he didn't see her. Adrian walked the length of the terrace, searching for her slender blond figure, but he saw no sign of her.

Rounding the corner at the far end of the house, he looked off toward an expanse of lawn on the eastern end. The duchess's grandchildren, a little girl of five named Hildy and a boy, Wilhelm, only four, offspring of a daughter who remained in Vienna, had arrived at the villa just that morning. The children were at play, their governess close at hand, but the woman tossing them a bright red leather ball was none other than the Countess von Langen.

Adrian watched her from his place on the terrace, oddly pleased at the sight of the lovely fair-haired woman laughing with the two even blonder children, throwing them the ball then running helter-skelter to catch it when one of them tossed it back. She seemed different today, relaxed and carefree as he had never seen her. With her golden hair slightly mussed and curling around her face, she looked younger, the way she had appeared the first time he had seen her. She seemed less sophisticated, more the impulsive young woman he had kissed in the garden last night.

Adrian watched for a while, till the warmth of the sun began to seep through his scarlet wool coat. He unbuttoned and shed the jacket, slung it casually over his shoulder, and made his way down the steps to the lawn where the children were at play.

The countess was laughing as he approached, a rich, slightly more full-bodied sound than he had heard from her before, her face glowing faintly and shiny with perspiration. He felt the strangest urge to join in the fun they appeared to be having.

He drew closer and she saw him just then, whirled in his direction the same instant the little boy let fly with the ball. The countess yelped as the ball bounced harmlessly off the top of her head then broke into vibrant laughter. The sound made something warm unfurl in Adrian's chest.

''Wilhelm hit you,'' the little girl said solemnly. ''He didn't hurt you, did he?''

The countess smiled, playfully rubbed the spot where the little boy's ball had landed. ''It was an accident and no, he didn't hurt me.''

Adrian leaned down and picked up the ball, tossed it to the boy. "Young Willie has quite an eye," he teased. "I think he is going to be rather good at the game when he grows up."

The countess looked at him and grinned. "Yes, I believe he is." She turned to the children. "Have you met his lordship, Colonel Kingsland?"

They shook their heads in unison, looking up at Adrian with a bit of hesitation.

"Then it shall be my pleasure to present you." She made the formal introductions and they responded with equal formality, Hildy making him an unsteady curtsy, Wilhelm making a rather too-stiff bow. All the while the little boy's eyes kept straying toward the ball.

The countess must have noticed, for she sent a questioning glance toward Adrian. *Surely you wouldn't consider playing with the children?* In answer, he reached down and plucked up the ball.

"I believe I shall throw this a bit farther than the countess," he said to the boy. "Do you think, young Wilhelm, that you might be able to catch it?"

"Oh, yes, my lord!" Even before Adrian raised the ball into the air, the little boy started running, grinning broadly, barely able to suppress his excitement. He missed the first toss and raced after it, then ran back and threw it with all his might in the colonel's direction.

"Try this one," Adrian said, tossing the ball into a higher arc, aiming it perfectly into the little boy's waiting arms. Wilhelm's squeal of delight brought a smile to the countess's flushed face and an odd thread of pleasure to him.

Willie tossed the ball back to Adrian and the four of them threw it in a circle for a while. It was the governess who finally put an end to the game, telling them it was time for the children to go in for their afternoon nap.

"I don't want to take a nap," Willie grumbled. "I want to stay and play."

"It's all right, Willie," Adrian said gently. "I believe her ladyship could use a nap as well, and I have a meeting to attend. Run along now. Do as your governess says. The sun will shine another day and we will play again.''

''Do you promise?'' little Hildy asked, lisping through the space between her two front teeth.

Adrian smiled. ''I give you my solemn word.''

''C'mon,'' the little boy said, taking his sister by the hand. ''The colonel will play with us again—a soldier never breaks his word.''

He watched them race off toward the house, leaving him alone with the countess.

''Is that true, Colonel?'' she asked as they moved out of the sun and walked toward the shade of the terrace. ''A soldier never breaks his word?''

''This one doesn't.''

She glanced away, then down at her pink satin slippers. He smiled at the grass stains that now marked the toes.

''You like children,'' she said. ''You're very good with them.''

''That surprises you?''

''In a way.''

''Because I have none of my own?''

''Ambassador Pettigru told me you were unmarried. I presumed that you did not.''

''As you do not, I am told.''

''No. One day I would very much like to have them.''

He studied her face, thinking he wouldn't have expected her to say that. For that matter, he wouldn't have thought to find her playing ball in the sun like a child.

He shrugged his shoulders. ''It is easy to be good with children. One simply treats them the way he should have liked to have been treated when he was of that age.''

She eyed him strangely, searching the lines of his face for what he left unsaid. His miserable childhood was none of her concern and not his favorite topic so he made no further comment.

''As a baron, 'tis your duty to produce an heir,'' she said. ''I'm surprised you have not yet started a family of your own.''

Adrian scoffed. "The title is mine by default. I care nothing for it nor what happens to it after I am gone. My life has always been the military. That is all I want."

She paused for several moments, as if his words had struck a disturbing cord, then started walking again. " 'Tis past the time I went in." She started up the steps of the terrace and Adrian kept pace at her side, escorting her to the tall carved doors at the rear of the villa. When she stopped, their bodies nearly touched, the skirt of her pink muslin gown brushing lightly against his high black boots.

The sight seemed to somehow unnerve her . . . or perhaps it was simply that he stood so near. "I—I must . . ." She straightened a little, her manner shifting, becoming more reserved. "As I said, my lord, I must be going in. The children quite wore me out. I am in desperate need of a bath and a rest before supper."

"Of course." He smiled slightly, but made no effort to move. "I enjoyed the afternoon, my lady. I hope you did as well." He bowed over her hand, brushing his lips against her fingers.

"Yes, I . . ." She glanced away. "Good day, my lord Colonel." Turning, she hurried to the door, almost running, looking back at him as if she were suddenly in danger. For a while, she had relaxed her guard, but the wariness had returned full measure.

Adrian turned back to the wide stretch of lawn, his mind returning to the picture of innocence she had made playing ball with the children. It occurred to him that perhaps the less he pursued her, the more chance he had of wooing her into his bed. After today, it was a goal that held more appeal than ever.

The resort town of Baden nestled at the southern end of the Vienna Woods, an area of rolling, densely forested hills that stretched all the way to the outposts of the Alps. It was a lovely little town, Jamison thought. Constructed around the site of its fifteen natural hot springs, it was an elegant little village of attractive cobbled streets and four-story baroque buildings in soft pastel colors.

Traveling through the city, enjoying the sounds of children playing and merchants hawking their wares, Jamison leaned back against the tufted leather seat, his friend Adrian Kingsland seated on the opposite side. They were headed for another meeting at the emperor's villa, more rhetoric, Jamison was sure, that seemed to cover little new ground.

The war and an Austro-British alliance was a subject they had discussed for endless hours last eve. At the moment, however, their conversation had turned to something else.

Jamison glanced over at his friend. "So she still refuses to see you."

Wolvermont smiled darkly, his eyes fixed on some undefined point on the carriage wall. "Unfortunately, yes. The lady seems to have little trouble resisting my considerable charms."

Jamison laughed softly. "Do not despair, my friend. 'Tis obvious the lady feels some attraction. Her composure seems quite ruffled whenever you are near."

The colonel grunted. "I do seem to have that effect on her. Apparently, however, I do not 'ruffle' her nearly enough." Adrian sighed. "I have to admit I find the young lady intriguing. She is vibrant and charming, quite intelligent, I should think, but it is more than that."

"Perhaps it is simply her beauty. You have always enjoyed beautiful women."

Adrian shook his head. "There is something about her . . . something I can't seem to grasp. Most of the time she appears to be exactly what she is, a polished, sophisticated young widow, well bred and perfectly in control. At other times, one would swear the girl is an innocent."

"An innocent! I daresay, Adrian, the woman has half the noblemen in Vienna panting after her. Pettigru is clearly besotted. Steigler seems no less charmed. An innocent, my friend, scarcely sets her cap for men like those."

"True." He toyed with the gold braid on his coat sleeve, but his eyes remained fixed on the carriage wall. "I wonder, does the lady realize the danger she courts in toying with Steigler? You know the sort of man he is, the kind of pleasure he enjoys. 'Tis certainly not for the tender or faint of heart.''

Jamison frowned, thinking how right his friend was. The general wasn't a man to trifle with, not even in a harmless flirtation. ''I have yet to form an opinion of the lady, myself. She is, of course, lovely in the extreme, and there are times, as you say, when she seems quite charming. At other times, I find her demeanor a bit too theatrical and mildly overblown.'' He grinned. ''But then I haven't explored her . . . virtues quite so thoroughly as you have.''

''No, and not nearly so thoroughly as I intend to explore them in the very near future.'' Wolvermont turned to stare out the window, drawn to the sound of vendors selling sausages in the narrow cobbled street. ''In any case, the girl is the choicest bit of baggage I have seen in a very long time. I want her in my bed and I mean to have her.''

Jamison said nothing more. He knew the determined look that had settled over his friend's suntanned features. Sooner or later, Adrian would have what he wanted. One way or another, the Countess von Langen would warm Lord Wolvermont's bed.

Elissa stood tensely behind the green baize table in the gaming room at Blauenhaus, watching Ambassador Pettigru lose at cards. One hand of whist after another, thousands of pounds being bet and lost, the ambassador's markers beginning to pile up on a corner of the table.

Colonel Kingsland had joined the game and was seated across the table, his not inconsequential winnings continuing to build. He was a good card player, exceptional, perhaps, his expression carefully bland as he laid down another winning hand. Several times his gaze caught hers, but Elissa forced herself to look away. She was determined to ignore him, to fix her attention on Pettigru, to do what she had come for.

She found it was no easy task. Not when her thoughts kept straying to the fun they'd had playing with the children on the lawn, to the way he had kissed her in the garden.

The ambassador swore beneath his breath, and Elissa's attention returned to the table. She realized the man had lost again. He was drinking too much, a propensity she had only recently discovered that made his playing even worse. She wondered if he could really afford to lose so much, if his wife and family would suffer at the loss.

Against all her attempts to remain objective, she had grown to like Sir William's bumbling kindness and fatherly attentions, a relationship she acknowledged with a sense of relief. It was her company, not her body, that attracted him, and the fact had spawned an odd sort of friendship between them.

Still, she didn't delude herself. The ambassador remained a suspect in her brother's murder, and she couldn't allow herself to forget that. He was a smart man, and well connected. If his gambling this night was any indication, he was also the sort of man who might need a great deal of money. It was not impossible Sir William was the Falcon.

It was also quite possible he was innocent. With that thought in mind and hating to see the poor man lose any more than he already had, she leaned forward and whispered beside his ear.

"I'm sorry to interrupt your game, Ambassador, but I would dearly enjoy a turn in the garden and you *did* promise to escort me. Do you think I might impose?"

He blustered a little, glanced down at his hand then back at her with what was surely a look of relief. "Of course, my dear. I should be delighted." He turned to the others. "I'm afraid you gentlemen will have to excuse me. Duty calls. The countess is in need of escort, and I am fortunate in being able to oblige—as I'm sure you will agree."

They smiled and mumbled their concurrence, took his unwanted cards and returned them to the pile across the table. The ambassador shoved back his chair and offered her his arm and Elissa accepted it with a smile. As she turned to leave, her eyes strayed toward the colonel and his mouth seemed to soften at the corners. It occurred to her that he had guessed exactly why she had interrupted. His expression remarked approval, touched with a note of something else.

Surely not jealousy. They did not know each other well enough for that. And yet there had been a quick flash of something. Whatever it was, it made Elissa's stomach flutter and her mouth go suddenly dry. She was grateful to be leaving the card room.

Walking together, they made their way out onto the terrace, stood for several moments at the wrought-iron railing, bathed in the flickering light of golden sconces mounted high on the rough stone walls.

"My dear, I shouldn't have played so long. I didn't realize that you were growing bored." He held a snifter of brandy in a slightly unsteady hand, and she saw he was drunker than she thought.

"Not bored, Sir William, I assure you. I simply needed some air." She smiled, watched him take another drink of brandy, and a notion that had risen earlier in the day began to surface once more. She tapped her fan against his shoulder. "As a matter of fact, I was just thinking . . . the night is still young, is it not? I believe I should enjoy a glass of sherry before retiring. Perhaps you might refill your drink, Sir William, and we shall sip them by the fire in the small salon."

A bushy white brow arched up. "Capital idea, my dear. Capital, indeed." Walking beside her across the terrace, he found a servant, requested a sherry for her and a brandy for himself. They carried the drinks into an intimate salon that only a handful of guests seemed to have discovered and sat down on an overstuffed plum velvet sofa in front of the fire.

It wasn't until several brandies later, the ambassador well into his cups and pining over the absence of his beloved wife, Matilda, and their only daughter, Mary, a young woman close to Elissa's age, that she began to probe his loyalties, hoping to discover the truth of where they lay.

"It must be a difficult job," Elissa said, "negotiating so important an alliance."

"Damnable war . . ." he mumbled, his head lolling forward over his half-empty glass. "Never good . . . never good."

"No it isn't, Sir William. I daresay it will be costly for the Austrians, with Napoleon knocking at their very doors. Perhaps our interference will only make things worse. Perhaps they would be better left alone."

"Need our money, they do. Archduke trying to launch an army, don't ya know. French . . . French don't want that. They'll try to stop 'em. Do anything . . . anything to see them fail."

"I imagine they would. Bonaparte would surely pay a fortune for information that would help to defeat them."

"Fortune . . . yes."

"A man could make himself rich."

The rustle of heavy fabric intruded, the sound of a man bending forward to lift the glass from the ambassador's nearly limp hands. "Or a woman," the colonel said softly.

His expression remained bland, but a dark brow lifted in disapproval at the state into which she had allowed the ambassador to fall.

"I believe, Sir William, the lady would like to retire," he said with a hard, pointed look in her direction. "Perhaps you would wish to retire as well."

The ambassador roused himself. "Yes, yes, of course. 'Tis well past the hour for sleep." Pettigru gave her a lopsided smile. "Will you excuse me, my dear?"

"Of course. I—I didn't realize it had gotten quite so late." Sir William rose, swaying unsteadily on his feet, and she glanced up guiltily at the colonel. "Might I impose on your kindness, my lord?"

He made a curt nod of his head. "I should be happy to see the ambassador safely returned to his quarters." His eyes ran over her, studying the way the color crept into her cheeks, and she wondered if he read her as easily as it appeared. "Good evening, my lady."

"Good evening, my lord." She watched him leave with Sir William, handling the man with gentle control, guiding him effortlessly out of the salon toward the stairs, saving the man from embarrassment.

She hoped he hadn't guessed what she had been doing.

Even if he had, and as guilty as she felt for taking advantage, she knew she would do it again if she got the chance.

Whether the colonel approved or not, no matter what it might cost, she had to be sure Sir William wasn't the man known as the Falcon.

Blauenhaus buzzed with activity the following day, as preparations were being made to mount a hunting party. There were chamois and roe deer in the area, wild boar and partridge. General Steigler convinced the duchess that the ladies should come along, those who enjoyed riding horseback, and mounts for the guests were provided.

Having always loved to ride, Elissa eagerly joined the party mounted on a dainty dapple gray mare while the general rode his own impressive white stallion. Elissa thought the keenest animal of the lot was the big black stallion ridden by Colonel Kingsland, perhaps the finest bit of horseflesh that she had ever seen.

They rode throughout the morning, through wooded mountain passes and open fields, pausing here and there while the men rode off in search of game. Just before luncheon they reached a small red-soiled valley surrounded by forested hills, and the men began setting up a makeshift camp. Elissa wandered toward the area where grooms had picketed the horses, strolling along the line, admiring one fine animal after the next, pausing in front of the colonel's impressive black stallion.

"Such a pretty boy," she crooned, stroking the animal's velvety nose. "And I should wager you can run like the wind." She had always loved horses, had been fortunate to live just down the hill from a wealthy squire who shared her passion and insisted she ride his fine-blooded animals whenever she wished.

The horse nickered softly, pressed its muzzle against her hand. "You're a fine one, you are. Your colonel has a very good eye for horses."

"Yes, he does," said the black-haired officer who stepped out from behind some bushes, Major St. Giles, she knew, for she had met him on several occasions. "As good an eye for horseflesh as he has for a beautiful woman."

Elissa glanced down, flushing a little, knowing the major and the colonel were friends, wondering if he knew about the night Lord Wolvermont had mistakenly come into her room.

She ran a hand along the horse's neck, felt the warmth of the sun absorbed by his soft dark coat. "You know him well, I gather."

He smiled. He was a tall man, leaner of build than the colonel, with an attractive, intelligent face and a self-assured smile. He seemed a gentler, less volatile man than the baron.

"The colonel and I have been friends since we were children."

"I give you credit then, Major, for the fortitude it must have taken to put up with so difficult a man."

"Difficult? Perhaps at times. Mostly stubborn and arrogant, a little bit spoiled, perhaps. Matched against his courage, his loyalty to those he cares for, his unflagging dedication to duty, there is no man I would rather call friend."

The words softened something inside her. She had sensed those qualities in him, but forced herself to ignore them, to see only his arrogance, his determination to have his own way.

"You've known him since he was a boy?"

He nodded. "We attended boarding school together. We were but five years old when we met."

"Five! Surely that was young to be sent away from home."

The major's face subtly tightened. "Our parents believed it the proper course. In my case, I am certain they came to regret it. Adrian's family never did. They were convenienced by his absence. He was a second son, you see, never meant to inherit and not of much worth in his family's eyes. As a matter of fact, the Wolvermont title actually came by way of a distant cousin."

She stroked the horse's nose, thinking of the lonely child he must have been. "I was luckier than either of you. My parents adored my brothers and me. We never had much money, but we never lacked for love.''

He smiled slightly. ''Then you are right, you were far luckier than we. Keep that in mind should you feel inclined to judge the colonel again.''

The horse's ears perked up and Elissa scratched them gently. ''I appreciate your honesty, Major, though I am surprised you would confide in me.''

St. Giles simply shrugged. ''Perhaps I shouldn't have. But for all your pretense it isn't so, I believe you have an interest in him. Should that interest grow, it might behoove you to understand him. Few people do.''

For a moment she said nothing, recalling the colonel's words when he played with the children on the lawn. *It is easy to be good with children. Simply treat them as you would have wanted to be treated when you were of that age.*

''Thank you for telling me, Major. I shall keep that in mind, though I doubt we shall become more than friends.''

The major nodded and looked off toward the center of the camp. ''I believe the men make ready to leave for the hunt. I trust you and the ladies will enjoy yourselves until our return.''

Elissa glanced at their lovely wooded surroundings, the thick black fir forests and fern-covered hills. An ancient crumbling monastery sat on a distant peak, and the scent of pine tinged the air. ''How could we not?''

St. Giles left her with a last warm smile and headed back to camp, leaving her to stroll back down the hill at her leisure. Halfway there, General Steigler intercepted her.

''Lady von Langen. I was wondering where you had gone. I was beginning to worry.''

She smiled. ''I was merely enjoying a walk. The scenery is quite breathtaking here.''

''Do not let the beauty of these woods deceive you, my dear. There is danger here, wild beasts and sheer rocky cliffs, treacherous, raging streams. You are safe here in camp, but do not stray overly far.''

''Of course not, General Steigler.'' But oh, she did so enjoy these lovely hills. Even with the general serving as her escort and the colonel's disturbing presence to unnerve her, she was glad that she had come.

"I shall be back in a couple of hours." His eyes skimmed lightly down her body. "Perhaps you will think of me while I am away."

A shiver ran through her. Elissa forced herself to smile. "You may be certain of it, General." But as he rode away, she breathed a deep sigh of relief that he was gone.

Chapter *Five*

Adrian sat comfortably in the saddle, riding at the rear of the group as they headed out of the valley. The sun beat down, warming the air at the slightly higher elevation, and he had taken off his jacket, leaving him in his full-sleeved white lawn shirt. His saber hung from his belt as it always did, and his musket balanced on the pommel of his saddle. Jamie rode beside him, also shed of his coat.

"You were speaking to Lady von Langen," Adrian said casually as they crested the rise. "What did the lovely young countess have to say?"

Jamie smiled. "That you had a good eye for horses."

Adrian's mouth curved faintly. "She liked Minotaur, did she?"

"Overly, it seemed. The lady appears to appreciate horses a good deal. She's a very fine rider, in case you hadn't noticed."

Adrian grunted. "There is little about the countess that I have not noticed." He glanced back toward the camp fading into the distance: the ladies in their riding habits, canvas awnings to protect them from the sun; a bevy of servants fluttering about; tables covered with linen and set with an array of delicacies, cold meats, fruits, and cheeses. "What else did she have to say?"

"She said that you were difficult."

His brow shot up. "Difficult? Why, I am the soul of congeniality."

Jamie laughed softly. "Actually, she implied that as your friend, I must be a paragon of virtue to have put up with you for all these years."

Adrian grunted. "The little minx said that?"

"I'm afraid she did."

"I suppose you agreed with her."

"Of course," Jamie said with a grin. "And you were right, she does have an innocence about her. I believe she tries to disguise it, but it is there just the same. Perhaps that is part of what makes her so attractive."

Adrian said nothing. He was thinking about the countess, recalling the joy in her face as she played with the children and wondering at her growing association with Franz Steigler. If Adrian's instincts were correct, the lady was getting in way over her head. Perhaps he would try to warn her. In this mayhap she would listen.

A huge hawk flew from the top of a tree, screeching a warning at the intruders passing below, and Adrian's attention returned to his surroundings. He was there for the hunt and he meant to enjoy it. He nudged the big black stallion ahead and the other men did the same, dropping out of sight over the rise.

It was several hours later before he rode that same trail in the opposite direction, making his way back to camp. A red stag roe deer, a brace of pheasants, and two plump partridges hung over the withers of a packhorse trailing along at the rear. Up ahead, the hunters reined in at the top of a ridge.

"What is it?" Adrian asked Jamie, coming up beside him.

"Wild boar. A big one. The general spotted it first. He has dismounted and moved into the brush in an effort to get close enough to shoot."

Adrian surveyed the nearby mountains, recognizing a huge granite cliff face they had passed on their way out. "I don't like it, Jamie. We're too close to camp. If the general should wound instead of kill, the ladies might be in danger."

Jamie followed his gaze toward the ravine the general had

ridden into, recognizing the same granite landmark Adrian had seen. "There isn't much we can do about it—except pray if he finds the beast, his shot is clean."

Adrian simply nodded, but he nudged the big black forward toward the front of the group of men, pulled up beneath a beech tree and checked the load in his musket. He pulled a pistol from his saddlebags, checked the load, and stuffed it into the waistband of his breeches.

The stallion began to dance beneath him, its ears going up, nostrils flaring. "Easy, boy." He slid a hand down the stallion's neck, gentling him a little while his gaze searched the forest and surrounding hills. No sign of Steigler.

He could hear the whispers of the men, the creak of their saddles beneath them, the shuffle of horses' hooves. A musket shot broke through the sounds, echoing across the valley, and Adrian set his heels to the stallion's ribs. Urging the horse down the hill, he rode off at a gallop toward where the shot had come from.

A second shot fired, a spare musket the general's servant carried for him, and Adrian reined the stallion off toward a cluster of low-lying shrubs, sliding to a halt just as Steigler swung up on his horse.

"Hurry with that musket, you fool!" he roared at the man working frantically to reload the first gun.

"Where is he!" Adrian shouted, and Steigler's head jerked up.

"Biggest damned boar I've ever seen. Took a shot to the lung and it didn't even faze him. He's a trophy, Colonel—a magnificent specimen—and I intend to bring him down."

"Which way did he go?"

"That way!" The general pointed toward the trail leading back to the camp and Adrian's blood ran cold. He set his heels to the horse, urging it up the hill, leaning over the animal's neck for greater speed. He didn't care about the general's trophy boar. He didn't care about anything but the unsuspecting women back in camp.

"That boar is mine, Colonel Kingsland, do you hear!" the general called after him.

Adrian didn't answer, just urged the stallion faster, riding full tilt back toward the camp. Dust and pine needles flew up from the horse's hooves, branches slapped him in the face, threatening to knock him from the saddle, but he plunged ahead, all the while praying the wounded animal had turned off the trail before it reached the camp. A trail of blood on the path in front of him said it wasn't so.

His heart pounded, pulsed in rhythm to the horse's thrumming hooves. Fear made his chest feel tight and his breath came in short, ragged gasps. The last rise loomed ahead. He crested the hill, looked down on the clearing, and his fears were instantly confirmed.

Adrian savagely cursed. Above the thunder of Minotaur's hooves and deep straining breaths, he could hear the terror in the women's shrill cries for help. As the trail angled downward, he spotted them clustered with the servants. He could see the huge black boar, its vicious tusks glinting in the sun, frothy blood oozing from the ball it had taken in its chest.

Adrian's gaze swung toward the women, unconsciously searching for the countess. When he finally saw her, his chest went so tight he could barely breathe. She was standing away from the others, on the opposite side of the boar, backed into an outcropping of boulders, her slender shoulders pressed against the trunk of a tree. She clutched a dry pine branch in her trembling hands and another woman, Lady Ellen Hargrave, a diplomat's daughter, wept frantically in the dirt at her feet.

Adrian's heart constricted. God's blood, the beast was set to kill them! He rode the horse flat out, coming as near to the boar as he dared, drew hard on the reins and swung down from the saddle before Minotaur had come to a sliding halt. With so many people scattered about, he didn't dare risk a shot. Even should the wound be fatal, the ball might ricochet off a bone and kill someone. He tossed the useless musket away and jerked the pistol from his breeches as he quickly made his way across the clearing.

"Colonel!" one of the women shrieked. "Oh, thank God

you've come!'' Several women started crying, but Adrian ignored them.

"I want you ladies to stay very calm. Just quietly back away."

"But the countess!"

"I'll see to the countess. Do as I say." They started easing backward and the boar caught the movement out of the corner of his eye. It viciously pawed the ground, flinging dirt beneath its sharp hooves, its small eyes fixed on the countess and Lady Ellen. Grunting, it began to fling its head, then took several threatening steps toward Elissa, trapped just a few feet away. Her makeshift weapon came up, but her face was as gray as the granite boulders behind her.

Her eyes searched him out. Fear was there and a look of such hope that a knot tightened in his stomach. "Don't be afraid, my lady. I'm not going to let him hurt you." But damn, it was impossible to shoot with the women in his line of fire.

He tried to work around to the side, looking for an opening, his heart almost beating its way out of his chest. He was almost there, would have made it if the woman on the ground hadn't panicked. The boar made a fierce, grunting squeal, and Lady Ellen shot to her feet, shrieking out in terror. Everything happened at once. The boar leapt forward. Adrian fired. Elissa screamed and swung her branch against the animal's shoulder, then darted to the side, shoving Ellen out of the path of the charging beast. Adrian unsheathed his saber and stepped in front of her just as the huge beast whirled, quick for a creature its size.

He swung the saber in a deadly arc, taking the boar behind the neck, and it crashed to its knees, flinging its head widely. A jolt of pain tore through him and he realized one of its razor-sharp tusks had ripped through the flesh of his thigh.

"Adrian!" Seeing the eruption of blood, Elissa raced forward.

"Stay back!" he warned, hacking down once more, tearing into flesh and bone, slashing until the great beast lay dead at his feet. Blood covered his breeches and a scarlet arc stretched across the front of his white lawn shirt.

"Adrian!" It was a measure of her fear that she had used his first name. Elissa rushed toward him, flung herself against him, and he held her trembling body in the circle of his arms.

"You're hurt," she cried, tears streaming through the dirt on her cheeks, her plum velvet riding habit torn in several places and covered with mud and leaves. "Dear God, your leg—please, you must let me help you."

He smiled at her softly, reached out to wipe the wetness from her face. " 'Tis a scratch, nothing more. What matters is that you are safe."

Her slender hands rested on his chest. "Because of you, we are safe. You risked yourself to save us." Her pretty blue eyes scanned his face. She gave him a sweetly tentative smile. "Thank you, my lord."

Adrian simply nodded. His leg was throbbing fiercely, pumping a steady stream of blood, but all he could think of was the way his name had sounded on her lips. She eased away from him, and reluctantly he let her go.

"Come," she gently instructed, taking charge as the women and servants rushed forward, the sound of their voices topped only by the pounding hoofbeats of the hunters returning to camp. "You must let me see to your leg."

He let her help him over to a tree stump, her slim arm beneath his shoulder though he could have easily made the journey on his own. She glanced down at his leg, saw that his breeches had been ripped open nearly to his groin and a goodly portion of his thigh was exposed. Her cheeks went from pale to rosy and her eyes swung up to his face.

"Th-that must be very painful."

He nodded. "Some. It needs to be cleaned and bandaged." Reaching down, he grabbed a handful of cloth and ripped an even longer gap in his breeches, exposing his leg to the knee.

The countess's hand flew up to the base of her throat. "Oh, my." Her eyes ran over the muscles and tendons that flexed each time he moved, and Adrian chuckled softly, surprised as he always was by her seeming naïveté.

"My dear countess. Major St. Giles is arrived back in camp. He has seen to my wounds any number of times and is far more accustomed to this sort of thing than you are. I appreciate your offer of assistance, but even should I accept, it would only be frowned on by the ladies. Perhaps it would be better if you saw to the supplies the major will be needing—something to use for bandages, some water, a needle and thread, if you can find them. And fetch me a decanter of brandy—we shall need it to cleanse the wound.''

To say nothing of the hefty draft he meant to take for himself. The damnable leg was starting to hurt like bloody blazes.

The countess nodded, but still did not move, just stood there staring at his leg. Then her head jerked up, and bright color flooded her cheeks. ''Of—of course, my lord. I shall see it done immediately.''

Smiling, Adrian watched her leave, thinking that no matter what she said, her aging husband must have done a very poor job of seeing to her wifely education.

Jamie strode up just then, a worried look etched into his face. He frowned down at the hole gouged in Adrian's leg. ''I gather you were right about the general and his boar.''

''Unfortunately, yes.''

''It appears the women are safe—thanks to you—but at no small cost to yourself.''

''A wound of the flesh. Nothing serious.'' He thought of Elissa's courage as she faced the savage beast and couldn't help feeling a surge of admiration. ''The lady was quite something herself. A fierce little thing, quite brave considering a pine bough was her only weapon.''

Jamie smiled. ''So I heard.''

Footsteps sounded. Elissa raced up, several servants in tow, and produced the items he had requested, setting them out neatly on what remained of a linen tablecloth she had torn into narrow white strips. ''I brought what you asked for—bandages, water, brandy. Lady Ellen contributed a needle and some embroidery thread. You are certain you'll be all right?''

He nodded. ''There is always the chance of infection, but hopefully, I'll be fine.'' Jamie sloshed a huge portion of brandy over his leg and Adrian hissed in a breath, clamping down on the oath he muttered.

"I know this was not my fault and yet somehow I feel responsible. Is there anything I can do, anything at all?"

His eyes traveled leisurely over her appealing dishevel, appreciating her softly feminine curves. "You know there is."

She colored prettily. "Surely you are not referring to your invitation for supper?"

"Exactly so."

Elissa softly smiled. "It would seem, my lord Colonel, after the gallantry you have shown this day, I have no choice but to accept."

Adrian smiled. "Tonight, my lady?"

"Tonight you need to rest. On the morrow, if your schedule permits, I shall be more than delighted to join you for supper."

Adrian's mouth curved up. He hadn't thought to go quite so far to win an evening in the lady's company, but all in all, it wasn't a bad exchange. "Thank you, my lady."

On the morrow he would see her, prove to her the attraction between them was real. Once he had done so, bedding her would be easy. Adrian could hardly wait.

Elissa turned once more in front of the cheval glass mirror, studying the sapphire blue taffeta gown trimmed with silver lace she had chosen for her dinner with the colonel. She shouldn't have agreed to go, she knew. Her time here was limited and she had a job to do, but dear lord, he had been so brave!

She would never forget the fierce look on his face when he had stepped between her and the charging boar. There was no doubt he would have laid down his life before he would have let the animal reach her. Her heart had nearly stopped beating and then, when she had seen him covered in blood— she'd felt a sharp, squeezing pain inside her chest.

Elissa smoothed the front of the gown, a favorite among those Gaby had provided. It set off the blue of her eyes, her friend had said, and the low, square neckline emphasized the swells of her bosom. She had worn it only once, had intended to save it to impress General Steigler.

Elissa's mouth thinned at the thought. Steigler. It was he who had wounded the boar. The general had given no thought to the women back in camp. He'd cared only for his enjoyment in making the kill. And the fact that Colonel Kingsland had risked himself to save them had only gained Steigler's ire. He didn't like being made to look the fool, and though Adrian hadn't done it on purpose, his heroic dispatch of the boar had certainly accomplished the task.

Adrian. She thought of him that way now. She had tried so hard not to and yet it had happened. She was drawn to him more every day though it was obvious their attraction could lead nowhere. Elissa was committed to finding the Falcon, and even if she weren't, the colonel wasn't interested in marriage. Not that she was interested in marrying *him,* of course. Life with an arrogant, domineering man like Wolvermont would probably be unbearable.

Elissa sighed as she drew her long white gloves up over her elbows. She shouldn't have agreed to go tonight, yet she meant to enjoy herself. Life was precious. She was involved in a dangerous business and she wasn't sure where it might end. She would take these few moments for herself. With a last glance in the mirror, she picked up her silver-trimmed sapphire taffeta reticule and headed for the door.

He was waiting at the foot of the stairs, taller than most of the men in the villa, black boots polished to a mirror sheen, gold epaulettes gleaming on the shoulders of his scarlet uniform coat. It took her breath away just to look at him.

"Good evening, my lord."

He smiled and reached for her hand, bent over it and pressed a soft kiss on the back. "I liked it better when you called me Adrian. Do you think you might manage that, at least for tonight?"

"Perhaps I could . . . Adrian."

His smile grew broader, and dimples appeared in his cheeks. He took her hand and they left the villa, descending the stairs to a carriage that waited out in front.

"Where are we going?" she asked, once they were settled inside and the carriage rolled over the cobblestone streets. A brass lamp burned on the wall inside, lighting the baron's handsome features, and it occurred to her the freedom a young widow possessed was definitely a thing to be envied.

"There is a restaurant near the center of the city, a favorite of the emperor. The food is supposed to be excellent. I trust you are hungry."

"Ravenous."

His eyes darkened for a moment, then he smiled. "As I have been of late, though food has been the farthest thought from my mind."

Elissa sat up straighter on the bench, her lips parting, ready to demand he take her home, but Adrian caught her hand.

"A jest, my lady. I am sorry if I offended. You are safe with me this night. I give you my word."

She relaxed against the seat. She trusted the colonel to keep his promise. He made no secret of his desire for her and yet she knew without doubt he would not take what she was unwilling to give.

"How is your leg this eve?" she asked. "I noticed you favored it only a little as we walked to the carriage."

"I told you 'twas only a scratch."

"A 'scratch' you would not have taken if it hadn't been for Steigler's thoughtlessness."

"True. With the camp so near, he should not have taken the shot." He looked as though he wanted to say something else, but decided against it. Elissa wondered what it might have been.

Watching the baron from beneath her lashes, she found herself comparing the two very different men. The colonel was demanding but he would never force her. She wasn't sure about Steigler. She knew what the general wanted, and that by pretending an interest in him, she was taking a serious risk. Unlike Wolvermont, should the circumstance arise, she feared General Steigler would not hesitate to take what he wanted.

Elissa shivered in the darkness of the carriage.

"You're cold," said the colonel, reaching for the lap robe that rode on the seat at his side.

"No, I—I'm fine, my lord, truly."

Still, he unfolded the robe and draped it over her lap, determined in this as he was in everything else. "Adrian," he corrected softly.

Elissa smiled, oddly comforted by the gesture. "Adrian," she said, and for her acquiescence got another of his charming dimpled smiles.

Supper turned out to be an elegant affair, served in one of the small private dining rooms above an inn called the Am Spitz. The building had once been a fashionable residence on the square, the doors richly carved and gilded, its windows hung with the finest Belgian tapestries. Even the elegant furnishings remained: carved Japan tables, chairs upholstered in velvet and trimmed in fine gold lace.

They dined on *Schnitzel cordon bleu,* a veal dish stuffed with ham and cheese, and trout *mullerin,* fried in butter. A *Leberknödel* soup was served, a meaty broth with liver dumplings, along with an array of sweetmeats and delicacies.

Conversation was matter-of-fact at first, the weather, the ball Empress Caroline would be holding at the end of next week.

"The guest list should be impressive," the colonel said. "Metternich will be arriving the first of next week and apparently even the archduke is planning to attend."

"This man Metternich . . . he seems to be quite an important figure."

The baron nodded, took a sip of his dry white wine, the product of a vineyard on the outskirts of the city. "He's one of the emperor's closest advisors. There is every chance that Francis will appoint him minister of foreign affairs."

Elissa sighed. "Austria seems determined to go to war. I should think after the losses they suffered at Austerlitz, they would not be so eager to face Bonaparte again."

"The Austrians are tired of French rule," Wolvermont told her. "Their army has never been stronger. Archduke Charles is ready to face Napoleon. It is only a matter of time before the alliance is official.''

Elissa started to say something else, but the colonel caught her hand. ''Must we speak only of war?'' He smiled. ''I thought ladies were supposed to find the subject boring.''

''How can a subject that could mean the lives of thousands of young men possibly be boring?'' And yet for him it must be a subject he grew weary of discussing. She relaxed against her chair and smiled at him softly. ''But you're right, Colonel Kingsland. There is enough talk of war during the day. We should leave such talk behind us at least for the balance of the evening.''

He lifted her hand and brought her fingers to his lips, pressing a soft kiss against the tips. A curl of warmth slid into Elissa's stomach.

''Thank you, my lady.'' He ordered *Sachertorte,* for dessert, a rich chocolate cake, and cups of thick black Austrian coffee. Throughout the meal, Elissa had merely picked at her food. It was difficult to eat with the colonel's fierce green eyes on her, as if she were a far more delicious dessert than the one placed in front of him.

The table was cleared and the door closed, leaving them alone in the private dining room, yet they remained in their seats, sipping anise-flavored cordials.

''I've been remiss in my duties,'' he said with a smile just for her. ''I have not told you how exquisite you look tonight.'' He sat closer to her now so that when he leaned forward his face was only inches from hers.

''Thank you,'' she whispered, suddenly a little bit breathless. She saw him lean forward but didn't move away, just closed her eyes and waited for his mouth to settle over hers. He fit them perfectly together, soft yet firm, warm, moist, and incredibly exciting. He cupped her face with his hand and kissed her more deeply, running his tongue across her bottom lip, coaxing her to open for him. She did so without hesitation, wanting to feel again the hot sensations that she had felt before.

His tongue swept in and heat seemed to melt through her

body. She barely heard the clatter of his chair sliding backward as he stood up, pulling her up with him, felt only the warmth of his scarlet wool coat and the beating of his heart beneath her hand.

"Elissa . . ." He tightened his hold around her, taking her mouth again, the kiss no longer gentle but fiercely possessive and sweeping her up in its wake. He kissed the side of her neck, pulled the lobe of her ear into his mouth and suckled gently, kissed the line of her jaw, then took her mouth again. His tongue thrust deeply and the warmth in her stomach radiated out to her limbs. She felt as if she were drowning, sucked into a spinning pool that drew her into its core.

"Adrian," she whispered, feeling the muscles of his chest flexing as her arms slid around his neck, his arousal pressing against her, thick and hot and determined. He kissed her throat and moved lower, bent his dark head and kissed the tops of her breasts. He slid the gown off one shoulder, giving him better access, and pressed his damp mouth against her thin white cotton chemise where it covered her nipple. His warm breath fanned her skin as he took the hard tip between his teeth.

"Adrian, oh, dear God . . ." She was losing control, she saw with a shot of panic. She should have stopped him before he had gone this far. Now it took her full strength of will to pull herself away. She pressed her trembling hands against his chest, and tried to shove him away.

"Adrian, please . . . I beg you. We must stop this at once. We cannot . . . we cannot possibly go on."

He gently bit the side of her neck. "Let me make love to you. It's what we both want. I can give you incredible pleasure. Let me show you how good it can be between us."

"No!" She shoved at his chest, but he held her fast. "Please, Adrian, we cannot do this."

He nibbled the lobe of an ear. "Why not? I've taken a room here at the inn. No one will know but the two of us."

She shook her head, her panic beginning to build. She should have known better than to come. A man like the colonel was not one to trifle with.

"You gave me your word," she said, fear replacing the desire she had felt just moments ago. "You said that I would be safe."

The colonel's face went hard and his tall frame grew rigid. His eyes bored into her even as he began to draw away. "You wanted me. Do not lie to yourself."

"It . . . it isn't a matter of wanting." She stared down at the table, embarrassed and shy all at once. "I'm sorry if I misled you. I—I truly did not mean to. Please . . . won't you just take me home?"

He studied her face, saw the way her bottom lip had started to tremble, and his anger slid away. "You're frightened. I can see it in your face. You've been with no other man but your husband. You've taken no lover since his death and you are afraid."

She glanced away, shaken still, uncertain how to respond. The best lies, she knew, were the ones that were closest to the truth. "No . . . there hasn't been anyone but my husband." She wished she didn't have to lie to him at all.

The tension drained from his body. He bent and pressed a feather-sort kiss on her lips. "I'm sorry I scared you. I didn't realize . . . I promise you it won't happen again." He smiled that charming smile of his. "The next time we'll go more slowly."

The next time? Sweet God, there couldn't be a next time. She said nothing as he pulled her cloak from the hook on the door, nothing as he swirled it around her shoulders and drew up the hood. They spoke only briefly during the carriage ride back to the villa. In the marble-floored entry, a servant dispensed with their wraps, and Adrian bowed over her hand.

"Thank you for a very pleasant evening, my lady. Perhaps supper again on the morrow—"

"No! I—I mean, thank you, my lord, but I have plans for the morrow. I trust your leg will continue to heal and that your duties will go well. Good night, my lord."

The colonel said nothing more, just stood staring at her as she retreated up the stairs. In her room, she walked straight to the bellpull, summoned Sophie, and hurriedly removed her clothes. After changing into a night rail, she climbed up in the big four-poster bed.

"Will there be anything else, my lady? You look a little pale. Perhaps a glass of warm milk?"

"No, thank you, Sophie. I just need to get some rest."

The dark-haired girl just nodded. "As you wish, my lady." She pulled the blue silk bed hangings closed, left the bed-chamber, and quietly closed the door.

Cocooned in darkness, Elissa stared up at the canopy. Her mouth still burned from Adrian's kisses. Her breasts felt swollen and tender from his touch. She shifted restlessly on the mattress, trying to ignore the odd, warm tingling that throbbed between her legs.

You wanted me. Don't lie to yourself. She had never known desire before. She didn't doubt she knew it now. Elissa took a long, shivery breath. The colonel was right—she was afraid. As he had once said, mostly she was afraid of herself.

Chapter Six

Adrian stepped through the doors of the Pagoda Room, an intimate drawing room reserved exclusively for the duchess's use. He was there in answer to a summons he had received that afternoon. He wondered why the woman wished to see him.

He saw her seated in the corner, a stout, robust figure dressed in a soft dove gray gown that brought out the silver in her once-blond hair. Adrian crossed the room in that direction, his bootsteps muffled by the Oriental carpet. Compared to other rooms in the house, which were mostly rococo in design, this room was filled with furniture and art from Asia: intricate japanned bowls and vases, spectacular ivory carvings, and tall teakwood screens inlaid with mother-of-pearl.

He approached the duchess where she sat waiting in a high-backed chair and made a formal bow.

"Your Grace, you wished to see me?"

She sat up a little straighter, cocked her head in a manner that made her appear to be looking down her nose. "Good afternoon, Wolvermont. I trust you are enjoying your stay at Blauenhaus."

He smiled slightly, took the seat to which she motioned across from her. "Your home is quite lovely, Your Grace.

Certainly it is an improvement on the tent I was sleeping in when I first arrived in Vienna.''

''And your leg? How is it healing?'' She motioned for a servant to bring him a cup of coffee, and a lovely porcelain cup and saucer steaming with the rich, dark brew was placed in front of him on a low black lacquer table.

''Quite well, thank you.''

''We all appreciate your heroics in saving Lady Ellen and the countess. God only knows what might have happened had you not arrived when you did.''

''I am sorry the ladies were put into that sort of danger.''

''Yes, well, as one gets older, one learns to accept that those things happen.'' She took a sip of her coffee, eyeing him over the rim, then returned the cup to its saucer. ''Your General Ravenscroft speaks very highly of you, Colonel. I thought you might be interested to know.''

A dark brow arched up. ''I'm flattered, Your Grace, that you have seen fit to ask about me. I wonder, however, why you have developed such an interest.''

''I am interested in you, my lord, because you have taken a more-than-casual interest in my friend Lady von Langen. Ravenscroft was generous in his praise of you. He was also quite blunt about your prowess with members of the opposite sex. It seems your appetites, Colonel Kingsland, are quite renowned.''

Adrian took a sip of his coffee, inhaling the robust fragrance. ''A man has needs, Your Grace. But if that is your concern, I am not a man to force his attentions on a lady who is unwilling.''

The duchess gave him a long, appraising glance. ''She is young, my lord. I realize she seems perfectly sophisticated and quite sure of herself, but I can assure you she is not up to a man like you. I ask you to keep that in mind should you continue in your pursuit of her.''

''As I said, I am not one to press my attentions where they are not wanted. Perhaps you would do better to have this conversation with General Steigler. He seems to garner far more time with the lady than I do, and I daresay, when it comes to women, he is not shy in taking what he wants."

The duchess said nothing. Steigler's reputation was not commonly known, but the duchess showed no surprise at the news. Apparently General Steigler had also been under the woman's scrutiny.

"I shall keep that in mind, Colonel Kingsland."

Adrian set his coffee cup down in the saucer and came to his feet. "If that is all, Your Grace . . ."

She eyed him up and down once more, as if she were taking his measure. "You like her, don't you?"

His mouth curved faintly. "Yes, I do."

She nodded. "Then perhaps between the two of us we can see that she is kept safe."

Adrian said nothing to that, but his mind churned with possibilities. So the duchess was worried about Elissa. She was a shrewd older woman, not known to give her affections lightly. It spoke well of Elissa that she had earned a place in the old girl's heart.

Still, he wondered at her concern. The Countess von Langen was a full-grown woman, a widow out of mourning with all of the freedoms that entailed. Among the aristocracy, a blind eye was turned on such a lady's indiscretions. If Elissa wished to have an affair, it was no one's business but her own.

Adrian took his leave of the Pagoda Room thinking of Elissa and the night they had supped together at the inn. He had enjoyed the evening even though he hadn't got what he wanted—the lady naked and willing in his bed. Damnation! He wanted to see her again, but the stubborn minx refused every overture he made.

Still, she must have some feelings for him or the duchess wouldn't have requested a meeting. He thought of what Her Grace had said about keeping Elissa safe and knew that he would indeed keep an eye on her.

In doing so, perhaps he would discover the real reason she refused him admittance to her bed.

*   *   *

Elissa spent the late morning hours in her room, waiting for the guests to depart for their daily rounds of business, or pleasure, or whatever they might do to entertain themselves. As for her, she was tired of talking, trying to coax information from Pettigru and Steigler when none seemed to be forthcoming.

Today she meant to take action.

Dressed in a simple day dress of dark green kerseymere, she opened her door and glanced around, checking to be sure no one was there. The hall was deserted. The ambassador's room, she had discovered, was ten doors closer to the staircase on the opposite side of the hall. Elissa headed in that direction. She wasn't sure what she might find, or even what it was she was looking for. She only knew she had to do something to unmask the Falcon.

Perhaps she would find a clue in the ambassador's room.

With a last glance around, she headed down the hall, quickly slipped inside the room, and quietly closed the door. Trembling, she leaned against it for support. She knew that he would be gone. She had seen him breaking his fast earlier that morning, a light repast of coffee, fresh fruit, and strudel.

Still, she didn't know his schedule, had no idea when he might return, and there was his valet to consider. The servant might show up at any time.

With that in mind, Elissa made her way to his velvet-draped bed, pulled open the drawers in the nightstand beside it, made a quick search that uncovered a book of William Blake poems and a pair of reading glasses, then moved on.

A search of his dresser revealed nothing except that there were holes in the ambassador's woolen drawers. She remembered a remark he had made about missing the tender care his wife had taken of him, and understood now what he had meant.

She carefully sifted through the items in the tall rosewood armoire in the corner, searched the trunk at the foot of his bed, and finally the small portable writing desk that sat atop it.

Nothing of interest. Nothing that might connect him with

the man they called the Falcon. Only his position as ambassador, which allowed him access to so many of the country's vital secrets, kept her from crossing him off her brother's list as a possible suspect.

She wondered if Karl had known something about him she did not.

Elissa made a last sweep of the room, checking to see that everything was left in the same order she had found it, though the ambassador wasn't the sort to keep much track. She carefully opened the door, glanced right and then left—gasped and quickly shut the door.

Sweet God, Adrian was coming down the hall, heading toward his room at the opposite end! She prayed that he hadn't seen her. She counted to ten, then began to count again. The third time she counted to twenty. Surely he would be gone by now, around the corner out of sight.

Taking a deep, courage-building breath, she eased open the door a crack and glanced down the hall to be sure he was gone. Her sigh of relief turned into a squeak of surprise at the sound of his deep male voice.

"I'm afraid the ambassador has not yet returned . . . but then I can see you know that already."

"A-Adrian!"

"Ah, so now you use my name. Curious how it only seems to occur to you when you are in some sort of peril."

"Peril?" Her chin went up. "I am hardly in peril. I was simply . . . simply . . ."

"Yes . . . ?"

"If you must know, I had a message for the ambassador of a rather personal nature. I left it on his bureau. I hardly think he would find that disturbing."

"A note, is it? Why don't we see?"

She gasped as he roughly caught her arm, opened the door, and pushed her in. "Where is this note you have left?"

Her chest squeezed tight. "All right, I—I didn't leave a note. I was going to, but I . . . I found his inkwell empty, and the more I thought about it the more I realized it wasn't a good idea. I started to leave, but I saw you coming down the hall. I was embarrassed, so I ducked back inside.''

Adrian watched as the countess chewed nervously on her lip. Turning, he walked over to the inkwell on the small portable writing desk on top of the ambassador's trunk. There were sheets of foolscap inside, a quill pen and a shaker of sand, but the inkwell, as the lady had said, was dry.

He relaxed a little. "We had better get out of here before someone sees us. I doubt you would care to explain to someone else what you were doing in the ambassador's bedchamber."

She nodded. He noticed her hands were shaking. What the devil was going on? Was she planning some sort of tryst? Damn, but the woman was vexing. He could have sworn her interest in Pettigru had gone no further than friendship, but perhaps he had been mistaken.

Or was it something else?

He didn't like the thought that crept into his mind. Pettigru and Steigler—two completely different men in every way. And yet they had one thing in common. Both men held positions of uncommon power. They had access to their country's most intimate secrets.

He studied Elissa as they walked down the hall back toward her room. Surely it was simply coincidence. There were any number of important men currently in Vienna. Pettigru and Steigler were two of them without doubt, but that didn't mean Elissa was after their secrets.

Still, he couldn't shake the notion she was lying about why she had gone into the ambassador's room.

"There is an opera tonight," he said when they reached her door. "I want you to go with me." It wasn't a gentle invitation. It was pointedly direct. After the incident in the hall, she would want to appease him. If she had done something wrong, she would say yes.

"I—I've made other plans."

Adrian arched a brow, but inside he was relieved. "Break them," he said, pressing her a little bit harder.

Her glance strayed down the hall. "Yes . . ." she whispered. "I believe I can do that."

Adrian's stomach tightened. Was she really that frightened that someone would find out? He made a curt nod of his head. "I'll be downstairs waiting at seven." Turning, he walked away, heading toward his room as he had intended before he saw her.

By the time he reached the door, he had convinced himself he was wrong. She was merely leaving a message as she had said. Elissa was young and impetuous, not governed by propriety as much as some. He had preyed on her embarrassment and bullied her into accepting his escort, yet he couldn't say he was sorry.

A reluctant smile pulled at his lips. What did it matter why she had agreed to go with him? He had been wanting to see her and now he had his wish. He would make sure she enjoyed the evening, and they would go on from there.

Elissa paced the floor at the foot of her bed. She had lied to General Steigler, told him she had forgotten a previous engagement and broke the date she had made to join him for supper. She had lied about who she was to everyone in Austria and to Adrian about being in Pettigru's room.

The lies were getting thicker, deeper, the danger rising closer to the surface, and yet she had no choice.

She glanced at the clock on the marble mantel above the hearth, saw that it was already past the time she should have been downstairs. Though she had dreaded the evening with Steigler, the hours with the colonel might be far worse.

She hadn't forgotten the dark look on his face when he had caught her in Pettigru's room. She had agreed to accompany him in order to appease him. Now she nervously paced and worried at the mood she would find him in when she joined him downstairs.

A last glance at the clock and she dragged in a quick breath for courage, marched out the door and down the hall, took hold of the gilded wrought-iron railing and descended the wide marble staircase. The colonel turned at the sound of her footfalls, and at the sight of the smile on his face, her whole body relaxed. He wasn't angry. Dear God, he had believed the lie she had told.

"Good evening, my lady." He bowed over her hand and she found herself returning the smile he gave her. Perhaps the night wouldn't be so bad after all. "My carriage awaits. Shall we go?"

She lowered her gaze. "As you wish, my lord."

The opera house, a lovely four-story building of marble and granite, was exceedingly crowded, yet the colonel made his way unerringly through the mob, escorting her to a private box on the second floor.

"I'm glad you agreed to come," he said as if he had actually given her a choice. "I hope you like opera as well as you like horses."

Elissa smiled brightly, beginning to get caught up in the excitement. "Oh, I do! Living in the country, we rarely got to attend the opera." She glanced down at the program she clutched in her hand, then back up at him through her lashes. "I am glad you asked me to come."

Adrian smiled. "I should enjoy your company far more often, my lady, if you would but agree."

Her own smile slipped a little. Adrian's company was indeed preferable to Pettigru's or Steigler's, but it was they she must spend her time with.

"The music begins," she said softly. "Perhaps we should take our seats." They sat down in plush red velvet chairs. Taking her opera glasses from where they rested in her lap, she focused on the stage, then closed her eyes and gave herself over to the music, Spontini's *Vestale,* first produced in Paris.

The evening passed swiftly. Adrian seemed to be enjoying himself as much as she was. When the opera ended they left the theater and stopped at a small cafe for coffee and rich chocolate pastries, then he settled her back inside the carriage. Instead of sitting across from her as he had done before, he took a seat beside her and pulled her into his arms.

A warm kiss followed, gentle yet insistent. "I have wanted to do that all evening." Another warm kiss, deeper this time, his tongue gliding in, teasing the inside of her mouth, arousing her until she felt dizzy. She had to stop this before it went too far, yet she didn't want to. Just a little while longer, she told herself, just a few more fiery kisses, and she would make it end.

She felt his lips against her jaw, felt the moisture of his tongue inside the rim of an ear, felt the hot pressure of his kisses along her shoulder. She didn't realize he had unfastened her gown until he eased it down, lowered his head and settled his mouth over her breast.

Elissa made a startled little cry then her head fell back as a wave of pleasure swept through her. His tongue encircled her nipple and it instantly puckered and tightened, began a soft throbbing that seemed to settle down low in her stomach.

"Adrian," she whispered, her fingers tangling in his thick, dark hair. "Dear God . . . Adrian."

His attention shifted to her other breast and he began to suckle gently, his hands moving to the hem of her skirt, shoving it up, then sliding beneath the fabric and easing up her leg.

She had to stop him. Dear God, she wasn't raised to behave like this. Her mother had never been overly strict or condemning, but she had raised her daughter to behave like a lady.

"Stop," Elissa whispered frantically. "I beg you—please, Adrian. Please don't go any farther."

His head came away from her breast, but his hand did not move from the warm spot burning into her thigh. "Tell me you don't want me. Tell me I'm not giving you pleasure."

Tears welled in her eyes. She could not tell him another lie. "It doesn't matter. I cannot do this. It isn't right." Tears spilled down her cheeks and Adrian cursed soundly.

"Good Christ, do not cry." He jerked a handkerchief from his pocket and handed it over, and she dabbed the embroidered *W* at the edge against her eyes. Wolvermont sighed. "You try my patience, Countess. The way you behave, one would think you an untried virgin."

She blanched and pulled even farther away, determined to

brazen things out. "You are the one who insisted I come. I have made it clear on more than one occasion that I do not wish to take you as my lover."

He stiffened, his tall frame coming so erect he nearly bumped his head on the top of the carriage. "You are saving that honor for Pettigru, I presume . . . or perhaps General Steigler?"

The blood drained from her face, making her feel slightly dizzy. "No, I . . . I enjoy the gentlemen's company. There is nothing wrong with that. And neither of them have behaved the least bit like you."

His mouth curved faintly. "I am extremely happy to hear it."

Elissa glanced away. "I'm sorry, my lord. I will not deny I feel a certain . . . attraction for you, but that is all it is."

He assessed her dishevel, the sapphire taffeta gown ruched up past her knees, the bodice unbuttoned and clutched against her bosom. "I should hope, Lady von Langen, that you feel at least something for me . . . considering what we have been doing and your current state of undress."

The blood rushed back into her cheeks. She hurriedly smoothed down her skirt, then reached behind her back to try and refasten the buttons.

"For pity's sake, turn around."

She flushed but did as he commanded, presenting her back so that he could reach where she could not. His big hands fumbled a bit, trying to slide the small pearls into the tiny loops.

"Having trouble?" she said a bit tartly. "I noticed you were quite adept at getting them undone."

The baron merely grumbled. "Unfortunately, I am far better at getting them undone than I am at doing them up."

Elissa ignored the remark. It bothered her to think that he did this with other women, that she meant no more to him than Lady Kainz or any other of his conquests.

It bothered her even more that she did not dare to see him again.

In the end, the confrontation she had feared with the colonel did not come. He was ordered back to his regiment on the outskirts of Vienna, and wouldn't be returning for at least a couple of days.

Relief made her almost light-headed. She didn't want to think about Adrian Kingsland. She didn't want to deal with her unwelcome emotions. Instead, she spent her time with the ambassador, and as much time as she dared with General Steigler, probing his loyalties, trying to win his confidence.

Surprisingly, he didn't press for her affections the way Adrian did. Unlike the volatile, passionate colonel, Steigler treated her as if she were a pretty moth he meant to capture, toying with her, letting her flit just out of his reach, all the while waiting with a net to trap her.

She thought there was a good chance he already had a mistress, that the woman cared for his needs and that bedding Elissa would merely be an interesting diversion. She had to become more than that if she intended to discover if he was the Falcon.

Elissa sank down on the tapestry stool in front of her gilded mirror and began to pull the silver-backed brush through her softly curling hair. She sighed into the empty room. The question loomed as it had before—how far was she willing to go to get what she had come for? Would she actually become Steigler's mistress? And if she did, how would she explain her virginity? The thought of his hands on her body, touching her as Adrian had, made her slightly sick to her stomach.

Then an image of Karl rose up, laughing at something she had said, tugging on the long blond braid she had worn when she was a little girl. She remembered the time he had taken her fishing and she had fallen into the pond. Karl had jumped in to save her, but he couldn't swim. He had wound up nearly drowned himself.

Karl was dead now. She would never hear him laughing again, never fish with him again, never know his teasing smile. She imagined him lying in a cold Vienna gutter, his blood running scarlet over the wet gray cobblestones. Tears burned her eyes and she blinked to keep them from falling.

When she thought of Karl, bedding Steigler seemed a small

price to pay for catching the man behind his murder. Unfortunately, Steigler might not even be the one. There were three men on Karl's list, she reminded herself. More and more, she was certain the ambassador wasn't involved. Major Becker, the third name on the list, wasn't, at present, anywhere near Vienna.

Steigler was right here in Baden. He had the means—and the disposition—to be an extremely accomplished spy, and though she had yet to discover a motive, he seemed most likely to be the one. A search of his room might aid her, if she could find some way into the emperor's villa where he was staying.

Perhaps when she attended the ball.

The thought was most disquieting.

A drizzle fell over Vienna and the plains to the east of the city where the British regiment was encamped. Even the Danube, usually a crystalline blue where it cut through the rolling hills, had turned a dull, sluggish shade of brown. Heedless of the mud clinging to his boots, Adrian strode through the camp, saluting soldiers here and there as he passed among the men of the 3rd Dragoons.

Eventually he reached his destination, removed his tall, visored shako and tucked it beneath his arm, lifted the flap of a canvas tent slightly larger than the others, and walked in. General Ravenscroft, a tall man with muttonchop whiskers and iron gray hair, stood behind a table across the small enclosure, several charts and maps spread out in front of him.

"It's good to see you, Colonel. I trust you are well."

"Fine, thank you, General."

"I understand you've been quite useful in Baden. I'm not surprised, but I am glad to hear it. Your background gives you an edge with these Austrians and we need all the help we can get."

"So do they, it would seem, General Ravenscroft."

"Quite so. As a matter of fact, that is why you are here. I wanted to give you an update on the way things are progressing and I wanted to do it in private. Lately there appears to have been a number of information leaks. As far as we know, it hasn't been serious, yet it is somewhat disturbing. I should like very much to know how the information is getting out, but so far we haven't a clue."

Adrian frowned. "I don't like the sound of that, General, not with Bonaparte breathing down our necks."

"Exactly so." He picked up a thin wooden pointer and leaned forward over the map. "Take a look at this, Colonel." He used the stick to indicate an area north and west of Vienna. "This is where the archduke's forces are beginning to assemble." He moved the pointer farther west. "This is the direction we think Bonaparte will be coming from. We aren't quite sure where he is at present, but his army is definitely on the move."

"If that is the case, and the archduke intends to confront him, they'll probably engage someplace along the Danube."

The general nodded. "I would say that is highly likely. Vienna will be Bonaparte's ultimate target and he will be set on that course."

"Should the war progress as you suspect, what will our orders be?"

The general clasped his hands behind him. "We've only a thinly manned regiment at our disposal, since our mission here is strictly a diplomatic one. Officially, we will be ordered to remain uninvolved. On the other hand, should Vienna fall into any sort of danger, I'm sure we'll be called upon to help evacuate the city."

"I see." He thought of Elissa immersed in the backlash of war, and a thread of uneasiness slid through him. Perhaps he could convince her to go home.

"That is one of the reasons I called you here, Colonel. As you well know, once plans for war are set into motion, things can progress rather quickly. There are any number of important people in Baden. As the time for confrontation draws near, someone opposed to the coalition might take it upon himself to do something to try and stop it. Keep your eyes open, Colonel." He smiled. "And don't let that pretty little countess you've been wooing get into the line of fire."

Adrian smiled dryly. Ravenscroft, like the duchess, always seemed to know what was going on. "I shall endeavor to do that, General."

He nodded. "Tonight a dinner is being held in our honor at the Belevedere Palace. I shall expect to see you there." A steel gray brow arched up. "Perhaps you will enjoy seeing an old friend of yours . . . Lady Kainz? I gather she will be in attendance."

Adrian said nothing, just gave him another dry smile followed by a sharp salute. As he turned to leave the tent, it occurred to him the last thing he wanted to do was attend a dinner party with Cecily Kainz. Knowing what she would expect, and as badly as he needed a woman, he knew he would not take her.

The lady he wanted slept in Baden this night.

Chapter Seven

A purple dusk hung over the hills rising in the distance, the last dying rays of light fading into the darkness of evening. Franz Steigler ordered his carriage to a halt near the outskirts of Baden in front of a moderately large, whitewashed residence belonging to a friend of a friend, a colonel of the Hussars, serving at present with the archduke's forces.

Franz smiled to himself. Being a general had its advantages, not the least of which was the ability to collect any number of favors.

He stepped down from the carriage, ordering the driver to return three hours hence, and made his way to the front door, which opened before he reached it.

"Good evening, Herr General." The butler, a stout little man who looked more like an innkeeper than a house servant, pointed toward the drawing room. "Your guests have already arrived."

A brow arched up. He expected his people to be on time, but he had almost hoped the girl would be a few minutes late. His blood went hot just to think of her cringing in fear while he administered a measure of justice . . . ah, but that was only part of the plans he had in store for her.

His jaw tightened as a memory of Elissa rose up. After the frustrating nights he had spent aching for her, he was more than ready for a little physical diversion. He had waited too long already.

He turned to the stout little butler. "Thank you, Klaus. That will be all for the evening. I presume you've informed the others I will not require their services for the balance of the night."

"Yes, sir. The house is empty as you requested. Good evening, sir."

The butler hurried away, and Franz removed his gloves as he walked into the drawing room, a large, sparsely furnished parlor papered with murals of Grecian ruins. The paper had darkened a bit with age, matching the worn Aubusson carpet that covered the floor. A fire had been laid in the hearth and it flickered and popped, casting long, wavering shadows against the walls.

A handsome blond man several years his junior arose from the sofa when Franz appeared through the open parlor doors. "Good evening, General."

"Major Holdorf"—Franz smiled, turned an assessing eye on the girl the man had provided—"I hope you've been keeping our guest entertained." The major's eyes swung toward the young woman seated on the sofa. She was dressed in the clothes of a peasant: cotton dirndl skirt, a brown linen bodice that laced up the front, and a white, full-sleeved blouse. Her long blond hair had been braided and looped beside her ears. "What is your name, girl?"

She came to her feet, smoothed the front of her simple skirt. "Helga," she said, flashing him a warm, seductive smile.

"Where are you from?"

"Modling, Herr General. Not far away."

No, not far. Just enough distance to be safe. And she wasn't new at the game, he saw, studying her practiced coquetry, satisfied with Holdorf's work. Though the pleasure was always heightened by an innocent, the tears and pleading afterward often resulted in problems. He wasn't in the mood for trouble tonight . . . at least not of that sort.

The girl started walking in his direction, the sway of her

hips making her simple skirt float seductively around her hips. She paused when she reached him, placed her hands on the front of his coat, ran them up and down his lapels.

"Let me help you out of your clothes, Herr General. I want you to get comfortable." She started to work the buttons, but Franz caught her arm.

"I don't think you understand." Long, dark fingers bit into her wrist. "I give the orders here. You are simply to obey them."

"But I thought you would enjoy—" He slapped her hard across the face.

"You aren't being paid to think. You are being paid to spread your legs and do whatever I tell you."

She wiped the blood from her mouth with a shaky hand. "Yes, Herr General." She glanced across at Holdorf, whose mouth formed a thin, lustful smile, then her eyes swung back to Franz, who studied her with a cool, unfeeling stare.

"You've been here only a few moments," he said, "and already you have displeased me."

"But I—"

He slapped her again. "You will speak when I tell you— not before. Do you understand?"

"Y-yes."

He began to pace in front of her, taking two short steps then turning. "What shall we do to remedy that, I wonder? Something must surely be done; some form of punishment meted out." Her face went a little bit pale and the sight made his pulse leap.

"Remove your clothes." She wet her lips, which were full and red and glistening with the moisture from her small pink tongue. "Do it now, Helga . . . unless it is your wish to anger me again."

"No! I mean, no, Herr General. I will take them off. I only wish to please you." She did so with trembling hands, tossing her simple garments over the arm of the sofa, then turning naked to face him.

"Take down your hair."

She pulled out the pins, set them carefully on the table

next to her clothes, and unbraided the long golden lengths, letting the pale strands fall around her shoulders and covering the rose aureoles at the tips of her heavy breasts.

"Come here," Franz softly commanded, his body hard now, beginning to ache and throb. He lifted away a long blond curl of hair, baring one of her breasts, slid his hand beneath it, squeezed it to test its weight, then let his hand drop away.

"In the army, a man who behaved with such disrespect would be flogged for insubordination." He glanced to Holdorf. "What do you think, Major? Perhaps a taste of the lash would teach the girl a lesson."

"No, please—"

"Silence!"

Holdorf started forward, a cruel smile on his lips. "Perhaps not a flogging," he said with a speculative air. "She isn't a man, after all, but merely a woman."

Franz cocked a brow. "True."

Holdorf walked up behind her, reached down to fondle the cheeks of her bottom, gave one a rough, thorough squeeze. When she winced, Franz's erection throbbed with anticipation.

Holdorf fondled a plump, milk white breast. "Still . . . as you said, some punishment must be meted out." Leaning down, he plucked up the riding crop he had tossed haphazardly on the table, its long, thick leather handle in contrast to the smooth, slim paleness of his hands. "Perhaps we should let dear Helga choose her own form of punishment. The whip might be wielded by one of us to teach her a lesson, or—" He placed the crop in her trembling hand, wrapped her fingers solidly around it.

"Or . . ." said Franz with a slight curl of his lips, "she might be ingenius enough to think of ways to use it on herself." He gave her a cool, warning smile. He stared with meaning at the shape and size of the handle. "Surely there is something entertaining you might do."

The girl looked aghast. "B-but that is not . . . I never agreed—"

His hand came down hard against her cheek. "Choose, my dear little Helga. You use the whip—or Major Holdorf will. The choice, my dear, is yours."

The girl eyed the whip and a shudder of revulsion rippled through her. It was clear the choice she would make. Franz smiled with satisfaction. He looked at Holdorf, whose lustful expression said he was equally pleased, then settled down to enjoy the show.

A little entertainment first, then some physical relief. As always, the major had done an excellent job. He would go a long way in his career. If things kept progressing as they had been, Franz would see to it personally.

Two more days passed. The rain had stopped though it looked as though another storm might be coming in. The colonel had not yet returned. It came as a shock when Elissa realized, to her chagrin, that she had missed him. For all his arrogance and demanding ways, he was still the most attractive man she had ever met and one of her most interesting companions.

He was well traveled and well educated. A bit too observant at times, perhaps, given the role she was playing, but there was no one with whom she would rather have spent her days.

Instead, while he was away, she passed a number of hours in company with General Steigler. Today would be another such occasion. The duchess had planned an outing, a picnic for her guests, and though the day was overcast, the sky a little cloudy, the ground had dried, and everyone was excited to be getting out of doors.

Elissa had invited the general to join them, figuring there was safety in numbers, and the open spaces would give her a chance to discuss the war without them being overheard. Traveling with the duchess in a line of expensive carriages, the group made its way to the outskirts of Baden, an area of gently rolling hills dotted with vineyards.

The servants had been sent ahead so the picnic site was already assembled, the ground spread with blankets, white linen cloths, china and crystal, as well as an assortment of delicious food: sausages and schnitzel; a fine haunch of beef the Austrians called *Spanferkel;* and roast suckling pig—which Elissa did not eat.

Steigler joined them on the hill, and he and Elissa sat together on a blanket a little apart from the others.

"You should eat more, Countess," he said, his black eyes scanning her scarcely touched plate. "A woman should have enough meat on her bones to provide a man with a proper cushion."

Elissa laughed. "Do I displease you then, General Steigler? Perhaps you would rather I was as plump as Lady von Szabo." She was the aging wife of a marquis, so wide in the girth she could barely bend over.

His lips curled a bit at the corners. "Heaven forbid." His gaze slid down to her bosom then darkened in a way that made her shiver. "You know that you please me very well. You are, in fact, a tender little morsel . . . if perhaps a bit unrestrained. A good man would not find that a problem. He would simply take you in hand, teach you your place."

Irritation trickled through her. Elissa forced it down. She smiled and changed the subject. "I heard a rumor today that the archduke will not be able to attend Empress Caroline's ball. Apparently duty called and he was unable to leave his men."

"Yes, I heard that as well."

"Do you think that means he makes ready for war?"

He looked down his sharply pointed nose. "Always you speak of war. One would think you a man instead of a woman."

She trilled a laugh at that, but a knot formed in her stomach. "La! You say the oddest things. War is exciting. I am simply amused by it. Since you are in a position to know things that no one else yet knows, I thought perhaps you might share some tidbit with me. I would never divulge a word, of course." She ran a finger down the front of his coat. "Surely you know me well enough by now to know that you can trust me."

A thick black brow arched up. He caught her hand, gripping it painfully tight, and moved it away from his chest. "I believe you are discreet enough. I am simply not sure of your loyalty. There are times I believe you are opposed to this war."

She eased her hand away and looked at him with earnest. "In truth, General Steigler, would that be so wrong?"

Angry color swept over him, turning the skin over his sharp cheekbones a dull shade of red. "Do not speak this way to me. You know my feelings on the subject, the position I am in. I tire of your constant need for gossip and I warn you, my lady—the time will come when I take retribution." He came to his feet, smiling coldly. "But all in good time. Never fear, Countess, you will learn your place well enough, once you are settled in my bed."

Turning, he strode away, leaving her to stare after him, his angry strides carrying him across the grassy knoll to the carriage he had arrived in. He made no offer to see her home and she was grateful. Her heart was hammering, thumping like a cannon inside her breast. She had angered him far more than she had intended. She had taken a chance that her boldness might somehow breach the barrier of his confidence.

Perhaps she had in some way. Perhaps that was why he had gotten so angry, why he had professed his loyalty to Austria to the point of fury. Perhaps she had crossed some line that she could make use of in the future. Whatever had occurred, it was certain the general was not a man to succumb to her wiles with ease. Unless she found something in his room, or overheard something, or someone came forward to implicate him in spying, odds were she would never catch him.

Elissa looked down at the delicious food now congealing in a cold lump on her plate. Her stomach rolled uncomfortably and she rose to her feet. The afternoon had grown chill and the flat gray clouds were growing denser. Still, she was glad to be out of the villa, and now that the general was gone, she might as well enjoy what was left of the afternoon. Picking up her yellow straw bonnet and wrapping her cashmere shawl more tightly around her shoulders, she headed off toward the vineyards, determined to stretch her legs before the party headed back into town.

After a three-hour carriage ride from Vienna, Adrian reached Blauenhaus in the middle of the afternoon. Eager to see Elissa, he walked into the marble-floored entry only to discover the place was nearly deserted.

"Her Grace planned an outing for her guests," the butler informed him. "They have not yet returned."

"And Lady von Langen? Would you happen to know if she was in attendance?"

"Yes, my lord. Her ladyship traveled with Her Grace in the ducal carriage."

"Thank you." He asked directions to the site where the picnic was being held then hurried upstairs to freshen up and change into his riding clothes, snug brown nankeen breeches and a full-sleeved white linen shirt. He pulled on a pair of high black boots, grabbed his cloak off the hook beside the door, and headed for the stable.

Minotaur nickered a welcome, fresh and full of himself, since the stallion had remained in Baden while he was away. A groom quickly had the animal brushed and saddled, and Adrian swung aboard, tossing the lad a coin for his trouble.

It didn't take long to reach the outskirts of town and the hills not far beyond. Even so, the sky had grown dark, the clouds much thicker than they had been earlier in the day.

By the time he reached the duchess and her guests, they were scrambling off the gentle hillside back into their carriages, dodging the first few drops of rain. Servants scurried about, gathering plates and glasses, stuffing the uneaten food back into baskets. Adrian rode past them, his gaze searching for Elissa, but he didn't see her. He found the duchess at the top of the hill, standing next to Ambassador Pettigru and the diplomat Robert Blackwood, staring off toward the mountains.

"Colonel Kingsland," Robert said as Adrian rode up and dismounted. "You are just returned to Baden?"

"Yes, just this afternoon."

"Then you have come here directly from the villa?" Pettigru put in with a note of urgency that drew Adrian's attention in his direction.

"Yes, why do you ask?"

"We seem to have lost Lady von Langen," the duchess said with obvious concern. "She was here a little while ago, sitting over there with General Steigler." She pointed to a spot a bit away.

Thinking of Elissa with Steigler, Adrian felt the heat at the back of his neck. "Perhaps she left with the general," he said through a jaw that felt suddenly tight.

"I don't believe so," Blackwood said. "I saw her sometime later, after he had already gone. She was walking off toward the hills, in the direction of the vineyards."

Adrian glanced in that direction, but except for the leafy vines, all he saw were empty fields and outcroppings of boulders.

"We searched the area as far as that abandoned stone cottage you can see near the top of the hill," Pettigru said, "but we didn't find her. We thought perhaps she had returned to the villa in someone else's carriage."

Lightning flashed just then and thunder rumbled across the landscape. Adrian glanced over at the duchess, surrounded by a handful of servants, one of whom held a parasol above her head.

"I'm sure you're right," he said. "The countess probably arrived at Blauenhaus just after I left and is sitting warmly in front of a fire." But he didn't really think so. Elissa had always seemed thoughtful of others and he didn't believe she would wish to cause the duchess needless concern.

Lightning flashed again, closer now, a long, jagged streak against the horizon. "You must see to the duchess's welfare," he said to Pettigru, "be certain she is returned home safely. In the meantime, I shall make a sweep of the area to be sure the countess is not here."

The duchess hesitated a long moment, her shrewd eyes assessing him from head to foot. With a slight nod of her head, she turned and took Pettigru's arm, letting him and the servants escort her back to her carriage.

"I'll stay and help," Robert offered, but Adrian shook his head.

"I'm well mounted. You're afoot. This storm is going to turn ugly and I can act more swiftly if I know I've only myself to worry about."

"But surely—"

Adrian laid a hand on Blackwood's shoulder. "Go back to the villa, Robert. If the lady is here, I will find her. Do not worry if we do not arrive forthwith. Once I have her safe, I'll seek shelter until the storm passes. Then I'll return her home."

Rain rolled off the brim of Robert Blackwood's tall beaver hat. "Perhaps you are right. Good luck, Colonel Kingsland." He made a slight bow of farewell, turned and walked off down the hill.

Pulling his cloak around his shoulders against the rain, Adrian swung up in the saddle to begin a systematic search of the valley and vineyards below. He wondered how far she could have gotten before the rain began to fall, and why she hadn't returned once it did.

Worry nagged him. Unless Steigler had returned for her, she was out there. She had taken refuge somewhere from the storm—or she was hurt. Ignoring the bright flashes of lightning and the heavy crack of thunder, he urged the big black horse into a gallop, calling her name, his circles growing wider, worry building by the moment.

The path he traveled carried him through several rows of leafy budding vines, but he saw no sign of Elissa. He rode up hills and into gullies, passed through another small vineyard, continuing to circle. Still no sign of her. The storm had turned to cold, pelting rain, and he tried to tell himself he was wrong, that she had indeed returned to the villa, but he couldn't make himself believe it.

His instincts said she was out there and that she was in trouble.

"Where the devil are you, angel?" The words disappeared

in the damp, chilly air. He rode into a low spot, puddling with water, traveled up a rise, and stopped at the top of a ravine. Lightning flashed. Thunder clapped a mere instant behind it. He knew he should be anywhere but where he was, but he couldn't make himself quit.

He started to rein away from the ravine, but the stallion nickered just then and his ears perked up. Adrian tensed as he spotted a flash of pale yellow at the bottom of the gully that seemed out of place against the red soil of the landscape.

The horse danced beneath him, sensing his sudden tension. "Easy, boy." He swung down from the saddle, his stomach knotted, and hurried to the edge of the drop-off. An area of fresh dirt showed where the earth had crumbled away. Through the low-growing shrubs, the swatch of yellow lengthened into a long strip of mud-spattered muslin, and Adrian's chest went tight. At the bottom of the hill, Elissa lay in a tangle of muddy skirts, her crumpled bonnet hanging from the pale yellow ribbon still tied around her throat.

He made his way down the hill as fast as he dared, then went down on one knee beside her, his hands suddenly unsteady. "Elissa . . . love, can you hear me?" Her clothes were soaked through and rain ran in rivulets down her smooth cheeks, but she made no attempt to answer.

"It's Adrian," he said softly, his hands moving with practiced skill over her arms and legs to check for breaks. Gratefully, he found none, discovered instead a great lump forming at the back of her head. "Can you hear me, Elissa? I'm going to get you out of here."

She moaned just then and her eyes fluttered open. "Adrian . . . ?" She tried to sit up, winced with the effort, and Adrian forced her back down. A thread of relief trickled through him. At least she was awake.

"Take it easy, love. You've taken a nasty fall, but nothing seems to be broken. Just relax and let me take care of you." The words seemed to ease her. Her eyes slid closed and the stiffness drained from her body. Careful not to hurt her, he lifted her into his arms and climbed the muddy embankment to where Minotaur stood waiting. It was difficult to mount, but by propping her in his saddle he was able to swing up behind her. Holding her against him, he enfolded her in his coat and started down into the valley and up the opposite side.

It didn't take long to reach the abandoned stone cottage Blackwood had spotted near the top of the hill. He said a prayer of thanks that the lightning had spared them, swung down from his horse and lifted Elissa down, then moved to the door.

Lifting the wrought-iron latch, he shoved open the heavy wooden planks with his boot and stepped inside. Instead of being empty as he had imagined, the cottage was merely out of use. Dusty white sheets enshrouded the furniture. A simple woven carpet covered the floors, and a stack of wood sat next to the small stone fireplace.

Adrian smiled with gratitude and swept the sheet off the sofa. As he bent to place the countess atop it, her long, thick lashes parted and her pretty blue eyes opened up.

Adrian smiled. "It's all right, angel. You're safe now. We've a roof over our heads and soon I'll have a warm fire going in the hearth. 'Twould seem God was looking after us this day."

Elissa turned her head and surveyed her surroundings, taking in the dimly lit cottage, its white-sheeted furniture and musty, unused smell, the single white candle Adrian had lit on the table in front of the sofa.

"What . . . what happened?"

He was busy at the hearth, stacking dry pine logs in the grate. "You took a pretty hard fall. No broken bones that I could find, but you've an ugly bump on the back of your head. Do you remember anything at all?"

She frowned, searching her mind, trying to recall what had occurred. "I don't know exactly. I was enjoying myself, walking through the fields along the edge of the vineyards. It felt so good to be out of doors I went farther than I intended. I remember I had climbed a small hill to the edge of a ravine when it started to rain. I remember thinking that the duchess would be worried and that it was past time I returned.

The next thing I knew I was looking into those bright green eyes of yours, and you were telling me you would take care of me.''

He finished lighting the fire and returned to the sofa. ''Which is exactly what I'm going to do. You are soaked clear through. You have to get out of those wet garments.''

Elissa stiffened, her hands coming up protectively over her bosom. ''Wet or not, if you think I'm disrobing in front of you, Colonel Kingsland, you are sorely mistaken.'' She was shivering, she realized, but it didn't make the least bit of difference. She knew Adrian too well. She wasn't removing her clothes.

A warm hand captured hers and he looked into her face. ''I am a lot of things, my lady. But I am not so low that I would take advantage of an injured woman.'' There was sincerity in the depths of his eyes and unmistakable concern. ''I care only for your safety, Elissa, I promise you.''

She glanced away, touched more than she should have been by the worry etched into his face.

''I'll try to find some blankets, something to warm you. Rest easy, love. You're in no danger from me.''

She relaxed against the sofa, bone tired and suddenly freezing cold. Her shivering increased until her teeth were chattering. She clamped them together, but couldn't seem to stop shaking. It occurred to her that Adrian must be equally as wet and cold as she, and the thought was oddly disturbing.

If he was, he did not say so. Just proceeded with his search of cupboards and chests then returned with a stack of blankets and colorful quilts.

''Do you think you can stand up?''

''I think so, but—'' He took her hand to help her, but the moment she tried, her head began to spin and the room turned black around the edges. ''Adrian?'' His arm held her steady. He guided her to a chair he had uncovered and sat her down there, turned the cushions on the sofa over to the dry side and fashioned her a bed.

''Your clothes will have to go. It is the only sensible course.'' He looked at her sternly. ''You must listen to me in this. You have my word as an officer of His Majesty's Army I will not take advantage."

She hesitated a moment more, then finally nodded. She was too cold to remain in her freezing muddy clothes and too unsteady to try and change out of them on her own. She sat in the chair as he unfastened the row of buttons down her back, then stood and leaned against him as he stripped off the soggy yellow gown. Wearing only her thin embroidered chemise, wet and plastered to her body, she stood before him, but as he had promised, there was nothing untoward in his manner. Not even as he knelt beside the chair and rolled down her torn and mud-spattered hose.

When he had finished, he carefully wrapped a soft woolen blanket around her. "The chemise must go," he said thickly. "Perhaps you could help me with that . . . seeing as I am still a man and by nature only human."

She smiled, feeling a soft warmth inside. "You are more than simply a man, Colonel Kingsland. You are my savior for the second time in a row. That makes you something of a hero, I should think."

His mouth curved faintly. "Yes . . . well, hero or not, I want you out of that wet garment. Can you manage on your own?"

She nodded. Wriggling inside the blanket, she pulled the chemise off over her head and handed it over. The colonel's eyes touched hers as he accepted the thin swatch of fabric she had worn next to her skin, and for an instant they darkened. Then the hungry look faded and he turned away, his attention focused on spreading the clothes over a chair to dry in front of the fire.

She watched him work with a guilty sort of pleasure, knowing it was her fault he had been forced out into the storm, unable to stop a surge of gladness that he had come.

"You must be cold and wet as well," she said, noticing the way his soaked shirt molded to the muscles across his chest, the way his breeches clung to the long, hard muscles in his thighs.

"I'm used to it. I'm a soldier, remember? We are often outside in the rain."

"It doesn't seem fair that I should be warm while you are cold. Perhaps you should dry your clothes as well."

His gaze swung to hers and he looked at her hard. "I should rather be cold than break my word. If you had any idea how fetching you look in that blanket, you would not dwell on the notion that I should remove a single stitch of my clothes."

Her stomach did an odd little twist. "Oh."

"Quite so. Now, why don't you rest for a while? The storm still rages like a banshee outside and poor Minotaur stands at the door. There is a lean-to behind the house. Perhaps if he is lucky, I'll find a bit of hay somewhere."

"Yes . . . I had forgot about your splendid horse."

Adrian smiled as she settled herself on the sofa. "I won't be long."

He returned a few minutes later, his wavy dark hair wind tousled, his greatcoat swirling around him. As he hung it on a peg beside the door and shed his soggy woolen jacket, she found herself staring at the muscles beneath his linen shirt, the ridges and valleys outlined by the damp white cloth. Where before she had suffered a faint pounding in her head, now all she felt was the increased thud of her heartbeat and a slightly dizzy sensation that had nothing to do with her fall.

She watched him from beneath her lashes. Encased in tall black boots, his legs were long and well muscled, his buttocks narrow, tight, and round. When he turned to face her, a ladder of muscle formed bands across his stomach, and Elissa felt an odd sort of tingling in her breast. Desire for him, she knew, a sensation she was becoming all too familiar with.

Sweet God, what would it be like to lie with him, to touch those beautiful, rippling muscles, to know the texture of his warm, sun-browned skin?

It was crazy. Pure, unbridled insanity, yet she couldn't help thinking about it. It occurred to her that she felt more for Colonel Kingsland than merely an attraction—much more. She desired him in a way she couldn't have imagined. He

made her think things, feel things, she had never felt before.
He was the bravest man she had ever met. He was handsome
and charming, but there was something else. Something she
had glimpsed in his eyes on occasion, a loneliness he usually
tried to hide.

She thought of the lost little boy he once must have been,
and it made her want to reach out and touch him, to hold him
so he wouldn't be lonely again.

An unexpected thought arose, surprising in its simplicity
yet hitting her with stunning force—dear God, she was falling
in love with him! She reeled as if she had been struck a
second blow and let her head fall back on the pillow. For a
moment the room grew fuzzy again.

Adrian crossed the room to where she lay and rested a hand
against her forehead. "Your skin is no longer so cold. You
still look a little too pale, but the color is returning to your
cheeks."

Elissa made no comment. She was still trying to grasp her
newly discovered feelings for Adrian Kingsland.

"Are you hungry?" he asked. "There seems to be no end
to what I might discover. Perhaps there is something—"

"No, no, I'm fine." She forced herself to smile. "How
was your horse?"

The dimples returned to his cheeks. "Minotaur is delighted
with his surroundings . . . he has hay enough for supper and
even a blanket to keep him warm."

"As you should have," she said softly.

He frowned. "I told you I am fine." He glanced off toward
the window to the gray skies beyond. "Our hosts are quite
thoughtful. I'll have to make certain they are properly rewarded."

"I believe the cottage sits on a portion of the Murau estate.
Some sort of retreat for the duchess's children when they
were young. I hope she does not worry overmuch."

"I have told them I would find you, then seek some sort
of shelter. The storm, however, does not abate. We may be
here till morning."

If he expected her to protest she did not. Instead her mind

was spinning, thinking about what she had learned of herself, thinking about Adrian and how much she desired him—about Steigler and the plans he held for her future. The question rolled over and over in her head: was she really willing to sacrifice her virtue to avenge her brother's death? The answer shot to the surface—a swift, resounding yes.

In truth, it wasn't just Karl. It was all the young soldiers who might die because of a traitor. Perhaps even her brother Peter.

Steigler's thin, dark face rose into her mind, his features harsh and somehow disturbing. Perhaps another woman would be too proper or too frightened to allow him into her bed. Elissa believed she could manage, if it meant unmasking the Falcon. And the more the general's ruthless nature surfaced, the more she believed he was the man for whom she had come.

Unless he canceled his invitation, he would be escorting her to the empress's ball on Saturday night. Sooner or later, perhaps even then, Steigler would find a way to take what he wanted. The general had made his intentions perfectly clear.

She glanced at Adrian, seated in the chair across from her, watching her with a face still darkened by concern. Just the sight of him made her mouth go dry and her pulse beat a frantic tattoo. He wanted her, she knew, and in some way, at least, he cared for her. And there was the matter of her virginity, a lie Steigler would unmask that Adrian could neatly dispose of.

She wasn't sure what she would tell Adrian about it, once it was a *fait accompli,* but she had lied to him before and he had believed her. There was a far better chance of convincing him of whatever story she concocted than she had of lying to Steigler.

And there was far less danger.

At least she thought there was. She still wasn't sure whom she could trust in matters of state and, unfortunately, that included Adrian.

But in this, the matter of making love, she trusted him completely. In this, there wasn't the slightest question, Adrian knew what he was about.

Chapter Eight

Another round of lightning flashed outside the window. Adrian could hear the patter of rain on the roof and the gray stone walls of the cottage. The fire crackled and an ember hissed against the iron grate in the hearth.

A few feet away, Elissa lay on the sofa, her head nestled into the soft goose-down pillow he had found in one of the chests, her golden hair dry now and shining like a halo, framing her face and making her look unbearably young and lovely.

His body throbbed with desire for her. Inside his breeches, he was hard and aching, his shaft rigid with need. He wanted to go to her, to peel the blanket away from her body and bare her breasts, to stare at their intriguing paleness until he got his fill. He wanted to touch her all over, to kiss her until she moaned his name and begged him to take her. He wouldn't, he knew, not tonight, not when she had been injured and he had given his word.

"Adrian?"

He knew she wasn't sleeping. He had noticed her soft, furtive glances as if she had reached out and touched him.

"Yes, love, what is it?"

"Do you think . . . do you think if you might bring your chair and sit over here?"

His body throbbed painfully and he shifted in his chair.

God, it was nearly impossible to restrain himself sitting four feet away. "Considering your state of dress—or undress, as it were—it's probably not a good idea."

She sat up on the sofa, holding the blanket over her bosom, the gently rounded curves barely visible at the edges of the fabric. "My neck is sore . . . from the fall I suppose. I thought perhaps . . . that you might rub it a little for me."

His brow arched up. He knew women well. Too damned well. This one was smarter than most. Did she know what she was asking? He took in a long, steadying breath and slowly let it out. Perhaps not. Perhaps he was reading more into her words than she intended, hearing what he wanted to hear instead of what she meant.

He sighed and came out of his chair, carrying it over closer to the sofa. "You would tax the honor of a saint, my lady." She only smiled, removed the two delicate pearl ear bobs she had been wearing, and set them on the table, then moved over on the sofa, giving him room to sit down.

"Are you certain you feel well enough for this?"

"I feel fine now."

He nodded. At any rate, this would keep her awake for a while, and sleeping wasn't the best idea with an injury of the head. He settled his hands over her bare shoulders and her body stiffened a bit, but as he kneaded the muscles and tendons, she began to relax.

She made a soft little purring sound, moved her head back and forth, rolled her shoulders from side to side. "That feels wonderful."

That was certainly the truth. Her skin felt as soft as rose petals, the small fine bones in her neck and shoulders exquisitely feminine beneath his big hands. Her short blond hair felt like silk where it brushed against his fingers. She turned her head a little to the side so that he might have better access, and his thumb moved along the line of her jaw. A fine tremor ran through her, and she turned her face into his hand, pressing a soft kiss against his callused palm.

"My lady," he said, his voice thick and rough. "There are limits to even my considerable control."

"Would you . . . would you kiss me, Adrian?"

His body went rock hard. "Kiss you? Good Christ . . . !"
He didn't wait a moment more, just bent his head and captured her mouth in a fiery kiss that made the blood surge into
his groin. His pulse was pounding, throbbing against his temples, and an ache tugged low in his belly. "I want you, Elissa.
God, you know how much I want you." He kissed her again,
cupped her face between his palms and took her deeply with
his tongue. A soft moan rose from her throat and her arms
slid around his neck.

"Let me make love to you," he whispered against her ear.
"Release me from my vow." When she didn't respond, he
kissed her again, deeply, thoroughly, till he could feel the
quick rasp of her breath, the fierce hammer of her heart.

"Say it," he coaxed. "Say you want me, Elissa."

"Yes . . ." she whispered. "I want you. Make love to me,
Adrian."

It was all the prodding he needed. He had played the part
of gentleman long enough, longer than he would have with
any other woman. Elissa wanted him and he wanted her.
There was no one here to stop him and he meant to have her.
His hand found the top of the blanket and he eased it down
to her waist, baring her breasts as he had dreamed. He paused
and drew away, allowing himself to look at them.

"Beautiful . . ." he whispered, reaching out to cup one. It
was heavy on the bottom, elegantly curved and crested with
a soft pink nipple. He took the end between his thumb and
finger, pebbling it gently, and looked up to see a warm flush
heating Elissa's cheeks.

"Perhaps we should blow out the lamp," she said softly,
glancing away.

"I wish to see you. I have thought of nothing else for
days." He leaned forward, prepared to take her nipple into
his mouth, but she stopped him with a hand against his shoulder.

"If that is your wish, then I should like to see you as
well."

He smiled then, pleased at her words. "All right, sweeting.

I hope you approve." In minutes he had stripped away his soggy shirt and boots, his damp nankeen riding breeches. Naked, he sat on the sofa beside her.

In the glow of the fire and the candle on the table, he could see the wonder in her face as her eyes traveled over his body, as well as a soft flush of embarrassment. He thought again that her aging husband must have taught her little of the art of love, and in an odd way he was glad.

"You're beautiful," she whispered, a slender hand coming up to touch him, her fingers threading through the curly dark hair on his chest. "Like one of Michelangelo's statues. Even your flesh . . . it is warm but it is as smooth and solid as marble."

Adrian glanced away, slightly embarrassed. "I'm glad I please you." Oddly, he was. Somehow it seemed important that she approve, and though he had never had a woman complain of his body, he had never known one to look at him the way Elissa looked at him now.

Her fingers trailed over the ridges on his stomach, and unconsciously the muscles there tightened. Her hand trembled faintly and she looked up at him from beneath her lashes. Her fingers traced an ancient saber scar and her gaze surveyed the spot then moved steadily lower, trailing down to his hardened arousal.

Her face went from rosy to pale. "You are . . . you are much larger than I had imagined."

Adrian chuckled softly. "I realize you are slender of build and that it has been some time since you were with a man, but we'll take it slow and easy and it shouldn't be a problem."

She started to say something else, but Adrian silenced her with a kiss. In minutes, she was kissing him back, her breasts pressing into his hands, her nipples pebble-hard and aching for his attentions. Outside the window the storm crackled and lightning flared. Rain pelted the roof above his head.

Adrian no longer noticed. He was moving with single-minded purpose, working to attain the goal he had set for himself the moment he had seen her lying in the big four-poster bed—to impale himself between her creamy thighs and finally make her his.

Elissa arched her back, a soft moan escaping, fierce heat coursing through her body. When Adrian bent his head to take her nipple into his mouth, she laced her fingers in his thick, dark hair. His kisses made her tremble. His hands sent currents of pleasure across her skin, and everywhere he touched, she felt as if she burned. Her heart was pounding, her blood pulsing. Her nipples ached, and there was a slick, odd dampness building in the place between her legs.

Desire made her dizzy. The feel of his body pressed against her, the solid strength of muscle over bone, made her ache for the touch of his mouth and tongue. Dear God, she couldn't have imagined!

And yet through the haze of pleasure, she felt the edge of fear. She had never known the touch of a man before, couldn't imagine what it must feel like to have a body as powerful as Adrian's tearing into her own slender frame. She knew there was pain the first time. Now that she had seen how big a man he was, she feared that pain would go beyond anything she was prepared for.

Her emotions swung in and out, vacillating from the height of burning passion, to the depths of icy fear. Adrian pressed her down on the sofa and his hand moved between her legs, urging them to part for him, then gently probing, separating the folds of her sex. He slid a finger inside and she squirmed beneath him, feeling the tightness, the unfamiliar intrusion, embarrassed and at the same time excited.

But even with the warm throb of pleasure, she couldn't help wondering how a man as large as Adrian could possibly fit inside her.

He stretched her a little, preparing her, it seemed, then his finger began to work the small, tight bud at the entrance to her passage. Pleasure shot through her. Dampness slid into her core. She felt him probe deeply again, felt the rhythm of his skillful stroking, and the pleasure built, pulsing in waves through her body. Adrian kissed her deeply, thrusting his tongue into her mouth even as he parted her legs and positioned himself above her, the tip of his arousal poised to thrust inside.

"Adrian?" she whispered, fear beginning to surface even through the building waves of heat.

"Easy, love." He pressed himself a little deeper, stretching her, her muscles tightening around him, her body going stiff against the intrusion. She felt filled to the point of bursting, pinned beneath his heavy weight, and suddenly wildly afraid.

"Adrian! Oh, dear God! Please don't—" His mouth came down in a fiery kiss that silenced her frantic plea. She tried to pull away from him, but he held her fast, a hand sliding under her buttocks, cupping her and bringing her more fully against him. He eased himself forward, spreading her legs even wider, thrusting himself deeper, and terror burst the last sweet bubble of pleasure that remained.

She tried to cry out, tried to shove him away, but instead he surged forward, tearing into her until white-hot pain shot through her body and a well of tears sprang into her eyes.

Poised on his elbows, Adrian went still, his body trembling as he fought for control, his skin damp with perspiration. He drew away to look at her and fury blazed in his eyes.

"For God's sake—you're a virgin!"

She blinked and the tears rolled down her cheeks. "I—I didn't think it would hurt so much."

"Bloody hell!" Clenching his jaw, he began to pull out, beads of perspiration forming in the dark hair at his temple. Elissa gasped as he stood up and cold air rushed over her bare skin. Embarrassment made the heat rise into her cheeks. Adrian didn't seem to notice. Naked, he tossed a blanket over her, turned away and began to drag on his clothes with quick, jerky, obviously angry motions. When he finally turned to face her, fury seethed from every pore.

"A damnable virgin! You're no countess! You've never been with a man—you couldn't possibly have been married. Who the devil are you?"

Misery seemed to swallow her. She had thought this whole thing through—how could it have turned out so wrong? She lifted her chin, fought to gather her composure. "I—I'm exactly who I said I was, the Countess von Langen. My husband was . . . was old, that is all. We never . . . we never . . . He was not capable of making love.''

His mouth went thin. ''You told me in no uncertain terms he was a virile, passionate man.''

''I—I didn't want you to think badly of him.''

''You're lying. I can see it in your eyes. Who are you?''

''I'm the Countess von Langen.''

''You're a liar.'' He rounded on her, so angry his eyes appeared a dark blackish green. ''Just as you were lying that day in the hall outside the ambassador's bedchamber. You may have fooled the others, but if you thought to fool me, you chose the wrong man.'' He reached down and gripped her arms. ''I want to know who you are.''

''He was old, I tell you. He was feeble. A-ask the duchess—she'll tell you it's the truth.''

''The duchess believes what you want her to believe. I'm not sure how you managed to dupe her, but I don't doubt that you have. Tell me who you are. Tell me now or I shall go to Pettigru and tell him my suspicions. There is every chance he'll believe you are a pretty French spy. God only knows what the authorities will do to you. Is that what you want?''

''No!'' Her hands were shaking. She was starting to tremble all over. She wasn't a spy. She was trying to catch one! How could this be happening? ''Please, Adrian, I beg you. You mustn't tell Pettigru. You mustn't tell anyone.''

Adrian looked at her hard. ''Then tell me who you are.''

''I . . . I cannot. Can you not trust me? Can you not simply believe that I am no spy?''

''You expect me to trust you when you have lied at every turn?'' Adrian studied Elissa's face, read her fear, her growing uncertainty. The girl had made a mistake. She had underestimated him badly. Her look said she knew it—and that she would do whatever it took to correct the error she had made.

He smiled wolfishly. Countess or not, spy or not, he had

ways of discovering the truth. In the meantime, he still wanted her in his bed.

"All right, *Countess,* you wish me to keep your secret?"

"Yes . . ." she whispered.

He picked up one of the ear bobs she had left lying on the table and studied it in the firelight. "I'll keep my silence on one condition."

"W-what is that?"

He tossed the shiny pearl back on the table. "What we started tonight is not finished. I want you—whoever it is you are. I'll keep your secret if you promise you will come to me—whenever, wherever I wish. Not ten minutes later, not later that night, but the moment I send you a summons."

Her face looked as white as the candle burning in front of her. "I could not possibly . . ."

"No? Then I shall go to Pettigru as soon as we are returned."

Her chin went up. Color replaced the pallor in her cheeks. "You are spoiled and arrogant, Colonel Kingsland. You command and expect me to obey. Do you always get your way?"

"Hardly," he said, thinking of the past, his lonely years in boarding school, the nights he had spent wishing he could go home. "I intend, however, to have my way in this."

She glanced toward the fire, her eyes on the flickering flames. "Then I shall have to do as you say. You have left me no other choice."

Adrian simply nodded. "I'll give you a couple of days to recover from your . . . experience . . . this evening. Monday night I shall expect you to accompany me wherever I might wish."

She nodded faintly, and Adrian turned away, striding off toward the window to check on the progress of the storm. On the morrow, he would send a courier to Vienna. There was a man there he had used before, an investigator of sorts who would make discreet inquiries into the lady's past.

Whoever she was, he would soon know the truth and hopefully the extent of her deceit. In the meantime, he would make her pay for that deceit with her sweetly desirable little body.

"The storm has slackened," he said to her over his shoulder. "I think we can safely return."

She glanced toward her clothes, drying on the chair before the fire. "I shall dress, then . . . if you don't mind."

He gave her a hard, unrepentant smile. "I don't mind in the least. As a matter of fact I'll be happy to help you." He crossed to the fire, dragged her clothes from the chair, and tossed them in her direction, but he made no move to turn around.

"Won't you please—"

"No."

Tears glistened in her eyes but she turned and quickly brushed them away. Still, the sight of them suddenly made his chest feel tight. God's blood, the woman—whoever she was—had the damnedest effect on him.

"I'll see to Minotaur," he finally said, his voice a little gruff, relenting though he didn't know why. Perhaps it was the sight of her virgin's blood on the blanket, silently accusing him, or the memory of how he had hurt her in his ruthless disposal of her innocence.

Bloody hell! The girl deserved what she got and more. And until he discovered the truth about her, he intended to see that she got it.

A soft knock drew the duchess's attention from the darkness outside her bedchamber window. It was nearly midnight. She had retired to bed, yet she hadn't been able to sleep. Worry for Elissa kept her awake and she had finally gone to sit beside the fire, keeping an ear cocked toward the door. She had left word that should the countess return, no matter the hour, she was to be informed.

Her little maid, Gretchen, opened the door. "She is safe, Your Grace. She suffered a fall but Lord Wolvermont found her. They took shelter and waited out the storm."

Relief trickled through her. At least she was home and no longer in danger. "Check on her, Gretchen. See if there is anything she needs before she goes to bed. Tell her I am glad that she is safe and that I shall be down to see her first thing in the morning.''

''Yes, Your Grace.'' The woman left, and Marie felt the last of her tension drain away. With a sigh she made her way to the bed and slid gratefully beneath the covers. She had been right in leaving the task of finding Elissa to the colonel. She had seen the worry in his intense green eyes. She knew the man would not stop until he found her.

Elissa was returned and yet she was worried about her. The girl was obviously attracted to the colonel, and Marie knew his rakish reputation. She hoped her old friend's daughter had the good sense to stay away from a man like the baron, but in truth, she wasn't so sure.

Elissa lay awake far into the night. Her breasts still tingled and felt oddly swollen. Her body throbbed painfully where the colonel's thrusting hardness had nearly rent her in two. She grimaced to think of it, embarrassed by her actions and their disastrous end; disappointed, though she was loath to admit it, that making love had been so abysmally unpleasant.

She had made a mistake last night—a bad one. She had misjudged the colonel, discovered too late that he wasn't so easily fooled as she had believed. Even the duchess wouldn't be able to convince him. Besides, she had asked too much of her father's friend already. She didn't want the duchess immersed any deeper in her lies.

Elissa tossed and turned, awakened several times, then fought to return to sleep. Morning finally came, sunlight slicing through the crack in the bed hangings so brightly she awoke with a pounding headache in back of her eyes. The dull pain persisted between her legs but it was fainter now, mostly a nagging memory of the fool she had made of herself.

Sophie came into her room sometime later, pulled the bed curtains, and delivered the duchess's command that she spend the day in bed—news she gratefully accepted.

''Her Grace will be down in half an hour,'' Sophie said. ''She wishes to be certain you suffer no ill effects from your fall.''

Elissa sighed. She wished she didn't have to face her. She wished she didn't have to face anyone ever again—especially not the colonel. She wished she could simply languish away inside her room, wallowing in oceans of self-pity.

Instead, with a Herculean effort, she propped herself up against the headboards. "Hand me my wrapper, Sophie. I refuse to greet the duchess lying here like a great lump in bed."

Sophie complied, bringing her a quilted blue satin robe, and Elissa drew it on over her night rail. Seating herself in front of the mirror, she poured water from the porcelain pitcher into the basin, washed her face, then pulled the bristle brush through her hair.

"Much better, my lady." Sophie smiled. "Her Grace will be pleased to see you are practically back to your old self."

Practically. Certainly not completely. She doubted she ever would be. Not when every time she closed her eyes, she felt Adrian's hands moving over her body. She remembered his deep, plundering kiss, and the feel of his mouth on her breasts. Elissa sighed to think of it. In the beginning, love-making had seemed so incredibly wonderful. Why couldn't it have ended with the kisses and the touching? Why was it so much of life turned out to be a bitter disappointment?

The countess knocked and Sophie let her in, then made her way downstairs to fetch them some refreshment.

"You ought to be in bed," the duchess said, eyeing the robe and the stool where Elissa had been sitting. She flashed a stern look down her nose. "I shall expect you to spend most of the day tucked securely beneath the covers."

"Yes, Your Grace."

"You are looking well enough. How do you feel?"

The ache between her legs throbbed annoyingly just then, and a slight flush rose into her cheeks. "I—I'm fine, Your Grace. Colonel Kingsland rode to my rescue once again. I should not have fared so well had he not been able to find me."

Shrewd gray blue eyes ran over her from head to foot.

"You were out there for quite some time. Your colonel played the gentleman, I trust?"

The warmth rose again, but Elissa fought it down. "He was quite gallant, Your Grace." *I was the one who behaved like a harlot.* Dear God and now he expected her to continue behaving like one.

"He is a very handsome man, my dear. He is wealthy and charming, yet I caution you. I am not so old I don't remember how it was with men like that. Before I was betrothed to my late, dear husband, God rest his soul, I fancied myself in love with a man much like your colonel."

"He isn't *my* colonel," Elissa said softly. "He is . . . he is merely an acquaintance."

The duchess eyed her with a glance that was far too knowing, as if she read the meaning of her unwelcome blushes. "Nevertheless, it is imperative you understand him. Women mean little to a man like that. Even should he care for you in some way, the military is his home. It is all that really matters. All he lives for. It is not the sort of life I would recommend."

"No, it is not at all the life I would choose for myself."

"A woman needs a home and family. Children to bring her joy when times grow troubled. Be careful of your colonel, my dear. Enjoy his admiration, but keep your wits about you. If you do, perhaps you will survive this little adventure of yours and emerge unscathed, as your mother would wish."

Unscathed. After last night, it was far too late for that. Her innocence was lost. Still, her heart had survived oddly intact. Considering the feelings she had begun to develop for Adrian, she felt fortunate in that.

"I shall remember what you have said, Your Grace." She *would* remember. She would keep the demands the colonel made on her body separate from the feeling he had once stirred in her heart. Should it come to it, she would have to do that with Steigler.

Surely she could do the same with the Baron Wolvermont.

Chapter Nine

Monday night arrived at long last. As he had promised, Adrian stood waiting at the bottom of the marble staircase in the foyer. He drew the watch fob from the pocket of his scarlet tunic and checked the time, then frowned to see that Elissa was late.

At ten minutes past the hour, she appeared at the railing, her chin held high, though her face was decidedly pale. She watched him a moment, her hesitation apparent, then stiffened her spine and gracefully descended the stairs.

Adrian smiled. "Good evening . . . *my lady.*" He bowed with exaggerated care over her white-gloved hand, wondering if the title had any basis in fact. Perhaps she was simply a clever little vixen who had skillfully duped them all.

"Good evening, my lord."

He studied her from beneath his dark, arched brow. "I thought perhaps you had changed your mind."

"Did you? And if I had done so, I suppose you would have had an interesting evening with Ambassador Pettigru."

His smile turned slightly mocking. "Exactly so." He extended his arm and she took it. "I've a carriage waiting out in front. I trust you're looking forward to the evening."

Her spine went a little bit straighter but she looked him in the eye. "Of course." She let him guide her through the doors and down the front-porch steps, and a footman opened the carriage door. Adrian settled a hand at her waist to help her climb in and realized she was trembling.

Inwardly he flinched. He didn't know who she was, but it wasn't like him to be overly cruel. He wanted her, yes, but he wasn't an ogre. She was young and she was frightened and he had hurt her before.

"I realize this is new to you," he said softly, "but there is no need for you to be frightened. Things went badly before. I intend tonight that they will be different. I promise I will not hurt you."

Her gaze came up to his face. "I am not frightened."

He smiled, admiring her bravado, recognizing the lie in her eyes as he had done before. "Good. Then you won't be afraid to trust me to see to your welfare. In this I know very well what I am doing."

Her mouth went a little bit thin. "I do not doubt it, my lord."

He smiled to himself, liking her spirit. In truth, he liked a great deal about her. The fact that she was a liar was not among them.

"Where are we going?" she asked with a glance out the window as the carriage rumbled along.

"I've made arrangements. There is a place I know . . . a spot where the mineral baths can be taken in private, if one has money enough. The place is ours for the balance of the evening."

Elissa's golden eyebrows went up. Her interest had been piqued, he saw, though it was definitely against her will. "We are going to the baths?"

"That is correct. The water is warm and relaxing. Surely you've heard it is supposed to have great medicinal qualities." Among other things, he thought. Like easing the fears of an innocent young woman who had yet to discover the pleasures of the flesh.

"I—I have been wanting to go there. I had meant to ask the duchess."

He smiled, pleased he had made the right choice. "Now you won't have to. I shall take you in her stead."

She said nothing more until their arrival, just leaned back against the tufted leather carriage seat. She was dressed elegantly but simply tonight, in a high-waisted gown of moss green silk bordered in black Belgian lace. She looked coolly reserved, but soon enough he intended to change that.

They traveled through town at a steady pace and arrived at a three-story building not far from the main spa in the park. Adrian helped her descend the iron stairs of the carriage and they made their way inside.

"There are dressing rooms through that door over there. You'll find towels and a sheet to wrap around you. The baths are found in a covered area at the rear."

She glanced in the direction he pointed, nervous once more, her pretty blue eyes dim with worry.

Adrian reached for her hand, which felt cold and a little bit shaky. "Listen to me, Elissa. There'll be no rush this night. You may enjoy the baths, as you have wished. In time I'll join you there."

She nodded, appeared to relax a bit.

"Turn around," he said, "and I'll help you unfasten your gown."

She hesitated only a moment, turned and let him push the tiny jet buttons through their loops. "Thank you," she said softly when he had finished, holding the bodice up over her breasts.

Adrian merely nodded. Already he was hard and aching, and the evening had only begun. He had meant what he had said. Tonight he wouldn't rush her. He watched her disappear into one of the private dressing rooms, then did the same himself, removing his clothes, hanging them on large wooden hooks along the walls. He wrapped a sheet around his waist and tucked it in, then padded toward the steamy chamber built over a bubbling hot spring at the rear of the building.

He was the first one there, which didn't surprise him. Tossing the towel away, he waded into the water and disappeared in the hot, dense steam.

*   *   *

With a sigh of resignation, Elissa wrapped the sheet around her, pulled it beneath her arms, tucked it securely between her breasts, and made her way to the bathing room. It was dimly lit, with a low-beamed ceiling and plain whitewashed walls. A single oil lamp burned on a table. A stone-lined pool filled most of the chamber, disappearing into the darkness, steam rising up in wispy drifts above the water. Broad, flat steps led down into the shallow depths that smelled faintly of sulfur.

She glanced around for Adrian, but she didn't see him. Perhaps he meant for her to enjoy the baths as he had said. Turning back toward the pool, she watched a soft spiral of steam float above the surface that seemed to beckon her forward. The sheet felt suddenly confining, and what did it matter? Adrian had seen her before, and even if he hadn't, he had come there with a purpose. She knew without doubt this time he would not be deterred.

Her hands were surprisingly steady as she untied the sheet, draped it over a wrought-iron bench next to the table against the wall, and started down the steps into the pool. The water felt exquisite as it swirled around her hips, immersing her in its soothing warmth, draining some of the tension from her body.

She sank down in the shallow pool and the water surged over her shoulders. Leaning back, she rested her head on the stones along the edge, closed her eyes, and forced herself to relax. Only the faintest movement of the water told her he was there, that he had been there in the shadows all along. He said nothing as he drew near, nothing as he sank into the water beside her, braced his hands on each side of her face and bent down to kiss her. She could feel his body brushing hers, as solid as she remembered, smooth, sun-darkened skin over muscles honed of steel, and her heartbeat suddenly quickened.

His kiss came more gently than she had expected, just a tasting of lips, the glide of his tongue, the warmth of his brandy-flavored breath. He lifted her arms around his neck and slowly came to his feet, bringing her up with him. Her body clung wetly to his, her breasts formed soft hills against his chest, and his springy dark hair teased her nipples.

A small flame ignited, a warm, teasing heat she hadn't believed she would feel. It blossomed as he kissed her, slanting his mouth over hers, molding them perfectly together. His tongue slid between her lips, tasting her, urging her to respond, and amazingly she did. Her blood was pulsing faster now, making her slightly light-headed. The water in the pool lapped slickly against her hips, the sensuous rhythm matching the thrust of his tongue. She tangled her fingers in his hair and kissed him back, opening her mouth to him, urging him to deepen the kiss.

His hands cupped her breasts, molding each one, budding the ends, making them swell and ache softly. Then his mouth slid there to ease the ache, but it only seemed to grow more fierce. He laved her nipples, circled them with his tongue, pulled the fullness between his lips and suckled gently.

Sensation overwhelmed her. Her legs felt suddenly weak and wildly unsteady. Her stomach sank as if the stones beneath her feet had suddenly dropped away.

"Adrian . . ." It came out on a soft breath of air and he recognized it for the plea it was. A big hand settled at her waist and he drew her closer, then he was lifting her up, setting her down on the steps at the edge of the pool, kissing her and filling his hands with her breasts.

"Adrian . . . dear God . . ."

Soft, moist kisses trailed along her jaw, down her throat, and across her shoulders. He kissed her breasts, then moved lower, across her rib cage, across her stomach. His warm tongue ringed her navel, then he moved lower, pressing her backward, his mouth hot and possessive, burning a path across the flat spot between her hipbones.

Her legs were slightly parted, she realized, and Adrian knelt between them, widening the distance between her thighs, his shoulders casting broad shadows against the surface of the water. Elissa gasped in shock as he settled his mouth over the tiny bud at her core. She tried to push him away, but he held her fast, his tongue sliding in, a hot wave of pleasure jolting through her.

Oh, dear God. Of all the things she had expected him to do, this was surely not among them.

He tasted her with steady purpose, his tongue slick and moist, and waves of heat scorched her insides. His hands gripped her thighs and he spread her even wider, took her even more deeply, and she thought that she might die of the pleasure.

It was wicked. It was sinful. It was surely the most incredible thing she had ever experienced. God in heaven—his hands and his mouth were everywhere, touching her, claiming her, and suddenly she was burning out of control. Something was happening inside her, a thick knot was forming, a spiraling heat that made every muscle and cord tighten inside her.

"Adrian . . ." she whispered, mindless with heat and need, feeling as if she were about to fly apart. A cry escaped, a moan of unbearable pleasure, and the world seemed to crash in on top of her. Bright lights flared. Pinpricks of sweetness rippled across her skin. Her body went taut then suddenly felt limp and boneless.

Adrian came up over her, his body raining droplets of steamy water. He kissed her again and she could taste her own musty scent, mingled with the maleness that seemed to surround him. Positioned on the steps between her legs, he began to ease his hardness inside her, and Elissa was too numb to be frightened, still too pleasantly absorbed to do more than allow him entrance.

"All right?" he asked once he had filled her completely. "This time I didn't hurt you?"

Elissa couldn't help smiling. "No, you did not hurt me."

Adrian's mouth curved in a slow smile of relief. For the first time she realized that he had been worried about her. He wanted to make this right for her. He wanted her to enjoy it. As he began to move his hips, thrusting slowly, setting up a rhythm, she discovered what she felt went far beyond enjoyment. She was feeling the most exquisite sensations she had ever encountered.

Her head tipped back, came to rest on the cool gray stone. Adrian kissed her, filling her again, sliding out and then driving forward, causing the water to lap around them in warm, gentle waves. The heat inside her began to build, the swirling pleasure she had known before. Her hands came up to his muscled shoulders and she arched her back, taking him deeper still.

He quickened his thrusts, driving into her harder, pounding faster, and still she wanted more. Her fingers dug into his shoulders. Her legs went around his hips and the tension increased in his powerful body. Still he drove on, so hard and deep she couldn't stop the pleasure from expanding, from tightening into a fierce, sweet coil, then bursting out of control.

She cried out his name as she reached her peak and her nails raked furrows in his muscular back. Adrian didn't seem to notice. Several more deep thrusts and his body went rigid. His head fell back and he groaned, his tall frame shuddering with pleasure, then he collapsed against her.

They lay motionless for several long moments, their bodies still entwined, hearts pumping, the water lapping softly against the stones. With a sigh and a last gentle kiss, he pulled himself away.

Bright green eyes held hers, sensual eyes, seductive even in their casual regard. "What happened at the cottage should never have occurred," he told her. "What we shared this night, my lovely little innocent, that is making love."

Her body still tingled from the way he had touched her, the intimate things he had done, and color rose into her cheeks. "Yes . . . I suppose it was."

A sleek, dark brow arched up. "You suppose? You are telling me you are still in doubt?"

She laughed then, softly, unexpectedly. "You've left no doubt, my lord. You have managed to show me very well."

Adrian smiled. "I shall take that as a compliment, my lady."

"It was meant as such, my lord."

He chuckled then, a rumble in his powerful chest. "I suppose we should get out. If we don't we shall return to the villa looking like a couple of shriveled grapes."

Elissa sighed. As much as she had dreaded to come, now she hated to leave. "I suppose so."

"On the other hand"—he pressed a light kiss into the palm of her hand—"there is a sofa in each of the changing rooms. Perhaps I could show you once more before we leave exactly what it is to make love."

She shouldn't. It was utter folly to allow him any closer, to chance that her feelings for him might grow. Still, life could be short—her brother's death proved that—and intrigue swirled around her.

"Perhaps you could," she said. "Perhaps there is something I have not yet learned."

Adrian grinned wickedly, bent and lifted her dripping body into his arms, then strode out of the pool splendidly naked. "That is one thing, sweet angel, of which you may be certain."

It wasn't until well after midnight that they returned home.

Adrian rode out of Baden the following morning. He left a brief note for Elissa telling her he'd been called away, nothing more. He stifled an urge to write something tender, something personal that spoke of the evening they had shared. Something held him back. The night was too memorably etched in his mind, and he didn't like the fact that it was. He didn't like the notion that bedding her had done nothing to decrease his appetite for her, had only made him want her more.

It was a dangerous and unwelcome sensation. He hadn't forgotten that the girl was a liar and a fraud.

Setting an easy pace into the city, he reached the outskirts of Vienna a little over three hours later and reined Minotaur up on a rise. Majestic baroque buildings paid homage to poetic bell towers, tall pointed spires, and glorious domes. In the distance, he could see the highest landmark in the city, the 390-foot spire of St. Stephen's Cathedral, and the impressive blue roofs of the Hofburg palace.

His first stop was a building on Kärntnerstrasse, the street that housed the office of Gerhard Mahler, the investigator he had used when he had been in Austria four years ago. The man's assignment had been easier then: simply track down the identity of and information on a lady he had observed on several occasions at the theater.

Gisela Handrick had subsequently provided quite a pleasant several weeks in his bed.

Seated in a chair in the investigator's small but tidy office, Adrian watched as Mahler, a small, thin, studious-looking man in his thirties, studied the notes of their conversation.

"If my understanding is correct, Lord Wolvermont, you wish me to unearth whatever information I can manage in regard to the Count and Countess von Langen."

"Exactly. Count von Langen is supposed to be from the town of Mariazell. Assuming that is true, information about him shouldn't be difficult to ferret out, though he has been gone from the country for a number of years."

The slender man looked down at his notes. "Living in England, you said."

Adrian nodded. "That is correct. Cornwall, as the story goes."

"Britain is quite some distance away. Information from such a distance will be difficult to unearth."

"I realize that. I'll take care of that portion of the inquiry myself. I've already posted a letter to London instructing my solicitor to hire an investigator there. If any portion of the girl's story is true, it shouldn't be hard to discover the facts." Still, it might take weeks, or even months. He was counting on finding the answers he needed here in Austria.

"I shall begin right away, my lord." He smiled from beneath a finger-thin mustache. "As I recall, you are a man who requires immediate action."

A corner of Adrian's mouth tipped up. "Exactly so. Thank you, Herr Mahler. I'm certain you'll do your usual capable job."

The little man smiled at the praise and Adrian left him to begin his work. From Kärntnerstrasse, he made his way across the city to his meeting with General Ravenscroft. This time he had been summoned to Ravenscroft's personal quarters, an elegant three-story residence on the edge of the city not far from where his troops were encamped.

A butler showed him into the house and Ravenscroft greeted him at the door leading into the study, a cozy, wood-paneled chamber smelling faintly of lemon oil and cigar smoke. "Colonel Kingsland, do come in."

"Thank you, General." Adrian waited while Ravenscroft returned to his seat behind a polished rosewood desk, then sat down in a deep leather chair across from him. He didn't miss the scowl pulling the man's thick gray brows into a frown, or the fatigue that appeared in purple smudges beneath his eyes.

"I sent for you, Colonel, because a matter of importance has arisen."

Adrian eyed him across the width of the desk. "From the look on your face, I assumed this wasn't a simple briefing."

"No, I'm afraid it isn't." He reached for a crumpled piece of paper lying on the green felt blotter and slid it toward Adrian, who picked it up and began to read.

" 'Ninety thousand troops marching into Bavaria under Archduke Charles. Unknown number under Hiller. Bellegard and his troops converging.' " Adrian looked up from the missive, staring in disbelief. "Good God, is this information correct?"

"I'm afraid so, Colonel."

Adrian shook his head. "You mentioned before that you thought there might be a leak. Apparently you were correct."

"Regretfully, that is so, and as you can see by that message, the matter has become extremely urgent."

"How many people are privy to this level of information?" Adrian asked.

"Unfortunately more than you might think. The emperor, of course, and a number of his top advisors. Several Austrian generals, including the three involved in the diplomacy at

Baden: Schnabel, Steigler, and General Oppelt. Our ambassador knows, of course; there are aides and couriers who might be able to find out. If the man were clever enough, he might have gathered the information from a number of separate sources and pulled the facts together.''

Yes, Adrian thought. *If the man were clever enough—or the woman.*

''The point is,'' the general continued, ''there is no longer a doubt we have a traitor in our midst. The only problem is discovering who it is.''

Adrian fingered the message, studying the neatly scrolled words penned in German. ''What is this mark at the bottom?'' A small round circle with an image in the middle. ''It looks like some sort of bird.''

''It seems to be an identifying seal of some kind. We have speculated on the type of bird it might be, but no one knows for sure.''

Adrian rubbed his chin, still staring at the letter, not liking the direction of his thoughts. ''Where did you get this?''

''It was discovered on a dead man in an alley outside Reiss's Tavern here in Vienna. The man was not in the military. He had no family or relatives that we have been able to locate. The truth is, we haven't a clue as to where this message might have originated and not a single notion where to look for who might have sent it.''

But perhaps Adrian did. He stared at the message and his stomach tightened. Surely the little fool wasn't really involved in spying. But remembering the night he had caught her coming out of the ambassador's room, he couldn't be sure.

The general stood up and so did Adrian. ''I want you to keep your eyes and ears open, Colonel. I realize you won't be returning to Baden for a couple of days, but perhaps once you are there, you'll be able to ask a few questions, see what you might turn up. Remember to be discreet. This war is getting closer every day, and with a spy about, the element of danger has just increased tenfold.''

"I'll do my best, General Ravenscroft." With a sharp salute, he started toward the door.

"And Colonel Kingsland—"

Adrian turned. "Yes, General?"

"One man is dead already. Do not underestimate the threat this man poses."

Adrian's jaw went tight. "I assure you I won't." Tucking his hat beneath his arm, Adrian left the study. Outside the house, a groom led Minotaur from the stable at the rear, and Adrian swung up on the stallion's back.

The general's words churned through his mind: *There is no doubt we have a traitor in our midst.* The urge to leave for Baden was strong, but he wouldn't be returning this night or the next. He needed to check in with his regiment, see that the tasks he'd assigned were completed, and assure himself that his men were faring well. Once he had done so, he could begin his latest task—and hope to bloody hell Elissa was not involved.

Elissa accepted the note Sophie handed over, the second from a gentleman she had received in the last two days. Unlike the first cool, unfeeling missive from Adrian informing her of his absence from Baden for the next several days, this one from General Steigler begged her forgiveness for his treatment of her at the picnic and apologized for his overzealous reaction to her innocent questions.

He inquired after her health, having just learned of the accident she had suffered that day, and mentioned his escort to the upcoming ball. He also asked that she join him for supper that evening at seven o'clock.

As she read the note, Elissa felt a pang of disappointment that the message was not from Adrian, and a measure of relief that Steigler's anger had faded. She would be spending time in his company once more, working to gain his trust, and she wouldn't make the mistake of angering him again.

Part of her was indeed relieved. Another, larger part dreaded the evening ahead. It was obvious the general was renewing his campaign to bed her, and she knew how deter-

mined he was to succeed. Still, with the injury she had suffered in the fall so freshly healed, she might yet be safe from
his advances.

The hours ticked past and Elissa mentally prepared herself.
The evening began rather well, considering how little she
wanted to be there, an intimate supper given by the wife of
a major named Holdorf in honor of the major's birthday. It
was held at a small but well-appointed residence at the edge
of town, a party of twelve including their host and hostess.

Dinner was superb: a thick bean soup; a boiled beef dish
called *Tafelspitz*; fresh vegetables; potatoes sautéed with on-
ions; *Knödel*, a bread dumpling; and a lovely raspberry torte
for dessert. Throughout the meal, Elissa made pleasant conversation with Frau Holdorf, a plump, loquacious woman in
her thirties, all the while avoiding the suggestive, heavy-
lidded glances cast her way by General Steigler.

"Your companion is quite lovely," she overheard Frau
Holdorf say as the company rose from the table at the end of
the meal.

"Yes . . ." her husband agreed, with a brief, speculative
glance in Elissa's direction. "I approve your taste, General
Steigler."

Though Elissa had immediately warmed to Frau Holdorf,
there was something about the major, a thin, slightly effem-
inate blond man, that Elissa did not like. She watched the
way his eyes slid over the swell of her breast, the faint edge
of a smile that seemed to settle on his lips as he watched her
with the general.

On the surface, the major was mildly attractive, yet there
was something about him . . . something oddly calculating
that reminded her of Steigler. Perhaps it was the reason they
were friends.

The evening passed without incident. Talk of war was kept
to a minimum, much to Elissa's chagrin, and much of the
conversation revolved around the empress's upcoming ball.
Finally it was time to leave, and thinking of the moments
ahead, Elissa's stomach knotted. She desperately needed to

be alone with Steigler, yet with equal desperation she dreaded what might happen.

They made their farewells and Steigler helped her into his shiny black calèche. "The hour is still early," he said, seating himself beside her on the seat. "There is a place I have use of where we might be private, perhaps enjoy a glass of brandy before I return you home." His eyes said he meant to enjoy more than brandy, and Elissa's stomach did a heavy roll.

She told herself to say yes. She needed to talk to him, to win his confidence and trust. Instead she found herself smiling but faintly shaking her head.

"There is nothing I should enjoy more, General Steigler. Unfortunately, the fall I took has left me with a few ill effects and my head has begun to throb unbearably." She reached over and laced her fingers through his, felt the long, slender bones. "When we are finally alone, I want everything to be perfect. Can you understand that, General?"

He frowned, his eyes going dark and unreadable. "I grow tired of waiting, Elissa. Should I discover you are playing some sort of game, I promise you will not enjoy the consequences."

The rattle of iron wheels over rough cobblestones filled the silence in the carriage. Elissa's heart thundered. Steigler was not the sort to encourage—God only knew the consequences. And yet she had no choice. Hoping he wouldn't see the worry in her eyes, she squeezed his hand and smiled up at him from beneath her lashes.

"I'm worth waiting for, General, I promise you."

He relaxed at that, raised her fingers to his lips. She noticed they felt dry and a little bit chafed, and a thread of revulsion slipped through her.

"I am usually a far more patient man," he said, a faint smile curling his lips. "However, my dear, where you are concerned, I find my patience is wearing thin. But you are right. I wouldn't want you feeling unwell."

Elissa settled back against the plush red velvet seat, angry with herself for her lack of courage, yet wildly relieved to escape him again. Relieved, that was, until she felt the general's hand at her waist, pulling her against him, felt his dry lips crushing down upon hers in a kiss. His hands moved over her breasts and through the thin silk fabric, he squeezed each one, testing the shape and size, lightly abrading her nipple.

Nausea rolled through her. Dear God, could she really allow this man to touch her as Adrian had done? Put his hands and mouth on her in the intimate way that Adrian had?

He broke off the kiss as the carriage rolled up in front of Blauenhaus. "I believe you are right, my dear. The wait appears to be well worth it."

Elissa said nothing, just let him help her down to the street and walk her to the door.

He bowed with great formality over her hand. "Good night, Lady von Langen. I look forward to escorting you to the ball." He smiled thinly. "I trust by then you'll be feeling far better."

Elissa started to tremble. "Y-yes . . . I'm certain I will be." Making her way inside the house, she hurried upstairs to her room. All the way there, her stomach roiled threateningly. Dear God, how could she let him touch her when every time he did, she thought she might throw up?

She closed the door and leaned against it, grateful for its solid support. Sophie had laid a fire in the hearth so thankfully the room was warm. Elissa crossed the bedchamber on unsteady legs and stood in front of the flames, rubbing her arms against the chill that had crept into her body.

Images of Steigler rose up, his thin, harsh features, his dry, chapped lips, the moisture in his palms when he had touched her. Was he really a traitor—the man responsible for the death of her brother? There was no proof as yet, but she believed him capable of it. She could sense his ruthlessness, his casual disregard for the people around him. For enough money, would he use his ruthless nature to further his own ends?

Images of Karl clashed with those of Steigler. Karl tall and fair, so brave and handsome. A memory arose of them as children, of Karl laughing as she trailed along behind him in her mother's blue silk gown. Knowing it was he who would get the thrashing if they were caught, Karl had still joined in the fun, donning Papa's best tailcoat and grinning at the sight they made in the tall cheval glass mirror.

She remembered him older, more serious. Karl was twenty-two, Elissa just eighteen when he came to her seeking advice about a girl named Allison Bainbridge, the daughter of a squire from a neighboring village. He had thought of proposing, since the squire seemed in favor of Allison's marriage to the von Langen heir, and he believed the girl would say yes. She was young and lovely and he thought that she would make a good wife. Elissa had simply asked him if he loved her.

Karl looked thoughtful, then he shook his head. He bent and kissed her cheek. "Thanks, Lis. I guess I have my answer." He joined the army the following week.

Now Karl was dead and no one seemed to care. Nothing had been done about his murder, and his urgent last request had yet to be fulfilled. She had to find the man they called the Falcon—for Karl and for the countries they both loved. She knew little of catching a spy, but surely she could find a way.

Elissa began to pace in front of the fire. Steigler was staying at the emperor's villa. Adrian was still in Vienna, and even if he weren't, from the tone of his coldhearted message, there was every chance, now that he'd had what he wanted, his interest in her had waned.

The thought made something squeeze inside her. Elissa forced herself to ignore it. Whatever happened between them, she had no one to blame but herself.

Her thoughts returned to Steigler and the task she had set for herself. The empress's ball was being held at the villa. If she could get into the general's suite of rooms, surely she could find some scrap of evidence that would connect him to the Falcon. Once she had it, she could take it, along with Karl's letter, to someone in authority. She could save herself from Steigler and discharge her obligation to her brother without having to compromise her honor.

The fire cracked and popped and the heat felt good against her skin. Elissa released a shaky breath and some of the tension drained from her body. Perhaps her scheme would work. There was no way to know until she tried, but at least for the present, she had a plan.

She crossed to the bellpull and rang for her maid, promising herself she would think no more of Steigler. It was a promise she found easy to keep. As the hours slid past, it wasn't the general, but memories of Adrian Kingsland and his powerful, hard-muscled body that tormented her restless sleep.

Chapter *Ten*

Elissa dressed with care for the empress's ball, choosing a gown of deep plum brocade shot with gold. It was her most elegant gown, the only one she had brought lavish enough for such an occasion. She smoothed the high-waisted skirt while Sophie floated around her, fussing over her hair and checking last-minute details.

"You mustn't forget this, milady." The slight, dark-haired girl handed her an elegant painted fan boasting an English sunset in colors of plum and gold.

"Thank you, Sophie." Elissa leaned down for a last glance in the mirror and surveyed her hair, pulling a blond curl back into place beside her ear. Tension sizzled along her nerves as she thought of the evening she had planned—a night that included invading the general's private quarters.

Sophie sighed. "You look beautiful, milady. I hope you have a wonderful time."

Elissa smiled. "Thank you, Sophie." With a last deep breath, she fled the room. In truth, the best time she could possibly have would be finding a connection between Steigler and the Falcon—and getting away *unscathed,* as the duchess would have said. Whatever the evening held in store, she prayed it would not include getting caught like a common thief.

She paused at the top of the stairs, her gloved hands gripping the gilded banister. On the marble floor below, in full-dress uniform—solid white except for a crimson collar and cuffs and row upon row of heavy gold braid—General Steigler stood waiting. The sight of his coolly ominous figure made the air compress in her lungs.

"Lady von Langen." His black eyes seemed to gleam with an unholy light as he surveyed the low-cut bodice of her gown, his gaze crawling over the tops of her breasts.

Elissa suppressed a shiver. "Good evening, General. I hope I haven't kept you waiting."

Something flickered in his expression, then it was gone. The general bowed over her hand. "A small wait is hardly important. Shall we go?"

Elissa took his arm and they made their way out to the carriage. There were others in their party, she saw as she climbed in, a colonel named Fleisher and his wife, who had attended Major Holdorf's birthday supper, as well as a general named Oppelt she hadn't met before. It was a small measure of comfort not to be riding with Steigler alone.

They chatted pleasantly on the way to the emperor's villa, a huge stone structure originally built as an abbey that had been added onto and restored over the years. With its rounded, cone-shaped towers and countless chimneys, the house had a slightly medieval air, yet the windows were large and plentiful, admitting the sunshine the emperor so enjoyed when he was in Baden.

The house was overflowing with dignitaries by the time they arrived. With the men in their flashy military dress, the women in their diamonds and pearls, they glittered like royalty, yet Steigler's presence, along with that of General Oppelt, caused a perceptible stir. It was obvious they were men of the emperor's innermost circle, for he greeted them personally and with noticeable warmth.

Which meant, Elissa thought, that Steigler had access to the emperor's most guarded secrets, just as she had believed.

Steigler smiled and took Elissa's hand. "Your Majesty, I should like to present the Countess von Langen." He bowed and drew her forward. "She has been eager to meet you."

Elissa dropped into a deep, graceful curtsy, trying not to feel guilty for the deceit she was committing in what she hoped was a very good cause. "Your Majesty, I am honored."

"The honor is mine, Lady von Langen." He was a tall, lean, elegantly built man in his early forties, thin-faced and graying, yet there was an aura of strength about him and intelligence in his eyes. "I was acquainted with your late husband," he said, "though we met on only a single occasion."

Elissa wet her lips, suddenly nervous again. "I—I didn't realize you knew him."

"As I said, we met only briefly." He smiled. "Perhaps you and I shall have the chance to become better acquainted." He surprised her by offering his arm. "Come, I shall introduce you to the empress. Perhaps after that you will wish to dance."

Elissa relaxed a little and smiled. She liked this man, Francis I. He was shrewd and he wanted to win this war against Napoleon. Perhaps, once she had proof of her claims, the emperor would help her.

The evening progressed hour by hour, Elissa smiling and dancing several times with Steigler, but instead of going off with his friends as he usually did, the general remained unfashionably close at hand. The sweeping grand staircase beckoned, leading to the rooms and suites upstairs. She knew which suite was his—she had bribed a servant to tell her, implying an illicit rendezvous sometime later in the evening.

It was embarrassing to pose as the general's mistress, even to a servant, when in fact she was doing everything in her power to keep it from being the truth. But she smiled and fluttered her lashes and learned that his suite sat at the far end of the east wing, the one with the wide double doors.

Now, if she could only get away from him long enough to steal upstairs, search his room, and return undetected . . .

He was standing just a few feet away. She watched him from beneath her lashes, saw a footman approach and hand him a note on a small silver salver. Steigler plucked the note from the tray, scanned it quickly, then ordered the servant to relay a message to the sender that he would soon be on his way.

Smiling, he closed the short distance to where Elissa stood, an unmistakable eagerness gleaming in his cool, dark eyes. "A courier has just arrived. Apparently there is news of some importance. The emperor has requested my presence. It probably won't take long, but I cannot say for certain."

He bent forward and whispered in her ear. "Enjoy yourself while I am away, Elissa. Just remember to keep me in your thoughts." His breath whispered past her ear in a moist, suggestive manner, and an unwelcome shiver passed down her spine.

Elissa firmly ignored it. She was her mother's daughter. Surely she could play this simple part. Gazing up at him through eyes liquid with warmth, she graced him with her most seductive smile. "I shall think of you, *mein General,* you may be certain. I shall be waiting with eager anticipation for your return."

He brought her gloved hand to his lips, lingered over it longer than he should have, finally turned and walked away.

Elissa breathed a sigh of relief. Sweet God, she really must be a competent actress if she could make him believe she found him the least bit attractive when in truth he made her skin crawl. She was pondering her success as she watched him disappear, worrying only vaguely how she would extricate herself from his clutches if her upstairs mission failed.

She counted to ten, turned toward the beautiful grand staircase—and stopped dead at the sight of the tall man lounging against the wall, watching her with menacing calm.

Adrian. Dear, sweet God, what is he doing here? She'd been certain he would still be in Vienna. Clearly he was not. Seeing his coldly furious expression, there was no doubt he had witnessed her flirtatious exchange with Steigler—anger seeped from every muscle and sinew in his body. Glittering green eyes speared her with silent accusation. Beneath his casual pose, his body thrummed with tension that tightened the lines of his face.

Her legs felt too shaky to move so she stood where she was, thinking surely he meant to confront her. Instead he turned and walked away.

Relief trickled through her, yet her heart pounded frantically. She felt an odd, regretful twist as she eyed the place he had been, then her gaze swung nervously toward the door leading out to the foyer. Did she dare to go forward with her plan? If she tried to go upstairs, Adrian might see her. As angry as he was, there was every chance he would follow. God only knew what he would do if he caught her in Steigler's room.

She stared at the doorway, wondering where he might have gone, then saw a footman rounding the corner in her direction. The man didn't stop until he reached her, his posture nearly as erect as Adrian's always was. Extending a white-gloved hand, he held out a silver salver and Elissa snatched up the folded piece of paper on the tray.

Inscribed in a man's bold hand, the words read simply: *The Roman Room. Now.*

Elissa stared at the footman, her pulse hammering madly.

"You will find the room at the rear of the house," the footman said. "The colonel will be waiting."

Her stomach knotted with dread. He had seen her with Steigler, flirting with the man like a brazen hussy. Dear God, what must he be thinking?

"Thank you," she said to the footman, who turned and walked away while Elissa still stood frozen. Adrian demanded she come to him and expected her to obey, as she had agreed. If she didn't, he would go to the ambassador, mayhap even broach his suspicions to the general.

Dear God, she couldn't let that happen. Forcing a stiffness into her spine that matched that of any soldier, she started across the room in the direction he had pointed, but Robert Blackwood stepped in her way.

"I couldn't help noticing the footman's approach, my lady, and you look a little pale. I trust nothing untoward has occurred?"

Elissa forced a smile. "No, no, it's nothing like that. I'm

a bit tired, is all. Thank you, Robert, for your concern.'' He made a slight bow, and she continued past him, out of the ballroom into the entry then down the hall to the room at the rear.

The door was closed. She turned the gilded handle and walked into a marble-floored salon hung with dark blue velvet draperies and lined with sculpted busts of Roman emperors. Since the waters at Baden had been used since the Roman occupation, she supposed it was fitting, yet their icy marble eyes were somehow disturbing.

A sound drew her attention. Elissa turned toward the tall man standing at a sideboard against the wall where he had poured himself a brandy. ''You're late.'' His scarlet tunic and white breeches glittered with buttons and braid, but they couldn't compete with the fierce glint in his eyes.

''I—I'm sorry. I came as quickly as I could.''

He said nothing as he approached, just stepped past her, closed the door and slid the latch, locking them inside.

Elissa moistened her lips, which suddenly felt dry. ''When ... when did you get back?'' She fidgeted beneath his close regard, nervously toyed with the fingers of her long white gloves.

''I only just arrived. Oddly enough, I found myself eager to return. I was looking forward to your company.'' A hard smile curved his lips. ''I could tell when I got here just how eager you were to see me.''

She flushed guiltily, damning Steigler and the situation she found herself in. Then she thought of the cold way Adrian had left her and forced her chin into the air. ''From the message you sent, I find it difficult to believe you thought of me at all. The general's escort was arranged some time back, and even if it hadn't been, whom I spend my time with is none of your concern.''

A muscle tightened in his jaw. ''You're right, *Countess.* You may do whatever you wish ... as long as I have no need of you. At present, however, that is not the circumstance.'' He set his brandy glass ringing on the table and walked behind the sofa that sat in front of the fire.

"Come here . . . angel." The rough male cadence of his voice slid out on a dangerous growl. His eyes, a deep jade green, moved with undisguised heat over her body. They left no doubt of his intention, and the fact that he meant to have her made a knot contract in her stomach. At the same time she felt oddly aroused.

She glanced with longing toward the door, wondering at the crush of people just beyond, then took a tentative step in his direction.

A sleek, dark brow arched up at her timid approach. "You're not afraid, are you?"

Her chin went up. "No. Should I be?"

"Not of what is about to happen. Of other things, perhaps."

She didn't like the sound of that, but she let it pass, continuing until she stood in front of him. The faint sound of laughter drifted through the walls and she thought that she must be wrong, that even Lord Wolvermont wouldn't have the audacity to make love in the emperor's drawing room.

"You don't really mean to—" He cut off her words with a kiss, a fierce, possessive invasion that showed her how angry he was. For a moment she stiffened, her hands coming up to his chest, pressing against the rigid muscles there, trying to free herself from his grasp. Then the kiss began to gentle. Hard lips softened to firm, warm promise, molding themselves to hers, sending a jolt of heat into her belly.

His hand cupped the back of her neck, drawing her forward as he deepened the kiss, tasting the inside of her mouth. Her knees felt weak and her breasts began to swell, her nipples rubbing painfully against the stiff brocade of her bodice. He must have sensed it for his hand moved there, slid inside to cup the fullness, gently kneading, teasing the ends into tight little buds.

A faint moan escaped and the hands on his chest crept slowly around his neck. She didn't want Steigler. If only she could tell him. It was Adrian she wanted.

He loosened several buttons at the back of her gown with the same deft skill he had shown before, allowing it to gape open, giving him freer access to her breasts. He squeezed each one gently, then lowered his head and took one into his mouth, sucking hard on the ends, making them stiffen and tingle.

Liquid heat moved through her, curling low in her stomach, fluttering over her skin. Her breath came in shallow little gasps and moisture slid into her core. She was trembling now, wanting him as she always seemed to, certain he wouldn't really take her—not here.

"Turn around," he whispered, hot kisses trailing along her neck, his teeth nipping into the lobe of an ear. She did as he asked, wondering what he meant to do, certain he would stop, beginning to pray that he wouldn't, that his mouth and hands would continue their magic.

The back of the sofa formed a soft blue velvet cushion beneath her stomach as he bent her over, dragged up her skirt and chemise and bunched them around her waist. Cool air rushed over her bare skin and she gasped, uncertain of his intention, embarrassment making her face go warm. She tried to turn, but he forced her back down.

"Take it easy. I'm not going to hurt you."

"But—"

"You agreed to this. By God, you'll keep your word."

She started to protest, to fight him if she must, but the notion died away at the feel of his big hands stroking over her hips. He kissed the nape of her neck, his voice rough and husky against her ear.

"Such soft, smooth skin. It feels like silk beneath my fingers." His hands cupped her breasts, gently teased the ends, and heat roared through her blood. His tongue ringed the rim of her ear.

"You want this as much as I do," he whispered. "I can feel it wherever I touch you." He proved it by sliding a hand over her bottom, gently kneading, sending warm shivers across her skin.

"Part your legs for me, angel."

She whimpered but did as he asked. His hand laced through the pale hair between her legs, and a finger slid deeply inside her. He stroked her, worked the tiny bud at her core, and she trembled.

"That's right," he said. "Give yourself over to me. Let me make it good for us both."

She heard the buttons on his breeches popping open one by one, felt the thick ridge of his shaft as he positioned himself behind her. He stroked her again, deeply, relentlessly. Parting the slick folds of her sex, he slid himself inside her, burying himself completely with a single deep thrust.

Elissa gasped at the feel of him, at the raging heat that tore through her body. For a moment he just held her, giving her time to adjust to his size and length, then he began to move. She could feel the heavy thrust and drag, and splinters of heat broke over her. He was gripping her hips now, dragging himself out, then thrusting deeply back in. Out and then in, out and then in. The pleasure was nearly unbearable. Unconsciously she arched her back, taking him even more deeply, and Elissa heard him groan.

His hands increased their hold. "Damn you," he swore, so softly she almost didn't hear him. Then the pounding increased and the memory of his harsh words faded away. She felt his body tighten, and her own responded in rhythm to his. Three more deep, pounding strokes and she climaxed in long, bone-melting waves, carrying Adrian to release in her wake.

In silence, they stood locked together, hearts pounding, heads bowed, neither of them speaking, both of them trembling. His arm tightened around her waist, pulling her back against his chest as they spiraled down. Eventually her senses returned and she was able to focus her thoughts. When she did, she felt the whisper of his handkerchief between her legs, then he was lowering her skirts and fastening the back of her gown, turning her to face him.

Except for the wayward dark brown lock of hair curling over his forehead, he looked as immaculately dressed and perfectly groomed as he had when he had arrived in the drawing room.

A glance in the tall gilded mirror across the way said her appearance, however—

Dear God, she looked like a just-bedded trollop!

She gasped at her image and her cheeks flamed bright red. Lips ripe and swollen from his kisses, a dappled flush of crimson over the tops of her breasts, wisps of her sleekly styled, perfectly coiffured hair curling in disarray around her face.

"Oh, dear God," she whispered, "what have I done?" Steigler was out there waiting, the emperor and empress, the duchess, and God only knew who else. She was supposed to be polished and sophisticated, a married woman who knew how to deal with such matters, but she wasn't—not really. At the moment she felt more like a lost little girl.

She lifted her gaze to Adrian, fighting to hold back tears. "I c-can't go out there. I c-couldn't possibly face all those people." She searched his face, but saw only a handsome, distant stranger. He had taken what he wanted, now he would leave her to face the consequences alone. She bit down on her lip, trying not to cry, but suddenly it all seemed more than she could bear.

Karl and Steigler. Losing her innocence to Adrian. Trying so hard not to fall in love with him. She swayed against the sofa, a sob escaping, a hand going up to hide the tears streaming down her cheeks.

Adrian muttered a curse. "Dammit, stop crying. You haven't done anything as bad as all that." Striding forward, he gripped her shoulders and turned her to face him. At her ravaged expression, his hard grip gentled, and a sigh whispered past those sensuous, ruthless lips.

"Stay here," he instructed. "Lock the door behind me and don't let anyone in until I return."

She looked up at him and felt a surge of hope. "You're coming back?"

"What choice do I have? I can hardly leave you like this."

She swayed against him, rested her hands on his chest. "Take me home, Adrian. Please . . . I just . . . I just want to go home."

He grumbled something she didn't quite catch, gently detached himself and stepped back. "Just stay here—and dammit, don't cry."

Dashing the tears from her cheeks, she followed him to the door and locked it behind him, then waited tensely for his return. It seemed like hours before she heard his footsteps in the corridor, though in truth less than fifteen minutes had passed. At the sight of his tall frame stepping through the door, her plum brocade cloak thrown over a powerful arm, relief swept through her so strong it made her dizzy.

"I've spoken to the duchess," he said, draping the cloak around her shoulders. "I told her you were indisposed, and that I would be seeing you home. She'll make whatever excuses are needed." He pulled up the hood, hiding her tear-stained face. "There's an entrance at the side of the house. My carriage is waiting. Let's go."

The stirrings of a smile edged her face. She should have known he wouldn't abandon her. It was his fault this had happened, yet in truth, she had wanted it as well. And it definitely could have been worse. Taking his arm, she let him guide her into the hall, around the corner, and out the door at the side of the house. In minutes they were cocooned inside the carriage.

She studied him from the shadows of her hood, uncertain what she should say, yet oddly unwilling to sit there in silence. "The hour is still early. I suppose you'll be returning to the ball."

He smiled thinly. "Considering our unscheduled departure, I think it's a good idea, don't you?"

She didn't answer. Deep down she was grateful to be leaving, grateful that no matter the reason, she had again been spared dealing with Steigler. She wondered how the general had taken the news of her departure, and a few moments later, Adrian mentioned his name.

"I realize, for the most part what you do is your own affair, but I want you to stay away from Steigler. There are things you don't know about him, things—considering your limited experience with men—I don't think you're ready to handle."

A chill swept through her, raising goose bumps over her skin. "What . . . what sort of things?"

Adrian frowned. "It's obvious Steigler desires you. He wants you in his bed and he's ruthless when it comes to getting what he wants."

A sound of disbelief came from her throat. "And you're not, Colonel Kingsland?"

A corner of his mouth curved up. Beneath the flare of a passing streetlamp, their eyes met and held. "Touché." He settled his broad shoulders back against the seat. "I'll grant I am used to having my way, but I've never raised a hand against a woman. What a man does in bed is his own business, which is why I've said nothing so far. The truth is, Steigler enjoys hurting women. He's usually willing to pay for his pleasures, but that doesn't mean he won't take what he wants if he's forced into that position. I don't want to see you get hurt, Elissa."

She glanced out the window, suddenly chilled to the bone. Still, her voice remained light as she responded. "Thank you for your concern, Colonel, I'll certainly keep that in mind."

Adrian swore beneath his breath. Leaning forward, he gripped her shoulders, his fingers biting in, shaking her until the hood slid off her head. "Stay away from him, *Countess*— do you hear? That is another order I expect you to obey."

Elissa said nothing. More than his words, the fierce look in his eyes kept her silent. Oddly enough, if ever there was a command she wanted to follow it was that one. She closed her eyes, knowing she wouldn't be able to, wondering how, if what Adrian said was the truth, she would be able to protect herself and still uncover the Falcon.

Chapter *Eleven*

Adrian went back to the emperor's villa as soon as Elissa was returned to Blauenhaus. Now he stood at the end of the huge gilt-and-mirrored ballroom, sipping a glass of brandy and fighting to keep the bored expression off his face. For the past twenty minutes, he had been listening to Lady Ellen Hargrave sing his praises and eye him over the top of her pink jeweled fan.

"You were magnificent, Colonel. Simply magnificent. The way you so courageously fought that boar—I vow we should both of us have been killed on the spot if it hadn't been for you."

Adrian was beginning to doubt it. He thought, in fact, that Lady Ellen could probably have saved herself simply by chattering away till the big boar spun on its heels and bolted, which was exactly what he wanted to do.

Instead he nodded and smiled and stared across the crowded ballroom, thinking of Elissa, remembering the feel of her body as he had thrust himself inside her in the Roman Room. When an image arose of her elegant breasts and slender hips, his body began to harden, and silently he cursed her, angry that she could make him want her again so soon.

He tried not to think of her embarrassment, the tears on her cheeks when she realized the extent of her passion. Who was she? he wondered. He might not know her name, but

she was, he'd discovered, the most intriguing mix of innocence and sensuality that he had ever encountered.

He listened to Lady Ellen, a robust, rosy-cheeked girl with
large, rather intriguing, breasts. Another time, he might have
enjoyed the view. Tonight his eyes strayed away from her
overripe cleavage to the cupid's-bow mouth that curled up at
the corners, all the while thinking of Elissa, pondering her
relationship with Steigler, recalling the intimacy the two had
shared that could not be mistaken.

Was she really attracted to the man? Some women were.
Steigler's dark, almost sinister appearance, his casual disregard of them, the way he remained aloof, seemed in some
way to entice them. Was Elissa the sort to be drawn to his
icy persona?

Or was it something else? Something that had to do with
the information being passed to the enemy beneath their very
noses. He couldn't help remembering her interest in Ambassador Pettigru. Several times he had seen the man imbibe
more than he should have, and each of those times Pettigru
had been with Elissa. Was it merely coincidence? Or had she
encouraged him, hoping to gain information? And what of
the time he had found her coming out of Pettigru's room?

He breathed a sigh of frustration, wishing he had the answer, and took a sip of his brandy.

"Enjoying yourself, Colonel?"

His head came up. Steigler stood in front of him, a hard
glint in his eyes. Still chattering away, Lady Ellen was making reluctant farewells. Steigler flashed her a thin, disinterested smile.

"It appears I am once again in your debt," he said. "I
was told the countess became indisposed while I was en-
sconced with His Majesty, and that you were good enough
to see her safely home."

A dry smile curved Adrian's lips. "Yes. By now the lady
should be warmly tucked into her bed." Where he would like
to be, Adrian couldn't help thinking—damn his bloody soul.
The woman could very well be a traitor, and all he could
think of was hauling her back to his bed.

The general smiled thinly. "As I said, I am grateful. However, I give you fair warning—in future, I shall be the one to see to the lady's welfare."

A ripple of tension passed through him. Adrian forced it down. "If that is the lady's wish."

"It is *my* wish. That is all that matters. From now on, the countess belongs to me. Do I make myself clear?"

Adrian's fingers tightened around the bowl of the brandy snifter he cradled in his hand. "Quite clear, General Steigler."

Steigler seemed to relax. "Good. Then we understand each other." His black eyes followed the robust figure of the woman who had just departed. "Lady Ellen seems to have more than a passing interest in you, Colonel. Perhaps you should fix your attentions there."

"The girl is in search of a husband. Since I am not in the market for a wife, I doubt her father would approve."

"Lord Hargrave is too busy to notice what his daughter is about. The chance for a bit of diversion might be worth the risk."

Adrian glanced at the girl. "Perhaps you are right," he lied, thinking that of all the women he had met, Hargrave's daughter, pretty as she was, held the least amount of appeal.

Steigler made a slight bow of his head. "I'm afraid I must be off. Good night, Colonel. I hope you have a pleasant evening."

Adrian watched the general leave, liking him less with each of their meetings. Four years ago they had clashed over another woman, an opera singer Steigler was particularly obsessed with. In the end, the general had taken her—once. By force, according to the woman, a fact she never mentioned to anyone except Adrian. She'd wound up bruised and battered—though Steigler had been careful the bruises didn't show—and sickened by the things he had done.

What would he do to Elissa? Steigler thought her an experienced young widow he could lure into his perverse world. Adrian knew the truth—or at least a small part of it. Until he had taken her, Elissa was an innocent. She was young and naïve and in way over her head with Steigler.

Damn her to bloody hell—if she wanted the man, he ought to let the bastard have her.

Adrian knew without the slightest degree of doubt that until the time came when he tired of her, Elissa would belong only to him.

"So what did your friend General Steigler have to say?"

Adrian glanced up to see Jamie sauntering toward him, his scarlet uniform perfectly tailored to his lean, sinewy frame, a champagne glass held in a slim, long-boned hand. "Something pleasant, I trust." Ellen Hargrave gave him a long, assessing glance as he walked past.

"The general pleasantly warned me to stay away from Lady von Langen. Apparently, he regards the countess as property belonging solely to him."

"Somehow I don't imagine that set well with you . . . considering you seem fairly proprietary about the lady yourself."

"I don't like to share what is mine."

"Especially not with Steigler."

"No, especially not with him." He took a sip of his brandy. "She encourages him. Damned if I know why. I tried to warn her, but I don't think she'll listen. She's a strong-willed woman, determined, and intelligent—but extremely naïve. When it comes to men, not nearly in Steigler's league."

"I gathered that." Jamie sipped his champagne. "Steigler won't see it. The countess is good at playing the sophisticate with him and the others. With you, she seems different." He smiled. "I haven't the foggiest notion why, but I think the lady likes you."

"Yes . . . well, she has an odd way of showing it." Adrian blew out a breath, let his gaze wander over the glittering assembly in the ballroom. "She's in trouble, Jamie. If she plays with Steigler, she's going to get hurt. I don't want to see that happen."

Jamie studied him over the rim of his glass. "Perhaps you entertain more than a casual regard for the lady yourself."

Adrian merely grunted. He wasn't sure what he felt for

Elissa Tauber besides a strong dose of lust, but worry for her was certainly on the list.

"How did your meeting go in Vienna?" Jamie asked, drawing a return of his attention.

"Not so well, I'm afraid. I was planning to talk to you about it."

"Now is as good a time as any. Why don't we go someplace where we can be private? The Roman Room is rarely in use and there is a lock on the door."

Adrian felt a quick shot of lust at the sharp memory of bare skin and heated kisses. "I was only too recently there. I'm afraid I might have trouble concentrating on the subject at hand. Perhaps the small library would suffice."

Jamie grinned, knowing him only too well. "The library then." He motioned in that direction. "After you, Colonel Kingsland."

With a last sip of brandy, Adrian left the ballroom, Jamie following in his wake.

Elissa spent the afternoon reading in her bedchamber. Everyone at Blauenhaus believed she was not yet recovered from the malady she had supposedly suffered last night. In truth, she was simply a coward, fearful she might cross paths with Adrian, embarrassed at the wild, unbridled passions he had aroused in her in the Roman Room.

Her eyes slid closed against a wave of humiliation, yet no matter how she tried, she couldn't block the memory of his big hands gliding over her hips, the pleasure of his hard length thrusting inside her. Dear God, she had gone to him resigned to uphold the pact she had made, thinking perhaps she could dissuade him, or simply detach herself from his casual use of her body.

There was nothing casual in what they had done. It was pure, raw passion at its zenith. Worst of all—God help her— she wanted him to do it again. He was arrogant and domineering, self-centered and possessive, yet when she was with him, he could seduce the very soul from her body.

Dear God—how could she be attracted to such a devil of a man?

Whatever the reason, the fact remained that she was.

She wondered what he thought of her, if he spared a single moment thinking of what they had done? He summoned her to care for his needs as if she were his whore, took her with ruthless demand, yet always she felt his care of her. It was there in his touch, in his kiss. In the gentle way he held her when his passion was sated. He had seen her with Steigler—there was no mistaking that—and nothing could disguise his anger.

He could have left her last night when his use of her was ended. If he were truly the unfeeling man he pretended to be, he would have. Instead he had protected her from the gossip that would surely have ensued and seen her safely home.

Elissa looked down at the novel she had been reading, *Titan,* by a German author named Jean Paul, and realized her attention had strayed. To understand the story, she would have to go back and reread the last five pages. Instead she sighed and put the book away.

It was nearly time for supper said the gold-faced ormolu clock above the mantel. Outside the window, darkness descended on the garden, and a linkboy moved along the gravel paths lighting torches.

Elissa squared her shoulders. She might be a coward, but nobody knew it. Rising from the sofa, she crossed the bedchamber and rang for her maid to help her dress for supper.

Perhaps she should tell him the truth. As Elissa took her place at the long linen-draped table, a seat opposite and two chairs down from Adrian, the thought rolled through her head as it had a dozen times in the past two weeks. She no longer believed he could possibly be involved in any sort of spying. He might be arrogant and demanding, but he was a man of honor, and from what she could discover, loyal to a fault.

Perhaps if she told him the truth about who she was and why she had come, he would help her.

She glanced in his direction, felt his eyes roam over her,

penetrating eyes, hot and devouring, yet she had known them
to reflect tender care. In the salon where the guests had gathered before supper, he had been excessively polite, pretending
to ignore the faint flush that rose in her cheeks, playing the
gentleman when his gaze said his thoughts were not at all the
gentlemanly sort.

In time she found herself relaxing, allowing him to charm
her as he invariably seemed able to do.

What would he say if she showed him the letter she and
her mother had received from Karl? Would he believe her,
try to help her? God knew she wasn't good at this spy-
catching thing. Adrian seemed good at whatever it was he
decided to undertake.

If only she could tell him, make him understand why she'd
had to behave as she did, convince him that she wasn't really
interested in Steigler, that she wasn't the loose sort of woman
he must certainly believe.

But as she tried to convince herself, the same unwelcome
thought she had faced before came crashing in.

What if he tries to stop me? It was the reason she hadn't
told him sooner, the fear that always held her back. Adrian
was a colonel in His Majesty's Army, and in his own right
a wealthy, powerful man. With hardly an effort, he could
force her return to England, end the work she had started as
if it were never begun.

Even if he promised to help, he might not be able to see
it done. The war was cranking up. With Napoleon closing in,
such a small detachment of British forces might be in danger.
They could be ordered to leave at any time. Adrian would
have to leave with them, even if he hadn't discovered the
Falcon. And odds were good, once he knew what she was
about, he would refuse to let her continue.

It wasn't worth the risk. Not yet. Not until she had some
proof the man was Steigler.

Elissa took a sip of her wine and studied the colonel from
beneath her lashes. Even from a distance, there was an aura
of power about him and a hard edge of strength that spoke
of the battles he had fought. His gaze met hers, dark green

and turbulent, probing till she had to look away. She wondered if he would summon her tonight, and a trickle of anticipation wound its way into her stomach. It was insane, and yet she couldn't stop the quickening of her pulse or the subtle shift in her breathing.

Pettigru sat in the chair to her right, his attention focused on a thick bowl of liver soup. He turned and smiled in her direction.

"It's good to see you, my dear. It seems it's been ages. Your legion of admirers, I suppose, have been keeping you too busy for an old curmudgeon like me."

"You are hardly old, Sir William." She smiled at him, warmed by his words. "But you are right—it has been too long. I don't believe, however, it is too late to rectify the situation. Perhaps we might enjoy a game of chess after supper." She *had* missed his company. And earlier she had been thinking that perhaps she could get him to talk about Steigler. Mayhap indirectly, the ambassador could be of some help after all.

"I daresay that sounds splendid. A game of chess would be just the thing." Pettigru beamed and dug into his soup with fresh gusto.

They finished the meal, their heads bent in pleasant conversation while Elissa ignored Adrian's scowl. It was harder to ignore Lady Ellen's blatant interest in him, especially when he turned to face her and flashed one of his devastating smiles.

Elissa glanced away as a sharp, unmistakable pang of jealousy stabbed through her. It shouldn't have surprised her—she knew how handsome the colonel was and that any number of women were attracted to him. But until tonight, he had never paid attention to any of them.

Fortunately, supper was almost at an end. The gentlemen retired to the green drawing room for brandy and cigars, giving Elissa time to refresh herself and regain her practiced calm.

An hour later, she met Sir William in the library where the chess board was already set up, and with no word from

Adrian—she told herself she was glad—they sat down to a long, challenging game before the fire.

They spoke briefly of the war, the ambassador looking almost gleeful about it.

"This coalition could be a major turning point. A fresh Austrian offensive is what we need. The country provides important passes through the eastern Alps and its waterways are vital to transportation. Napoleon needs control and we must wrest it from him."

Elissa moved a pawn two squares ahead. "Archduke Charles seems more than ready for war."

"Good ol' Charlie." Sir William, chuckled, countering her move with one of his own teakwood pawns. "He'll do his damnedest, you may be sure, and we'll do our best to support him."

Elissa slid her ivory bishop across the board. "General Steigler also seems eager for war."

The ambassador grunted. "Steigler is a zealot. He would fight even if there wasn't the slightest chance of winning."

Elissa cocked a brow at the tone of the ambassador's voice. "Do I detect a grain of dislike for the general?"

His gaze came up from the board to settle on her face. "General Steigler fights on the side of a country soon to be our ally. I am hardly at liberty to discuss my feelings about him. Since you have asked me and we are friends, I will tell you I have little regard for the man." He eyed her darkly. "I would advise you, my lady, to consider very carefully your association with the general."

Elissa looked away from him, her gaze returning to the board. She jumped her knight up two spaces and over one. "I heard he lost most of his family lands four years ago, during the last campaign." She had heard the story yesterday morning, from Major Holdorf's wife as she and several others sipped coffee out on the terrace.

Pettigru nodded. "While Steigler was away at war, his father managed to lose what little was left of the family holdings. Fortunately, his rank carries a great deal of privilege, and the pay is enough for a comfortable retirement." He moved his queen across the board, capturing her bishop. In his next move his castle took her queen. Bushy gray brows pulled together as he studied her over the tall carved pieces.

"You're not paying attention tonight, Elissa. You're usually a far better player." He arched a brow in subtle warning. "Perhaps it would be better if we discussed another subject."

"Yes . . . yes, of course." She forced herself to smile. "Tell me about your wife, Sir William. Have you heard from her lately? How does she fare?"

His easy manner returned as he launched into an accounting of his wife's latest letter. Elissa smiled and nodded, all the while mulling over his words. So the rumor was true—Steigler had lost whatever fortune his family'd once had. A comfortable retirement might not be enough for him. Money was always a motive for deceit.

Perhaps the general's zeal for war was in truth merely a cover for his breach of faith. It might be a very thick smoke-screen. Enough to cover a very hot fire.

Adrian studied Elissa through the door to the library, wishing he could hear her conversation with Pettigru. As far as he knew, the ambassador wasn't the sort to be loose with his words, but a woman as lovely as Elissa might be distracting enough—and clever enough—to learn something of value.

Odds were Pettigru had been informed of the leak just as he had. Hopefully the news would be enough to keep the country's secrets safely locked behind his tongue. For everyone's sake, Adrian hoped so.

He watched them a moment more, listening to Elissa's easy laughter, feeling his body stir, wishing he could send another message demanding she come to him, that he could make love to her again. Unfortunately, he had other, more important matters to attend to.

Half an hour later, dressed in simple brown breeches and a full-sleeved homespun shirt, he made his way out to the stables at the rear of the house. Jamie stood waiting, also dressed simply in black nankeen breeches and a muslin shirt, a nondescript bay and a plain-faced sorrel saddled and ready to go. Minotaur and Jamie's own regimental black were too remarkable, too easily recognizable, for the task they were about.

They were headed to the Bratis Tavern, a seedy, run-down inn on a back road leading out of Baden, a place his questions had led him, a place often frequented by men at the edge of society, men who could be bought for any number of nefarious tasks—if the price was high enough.

It was also a meeting place of the disgruntled, of radical, cynical men discontented with their lot in life. Men who blamed the emperor for their failings, men opposed to the war. It was a good place to begin looking for a traitor.

Adrian made his way across the low-ceilinged smoky taproom to the long, scarred plank bar, Jamie walking beside him, his gaze going right and then left, traveling over the patrons in the dimly lit tavern, silently taking their measure. His friend was lean, but hard muscled and wiry, a good man to have at your back in a place like this.

They ordered two tankards of beer.

"You are new around here," the innkeeper said. "I do not think I have seen you in here before."

"I haven't been often to Baden," Adrian said simply, allowing his German to slide into the less polished usage of the common man. "I came only to deliver a message."

The innkeeper, a barrel-chested, black-bearded, hard-faced man, eyed him with cold, squinty eyes. "What kind of message?"

"One that could make a man a tidy sum of money."

"Go on."

"Word is, someone may be working the other side of the fence . . . carrying messages to the Frenchies. The Brits don't care who's being paid to carry them. What they want to know is where the messages are coming from. They'll pay big for that information. Very big."

The innkeeper shook his head. "Then it is a shame none of us knows anything about it."

"Yes . . . a very big shame." He leaned closer to the man across the bar. "But just in case someone does know something, I'll check back in a couple of days." He drew a small leather pouch from his waistband and tossed it onto the bar. The coins clanked pleasantly as they landed. "That's for listening. There'll be more if you find out anything useful."

"I told you, no one here knows anything about it."

"I'll be back on Tuesday," was all Adrian said. He up-ended his tankard of beer and so did Jamie. They set the mugs back down on the bar and turned and walked out through the low oaken door.

Outside the air was cleaner, smelling of wood smoke and pine, the night air brisk as they swung up into their saddles.

"Think he'll come up with something helpful?" Jamie asked.

Adrian rubbed his jaw. "Hard to say. The information may not have even come from sources in Baden. The courier was killed in Vienna. The source could have been anywhere."

"Word may get out that we're on to him."

"If it does, it won't matter. If he's got information, he'll want it to get to the French. Hopefully, sooner or later, the money we've offered will be enough to lure someone forward—here or in Vienna. We'll be heading back there in the next two days."

"What?"

"Word's come in. That's what the emperor called Steigler in to discuss last night. Napoleon is moving toward Bavaria. Things are heating up quickly, and the emperor wants to be back at the palace when it does."

Jamie glanced down the road at the yellow glow of lights in the distance. "Baden will be empty by the end of the week."

Adrian nodded. "Exactly so."

"And the countess? Will she be returning to Vienna as well?"

A muscle worked in Adrian's jaw. He still knew nothing about her, only that she was a liar and perhaps she was a spy. Still, his body hardened just to think of her. He wanted to be inside her, wanted to return to Blauenhaus and summon her to his bed. He wouldn't, not at such a late hour, but as soon as he returned to Vienna he would take her again. The notion occurred that perhaps he would establish her as his mistress, at least for the short time he had left in the country. He could keep a closer eye on her, and perhaps by then Mahler would have discovered who she was.

"I imagine the countess will be returning to the city with the duchess," he said. "She's made no mention of going back to England, though God knows it would be the smart thing for her to do."

"Certainly it would be the safest." Jamie smiled. "But I don't imagine you'll protest her staying overmuch. It will certainly suit your purpose."

Adrian grunted. "It will, indeed." He was glad his friend didn't know the girl had been a virgin. The amused smile on the major's face would no doubt be a scowl of disapproval. Jamie was too damned noble. Adrian's nobility had a very strict limit, and lying little frauds like Elissa fell well beyond the bounds.

Adrian ignored the mocking voice that said he would have taken her no matter who she was. That he had wanted her, and one way or another, he would have had her. The irony was, as he thought of her now, his groin thick and heavy with desire for her, at times it seemed as if Elissa were the one commanding him.

The emperor and empress left Baden two days later, a steady stream of diplomats, military leaders, and aristocrats following in their wake. Francis I was returning to his palace at Schönbrunn, where many of the more important diplomats and military officers would be housed. Others, like Adrian, would be returning to their private quarters in Vienna, in his case, a town house he shared with Jamie situated on Naglerstrasse, a street running along the old Roman ramparts.

The residence was built in the fifteenth century, given a classical façade in the 1700's, and ornamented with a colored relief of the Virgin Mary sometime later. The interior was elegant, providing large private suites for each of them upstairs, several marble-floored drawing rooms, a library and study, and a staff of servants to take care of them. It felt good to return to the place he had come to think of as home, yet oddly he missed the excitement of Blauenhaus.

Or was it, perhaps, that he missed his challenging, blood-heating, often fiery encounters with Elissa?

He knew she had arrived in the city along with the duchess and that soon he would see her. Though talk of war had escalated and people were somewhat uneasy, Society went on as it always did, as if naught were amiss. A musicale was planned, the affair to be held at the palace of the Duke of Webern, a magnificent baroque structure in the Innere Stadt near the Hofburg palace. Adrian discovered the invitation upon his arrival in a stack of long-waiting correspondence, all of which, he grimaced to think, were in need of some reply.

He'd been late in returning to Vienna, had stayed in Baden to make further inquiries about the possible source of the information leak, but the extra days had proved fruitless. His questions led to naught and no one came forward at the Bratis Tavern. He had left word where he could be reached in Vienna, but he didn't really believe anything would turn up. He was beginning to think the leak had not originated in Baden.

Or perhaps, considering his suspicions about Elissa, that was simply what he wanted to believe.

At any rate, he would most likely see her at the musicale. He wondered if she had heeded his warning about Steigler, but something told him she hadn't.

Unconsciously he clenched his fists.

Chapter Twelve

Elissa stood in the garden. Only a sliver of moon reflected above the houses and spires of Vienna. A thin layer of clouds covered what few stars peeked through the overhead gloom. In a gown of white satin edged with silver tulle, her slender form stood out against the blackness, and she silently wished she had chosen a more somber shade, one that would hide her in the soft midnight shadows.

Then again, she hadn't expected to be sneaking around in the dark, hiding in the shrubbery with her ear pressed against the windowpanes, hoping to catch at least some portion of the conversation between the two men inside, Major Holdorf and General Steigler.

Since her return to Vienna, she had spoken to the general only briefly. In return she had received a clipped, unfriendly greeting, and a harsh, disapproving scowl. He scared her when he looked at her that way, his eyes raking over her breasts, menacing in the way they seemed to press into her flesh. God's breath, if only she could be rid of him, certain one way or another whether he was the Falcon. If only she could have gotten into his suite of rooms.

An owl hooted somewhere over her left shoulder, and Elissa jumped several inches, a shiver skimming along her spine. She wore only a light cashmere shawl over her gown and suddenly it wasn't nearly warm enough. Her heart was clattering and her insides felt trembly, partly from fear, partly in the hope that at last a miracle would occur and she would uncover some clue for her efforts.

The crack of a twig snapped behind her. She was certain someone was following her, and she snapped her head around. Her hands were shaking, her palms damp. Her eyes searched the darkness but no one was there. It was only her imagination. She was standing deep in the shadows at the side of the house, safe, she was sure, from anyone who might wander out into the garden.

The general laughed—she could hear that very clearly—and she fixed her attention back on the two men seated in the study, watching them through the crack in the heavy gold velvet draperies. They had left the musicale before it was ended, slipping quietly away during a rendition of Beethoven's Piano Concerto No. 5, "The Emperor," played in His Majesty's honor. The general had summoned the major with a look that seemed most urgent.

Now, through the split in the curtains, she saw Holdorf smile.

"I'll make the arrangements myself," he said, "be certain the message gets through."

Message? Elissa's pulse went faster. She edged closer, held her breath. Was he talking about passing secrets to the French?

Steigler lifted his wine glass, waving it expansively then brandishing it up and down in staccato jabs to emphasize his point. "I don't want any mistakes, do you hear? This is too important. I won't tolerate any mistakes."

"I haven't disappointed you yet, have I, General Steigler?"

He lowered the glass and smiled. "No, Major Holdorf. So far your record is unblemished."

"I intend to keep it that way."

Steigler took a drink of his wine. "When will you leave?"

"In the morning. It shouldn't take long to reach the first relay point. After that there is less danger."

Elissa leaned her head against the rough stone wall, her

heart trying to pound its way free of her chest. This was it. The first real indication that Steigler was actually involved in passing information. It wasn't tangible evidence but it renewed her hope—and her determination.

"Well, well, well . . . if it isn't my lovely little angel." The lazy drawl drifted from the shadows a few feet away. "Imagine . . . finding you out here all alone." He moved forward with an easy grace in a body simmering with tension. Leaning down to peer through the curtains, he saw Steigler and Holdorf in quiet conversation and a muscle leapt in his cheek. "Ah, but then you had plenty to hold your interest, didn't you, *Countess*?"

"I was . . . I was . . ." She swallowed hard, groping to find something to say. "It was overly warm inside. I—I needed a quick breath of air."

He moved closer, gripped her arm and dragged her away from the building, deeper into the shadows of the garden. "I'm certain you did," he said, the gravelly texture of his voice made rougher by the anger that quivered through each word. "That is why you were hiding out here in the darkness. Because it was cooler, more private. It had nothing to do with the fact you wished to eavesdrop on the general's conversation."

"No! Of course not!"

He hauled her deep into the foliage and hard against his chest. "You're a liar." She tried to twist free, but his hold only tightened. "Tell me who you are."

"Y-you know who I am. I'm the Countess von Langen. I'm here from England to visit the Duchess of Murau."

"I want the truth! I want to know who you are!"

She only shook her head. "Elissa Tauber, Countess von Langen."

His hand smoothed down along her cheek, yet there was nothing of tenderness in his touch. "Such a beautiful little liar."

Elissa glanced away, unable to look into those hard green eyes a moment more. "I would tell you if I could," she said softly. "I never wanted to deceive you. Give me some time. All I need is a little more time."

The bright glow of his anger seemed to dim as he fought for control. He moved a few steps away, deeper into the darkness, his big hands fisted at his sides. His breath whispered out into the night, edged in white in the cold evening air. When he finally spoke, his words sounded husky in the quiet of the garden.

"Come here, Elissa."

Her breathing quickened. Something had changed. She could hear the difference in the thickening drawl of his voice.

"W-where are you?" she asked, though she could see the glint of gold braid flashing behind a tree in the thin rays of moonlight slanting down through the leafy foliage.

"You know where I am. Come to me, Elissa. Now."

He wanted her, she knew. She could hear it, feel it. He was angry, but he wanted her still. She made her way toward him on unsteady legs, uncertain what he meant to do. She was a little bit frightened, yet desire stabbed its sharp, keen edge at the thought of his hands and his mouth.

She paused a few feet from where he was seated on a low stone bench in the shadows, his scarlet tunic unfastened at the collar and unbuttoned partway down. She recalled the thick bands of muscle that lay beneath the coat and her fingers itched to touch them.

"I said for you to come here."

She crossed the last few feet between them, floating more than walking, lured like a moth by the heavy timbre of his voice.

"You belong to me, Elissa. You know that, don't you?"

"No, I—"

"You know it. Don't you?"

She moistened her lips. "Yes." She could see his eyes, glinting like emeralds in the moonlight, and need reared up in a thick, hot wave.

"Raise your skirts. Lift them slowly and let me see your legs."

For a moment, she faltered. Sweet God, it was hardly her

nature to behave like a cheap tavern whore. Then the image of what he might do slid into her mind. Her body tightened with longing and she thought that perhaps it was her nature after all.

Her hands trembled slightly as they slid down her narrow white silk skirt, and she slowly raised the hem, baring her legs to well above her garters.

"Higher," he commanded. "I've thought of nothing but you all week. I want to see you in the moonlight."

She clamped down on her lip, but it didn't stop the wave of heat that scorched through her. She looked into those hot green eyes and felt a sudden burst of power to think that she could make him want her so badly. Lifting the skirt and her embroidered lawn chemise, she raised them to just below the curve of her bottom. She gasped as Adrian ran a hand along the inside of her thigh, stroking her skin, making goose bumps spread across her flesh. Then he settled his big hands at her waist and lifted her astride him, her legs splayed apart by his muscular thighs.

"I want you, Elissa. Shall I show you how much?" His hand cupped the back of her neck and he dragged her mouth down to his for a fierce, scalding kiss. It was burning with heat and need, his tongue lashing out to take possession, making her whole body go taut. Wet heat slid through her, settled low in her core. Dear God, until she'd met him, she never would have guessed, never could have imagined what it might be like to know a man in this way.

Adrian deepened the kiss, demanding more, tasting her more fully, and Elissa softly moaned. Her hands slid into his thick, nearly black hair as he angled his head to claim her more fully. Then, one by one, the buttons popped free at the back of her gown and he filled his hands with her breasts. They spilled out eagerly, wantonly, and he fastened his mouth there, nipping the crest of one, making it pucker and tighten. He took the weight of it into his mouth and began to suckle gently, the rhythm tugging deep in her womb.

She barely noticed when he parted her thighs, spreading her wide for him, leaving her exposed, vulnerable to his intentions. He kissed her hard and thoroughly as his big hand found her and a finger slid deep inside. Pleasure lanced through her, a searing fire that roared in her blood. He stroked her with expert skill and Elissa bit her lip to keep from crying out at the white-hot flames scorching through her.

She barely heard the sound of his buttons popping free, barely noticed the smooth, thick head that probed for entrance, simply gasped at the deep intrusion of his hardness inside her.

"Adrian . . . dear God . . ." Whatever else she might have said slid away on a wave of heat. Her fingers dug into his shoulders, felt the thick muscles bunch there as he moved. His hands encircled her waist and he held her steady, driving himself inside her, his thickness pulsing, throbbing against the walls of her passage. Need stretched her muscles taut. Her head fell back and Adrian fastened his mouth on her throat. He rode her hard, and she rode him, the pounding rhythm forcing her to climax.

Adrian followed, a deep groan erupting from his throat, the thick muscles straining, the veins standing out against his sun-darkened skin.

She clung to him for long, timeless moments, her head against his shoulder, not caring this time that her gown was ruched up, her coiffure in disarray, trusting Adrian to take care of her, believing that he would.

"Tell me who you are," he whispered against her ear. "If you're in trouble, let me help you."

She was in trouble, all right. But the biggest problem she faced was her unwanted feelings for him.

"I need time, Adrian. Trust me just a little bit longer."

A harsh sound tore from his throat. He lifted her to her feet and set her away. "My lovely little angel—what makes you think I trust you at all?"

Elissa didn't answer. One look in those hard green eyes and, even in the darkness of the garden, she could see there was no trust there.

*   *   *

He closed the door with a soft, nearly soundless click and moved across the study with anticipation. He didn't particularly like the room, with its low-beamed ceiling, smoky hearth, and thick stone walls. He preferred something more elegant, more sophisticated. Yet as he seated himself behind the simple oak desk in the house that served as his temporary quarters, it fostered the same excitement, the same surge of power he always felt when he sat down to this task, this duty that he had undertaken.

Strength flowed through him, almost godlike in its proportions, as if he held the fate of the world in his hands.

He reached for a clean white piece of foolscap and placed it on the table precisely in front of him. Dipping the quill pen in the inkwell, he began to write in clear, concise blue letters.

Ratisbon. Combined forces of a million men seeking to trap Marshal Davout's forces. If you can split the archduke's army, you can win.

He particularly enjoyed the last bit—giving advice to Napoleon himself. The little corporal might not heed it, might not recognize it for its brilliance, but he thought that perhaps he would.

It would be interesting to see.

The best part came last. Taking the heavy gold ring from a drawer of his small portable writing desk, he inked it carefully on the flat surface on top, not too much or the image might smudge, not too little or the picture would appear too faint, then he pressed it hard in the lower right corner. He lifted it away to study the outline of the bird on the page, making certain its eyes and beak were discernible inside the thin blue circle.

Satisfied with his efforts, he worked the sand shaker over the paper, waited for the ink to dry, then shook the loose grains into the wastebasket and carefully folded the message. A drop of wax to be certain it was sealed from prying eyes, and it was ready for delivery, ready to begin its long journey west.

That was the only part he didn't enjoy, since the outcome was no longer in his control. It was also the most dangerous. Which was why he took considerable precautions to see he was removed from the process. He smiled as he stood up from the desk, picked up the message, and headed for the door.

Adrian took a seat in Mahler's small, tidy office and tried to ignore the tightness that had sat like a rock in his chest since the investigator's note had arrived that morning. "What have you discovered?"

"Only the barest facts, but I thought you would wish to know."

"Yes, you did right in sending for me."

The slender man peered at his notes through a pair of gold-rimmed glasses. "It appears as though, some years back, the Von Langens were quite wealthy. They owned a great deal of land near Mariazell and a castle that was passed down for more than ten generations. Then the fortune began to erode. Difficult economic times, combined with a penchant for gambling and excessive living, caused the money to dwindle away. Maximilian Tauber, the countess's husband—"

"Assuming she is really his wife," Adrian put in.

The smaller man glanced up from his notes. "Assuming, as you say, that she is indeed his wife. At any rate, von Langen was forced to sell the castle and what remained of the lands. He left the country with the proceeds and went to England, ostensibly to avoid the embarrassment of such a circumstance. Friends said they believed he would return, and apparently he did on several occasions, but he never stayed long and he always went back to Cornwall."

"Cornwall," Adrian muttered. "So that much of her story is true."

"My lord?"

He waved away the man's words. "Did he bring his wife when he returned to Austria?"

"A wife and three children. Obviously not *this* wife, however. The woman was an English actress some years senior to the woman in question. Apparently this is the count's second marriage.''

Adrian chewed on this. Second wife, perhaps. Or a complete and utter fraud. "Do you know what happened to the first wife? Or to any of the children?''

"Not yet, but I hope to discover more soon. I'm planning a trip to Mariazell. What I find out there is bound to be of some help.''

Adrian nodded, disturbed that so little had surfaced when he was hoping for more. Much more. He stood up from his chair, sweeping it back with a grating sound on the bare wooden floor. "Thank you, Herr Mahler. You know where to find me should you uncover anything else.''

"Certainly, my lord. Perhaps you will hear something from your inquiries in London.''

"Perhaps.'' But he didn't really think so. At least not in time. The war was nearly upon them, the stakes of his silence growing higher every day. He wasn't sure how much longer he dared not to voice his suspicions, when duty and honor would finally override his uncertain feelings for Elissa.

He prayed that before that happened, she would tell him the truth.

Jamison sat in the drawing room of their town house after supper, watching Adrian brood, sip brandy, and ignore the long cigar turning to ash in the crystal tray beside him.

A frown marred his friend's dark brow. Tension formed a tight edge along his jaw, and his eyes looked tired and distant. He couldn't remember seeing him so withdrawn since they were children. Not since the days after one of Adrian's two brief yearly sojourns to his family's home in Kent, when he would sit alone in the dormitory, thinking of his parents, remembering how his mother had ignored him, and his father had called him names.

Jamie knew the story, which was always the same. He was eventually able to coax Adrian into telling him, which usually lightened his best friend's mood.

"They hate me," Adrian would say. "My father says I'm nothing but a nuisance. Whenever he sees me, he pretends I'm not there. They love Dickie." Adrian's older brother. "He doesn't have to go away; he has tutors who come to the house. Why don't they like me, Jamie?"

"They must like you, Ace. They gave you a brand-new red wagon, didn't they? They gave you a whole army of toy soldiers."

"You may have them," Adrian said dully. "I just want Mother and Father to like me. I just want parents like the other children have."

But he never had them. Jamison wasn't quite sure why, but Adrian never really had a family at all. They were partial to Dickie Kingsland, just like he said, though as far as Jamison was concerned there was no comparison between the two men. Where Richard was whiny and weak and not particularly smart, Adrian was strong and brave and intelligent. They didn't deserve a fine son like him, Jamison had told them once. He wasn't allowed in their house again.

Now Adrian's parents were dead and even Dickie was gone. Adrian had shoved his lonely childhood into the past and only one other time, years later, had those same dark feelings surfaced. Jamison wondered what Adrian could be pondering with such bitterness now.

"Want to tell me about it, Ace?"

Adrian's head jerked up. Jamison hadn't called him that in years. "Nothing important."

"Doesn't look like nothing. Looks as though something's got its teeth into you. You know you'll feel better if you tell me. You always do."

Adrian sighed and sat up straighter, raked a hand through his thick chestnut hair. "It's the Tauber girl."

"The Tauber girl? You mean the countess?"

He nodded, looking even more glum. "She isn't a countess. At least I don't think she is. Before I took her to bed, she was a virgin. In my book that means she's never had a husband. I don't believe she has ever been married."

"The girl was an innocent? Good God."

"Exactly so. I didn't know it until it was too late, but in all honesty, I don't know if that would have stopped me."

Jamison said nothing. He knew his friend well enough to believe that nothing would have kept him from taking the girl to his bed. He had wanted her that badly. Adrian rubbed a hand over his face, but the turbulence in his eyes did not lessen.

"I can see there is more," Jamison said. "You might as well tell me."

A long, harsh breath whispered out. His eyes fixed on the wall a few feet away. "I'm afraid she's the spy Ravenscroft is after."

"What! That is insane. According to you, she is barely a woman. You said yourself—more than once—that she is naïve. Until a few weeks ago, she was a virgin. I hardly think that is the description of a dangerous spy."

Adrian took a long draw on his brandy. "You have no idea how much I hope you're right. But the fact is, I caught her sneaking out of Pettigru's room when she thought no one was watching. I caught her in the garden eavesdropping on Steigler's private conversation. There were other incidents, a number of odd little things that all point in the same direction. I'm afraid she is somehow involved."

Jamison leaned back in his overstuffed chair, letting the words sink in, trying to visualize pretty blond Elissa Tauber spying for the French. As hard as he tried, he couldn't bring the image into focus.

"I'm afraid this time, Colonel, I have to respectfully disagree."

Adrian cocked a brow. "On what grounds?"

"Instinct. You've always been a big believer in that. My instinct tells me Elissa would be fiercely loyal to her beliefs. She's English and Austrian. I don't think she would betray either of those countries."

"She has lied about other things. Perhaps she is French."

Jamison pursed his lips. "In that case, she would see herself as a patriot, not a spy. Which might explain her motivation, but I don't think she would know how to deal with the element she would have to consort with in order to pass on the information." He leaned forward in his chair. "Can you really see Elissa Tauber in a place like the Bratis Tavern? I don't think so. No, my friend. Whatever she is doing, she isn't spying. If you weren't so worried about her, you would see that for yourself."

Adrian sipped his brandy, pondering the thought. "Then you don't think I'm being derelict in my duty by not telling Ravenscroft about her."

"Not at this point. You've a certain duty to her, as well, my friend. After all, you did seduce her. Which brings up the unwelcome subject—what do you plan to do should you get her with child?"

Adrian shrugged. "I'm not a monster. I would take care of her and the child. Finances are hardly a problem these days."

"I'm not talking about finances. I'm talking about marriage. It isn't a dirty word, you know."

Adrian grunted. "It is to me. You know what I'm like, Jamie, the kind of life I lead. I'm not interested in marriage. I never will be."

Jamison didn't argue. He knew the way Adrian felt—or thought he felt. Jamison simply did not agree. He thought the right woman would be good for his friend. Someone to give him the love he never had. He thought Adrian had the qualities to be a good husband, if he ever decided that was what he truly wanted. But Jamison didn't say so. It was none of his business and Adrian wouldn't listen if he did.

"Whatever you do," Jamison said, "you owe her some measure of loyalty, some degree of protection, at least until you can find out what is going on."

Adrian relaxed in his chair, and the tension in his body seemed to ease. "I'll give it a little more time." He flicked Jamison a glance. "But I'm damned if I'll let her far out of my sight."

Jamison chuckled softly. "Capital idea. I think you should keep the lady well in hand till you've found out the truth."

Adrian relaxed even more. He picked up the dwindling

cigar and rekindled the flame, then leaned back and blew a smoke ring into the air. "Exactly so," he said. "It's a matter of duty."

Jamison almost smiled. If the whole thing hadn't been so damned serious, if his best friend weren't involved, he might have found it funny. As it was, he just prayed he was right about the girl and that whatever feelings Adrian harbored for her didn't get them all into very deep trouble.

Elissa tried not to think of Adrian. It had only been two days since she had seen him, but during each of those days she remembered with vivid clarity the moments they had spent in the garden. Hot moments, extraordinary moments. Moments she would never forget. She wondered if Adrian would give them a second thought.

She wondered if he would reappear, or if at last he'd had his fill of her. She only had to recall their first meeting and his affair with Cecily Kainz to know he was a man of virile appetites. Still, the thought that he might already be seeking another conquest made her heart twist painfully against her ribs.

Elissa sighed as she descended the wide marble stairs of the duchess's palatial residence. Whatever he was about, she had other work to do and she intended to see it done. That meant concentrating on Steigler and somehow unmasking the Falcon. She recalled the general's conversation with Holdorf, certain the men had been discussing national secrets, certain as well that the major must also be involved in spying.

What she needed was proof, though she was still unsure how to get it. Sweet Judas, she wished Karl were here. Karl was the smartest of the three Tauber children, the best at chess, the deftest at cards, the quickest in school. Karl would have known what to do.

Unfortunately, Elissa had never been involved in a matter of intrigue. Her only option was to rely simply on opportunity. Time to be with the general, learn more about him—but time was running out. According to the duchess, the general would be leaving Vienna to join his troops the day after tomorrow, which meant her chances were growing even more scarce.

Just when things looked impossibly grim and no answer came as to what she should do, a footman arrived, carrying a message from Steigler, a flowery summons, seeking the pleasure of her company for a carriage ride through the park.

Hope reemerged in a heartbeat. The afternoon was sliding away but the sun still slanted through the trees, and the air was pleasantly warm, the weather growing milder every day. Surely she could put up with Steigler for a few brief hours, and perhaps this time she would learn something useful, something that, combined with what she had overheard, she could take to the authorities.

Steeling herself against the revulsion she felt, she joined him in the marble-floored entry of the palace and let him lead her out to his waiting carriage.

Chapter Thirteen

Adrian crossed the gravel drive of the duchess's palatial home and climbed the wide stone steps to the door. He knew it wasn't proper to arrive after dark and uninvited, but dammit, he didn't care. He wanted to see Elissa, to assure himself she was staying out of trouble. And dropping in unexpectedly gave him a bit of an edge—which he damned well needed where this lady was concerned.

A pair of liveried footmen showed him into the foyer, then the butler arrived, a gaunt blond man with high, carved cheekbones and a slightly arrogant smile.

"I shall have to see if the countess is at home this evening, my lord. If you will please follow me, you may wait while I inquire." Without checking to be certain Adrian followed, the butler led him into the drawing room.

Drawing room, hell, Adrian corrected, admiring the elaborate baroque salon done in black and gold marble. With its huge gilded sconces and high-domed ceilings painted with scenes of the Crucifixion, it was more like a ballroom. As magnificent as Castle Wolvermont was, it couldn't compare to the palaces in Vienna.

"I shall return forthwith," the butler said, guiding him over to a gold brocade sofa. Adrian sat for a moment, then sprang nervously back to his feet, irritated more than a little that the notion of seeing her had the blood running fast through his veins. He hadn't been like this over a woman since he was a randy schoolboy.

Even Miriam hadn't been able to affect him this way.

The thought came out of nowhere, bringing a bitter taste to his mouth. It slithered away at the sound of footfalls ringing on the gray marble floor. The butler reappeared, a woman padding softly along behind him. It wasn't Elissa. It was the Duchess of Murau.

"Good evening, Lord Wolvermont."

He shifted a bit uncomfortably. "A pleasure to see you, Your Grace." He gave her a bright, charming smile. "I realize you weren't expecting me, but a matter of some importance has come up and I wished to discuss it with Lady von Langen."

The duchess's graying blond brows drew together. Obviously his effort to be charming was lost on this particular woman.

"Ordinarily, Colonel, I would frown on your impertinence in arriving unannounced, but as it is, I am glad you are here."

Unease trickled through him. Instinct warned him that something was wrong.

"Normally I might not be so blunt," the duchess continued, "but under the circumstances, I don't see any choice. The truth is, Colonel, I am worried about Lady von Langen."

His mouth went dry. "Why is that, Your Grace?"

"Several hours ago, the countess received an invitation from General Steigler asking her to join him for a carriage ride. According to her maid she was supposed to have returned before dark."

"Perhaps they were simply enjoying themselves and time got away." But he didn't really believe it and the claws of tension sank into him deeper still.

"I wish I could agree with that, Colonel, but you see, I had her followed. General Steigler is quite discreet in his activities, but word of such unusual . . . pursuits . . . has a way of leaking out. I know his reputation. And that his interest in the countess has been growing. I also know he will be leaving Vienna the day after the morrow. When I learned Elissa intended to accompany him this afternoon, I feared he might not be willing to postpone his pursuit.''

''Where has he taken her?'' The hand at his side unconsciously fisted. His heart pumped angry spurts of blood through his veins. He had tried to warn her. Dammit, why hadn't she listened?

''General Steigler is a member of a particular gentlemen's club in Kohlmarkt. It has a certain . . . reputation.''

''Yes, I've heard of it.''

''My footman followed him there, to a door in the alley at the rear. He was carrying a heavy bundle when he climbed the back stairs. I only heard the news just moments before your arrival. I wasn't certain exactly which course to pursue, but now that you are here—''

Adrian didn't wait to hear more, just spun and started striding toward the door. His chest felt tight, his stomach as leaden as if he'd swallowed a dozen musket balls.

''Bring her home, Colonel,'' the duchess called after him. ''Don't let him hurt her.''

Adrian just kept walking. He would bring her home—of that he was certain. The question was, would he reach her in time? And if he didn't, what condition would she be in when he found her?

His stomach grew even more leaden.

Elissa awoke to the soft glow of an oil lamp burning beside the bed. Her mouth felt dry and shadows danced on the ceiling above her head. She sat up inch by inch, feeling a slight ringing in her ears, trying to remember where she was, to think what might have happened.

The last thing she recalled was drinking a cup of coffee heavily laced with cream that the general had stopped to purchase before they entered the park.

''Ah, so at last you are awake.'' She turned at the sound of his voice. He handed her a glass of water. ''Drink this and you will begin to feel more yourself.''

She accepted the glass with a hand that trembled only faintly. ''What happened?''

"You swooned, my dear. Perhaps the air was still too chill, or you were simply a bit fatigued. One never knows what might send a lady into a swoon."

Frowning, she took a deep drink of water and her head began to clear. "The air was pleasant, and I don't believe I have ever fainted." She glanced at her surroundings, a small, nondescript bedchamber, clean but spartan, with a dresser against the wall, a chair where her cloak had been draped, an oak armoire, and of course the big iron bed she sat on.

She dragged herself up from the mattress, suddenly uneasy, swung her legs to the floor and stood up. She swayed a moment, then steeled herself. "Where are we?"

"A place near the park I enjoy upon occasion. It was near and I was concerned."

Why didn't she believe him? "I appreciate your worry, General, but I am quite all right now. The duchess will be wondering where I am. I must be returning home."

He only smiled, a thin line of red in a harsh, unsympathetic face. "Then she will simply have to worry. I have different plans for you this evening, Elissa, ones that don't include your leaving for quite some time."

Her chest squeezed into a knot but she lifted her chin, fought to get a grip on the fear sliding into her stomach. "I want to go home, General Steigler. I am asking you as an officer and as a gentleman to take me."

He moved closer, took the glass from her trembling fingers and set it on the nightstand beside the bed. "There is no need to be frightened, my dear. We have both known this moment was coming for quite some time. Now it has finally arrived." He bent his head and covered her mouth with his lips. They felt dry and slightly rough. He tasted of the coffee they had been drinking.

Elissa pulled away. "You drugged me, didn't you?"

His thin mouth curved. "You left me no choice. I warned you what would happen if you tried to play games."

She fought to think as he drew her into his arms and kissed her again, a wet kiss now, slick and disgusting, yet she forced herself to endure it, to let his tongue slide into her mouth.

She had known this moment might come, had known it from the start. She had told herself she would get through it, that she would let him take her if she had to. She had said she would do anything to win his trust, anything to keep the promise she had made to find the man who murdered Karl. She thought of him now, lying dead in an alley, of the secrets he must have discovered, of why she had come to Vienna. If she turned Steigler away, she would have failed.

She steeled herself, battled down her revulsion, slid her arms around his neck and kissed him back. She could feel his lips curve with satisfaction.

"Very good, my dear. Very good, indeed." His mouth returned and his tongue slid in. She swayed on her feet and thought she might be sick. His hands moved over her breasts, slid into the bodice of her gown, cool hands, slightly damp. They pinched her nipples, then began to squeeze the fullness. His breath whispered into her mouth, as wet and sticky as his tongue, and one of his hands began to move down her body. When he reached the vee between her legs, he cupped her there, and the feeling was so revolting, so incredibly vile, she jerked away.

"I—I can't do it. I—I'm just not ready. I haven't been that long a widow." Tears threatened. She desperately forced them away.

"Nonsense. It's been almost three years."

"I'm sorry, General. I know—"

"Franz," he corrected, "my name is Franz. I wish to hear you say it."

She tried to smile. Failed in the attempt. "I know you are disappointed . . . Franz, but I just can't go through with this. At least not yet."

His smile was swift and hard, a ruthless curve of the lips that held an edge of anticipation. "Do you really believe you have a choice?"

She backed away from him then, till her knees hit the side of the bed. "What—what do you mean?"

"This place I have brought you is private. There is no one

who will come to your aid. I am in charge here, not you. You will do exactly as I tell you.''

He cocked his head toward a panel in the wall she hadn't paid attention to before. ''Come in, Major Holdorf. It is time for you to join us.'' Someone shoved the panel back and the major walked in from a room on the other side.

''Good evening, my lady.'' He made an excessively formal bow. ''How good of you to come.''

Cold fear seized her, an icy talon that ripped into her stomach. ''I—I must get back to the duchess. Her Grace will be worried.'' She glanced toward the door, but the general stood in the path of escape. Her gaze swung back to the slender blond man who had just walked in. ''Major Holdorf, it is your duty—''

Steigler's hand came out of nowhere, a swift, hard stinging across her cheek. Her head snapped back, the vicious blow turning her skin bright red.

''Major Holdorf's duty is to me, not some lady whore who has played the tease far too long.''

''But I—''

''Silence!'' He slapped her again, harder this time, cutting her lip and bringing a trickle of blood to the corner of her mouth. ''I gave you a choice and you made it. I would have made love to you, taken you with care, but you refused. Now Major Holdorf will take you, and I will please myself by watching. When he has finished, you will be mine.''

A wave of nausea swept over her and the room grew dark around the edges. This time she thought she might faint in earnest. ''Please, I beg you—''

He seized her arms before she could finish, dragging them up behind her, pain knifing into her shoulders. ''Gag her, Major. I am tired of hearing her whine.''

A length of white cloth appeared in the major's pale hands. He tied it around her mouth and secured it behind her head, while the general held tightly to her wrists. She stood there feeling numb, knowing it was useless to try to fight them, knowing there was no chance of escape yet unwilling to give in. For a moment, she surrendered to the building terror, overwhelmed by it, and more afraid than she had ever been in her life.

No! she silently whispered. *I won't let it happen. Not like this. Not like this!* Gathering her strength, she jerked free of the general's hold and started to fight them, lashing out with her feet, scratching and clawing, raking her nails down Holdorf's cheek, feeling a surge of triumph at the sight of a thin line of blood. Steigler hit her again, another brutal slap across the face. Twice more she felt the stinging blows, but she kept on fighting, then a hard punch to the jaw sent her spinning into darkness, landing in a painful heap on the floor.

She awakened spread-eagle on the bed, naked except for the tiny gold locket on a chain around her neck, a present from her mother. Dear God, how she wished she were home with her mother now. Her jaw was throbbing, bruised and beginning to swell. Her muscles ached, and her heart slammed in quick, sharp jolts against her ribs. She tugged on the sash that lashed her wrists to the painted iron headboard, but the knot only went tighter. Another sash bound each of her ankles to a corner of the footboard.

She tried to cry out but the sound was cut off by the gag stuffed into her mouth, and she didn't think anyone would come to her aid even if they heard her. Her eyes moved helplessly toward the man who stood just a few feet away.

The general sipped a glass of white wine, his mouth a narrow red gash in a face without the least trace of pity. His black eyes seemed to glow, lit from within, burning with an evil light unlike anything she had seen in him before.

She noticed his jacket was torn but his hair had been carefully combed back into place, leaving only faint evidence of their struggle. Holdorf had mopped the blood from the scratches on his face, but the damning evidence remained, giving her a shot of satisfaction. Anger sparked in the major's pale blue eyes. He was stripped to the waist, his thin chest bare, spidery curls of nearly white hair forming a fine web over his fair skin.

Elissa closed her eyes as he moved toward her, reached down toward the buttons on his breeches. Tears burned her eyes and began to slide down her cheeks. Dear God, she had never believed it would end like this.

Adrian shoved his way through the doors of the Neue Burg Private Gentlemen's Club on Kohlmarkt Street. It was quiet inside except for the soft female laughter coming from one of the drawing rooms. The faint odor of cigar smoke rode the air, and the music of a pianoforte seeped through the walls of a room deeper in the interior.

A man in the gold and crimson livery of a footman with a body twice too large stepped in his path as he started for the stairs.

"Where do you think you are going?"

He forced his temper down, fought to make himself think, to ignore the too-rapid thudding of his pulse and the worry for Elissa that coursed like a river through his veins. He had to find her. This was his chance if he could just stay in control.

"I've an urgent message for General Steigler. I am told he is here." He glanced at the line of rooms at the top of the stairs. "Which room is he in?"

Big beefy arms came up and folded across the man's broad chest. "You cannot come in here. This is a private club only for members. *You* are not a member."

Adrian clamped down on his jaw. It took every ounce of will not to hit him. "I told you I've got important news for Steigler. I'm a colonel in the British Army and I need to see him. Now tell me where he is." When the man said nothing, Adrian moved forward till their faces were inches apart. "Do you want to be the one to tell him there was a colonel here with news of the war but you wouldn't let him in?"

For the space of several heartbeats, the huge man didn't move. Then his arms fell away from his chest and he took a step backward, clearing a path up the stairs.

"Room fourteen. Last door in the hall to your right. Knock before you go in or you won't be a colonel much longer."

Adrian made no reply, just took the stairs two at a time up to the second floor and strode down the hall. Tension ate like acid into his stomach. Fear tightened a knot in his chest.

When he reached the door, he paused, an unwelcome thought rising up from the darkest part of his mind—*what if this is what she wants? What if it is Steigler she has wanted all along?*

He prayed it wasn't so, knew he would look like a damned bloody fool if it was. Forcing down the thought, he turned the knob and shoved open the door. Any doubts he might have had slid away at the sight of the woman on the bed. *His* woman. Staked out like a banquet for Holdorf and Steigler, beaten and battered and bruised.

A low growl erupted from his throat. He leapt forward, wrapped a hand around Holdorf's neck and jerked him off the foot of the bed. Slamming a fist into his stomach, he whirled the man around and punched him hard in the jaw, sending him flying into a corner.

Adrian's breath came hard, burning sharply in his chest. He turned to Steigler, who stood calmly a few feet away.

Steigler's mouth curved thinly. "I would suggest you rein in your temper, Colonel Kingsland. Before someone gets hurt." A small pearl-handled pocket pistol appeared in the general's hand. "As a matter of fact," Steigler continued, "I strongly suggest that you leave."

Behind him Holdorf groaned. He could hear Elissa whimper, and a sudden calm descended over him. It was the same calm he felt before a battle, the same icy purpose.

"But you know I won't do that, don't you? Not without the girl."

A sleek black brow arched up. "You would risk a bullet for her?"

"Let her go," Adrian warned, moving closer, his gaze locked on Steigler's harsh face. "Cut her loose, or I swear I'll kill you."

"You seem to be forgetting, Colonel. I am the man holding the gun."

Not for long, Adrian thought, easing a few inches closer. He looked down at Steigler's olive-skinned hand, saw his finger tighten on the trigger at the same instant his foot lashed out, slamming hard against Steigler's wrist, the pistol flying free, sliding across the floor.

Steigler bolted to retrieve it, but Adrian caught his arm and spun him around, slammed a fist hard into his stomach, then smashed a blow to his face, knocking him backward across the edge of the bed and onto the carpet. Blood erupted from his nose. Scarlet drops scattered across his pristine white uniform coat.

He noticed it was torn, as he had noticed the scratches on Holdorf's face, and felt a fierce glimmer of pride that Elissa had fought them.

Adrian bent and scooped up the pistol. "Step away from the bed," he warned, pointing it at Steigler's heart as he bent and slid a thin-bladed knife from the top of his boot.

"You'll pay for this, Colonel. I'll see you stripped of rank—you'll be a private by morning."

"I don't think so." Adrian leaned over the bed, sliced through the bonds on Elissa's wrists, moved down to sever the sashes that tied her ankles to the footposts of the bed. "I think you'll keep your mouth shut, just as you knew the countess would have been forced to do. If you don't, your reputation will be in ruins. Your dirty little secrets will be spilled all over Vienna."

A pile of torn peach muslin on the floor told him the fate of Elissa's clothes. He jerked her cloak off the chair and swirled it around her shoulders while she sat up unsteadily and swung her feet to the side of the bed.

Steigler's fist began to shake, his black eyes so full of hatred they glowed in the light of the lamp. "You'll regret this, Colonel. Both of you will regret it—I promise you that."

Adrian ignored him, turned instead to Elissa, who had removed the gag and pulled the cloak more closely around her.

"Can you make it?" He tried not to think what she had endured, hoped the scene he'd walked in on—Steigler still dressed, Holdorf unbuttoning his breeches—meant they hadn't yet had time to force themselves on her.

Elissa nodded, wetting her lips, which looked dry and swollen, a corner stained with dark blood. "I can make it."

Still, she swayed on her feet as she stood up, and leaned against him when she reached his side. He slid an arm around her waist to steady her, felt the tremors running through her slender body, and his finger tightened on the trigger of the pistol.

He had never wanted to kill a man so badly. "I'd advise you both to stay where you are until we're gone. I'll shoot the first man who tries to follow us." He turned to Elissa. "Hold on to me. It's past time for us to leave."

Easing her backward, his arm still tightly around her, he stepped out into the hall and closed the door. He slid the pistol into the waistband of his breeches, and the moment he did, he saw her knees begin to buckle beneath her. Cursing Steigler, wishing he *had* pulled the trigger, he turned and scooped her up in his arms. Long strides carried them down the back stairs and out into the alley. Her arms went around his neck to brace herself, and he could see the glitter of tears on her cheeks.

They rounded the building and he spotted his carriage waiting on a side street. He strode toward it. With a grateful nod at the driver, Adrian opened the door and climbed in.

The wheels began to turn a few seconds later, the driver snapping the whip above the horses' heads. They picked up speed, carrying them farther from Steigler and Kohlmarkt Street, and Elissa relaxed in his arms. He held her in his lap, her head nested into his shoulder, her body burrowing against him, seeking his care and warmth.

"You're safe now," he whispered, kissing the top of her head. "I promise you, Steigler will never touch you again."

She lifted her head. Tear-filled eyes came to rest on his face. "I led him on. I didn't want to do it, but I had to. Tonight, before Holdorf came in, I let him kiss me. I meant to give in to him, to let him make love to me. I told myself that even though he'd drugged me, even though it sickened me, I could do it. That I had to do it for Karl. But I couldn't go through with it." She sucked in a teary breath. "I thought of you, and I couldn't stand for him to touch me. Not the way you did." She shook her head and tears rolled down her cheeks. "I couldn't do it, Adrian. I failed my brother. Worse than that, I failed myself."

She started to cry then, deep, wracking sobs that squeezed a tightness around his heart. He held her against him, cradled her like a baby, stroked her hair, and kissed her forehead.

"I'm sorry, love, so damned sorry. I wish it hadn't happened, but it did. Perhaps it wouldn't have if you had trusted me." He tipped her chin up. "Surely you know you can trust me now. Don't you think it's time you told me the truth?"

She looked at him through wet, spiky lashes, her lovely face pale and bruised, yet even more attractive for the spirit it reflected. "Yes," she said softly. "It is past time I told you the truth."

Chapter *Fourteen*

The carriage wheels hummed. Through the window Elissa heard the faraway tolling of a bell in St. Stephen's Cathedral. The music of an orchestra playing in the park drifted on the cool spring air. As she rested in Adrian's arms, the rough wool of his scarlet coat rubbed comfortingly against her cheek. His heart beat steadily beneath her hand.

She didn't want to rouse herself, to remember what had happened to her this night. She wanted only to stay where she was, feeling safe and warm and protected. She turned to study the profile of his face, the strong planes and valleys, his straight patrician nose, the hard line of his jaw.

"How did . . . how did you know where to find me?"

Adrian shifted her on his lap, his hold unconsciously tightening. "The duchess was concerned when you left with Steigler. Apparently she knows him far better than you. She had you followed. Fortunately, I happened along shortly after the discovery of his plans."

"Are you taking me home?"

Adrian smiled softly. "To my home, yes. We need to talk, and I don't think you're ready to face the duchess quite yet."

Naked except for her cloak. Battered and beaten. No, she wasn't ready to face anyone yet. "Thank you. You always seem to know what is best."

His chest rumbled slightly. "Not always, angel, I assure you."

They said no more until he reached his town house in Naglerstrasse. Wrapping her securely in her cloak, he lifted her out of the carriage and carried her into the house. A tall dark-haired man she recognized as Major St. Giles stood at the top of the landing, a navy blue dressing gown tied around his waist, a book in one hand. A look of surprise came over his face as Adrian carried her into the entry and began to climb the stairs.

"Good Lord, what's happened?" Cloaked as she was, St. Giles could see only a portion of her face, but the blood at the corner of her mouth and the swollen, purple bruise along her jaw told most of the ugly story.

"She had a run-in with Steigler." Adrian's voice sounded gruff. "Thanks to the duchess, I arrived in time to alter his plans for the evening." He made his way to the guest room, and the major rushed to open the door. Adrian headed straight to the four-poster bed, pulled back the plum satin counterpane, and settled her between the pristine sheets.

"She hasn't a thing to wear," he said to the major. "Perhaps you could fetch one of my robes."

"Of course." St. Giles left to do his bidding, and Adrian returned his attention to her.

"I'm afraid the robe will have to do. I would offer you a night rail but I don't own one, since generally I sleep in the nude." He smiled a bit roguishly. "That is one point on which we apparently agree."

Elissa found herself blushing, thinking of their first encounter, glad for the brief distraction from her thoughts about Steigler.

"You're smiling," Adrian said. "That's a very good sign."

Elissa looked into his face. Such a beautiful face, so incredibly male yet so disturbingly handsome. "You have dimples when you smile," she said. "Not always. It takes a certain wicked glint for them to appear."

His lips curved faintly. He reached out and took her hand,

brought it to his lips and gently kissed the palm. "I don't really feel like smiling. Not when I think what that bastard did to you."

A shudder rippled through her. A queasy feeling rolled through her stomach. "He didn't . . . he didn't force himself on me. You got there before either of them had the chance." She glanced away, but her voice caught. "If you hadn't come when you did—"

"None of that now." He squeezed her hand. "I came and you are safe. What matters is that you tell me what this is about."

Elissa stared off in the distance, tears stinging the backs of her eyes, her thoughts cloudy with images of Karl and Steigler and all that had occurred these past few months. "I'm not quite certain where to start."

"The beginning is usually best. How about telling me your name?"

Surprise made her eyes go wide. "My name is Elissa Tauber. I didn't lie about that." She sighed. "But I'm not a countess—my mother is. Count von Langen is my father."

Both dark brows went up. She wondered what identity he had imagined. "The count is your father?"

"Yes."

A knock sounded just then and Adrian strode to the door. He accepted a bundle from the major, said something she couldn't hear, closed the door, and crossed to the bed.

"Apparently Jamie has come through as he always does. He has supplied a night rail and one of my dressing gowns. Do you feel well enough to put them on or shall I help you?"

Warm color rose into her cheeks. "I can do it." Adrian nodded, his face stoic. He handed them over and turned away, allowing her to shed the cloak that was all she wore and pull on the soft cotton nightgown. It was a man's, she saw, the major's apparently, and a good few sizes too big. But it was soft and warm and she was grateful for it.

"You were telling me about your father," Adrian gently reminded her, his broad back still turned away.

"Most of the story you heard was the truth. The count died

three years ago, leaving my mother—his widow—behind. What I didn't say was he also left three children, my older brother Karl, my younger brother, Peter, and me." She leaned back against the pillow. "I am dressed now, my lord. Please thank the major for his kindness."

He turned, his gaze warm on her face, yet a hint of worry lingered in the green of his eyes. "You may thank him yourself on the morrow. In the meantime, I should like to hear the rest of the story."

Elissa sighed, feeling suddenly tired. Her head throbbed and her jaw ached where Steigler had hit her, but she owed Adrian the truth.

"In a way this began with my father. He was a wonderful man and all of us loved him, especially my brothers. He lost most of his fortune and was forced to leave Austria as a young man. As far as I know he was happy with the life he led in England, but he was fiercely loyal to his homeland. He instilled that loyalty in us. My mother's mother was half Austrian, so German was spoken as well as English in our home. After he died, Karl and Peter joined the Austrian Army."

Adrian frowned. "Your brothers are here?"

She thought of Karl and sadness filtered through her. "Only Peter. Six months ago Karl was killed, murdered here in Vienna. No one has discovered who did it, but the letter my mother received just before he died said he had stumbled upon a traitor, a man who called himself the Falcon."

Adrian fell silent for a moment. "The Falcon. That is his name?"

"Yes. Why? Do you know something of him?".

He didn't answer, but the look in his eye said he had just made some sort of connection. She wondered why he evaded the question, and a whisper of unease crept through her.

"Go on," he softly urged.

"For whatever reasons, Karl was certain the Falcon was one of three men: Ambassador Pettigru, General Steigler, or an aide to General Klammer by the name of Josef Becker. Karl was trying to discover which of the men was a spy when he was killed."

Adrian pondered that for several long moments. "So that is why you came to Vienna—to finish the job your brother started."

"That's right. It was Karl's most fervent wish that, should something happen to him, we would see the matter of the spy resolved."

"Surely he didn't expect his younger sister to travel to Vienna in search of a traitor."

"I'm sure he didn't, but there seemed no other choice. We had no proof, no idea whom we could trust. My mother wrote to the duchess. She was an old friend of Father's, and we thought that she might help us, since her country's future was at stake. The duchess agreed and she has done so. We decided to investigate Sir William and the general first, since they were here in Vienna. Becker is with General Klammer, somewhere with the archduke's forces."

"And your brother, Peter?"

"He's a lieutenant with Kinsky's Chevauxlegers, wherever they are presently stationed. He knows nothing of this. I had hoped to seek him out, but so far there hasn't been time."

Adrian walked to the side of the bed, his dark brows pulled together in a frown. "I understand your grief for your brother. I applaud your wish to see justice done, but I am surprised your mother would allow an innocent young woman to embroil herself in something as dangerous as this."

Elissa shrugged. "Perhaps she wouldn't have, except that she suspected I might come on my own. She is quite independent herself, you see. She would have come in my stead but she has been ill of late. And she was right—I would have found a way to come even without her assistance. Now that I have, I intend to put an end to Steigler's spying—"

"Steigler? You have proof that Steigler is the spy?"

"Not yet, but sooner or later I will. That is the reason I decided to submit to his advances. I thought that as his mistress, he would trust me with his secrets. It wasn't what I wanted, but there was a time I believed I could go through with it."

Adrian leaned forward, tipped her chin with his hand. "But

you couldn't, could you, angel? You aren't cut out for that sort of thing.''

Elissa glanced away. ''My mother was an actress. I thought I could play the part, but I could not.'' She set her jaw. ''It doesn't matter. I won't give up—I'll find another way.''

''What makes you believe it is Steigler?''

She told him about the conversation she had overheard outside the garden window, explained about the lands the general had lost and his need of money, and reminded him of Steigler's brutal, unconscionable nature. ''It has to be him. After tonight, how can you doubt it? It is plain the sort of man he is.''

''I know very well the sort Steigler is—a disgusting bit of humanity that walks in the guise of a man. That doesn't, however, mean that he is also a spy.''

''But—''

''To begin with, Austria is on the brink of war. The conversation you overheard could have been in regard to any number of things—troop movements, supplies. There are countless reasons they might have such a conversation.''

''But Holdorf said he'd make certain the message got through—as if he might be crossing enemy lines. He talked about relay points. He said—''

''You have told me what he said, and I have told you there is nothing in his words that is the least bit extraordinary for a man in his position.'' He brushed a lock of her hair back from her forehead. ''As much as I detest him, I don't believe the general is a spy. I think you are confusing Steigler's brutality with the notion that he is disloyal to his country. They are not necessarily one and the same.''

He dragged the covers up to beneath her chin, tucked them securely around her. ''Did your investigation happen to disclose that both of Steigler's brothers died at the hands of Napoleon's Grande Armée? They were killed four years ago in the fighting at Austerlitz. Since then, Steigler has become fanatic in his hatred of the French.''

''I thought . . . I thought perhaps that was a cover to mask his role as the Falcon.''

Adrian shook his head. "I don't think so."

Elissa chewed on that. "I don't think it's Pettigru. He isn't the sort for spying and I found nothing suspicious in his room." She yawned behind her hand, the throbbing in her head beginning to intensify while her eyelids drooped with fatigue.

"I don't think it's Pettigru, either, but we can talk about that in the morning. You have told me enough for tonight and you need to get some sleep."

She wanted to argue, to ask him what he might know of all this and if he would agree to help her, but she was simply too weary. As Adrian said, they could discuss it again on the morrow.

Her eyes began to drift closed. "I should love a bath," she whispered. "I want nothing more than to wash away Steigler's touch, but I am just too tired."

Beside her Adrian stiffened. "You'll have your bath, love, I promise you. For now, get some sleep." Quietly, he turned and left the room.

Jamison sat across from Adrian in the study of the town house. They had spoken briefly of what happened between Elissa and Steigler, then Adrian had fallen unaccountably silent. Jamison knew there was more to the story. He wondered when his friend would tell him. It was well past midnight, yet Adrian seemed not the least bit ready for sleep. Instead he stared into the brandy glass in his hand as if it held the secrets of his existence.

"You're brooding again, Ace."

Adrian's head came up. He sighed across the distance between them. "I'm sorry. My mind is elsewhere, I guess."

"Perhaps on the lady upstairs?"

He took a sip of his brandy, swirled the amber liquid around in the bowl of the glass. "I told you what happened. I didn't tell you the rest." He shook his head, then a muscle flexed in his cheek. "She wasn't a spy, Jamie. She was trying to catch one."

So his instincts had been right after all. "Well, that's a relief."

"To some extent, yes." Adrian went on to relate Elissa's story, a tale that little by little fit together in Jamison's mind like the final pieces in a heretofore-unsolved puzzle.

"I should have known she wasn't involved," Adrian said. "I should have seen it as you did, but I didn't want to. I wanted her, Jamie. I wanted an excuse to have her and she gave me one. I blackmailed her, Jamie. I told her I'd go to Pettigru if she didn't do what I said. God, I behaved little better than that foul beast Steigler."

Jamie swirled the port in the glass he was sipping. "I daresay, you weren't exactly the model of gentlemanly behavior. On the other hand, I've seen the way she looks at you. Did it ever occur to you she might have cared for you enough to agree to your advances, that perhaps you simply gave her an excuse to do what she wanted to do all along?"

Adrian scoffed as Jamison had known he would. "She was an innocent," he said.

"She is a woman. A lady of courage and fire. I find it hard to believe you could have forced her to do anything she didn't want to no matter what you did. Steigler couldn't manage it. Perhaps her caring for you was the reason you were able to succeed where he could not."

But the look on his face said Adrian didn't believe it. In his thirty-two years, his friend had never believed himself worthy of that sort of love. His parents hadn't loved him. Why should anyone else?

Jamison took a drink of his port, set it down on the piecrust table. "If you feel so guilty, there is a way to ease your conscience."

Adrian scoffed. "You're speaking of marriage again."

"What if I am? Your ten-year enlistment was up years ago. 'Twould seem you could do far worse than Lady Elissa."

Adrian grunted. "I started down that road once before, if you will recall. It was an utter disaster. I don't intend to engage in that folly again—not now, not ever."

Jamison said nothing more. He remembered only too well

the year Adrian had courted Miriam Springer, the daughter of a moderately wealthy nobleman. Miriam had agreed to the marriage, and an extravagant wedding was planned for the fall of that year.

From the start, Jamison had been skeptical. With her long auburn hair and creamy complexion, Miriam was a beautiful girl, but she was also shallow and selfish, not the sort who could give a man like Adrian the kind of love he needed.

In the end, Jamison had been right about her and the marriage had not taken place. Unfortunately, Adrian blamed himself for what happened, another nail in the tightly built wall he had built around his heart.

"What will you do?" Jamison asked into the silence of the room.

"Stay away from her. I owe her that much. I can hardly press her into my bed after what has occurred. Even I am not that big a cur." He sighed, looking far more weary than he had when he had walked in. "I'll see Ravenscroft first thing in the morning, tell him what I've learned. There is more to Elissa's story, but she was so exhausted I didn't have the heart to press her. I'll talk to her again in the morning when I return."

Jamison simply nodded. He had no idea where the pair was headed from here, but somehow the notion of them staying apart didn't seem a good bet, either.

Adrian felt like pacing. Instead he stood stock-still, his bearing perfectly correct, in the center of the canvas tent that served as General Ravenscroft's regimental headquarters in the muddy field outside Vienna. A weak morning sun filtered in through the dingy canvas, lighting the room with a dim yellow glow, and a chill tinged the moist dawn air.

The general sat behind his battered work desk listening to Adrian's report, a half-empty tin cup of coffee growing cold near his elbow. "That is quite a story, Colonel Kingsland."

Not by half, Adrian thought, his thoughts returning to the night before. But he wasn't about to tell the general about Elissa's disastrous encounter with Steigler. "It's something to go on at least. I was hoping you could look into the death of Karl Tauber, as well as locate Lady Elissa's brother, Peter.''

"I'll get on it straightaway. Finding Lieutenant Tauber shouldn't be a problem. Unfortunately, getting to Becker is going to be a whole lot harder."

"Why is that, General?"

He shoved his cold mug of coffee away, a few drops spilling onto his battered desk. "You might have noticed a bit of activity around here this morning."

"Actually, sir, I did." There was an excitement in the air he had noticed the moment he'd set foot in the camp, a stirring among the men, a heightened anticipation no military man could fail to detect.

"Word came down just this morning. Bad news, I'm afraid."

"Sir?"

"Four days ago, the archduke and his forces clashed with Marshal Davout and Lefebvre's 7th Corps near Ratisbon at a place called Abensberg. Marshal Lannes showed up in time to split Charlie's forces. Half of them retreated to Echkmuhl, the other half to Lanshut. There may be as many as seven thousand Austrian casualties."

"Bloody hell."

"Exactly so, Colonel."

"Four days, you said, and there's been no further word?"

"Not yet. In the meantime, stopping this traitor is becoming all-important. Since the Tauber girl is the only lead that's turned up so far, I want you to stay with it. You've leave to take whatever action necessary in order to pursue this matter to its resolution. We've others looking into it as well. Hopefully someone will turn up something."

Adrian nodded. "I'll look into the Tauber murder, see how it might be connected, then go after Becker."

"Sounds good. In the meantime, I'll keep an eye on Steigler, just in case."

"And Pettigru?"

"I don't think he's our man, but we'll watch him, too."

The general rose from behind his desk. "Good luck, Colonel."

"Thank you, General." With a smart salute, Adrian turned and left the tent.

Chapter *Fifteen*

Elissa awoke to the gentle prodding of her lady's maid, Sophie Hopkins. Dressed in a simple white skirt and blouse, with her dark hair and big dark eyes, Sophie looked like a fragile waif. Fortunately, she was sturdier than she appeared.

"Wake up, milady. Your bath is ready and waiting. You don't want the water to get cold."

Elissa blinked groggily, then remembered she was sleeping in the guest room at Adrian's town house and her eyes popped open. "Sophie! How on earth did you get here?"

"Colonel Kingsland sent word to the duchess last night. She sent for me first thing this morning, told me the colonel's carriage would be coming to pick me up and that I should bring you some fresh clothes to wear. I hung 'em over there in the armoire."

Elissa smiled, thinking that Adrian always seemed to take care of things. As he had done with Steigler. As long as she lived, she would never forget the sight of him bursting through the door to save her. Or the fury in his eyes when he had seen what Steigler had done.

Her gaze swung back to her maid. "Did I hear you mention a bath?"

"Aye, milady. The water is hot and I put in some lilac scent I found with the towels on the dresser."

"Thank you, Sophie." The girl helped her out of bed,

Elissa wincing as her stiff, aching muscles began to move.

"I know it's none of my business, milady, but it wasn't . . . it wasn't the colonel who hurt you?"

Elissa shook her head. "The colonel is a gentleman." She smiled. "He might not know it, but he is. And he would never hurt a woman."

Sophie nodded, apparently satisfied with that. It wouldn't take much for the girl to figure out it was Steigler who had treated her so badly. Fortunately, the willowy little maid had been the model of discretion since they had left England.

She crossed the bedchamber, drawn to the wonderful lilac scent. Sophie helped her strip off her borrowed night rail and slide into the small copper bathing tub. With a sigh of pleasure, Elissa sank down in the steamy bubbles, drew her knees up beneath her chin, and settled back against the rim of the tub.

She soaked for a while, absently trailing hot water over her skin, then Sophie washed her hair and scrubbed her back. It felt wonderful to be clean once more, to wash away the awful memories of Steigler, the feel of his long-fingered hands on her body.

"Are you finished, milady?"

Elissa shook her head. "I'd like to soak a little while longer. The water feels so wonderful and it isn't cold yet."

Sophie smiled. "All right, I'll come back in a bit. In the meantime, it'll do you good to relax." The girl left the room, the door closing softly behind her.

Elissa must have drifted off for a time. The water was chill and when she opened her eyes, most of the bubbles were gone. A shadow fell over the edge of the tub and her glance shot in that direction, lighting on a pair of tall black boots.

Elissa sat up straighter in the tub. "Adrian! I—I didn't hear you come in."

"I'm sorry. I didn't mean to startle you. I was worried about you, is all."

His eyes skimmed down to her breasts, glinted, then grew oddly dark. Something tightened in her stomach and her nipples went hard. Unconsciously her hands came up to cover them.

Adrian cleared his throat and turned away. "I'll fetch your maid," he said gruffly, starting for the door. "The water's bound to be cold. You'll catch a chill if you stay in there much longer. When you're dressed, I'll come back and we can finish our conversation."

"I'm feeling much better. If you don't mind, I'd rather join you downstairs."

He made a brief nod of his head. "I'll have cook prepare something for you to eat." She watched him close the door, her nipples still taut, feeling oddly disappointed. What had she expected? That he would drag her out of the tub and ravish her there on the floor?

Her stomach fluttered pleasantly. Sweet God, it didn't sound all that bad.

Elissa shot to her feet, ashamed at her wicked thoughts. Dripping onto the floor, she reached for the towel on the dresser just as Sophie walked in and rushed to hand it over. Twenty minutes later she was walking into a small sunny room at the rear of the town house. The aroma of coffee floated on the air, and a pot of the rich black brew laced with hot milk, a drink they called *Melange,* sat in the middle of the table next to a large fresh fruit compote and a big silver tray of fresh pastries, including a strudel of apple and pot cheese.

She reached out to steal a bite off one corner, then snatched back her hand when she caught a glimpse of Adrian's tall frame leaning against the wall in the corner. He moved away with casual grace, a soft chuckle rumbling in his chest.

"Don't let me stop you. If I hadn't eaten already, I'd be hard-pressed to resist."

Elissa smiled and let him seat her, then he took a chair across from her, his uniform spotless though she remembered earlier his tall black boots had been edged with mud.

"You're looking much better this morning," he said. "How do you feel?"

"Much improved, I'm happy to say. The bath was a god-send. Thank you, Adrian."

His eyes touched hers for a moment as he remembered the sight of her sitting naked in the tub, and she didn't miss the heat in his gaze. Then he glanced away, handing her the fruit compote, which she accepted and spooned onto the gold-rimmed porcelain plate. She took a pastry while Adrian poured hot coffee into her cup.

She straightened the napkin in her lap. "What about you? Are you sure you aren't hungry?"

He shook his head. "I've been up for hours. As a matter of fact, I've already been to see General Ravenscroft. We went over the matter you and I discussed last night, and he has agreed to look into the death of your brother."

Pain mingled with relief, then uncertainty arose. "Are you sure we can trust him?"

"The general is an honorable man—I have known him for more than ten years. And he was already aware of the spy in our midst."

"He was?"

"Yes."

There was something in his manner that reminded her of last night when she had mentioned the Falcon. "You know more about this than you are saying. I have told you all I know yet you are holding something back. What is it?"

For a moment he didn't answer, his features inscrutable, his eyes assessing her. Trust, it seemed, came as hard for him as it did for her.

"Several weeks ago, a man was killed here in Vienna. Apparently the man was passing secret information. A note was found, but there was no clue as to who might have sent it. There was no signature, but there was a mark, the image of a bird made by a ring or a seal of some sort. From what you have said, that bird must signify the Falcon."

Excitement filtered through her. For the first time since she had come to Austria, she felt as if she might actually be getting somewhere. "But that's wonderful! Surely that is a valuable clue."

"When we talked about the letter your mother received, you didn't mention *why* your brother believed the traitor was one of the men he named."

"I'm afraid I don't know. Karl must have had some reason to think so. He wasn't the type to make unsubstantiated claims."

"Yes, well, whatever his reasons, we can't know them now. But at least we have something to go on."

Elissa reached over and gripped his hand. It felt warm and strong, and an image flashed of the tender way he had held her in the carriage.

"I don't know how to thank you. You can't know how much it means to know you're going to help me."

Adrian arched a brow. "Help you? My lovely little angel, of course I'm going to help you. I'm going to do my best to find out who this man is, and in the meantime, you're going home."

Elissa blinked, struggled for a moment, trying to grasp the meaning of his words. "Home? What are you talking about?"

"I'm talking about the war, love. It's breathing down our necks. Four days ago the archduke's forces clashed with Napoleon's Grande Armée. Charlie lost the encounter and was forced to retreat. God knows what will happen next, but one thing is clear—unless the Austrians can stop him, Napoleon will be marching on Vienna. I want you home where you'll be safe."

Very carefully, she set her coffee cup back in its saucer and blotted her mouth with the crisp linen napkin in her lap.

"I don't think you understand, Adrian. I told you all this because I trusted you. I believed you would help me find the man who killed my brother and perhaps find a way to stop a traitor. I don't intend to leave Austria until that goal is accomplished. I did not tell you so that you could send me away."

The gentleness in his expression vanished. Adrian fixed her with a hard green glare. "Need I remind you, sweeting, of the beating you suffered last night? If you don't recall, Steigler very nearly raped you. Aside from that, your brother has been murdered. One of the Falcon's couriers was murdered. This is dangerous business, Elissa. A woman has no place in it. It's time for you to go home.''

Her chin angled up. ''No.''

''Be reasonable. There is nothing more you can do.''

''I said I'm not going.''

Adrian's fist slammed down on the table. ''Yes you are!''

''No I'm not!''

''By God, you're going back to England if I have to tie you up and hire someone to drag you there!''

She shoved back her chair and surged to her feet. ''You are not my keeper, Colonel Kingsland. I'll return to England when I'm good and ready and not a moment before. Need I remind *you* that I'm a grown woman? I have friends and relatives here who will not allow you to run over me as you are attempting to do.'' She stiffened her spine. ''Now, if you will please call for your carriage, I should very much appreciate a ride back to the palace.''

A muscle leapt in his cheek. Fury glittered in those hard green eyes. ''You are the most stubborn, most reckless, most willful woman I have ever met!''

''And you, Colonel Kingsland, are the most arrogant, most domineering, most irritating man *I* have ever met!''

For long seconds they just stood glaring, till the major's amused voice sounded through the open door. ''I see you two have sized each other up fairly well. Now, do you suppose we might sit down and discuss this matter like adults instead of ill-tempered children?''

Adrian swore softly. '' 'Tis the lady who behaves as a child—and should she continue, she may well find herself over my knee.''

Elissa shrieked in outrage. ''Don't you dare threaten me, Colonel Kingsland! I'm leaving—with or without your assistance.'' Turning away from him, she marched past the major, calling up the stairs for her maid.

Adrian swore a savage curse, fighting to ignore Jamie's

soft laughter and rein in his formidable temper. "Damnable woman. She's a handful, Jamie, I tell you."

His friend merely smiled. "Perhaps she is right. Have you thought of that?"

"What are you talking about?"

"I'm talking about a way to get close to Josef Becker. She managed to intrigue General Steigler, and Pettigru was clay in her hands. Perhaps there is a way she could help."

Adrian shook his head. "It's too bloody dangerous."

"She isn't going to leave, Adrian, and you can't make her go. Wouldn't she be safer with you looking after her than going off by herself, trying to find this man on her own?"

"She won't do that. She hasn't the foggiest notion where Becker is, and even if she knew, she couldn't get to him." He shook his head. "No, I'm keeping her out of this and that's final."

Jamie looked amused and Adrian grumbled a curse. Brushing past his friend, he started for the door, arriving just in time to see Elissa tying her cloak beneath her chin with quick, jerky motions, then bending to pick up the satchel she had carried down from the guest room. Her lady's maid hurried down the stairs behind her.

"It's all right, Adrian," Jamie said, walking forward to take the bag from Elissa's hand. "I'll be happy to see the lady home."

Adrian glared at Elissa, who turned and started walking away. "Fine," he said. "And while you're at it, see the little vixen stays out of trouble."

Jamie only laughed as the little group marched out the door. Damn her, Adrian thought. How could a single female cause him so much trouble? And to make matters worse, he couldn't even bed her. Damn her to bloody hell.

Then again, perhaps this was for the best. He was getting too involved with the girl and that was the last thing he wanted.

He would do his work, he vowed, and when he was done, perhaps he would pay a call on Cecily Kainz. She might not set his blood on fire the way Elissa did but she was certainly far easier to manage.

Elissa stared out the window of the carriage, watching the tall baroque buildings pass by, listening to a newsboy on the corner hawking the morning paper, all the while fuming at Adrian. She never should have trusted him. She should have known he would behave like the arrogant lout he was. She should have known he would behave like a high-handed brute!

"I realize you are angry." The major's voice drifted toward her from the opposite side of the carriage. "But it is worry for you that makes him behave that way. He feels responsible for you. He doesn't want to see you get hurt."

"He isn't responsible for me. I can take care of myself."

"The way you did last night?"

Her face went warm. She didn't like to think about Steigler. "I'm grateful for what the colonel did. I will always be in his debt, but I can't let that stop me from doing what I've come for."

"You're grateful. Is that all you feel for him—gratitude? Or is there something else?"

Why was he pushing, forcing her to face her feelings when she was trying so hard to ignore them? "I admit I have come to . . . to care for the colonel—at the moment I am at a loss to understand why—but the fact is I do."

"As he cares for you," the major said. He leaned toward her across the carriage, flicking a sidelong glance at her maid. "I realize now is not the time to discuss this, but I think you should know Colonel Kingsland is not the sort to allow his feelings to guide him in matters as important as these. His emotions run deep and he guards them well. It is a measure of his affection that he is so concerned."

Affection. That was what Adrian felt for her? So bland a word couldn't begin to describe her feelings for him. Dear Lord, if he only knew!

"Thank you, Major, I shall certainly keep that in mind." Along with the knowledge of her own unruly emotions, and the fact that she had fallen in love with him. She wouldn't tell him, of course. It had only been since last night—during the long, unbearable moments with Steigler—that she had realized the full extent of her feelings for Adrian.

Until last night, she had always believed she would fall in love with a kind, gentle, comfortable man, a man of letters, perhaps, or a clergyman.

It wasn't what her father had wanted, of course. He had wanted her to marry a nobleman, someone of rank and power. He'd said she needed the sort of man who would challenge her, someone who would appreciate her spirited nature but wouldn't be intimidated by it.

Elissa had always just laughed. Until she met Adrian. Now she couldn't imagine life with a man of less passion, less magnitude. Wolvermont was larger than life, and when she was near him, she felt that way, too. That she could do anything, be anything, accomplish anything she set her mind to. What it was about him she could not quite say, only that she was drawn to his powerful presence as she never had been to another man.

"We are arrived, my lady."

Elissa nodded at the major, let him help her down from the carriage, and thanked him for his kind escort home. She was inside the palace and halfway up the sweeping staircase before Fritz, the duchess's butler, called up to her from the marble floor below.

"Lady von Langen, I am sorry to disturb you but the duchess wishes to see you. She left word that I should summon you to her presence immediately upon your return."

Elissa released a breath. She should have known she wouldn't get off so easily. "Where is she?"

"The Yellow Salon. If you will please follow me."

She trooped along behind him, grateful Sophie had arrived at the colonel's town house with appropriate clothes, and stepped inside the drawing room. It was done in ivory and a bright lemon yellow, with yellow striped draperies on the windows, yellow overstuffed sofas, and huge potted plants along the walls. It was cheerful, even on an overcast day like this one; it was one of Elissa's favorite rooms in the palace.

"Come in, my dear." The duchess's voice floated up from among the silk cushions of a deep saffron chair near the fire. "Come here so that I may have a look at you."

Elissa flushed. She had used a bit of rice powder to disguise the bruise on her jaw but the faint blue shadow still remained.

The duchess frowned as Elissa approached, her thin, nearly gray brows pulling down toward her slightly long, too thin nose. "I suppose I shouldn't be surprised. Your colonel explained a bit of what happened in his note." She reached out and caught Elissa's chin, turned her head from side to side. "It could have been worse, I suppose. Thank God the baron reached you as quickly as he did."

Elissa smiled, warmed by the memory of Adrian's daring rescue. "Colonel Kingsland is an amazing man." He was that and more. As angry as she was with him, she couldn't stop a surge of admiration. "He is the bravest man I have ever met."

"Yes . . . well, we are all of us grateful for his efforts."

"Steigler is ruthless and without a trace of conscience. He should be stopped, Your Grace."

"He is useful to the government. As long as that is the case, he'll be able to do more or less as he pleases. Were you able to discover any proof that he is the Falcon?"

Elissa shook her head. "I'm afraid not. In fact, the colonel believes I am wrong about him."

The older woman shifted in her chair, the rings on her bony fingers flashing in the light of the lamp on the table beside her. "What do you believe?"

"To tell you the truth, I'm not sure anymore. He is certainly capable of being a traitor. His behavior last night proved that. If only I could have gotten into his room at the emperor's palace I might have found something . . ." Even before she finished the sentence, an idea burst forward, slamming into her brain with the force of a blow.

"What are you thinking?" Shrewd pale blue eyes drilled into her with almost equal force.

"That perhaps it isn't too late. The colonel says the fighting has begun, that the archduke has encountered the French."

"With unfortunate results, I'm afraid."

"Surely the general will be called to duty."

"He has already left Vienna."

"Then there is no reason why I can't search his house. From what the colonel has told me, there is a ring or a seal of some sort that signifies the Falcon. If Steigler has the seal, it might be somewhere in his suite of rooms."

"The odds of that are unlikely. If there were such an object, most surely he would carry it with him."

"True, but there is always the chance he left it behind. Since the emperor is here, this must be where most of Steigler's information comes from. He might have left the seal here, and since he is already gone, there is very little risk of my being caught."

"If you could manage to get in."

Elissa chewed her lip. "That could very well pose a problem."

The duchess leaned back in her chair, her pale blue eyes gleaming with speculation, the scent of her sweet perfume, jasmine perhaps, tinged with cinnamon or some other spice, floating heavily in the air. It wasn't Elissa's favorite.

"I believe I could be of some help," the duchess said. "My footman Hans has a number of useful skills. His youth was a bit disreputable. He claims there isn't a lock that's been made that he cannot open."

Elissa clapped her hands, controlling an urge to grin like a fool. "Oh, thank you, Your Grace. You're incredible!"

The older woman watched her, her features inscrutable. "Do you not wonder why it is I would help you in a plan as dangerous as this? Your scheme is, after all, hardly something a young woman of your station should involve herself in."

"I suppose because you wish to catch a spy who might harm your country."

"That is true. But mostly because you are trying to accomplish something few women would ever attempt. In doing so,

you are living a grand adventure, the sort a woman is never
allowed to live. I used to dream what it might be like to be
free of responsibility, able to go out and seek my own des-
tiny. It was foolish, of course, not something a sane woman
did, especially not a duchess.''

She shifted in her chair, her face flushed with reminiscence.
''Ah, to be free of society's strictures—even for a little
while—to experience life to the fullest measure. That takes
courage, my dear, and I admire you for it.'' She eyed Elissa
down the length of her nose. ''Just be certain to temper it
with wisdom if you wish to survive this affair.''

''I will, Your Grace, I promise you.''

''Now what of Steigler?''

''The general told me he lives in a town house across from
Karlskirche.''

''Yes, I know where it is.''

''Then there is no reason I can't go there tonight.''

''You will have to be careful,'' the duchess said. ''Whether
he is there or not, you will be breaking the law.''

''I'll be careful. More than careful. If I find nothing there,
I'll presume he is not the man we want. I'll steer my search
toward Becker, discover his whereabouts and find a way to
approach him.''

''First things first,'' the duchess said, waving a thin, heavily ringed hand. ''It would be far better for us all if Steigler
proved to be our traitor.''

The soft chant of crickets drifted on the still night air. Thin
patches of moonlight filtered through the passing gray clouds
as Adrian swung a leg over the windowsill of Steigler's town
house and eased himself down to the ground below. The rear
of the house fell in shadow, dark except for the glow of a
lamp in one of the servants' third-floor bedchambers.

Dressed in black from the scarf tied around his neck to the
bottom of his Wellington boots, Adrian disappeared easily
into the darkness, his task completed, staying close to the
walls of the house, heading for his carriage, which waited on
a side street half a block away. He had just reached the corner

of the house when the muted whisper of voices seeped toward him.

Adrian paused, backing farther into the shadows, straining to hear, wondering whom it could be. Two people, he saw, one tall and lean, the other small and slender, both of them cloaked in black. A grating sound, quickly muffled, ruptured the evening quiet, the turning of a lock, Adrian knew, but he didn't think the man was using a key. Then the pair disappeared inside the house.

Adrian moved closer, creeping stealthily toward the back door. Who was it? And why would they be breaking into Steigler's house? Even as the thought took form, an odd suspicion tingled up his spine.

She wouldn't dare, he thought. Not after he had warned her, not after her last encounter with the general. But the size and shape was right, and deep down he knew she would do it. There was very little Elissa Tauber would not dare. Anger made him bolder than he should have been. He opened the back door and climbed the servants' stairs up to Steigler's private suite of rooms.

Pressing himself against the wall, he peered through a narrow crack in the door to see the tall, lean man moving silently around the small upstairs sitting room. With practiced skill, the man opened drawers and chests, quietly examining one object after another. Ignoring him, Adrian opened the door to the general's bedchamber and silently eased inside, slipping behind the draperies to watch the slender figure who had shoved back the hood of her cloak, whose cap of shiny blond hair glistened like gold in the light slanting in through the window.

She was opening and closing drawers, stopping to riffle through the pages of Steigler's books, examining the papers on his small writing desk.

The same things Adrian had done the hour before.

He watched her work with steady purpose, making her way in his direction. As she turned to pull open a bureau drawer, he stepped close behind her, sliding an arm around her waist and hauling her against him. At her sharp squeak of surprise, he clamped a hand over her mouth and leaned down to her ear.

"Looking for something, angel?"

The sound of his voice made her stiffen even more, then the tension slowly seeped from her body. He took his hand away and the fear in her eyes receded into anger.

"What are you doing here?" she hissed as she turned to face him. "You said you didn't believe Steigler was a spy."

He grinned at that. "I don't, but there is always the chance—remote as it might be—that I could be mistaken."

She settled her hands on her hips. "If that is the case, I suggest you get to work. It would hardly look good on your military record to be arrested as a thief."

He chuckled softly, enjoying himself far more than he should have been. "I've already searched the house. I didn't find a damnable thing."

"Did you look in the study? Perhaps there is something—"

"Every drawer, every book, every file. If there is something to be found, he has taken it with him."

"Damn," Elissa muttered, and Adrian grinned again.

"Come on, little heathen. Summon your cohort in crime and let's get out of here."

She agreed with a sigh of disappointment and started toward the door, Adrian following behind her.

"Who is he, by the way?" he asked. "Some other poor sod you have charmed into doing your will?"

Elissa tossed him a glare. "He happens to be the duchess's footman, a trusted family retainer."

"Who just happens to know how to pick locks."

"Yes. 'Tis rather convenient, I would say." She motioned to the footman, who stiffened when he saw Adrian standing at the door. The man relaxed at the calm in Elissa's face and joined them in the hall.

A few minutes later they were standing outside in the shadows at the rear of the town house, feeling the chill through their clothes.

"Tell your footman to take the carriage and go home.

There are things we need to discuss. When we have finished, I'll see you safely returned.''

She eyed him with a bit of interest, then turned and repeated his orders to the tall, lean man a few feet away.

"You are certain, my lady, that you will be all right?" the footman asked, tossing a glance in Adrian's direction.

"I'll be fine."

He made a polite bow of his head. "As you wish, my lady." With a final assessing glance, he jogged off in the direction they had come, and Adrian led Elissa away.

"My carriage is just down the block."

She lifted her skirts above the mud in the garden, and when they reached his conveyance, he helped her climb in, choosing the seat across from her although he would far rather have had her sitting in his lap as she had done the night before.

They passed beneath a streetlamp and he noticed the firm set of her jaw. "All right, Colonel. What is it you wish to discuss?"

"I could say your lunacy in breaking into the general's quarters, but since I was doing the same thing, I shall restrain myself."

"Good idea," she said.

Adrian leaned back against the tufted black leather, watching her fidget beneath his regard, enjoying the soft play of moonlight on her bouncy golden hair, the full pink curve of her bottom lip. When his body began to grow hard, he glanced away.

"Well?"

He raked a hand through his hair. "Dammit, I don't bloody like this."

"You don't bloody like what?"

He frowned. "Now you're cursing. First you are breaking into houses and now you are cursing."

"I'm not cursing. You are the one who is cursing. I am merely trying to discover what it is you are talking about."

"I'm talking about catching a spy—that's what. You won't go back to England. Obviously you're not going to heed my warnings, which leaves me no other choice."

"I still don't understand."

"You win, dammit. I'm going to let you help me."

Her eyes went wide. "You are?"

"For now. But we're going to do this my way and you are going to follow my orders—every last one of them."

Elissa made a bubbly, joyous sound in her throat and smiled at him so brightly something tightened in his chest.

"You won't be sorry. I'll do whatever you say. I'll follow your orders completely."

He chuckled softly. "I'll believe that when I see it. In the meantime, I want you to keep your eyes and ears open. I'll let you know what's going on, and as soon as I locate Becker, we'll go after him."

She grinned at him, flashing a bright white smile in an achingly lovely face. She squared her shoulders and gave him a smart salute. "Aye, Colonel Kingsland. Whatever you say, sir." Reaching over, she took his hand, gave it an excited squeeze. "Thank you, Adrian."

He sighed into the darkness of the carriage. "Whatever you do, don't thank me. Not until this is over and you are safe again in England. In the meantime, I had better get you home."

Elissa nodded, but as he watched her smile, as he felt the warmth of her hand in his, he found that home was the last place he wanted to take her. To bed—most assuredly. But in that moment, he discovered he would be happy just to sit with her as he was now, to watch the excitement in her eyes, to see her smile, and listen to the laughter in her voice.

The knowledge was so frightening, so totally unexpected, a knot of fear rose in his chest and he felt slightly sick to his stomach. Adrian steeled himself, suddenly grateful he was taking her home and that soon he would once more be alone.

Chapter Sixteen

Adrian shouldered his way through the crowded Reiss's Tavern, Jamie a few steps behind him. The smoke-filled, low-ceilinged building sat in the northern section of the city in a rundown area at the edge of the Leopoldstadz, a place teeming with a gaudy mix of men, an assortment of Greeks, Turks, Poles, Jews, Croats, and Hungarians, all dressed in their bright, traditional clothes.

Adrian and Jamie were garbed far more somberly, in simple dark breeches, and full-sleeved homespun shirts. Reiss's was the place the Falcon's courier had been killed, but so far no one in the tavern even recalled the events of the night. Then the barkeep pointed toward a stout, bald-headed Turk sitting by himself in a corner.

"You might try him. If Janos cannot help, I am afraid no one can."

Adrian tossed a coin on the bar and the barkeep, a rotund man with a thick, pointed beard and wary gray eyes, picked it up and slid it into the pocket of his leather apron. "I appreciate your help."

He and Jamie strode toward the man in the corner, who tilted his chair back against the wall, stretching his short, muscular legs out in front of him.

"Your name Janos?"

"Who wants to know?"

"I do." Adrian flipped a coin on the scarred wooden table. "I'm looking for a little information. There's gold in it for the man who knows something. The barkeeper said you might be that man."

"What is it you wish to know?"

"A couple of weeks ago, there was a man in here, black-haired, average in height, a lean, wiry build. He wound up dead in the alley. Were you here the night it happened?"

Janos sat up in his chair, the muscles flexing beneath his powerful shoulders. "I was here, but I didn't kill him."

"Do you know who he was?"

"I had seen him a couple of times. He was in here every once in a while but I had never spoken to him until that night. He said he had traveled a good ways that day."

Adrian tossed another coin on the table, watched it roll into a deep groove whittled into the wood and flip over onto its side. "Could you make a guess where he might have come from?"

"He was Hungarian, by the look of him, dark and scowling, his eyes always darting around. If I remember, he mentioned he had come from Süssenbrunn, that is north and east of the city."

"The barkeep said there was some sort of altercation. A card game or something."

"Ya, that is so. He was drinking schnapps, downing it faster than that poor wench, Lissel, could carry it to the table. He wasn't supposed to stop in Vienna, he said. He had more important things to do—that is what he said—but he was thirsty and he could make time for a game of cards."

The bald Turk shook his head. "He should have minded his business. If he had, he would still be alive."

"Why is that?" Jamie asked.

"He was cheating," Janos said as if that made everything perfectly clear. "They found him in the alley that next morning, his throat cut and his purse gone. The men who play here don't like to be cheated."

Adrian added a last coin to those that had gone before. "Thank you, my friend."

The burly man nodded and leaned back in his chair, took a long drink of the stout dark beer he was drinking, then set the empty mug back down on the table.

"Not much of a lead," Jamie said as they walked out the door.

"Maybe more than you think. If the barkeep is telling the truth, the courier didn't come here from Baden. That means the information didn't come through any of the emperor's people or the diplomats who were there for the negotiations, which eliminates both Steigler and Pettigru."

"The archduke's forces were assembling north and east of here just about the time of the murder. General Klammer was with them."

"And Major Josef Becker."

Jamie smiled. "Karl Tauber may have been right."

"Elissa thinks so."

"What's your next step?"

"I need to talk to her, see if she knows anything else about her brother's murder."

"It's been four days, she'll be angry you haven't gone to see her before this."

Adrian scoffed. "I haven't gone to see her because every time I do all I can think of is tearing off her clothes and dragging her beneath me. God's blood, I get hard just watching her smile."

Jamie smiled. "Maybe you're in love with her."

Adrian pierced him with a glare. "I'm in lust with her luscious little body. In love? Never. Love is for fools and dreamers. I am neither of those things." An image of Miriam Springer rose unbidden into his mind, beautiful and tempting, but not for him. Never for him. "At least not anymore."

Jamie said nothing, just followed him to the stable at the rear of the tavern where the horses were tied, and they swung up into their saddles.

It felt good to be mounted again. Adrian realized he had missed it, missed the freedom of riding with the wind in his face, the pleasure of being one with the powerful animal beneath him. He would always love horses and being out of doors, no matter where life carried him.

This last thought was oddly unnerving. He had never envisioned any sort of life beyond the military. Even the shadow of a different notion surprised him. Where had it come from? he wondered. Why had he thought it at all? He shoved the unsettling idea away.

"Tauber's murder is next," he said to Jamie as they rode along. "Perhaps someone saw something or heard something that will help."

"And Elissa?"

"Will simply have to be patient."

"But you *are* taking her with you when you go after Becker."

Adrian pinned him with a cool green stare. "You heard the report this morning. With Napoleon bearing down on us, I can't possibly take her along. The girl will have to stay here."

Jamie hid a smile of amusement. He wondered how his friend intended to manage that.

Four days had passed with no word from Adrian. News of the war had come and it hadn't been good. After the fighting at Abensberg, the archduke's forces had been split, the larger wing falling back to Eckmuhl, a town to the east, while General Hiller and his army turned south over the Isar River to Lanshut.

The French general, Lannes, caught up with Hiller outside the town, and though the Austrians fought with valor and determination, Napoleon's arrival on the battlefield had rallied his men and quickly sealed Hiller's fate. Austrian casualties were reported as high as ten thousand men.

At Eckmuhl things hadn't gone much better. The fighting started with the archduke in a superior position against the French and ended in defeat when Napoleon ordered Lannes and his troops to hasten northward from Lanshut. An army of thirty thousand arrived to aid Marshal Davout against the archduke and his army. Seven thousand Austrian men were lost and nearly five thousand were captured.

Charlie had withdrawn, retreating toward Ratisbon with Napoleon hot on his heels and everyone in Vienna anxiously awaiting word of what would happen next.

And yet, as Elissa sat in the Gold Drawing Room of the duchess's palace it was a minor topic of conversation. Ladies didn't belabor such things, and though Elissa knew she could discuss the war with the duchess, she refrained. The older woman looked even thinner than she had a few days ago, her eyes sunken and her face lined with worry.

Elissa was worried, too—worried about her brother, terrified he might be among those wounded or killed. She should have gone to him when she had first arrived in Austria. She should have told him how much she missed him, how much she and her mother wished he were safely back home.

But she had been too concerned with finding the traitor responsible for Karl's murder.

If only Adrian would come. Perhaps he would bring news. He had promised to help her find the Falcon, but so far she hadn't seen him. And with every passing hour, the need to stop the traitor grew more crucial.

The butler walked in through the open sliding doors, announcing the arrival of another guest to the intimate gathering of a few of the duchess's friends.

"Good afternoon, Your Grace," the woman said. "It was kind of you to allow me to call."

"Nonsense," said the duchess. "You know you are always welcome here."

The viscountess smiled and started in the older woman's direction, walking with a confident grace that drew the eye of every woman in the drawing room. Lady Cecily Kainz was beautiful and charming, her golden blond hair sweeping up in a crown above her head, her gown of embroidered cream silk falling over unmistakably feminine curves.

"Lady Kainz, I believe you know everyone here. Lady Ellen Hargrave, Lord Hargrave's daughter; the Honorable

Mrs. Robert Blackwell; General Oppelt's wife, Berta; and of course the Countess von Langen.''

"Yes . . . I believe I've met them all. Good afternoon, ladies.'' She was smiling, but the smile slipped a little when it came to rest on Elissa. Why, she wasn't quite sure. She had met the viscountess once before. Elissa couldn't say she had liked her. The woman was a bit overblown and full of herself as far as Elissa was concerned.

"Why don't you sit down, Cecily?'' the duchess suggested in that way of hers that was actually a command. "Tell us how you have been keeping yourself occupied while you've been away.''

The duchess signaled for a servant, who returned in moments with a delicate porcelain cup of coffee, a plate of miniature tortes, and a slice of delicious Viennese sponge cake called *Guglhupf,* which he set on the table next to where the viscountess perched in an overstuffed chair.

"It has certainly been a trial,'' Lady Kainz was saying, flashing a sensual smile as she launched into a tale of her days in the country with her rapidly failing husband. "I just don't know what I would do,'' she said a few minutes later, "if my poor, dear Walter should die. I can't imagine life without him.''

Even the duchess looked askance at this, and she seemed willing to indulge Lady Kainz in nearly any of her fantasies. As for herself, Elissa imagined the woman would do just fine without a husband, as she had been doing all along. Adrian could certainly attest to that.

Adrian. The thought of him with Cecily Kainz sent a hot stab of jealousy slicing through her. It was easy to imagine them together—Adrian handsome, powerful, and charming; Cecily beautiful, sensual, and exciting.

It was obvious why they would be drawn to each other, yet the image did not seem to fit. She couldn't envision Adrian looking at the viscountess the way he looked at her, couldn't image the searing green of eyes that seemed to burn right through her, the smile that melted her heart. She couldn't convince herself he would make love to the woman with such unquenchable passion.

She knew it was a lie. Adrian was a virile, masculine man, one who satisfied his needs with whomever he was enamored of at the time. For now it was Elissa. Or at least it had been. Her stomach clenched to think of the pointed way Adrian had been avoiding her. Perhaps he no longer wanted her. Perhaps after seeing her with Steigler, she repulsed him. Perhaps the fascination was simply gone.

She wondered at the truth even as the viscountess ended her story on a note of laughter, excused herself from the others, and made her way over to where Elissa stood beside the hearth.

"Lady von Langen. I am surprised to find you are still in Vienna."

Elissa glanced up. "Oh? Why is that?"

"With the war so close, I would have thought you would have gone home."

"Austria is my home. It was my . . . husband's. Therefore it is mine."

"And you aren't afraid?"

"I have faith that the army will protect us. Besides, I have business here."

"Business . . . ? You are referring to Colonel Kingsland, perhaps."

Elissa's hand trembled. Her coffee cup clinked as she set it down in its saucer. "Colonel Kingsland and I are merely friends."

"Friends . . . yes, I believe that is what he said the last time I saw him. That you and he were merely friends."

An uneasy tension gripped her. Something tightened in the pit of her stomach. "The last . . . the last time you saw him? When was that?"

"He was staying in Baden, I believe, but he had business here in Vienna. There was a dinner party at the Belevedere Palace. Adrian was kind enough to . . . escort me home."

The words fell like a blow. Her stomach clenched then rolled over. Elissa remembered the trips Adrian had made from Baden to Vienna, and the woman's meaning couldn't have been more clear.

"I have seen him several times since, of course," the viscountess was saying. "We understand each other, you see. I make no demands on him, and I know how to please him, since we have been . . . *friends* far longer than the two of you."

Elissa felt sick. Her heart was squeezing, crumbling inside her chest. Dear God, had she meant so little to him then? She had thought that he cared for her at least in some fashion. She fought to hide the ache welling up inside her, the tightness that was gripping her chest. Instead she lifted her chin, facing the woman as if she found the news only remotely interesting.

"I'm glad the colonel found a way to amuse himself while he was away. The next time you see him, give him my regards, won't you? From one *friend* to another." She set her cup and saucer on the table. "In the meantime, if you will excuse me, Lady Kainz, I have some letters to finish upstairs."

With a casualness that was the last thing she felt, Elissa walked away, pausing only long enough to make her excuses to the duchess and her friends. Once she was safely in her bedchamber, the mask she wore crumbled away. She thought of Adrian, of the way he had saved her from Steigler, of the tender care he had shown her, and collapsed into tears on the bench at the foot of the bed.

If what the viscountess said was true, if Adrian had sought out Lady Kainz when he had made her believe he wanted her, cared for her, everything she believed about him was a lie. He had used her. He was as callous and unfeeling as he often appeared to be. He took what he wanted and gave nothing of himself in return.

And there was so much that she had wanted to give him. She was in love with him. The pain she was feeling made the depth of that love abundantly clear. More than anything, she wanted him to love her in return.

It wasn't going to happen. He wasn't the sort of man to

feel love for only one woman. She had known that from the start. Pressing her cheek against the bedpost, Elissa felt the ache of loss sweeping over her. She closed her eyes and gave in to her tears.

Adrian paid a call on her the following evening. By then she had finished crying and pulled herself together. She was insane to let her feelings get the best of her, a naïve, silly fool to believe a man like Adrian cared more for her than he did for any other of his women.

From the start, she had known the kind of man he was— even the duchess had warned her—but she had refused to listen. If anyone was to blame, it was she and not he. And in truth, she was the one who had seduced him, practically begged him to take her that night in the tiny stone cottage. What happened after, the demands he had made, perhaps that was partly her fault as well. He had blackmailed her, true, but she had wanted him to make love to her. His outrageous demands had merely given her an excuse.

But things were different now. The viscountess's words had tempered her feelings for him. She had to guard her heart now, or suffer a good deal more pain.

She waited for him in a small salon she favored at the back of the house, tension running through her even as she worked to steel herself. The room overlooked the formal gardens, whose pathways this time of night were lit by flaming torches. A marble fountain crowned by a cherubic angel spouted a shower of water into a mossy reflecting bowl.

Staring out the window, she heard his heavy footfalls and turned at his approach, saw the worry on his face and the rigid set of his shoulders as he walked in her direction. His face looked as hard as granite, and his eyes were cloudy and dark. Something was wrong, she knew, and as dangerous as it was to care, as much as she wanted to ignore it, worry for him slid into her stomach. She fought an urge to go to him, slide her arms around his neck and give him comfort from whatever it was.

"What's happened?" she asked. "What's wrong?"

A muscle jumped in his cheek. "Charlie's been routed at Ratisbon. He was escaping north across the Danube, leaving a rear guard to defend the city. The cavalry went in. At first the French were repulsed, but Napoleon ordered Lannes to storm the walls. By the end of the day, the entire city and its nine battalions of defenders had fallen into French hands."

"The cavalry?" she whispered, her heart constricting with worry for her brother, her chest aching with fear. "What regiments were involved?" Dear God, he could have been there in the fighting, could have been among those killed!

"I don't know yet. There's only been the briefest word."

"What . . . what were the casualties?"

"Not good. Perhaps a thousand men. But Charlie made good his escape. He's crossed the Danube. He'll find someplace to rest and re-form his troops."

Her fear began to spread, making her insides churn. "Is there no way to discover if Kinsky's Chevauxlegers were involved in the fighting?"

"Not yet, but soon we'll know more."

Elissa's head drooped forward. Burning tears collected and began to slip down her cheeks. "I've been worried. But until now it all seemed so very far away. My brother might be dead and I have been downstairs sipping coffee, chattering with a bunch of women about which gown to wear." She pressed her fist against her mouth. "I can't bear it, Adrian. I've lost one brother. I cannot bear to lose another."

Adrian pulled her into his arms and she let him, knowing she should protest, that it would only make things harder. She rested her cheek against his chest, comforted by the rough wool of his coat.

"You aren't going to lose him," he said gently. "There is no reason to think he is dead. If I had thought this would upset you so badly, I wouldn't have told you."

Elissa shook her head. "I would have found out soon enough. The duchess has a network of people who are paid to carry such news."

"He'll be all right, Elissa. You must believe that."

She nodded, knowing he was right, that it wasn't fair to

Peter to imagine the worst. She drew herself away, and he brushed the tears from her cheeks with the pad of his thumb.

"I'm sorry," she said, accepting the handkerchief he gave her. She dabbed it against her eyes. "I'm just so afraid for Peter." Lifting her gaze to his face, she saw the strength there, the driving purpose, and it gave her strength as well. "We have to get to Becker. God only knows what part the Falcon may have played in all of this. There is no more time to lose."

Adrian caught her shoulders. "Listen to me, Elissa. Napoleon is marching toward Vienna. At this point we don't know if Charlie will be able to stop him. If you leave here now, head south into Italy, you can still get safely back to England."

"I told you I'm not leaving."

"Dammit, it's not safe for you to stay here."

"It isn't safe for my brother. It isn't safe for you."

"That is different."

"Why, because I'm a woman? I can help stop a traitor. It is what I came here to do. I'm going to find Becker—whether you come with me or not!"

He straightened to his full, imposing height, looking furious and dangerous and so incredibly handsome her heart turned over.

"And just how, if I may ask, do you plan to reach Becker? He is traveling with the archduke, moving from place to place with the rest of the Austrian Army. You can't just appear outside his tent."

For the past week she had been thinking exactly that same thing and she had come up with a plan. "There are women who travel with the army. Wives of the soldiers, women who wash their clothes and cook for them, mend the holes in their uniforms."

"A camp follower?" His expression turned incredulous. "You want to travel with the army as a camp follower?"

She glanced away from him, refusing to be intimidated by the hard look in his eyes. "I'll admit it would be easier if you were with me. If I posed as your . . . as the woman who takes care of you. I could pretend an interest in Becker without worrying about being set upon by the rest of the men.''

''This is insane.''

''It isn't insane. You have probably traveled with a woman before, many of the officers do.'' His cheekbones flushed a bit and she knew it was true. She forced herself not to think of how many women he had been with, but it wasn't easy to do. ''We have to do something. This is as good a plan as any.''

Adrian paced away from her then returned. ''I came here tonight for two reasons. Aside from the news I carried, I came to ask if there was anything else you could tell me about the death of your brother. Where it happened. What he might have been doing at the time.''

''I know nothing else. His commanding officer would probably know the details. A colonel named Shultz wrote the letter informing us of Karl's death, but most likely he's campaigning with the army. If we go there, we can talk to him, see what he might know.'' *And I can find Peter, be certain that he is safe.*

''I don't like this, Elissa. A woman has no business in the middle of a war.''

''I'm not asking you to like it. I'm asking you to do the most expedient thing.''

His eyes bored into her, hostile eyes that demanded she retreat. Elissa's gaze did not waver. Another silent moment, and Adrian released a slow breath of air. His posture shifted, and resignation altered his features.

''It won't be easy. Living out of a tent is hardly the same as living in a duchess's palace.''

''I lived a simple life at home. I am tougher than I look, and I am not afraid of hard work. I can cook and wash and mend—''

''All right—you can go. Again, you leave me no choice.''

''You are saying you'll come with me?''

''I'm saying that since I had already made plans to seek out Becker and you are so damned stubborn, you may come along. I can hardly let you go off on your own.''

Why not? she wanted to ask. Because you care about me? If he did, he didn't care enough. She thought of Cecily Kainz and her chin went up a notch. "I'll cook and clean for you, but I'm not sleeping with you."

A muscle tightened in his cheek. "I didn't expect you to." A cynical twist moved his lips. "After all, I've nothing to blackmail you with now." There was a bitterness in his tone she hadn't expected, and perhaps a tinge of regret. She started to tell him the truth, that his threats had never been the reason she had given herself to him. She had done it because she was in love with him, though she hadn't realized it at the time. She had done it because she wanted him as much as he had seemed to want her.

She bit back the words. He had too strong a hold on her already, and there must have been dozens of women who had loved him. He would only think her weak for becoming another one of them.

"How will you explain your arrival?" she asked. "A British soldier in the midst of the Austrian Army."

His mouth curved faintly. "Ravenscroft has seen to that. Since England is still in the process of forging an alliance, I have orders to report to the archduke in an advisory position, to show our support for his cause."

"When do we leave?"

"Tomorrow morning." A hint of mockery touched the corners of his mouth. "As you said, there is no time to lose."

Dawn broke crisp and clear over a cloudless blue sky. Adrian arrived with the sun, riding up to the duchess's front door on his magnificent black stallion, leading a dapple gray mare sporting a worn leather saddle.

Elissa joined him in the foyer, dressed in a plum velvet riding habit trimmed with white lace, carrying a small tapestry traveling satchel.

Adrian scowled at her appearance, surveying her expensive riding clothes with a look of disdain. "I hope you've brought something more practical. Marching behind an army of men is hardly the place for fashion."

Her chin hiked up. "I've purchased some simple garments from one of the maids. She is about my size and the clothes are quite sturdy. I prefer my habit for riding, but if it doesn't suit you—"

"It'll do for the present. We won't reach our destination for at least several days. What you wear now doesn't really matter." He seemed remote and impatient, yet his eyes followed each of her movements as a footman cupped his hands and gave her a lift up onto the saddle. Riding astride as she was her stockings showed nearly to her knees, but she forced herself to ignore it.

"You're sure you are up to this?" he asked. "I haven't time to coddle you, and I mean to push hard."

"Worry about yourself, Colonel Kingsland. I assure you I shall be fine."

He hadn't lied about the pace. They rode the horses till both animals were lathered and sweating beneath the fierce May sun and Elissa was hot, dusty, and exhausted. She hadn't ridden this hard since she was a girl, racing across the moors with her brothers, and she ached from neck to ankle.

The colonel glanced at her several times, but she didn't ask for quarter and he gave her none, stopping only briefly to rest and water the horses, then moving on. It wasn't until the sky turned to shades of dusky orange that he finally reined up in front of a small, well-appointed inn. Griensteidl Haus read the red-painted sign out in front.

The little dappled mare hung its head and blew out its sides with fatigue, apparently as tired as Elissa. She watched Adrian dismount, wishing she had half the energy he still seemed to have, and gathered her strength to do the same, praying her aching limbs wouldn't be too shaky to hold her up. She sighed and leaned forward, her hand trembling on the pommel, then felt Adrian's hands at her waist, lifting her from the saddle more gently than she would have expected, setting her carefully on her feet.

"Are you all right?"

She smiled with weary gratitude. "Just tired is all. I'll be fine once I've rested."

"You did well," he said a bit gruffly, glancing away when she looked into his face. "We'll get a good night's sleep and perhaps by tomorrow your body will be more accustomed to the saddle."

She only nodded, grateful for the hand he kept at her waist as he guided her on unsteady legs through the inn's heavy door. He surprised her by ordering two rooms instead of one, and she felt an unexpected twinge of disappointment. It was silly, considering his recent liaison with Cecily Kainz, but the unwelcome feeling remained.

"I thought I was supposed to be your mistress," she said so that no one could hear.

"Nothing so fancy as that. Not out here. Here you are merely my woman. It is as simple as that."

"Then why—"

"We'll be confined together soon enough. Perhaps this way we'll both be able to get some sleep."

She wasn't sure what he meant, but she forced a smile and accepted the key he gave her, then they followed the innkeeper up the steep wooden stairs to their second-story rooms.

"I can have your supper sent up," the innkeeper offered, a thin little mustached man with round eyes and spectacles that gave him a constant look of surprise. "But you will be charged for it. Otherwise you must eat in the taproom."

Adrian took one look at her wan, pale face, the fatigue that darkened patches beneath her eyes, and ordered the man to send their supper upstairs.

Elissa flashed him a tired, grateful smile. "Thank you."

"It's been a long, dusty day. I'll have a bath sent up, then you can eat and go straight to bed."

She simply nodded, wanting only to put her head down on the pillow and drown herself in sleep. Adrian opened the door and tossed her satchel on the ladderback chair against the wall. She walked in behind him on legs that trembled beneath her riding skirt and stood there swaying on her feet. Adrian left and she sat down on the bed. She must have lain down and drifted to sleep, for the next thing she knew, he had reappeared in the room and was muttering a curse at her bedside.

"Dammit, I told you this would be hard but you wouldn't listen. Now you're so exhausted you didn't even wake up when your bathwater arrived."

She rubbed the sleep from her eyes and sat up on the bed, her muscles screaming at the torture of that simple movement. Her dusty velvet riding habit was ruched up around her knees, rumpled and stained with perspiration.

"I'll be fine in the morning," she said, knowing it was a bald-faced lie. "But thank you for waking me."

"Come here and turn around," he grumbled. She started to tell him she didn't need his help, but she was too tired to argue. Adrian worked the buttons at the back of her dress with the same skill she recalled from the night they made love in the bathhouse. It unsettled her to think of his expertise with women, yet her thoughts wandered back to that evening, to the intimate things they had done and the thrill she had felt when he had been inside her.

She forced the unwanted images away, hoping he wouldn't notice the tinge of color that had crept into her cheeks.

"Tomorrow wear something more comfortable," he said, stripping the gown off her shoulders with quick, purposeful motions. When she stood in front of him in only her thin chemise, his eyes shifted away and focused on a spot on the wall.

"Get into the tub," he said with authority. "And don't fall asleep. I'll be back to check on you before I go to bed."

With a weary sigh, Elissa watched him walk away, his wide shoulders perfectly straight, his narrow hips moving with the strong sense of purpose that always seemed to surround him. He was such a virile man. Too arrogant by half, too stubborn, too demanding, yet in Adrian she found those very qualities appealing. It was insane to love that sort of man, yet the feeling doggedly remained.

Sighing at the thought, Elissa stripped off her chemise, sank into the warmth of the tub, and leaned her head back. She wouldn't stay long, she told herself, but it did feel good to wash away the dust; and the heat of the water soothed the ache in her back and thighs.

She was out of the tub, in bed, and drifting off to sleep when the colonel stuck his head through the door to make certain that she was all right. Whatever he felt for her, he meant to keep her safe. The knowledge brought the faintest touch of a smile.

Chapter Seventeen

Adrian stood in the doorway of Elissa's tiny room at the inn, watching her eyes droop closed, listening as her breathing settled into a peaceful sleep. Her golden blond hair, still damp from her bath, curled in soft little ringlets around her face. Her fingers fisted the blanket. Her body curved protectively into itself as if she were warding off danger.

The only danger Adrian sensed in the comfortable little inn was himself. He wanted to go to her, to pull back the light woolen blanket and slide into the bed beside her. He wanted to make slow, languid love to her as he had done that night in the bathhouse.

He had rarely slept the night with a woman. Usually, once his appetite was sated, he wanted simply to be rid of her. He didn't like the feeling of awakening next to a woman, hated to see that look of expected commitment in her eyes when he felt only a sense of gratitude for the temporary use of her body.

Yet now, looking at Elissa, he thought that he wanted nothing so much as to join her there in bed, to bury himself deeply inside her and ease his frustrations, to wake up with her slender body pressed against his and make love to her again in the soft light of dawn.

He wouldn't, he knew. He had pressed her before, demanded she give herself to him, taken her with little concern for her feelings. He wouldn't do it again. He wouldn't bed her unless it was what she wanted as well, unless her need of him was as great as his need of her.

He didn't think that would happen, and if it did he wasn't certain he would like the consequences. Commitment wasn't part of his nature. He knew he would never marry, and it wasn't fair to Elissa to use her and cast her aside.

Still, just watching her lying beneath the rumpled covers made something tighten inside him. His blood began to thicken, settle low in his groin, and his shaft pressed hard against his belly. Damn, there were times he wished he had never met her. But as Jamie had said, he needed her. As much as he hated to admit it, her plan was a good one, and he thought that she would be safe as long as he was there to protect her.

He owed her that much, since he had been the one to steal her innocence. And he knew how much this meant to her. It was hard to imagine the emotion she felt at the loss of her brother, the fierce family ties that bound her to her mother and father, to Karl and to Peter. He had never known that sort of love. The loss of his brother, of his mother and father, had made him sad, but only to think of the feelings for each other that they had never had.

He glanced back at Elissa, feeling the ache of wanting, his unending desire for her, not liking the train of his thoughts. Once their mission was completed, he would send her home and be damned glad to see her gone. At least he told himself that as he returned to his lonely room, climbed into a cold, empty bed, and tried to fall asleep.

They crossed the Danube at Krems the following day. It was a bustling, walled city of narrow streets and baroque and rococo buildings. The town had prospered from the wine trade, the steep vineyards on the hills producing some of the best wines made in Austria. An open-air play, a comedy of some sort, was being staged in the Hoher Markt.

Elissa watched the actors with a wistful eye, wishing they could join the animated crowd, but Adrian gave them no time to linger. They watered the horses, purchased food to eat on the road, then set off again, headed toward the town of Zwettle, hoping to cut the path of the archduke's forces.

"He'll have wounded men to tend," Adrian said as they rode along. "He'll be pushing them hard, but I don't think it's possible he could have made it this far yet. Perhaps tomorrow or the next day we'll find them."

That night was the same as the one before, though she didn't ache quite so badly. As Adrian had said, her body was beginning to grow accustomed to the long hours in the saddle. The inn they stayed in sat at a crossroads, but nowhere near a town. It was more a tavern than an inn, its furnishings worn and faded, dirt accumulating in musty piles in the corners. There were only a couple of rooms upstairs. Though Adrian could have purchased them both, he did not.

She thought perhaps it was because of the disreputable-looking men in the taproom who kept staring at her with too bold eyes. Forcing herself to ignore their muttered comments and ribald jokes, she climbed ahead of Adrian up the stairs and walked into the shabby little room he had let for the night.

"You may have the bed," he said. "I'll make up a place on the floor."

The bed didn't look any more appealing than the rest of the room, just a lumpy corn-husk mattress over a framework of rotting wood and a web of sagging ropes, but she was so tired she didn't care. Her head was pounding, and the muscles in her back and legs felt as knotted as the rope beneath the bed.

Beyond that, she was hungry, her stomach growling so loudly she was certain Adrian could hear it.

"What about supper?" she asked. "I'm even hungrier than I am tired and the tavernkeeper doesn't look the sort to carry it up to us. I suppose we shall have to go down to the taproom."

Adrian shook his head. "I'll bring up something for you. I'll eat downstairs. Perhaps I'll hear news of the war or the army that we might not yet have heard."

She smiled, grateful she didn't have to face the lascivious looks of the men. "Thank you."

He left her to bathe as best she could with the water in the chipped bowl and pitcher on the dresser, then returned with a small tray laden with a portion of goulash, a hard crust of coarse brown bread, and a flagon of wine.

"Lock the door when I leave. Don't open it for anyone else."

She nodded. She didn't like the place any better than he did, but she wasn't really afraid. Not as long as Adrian was with her.

She changed out of the plain brown skirt and unbleached muslin blouse she wore, thinking about him, wondering at the stiff formality he had adopted whenever he was with her. She wondered if he still desired her. She would have been certain that he did not if it weren't for the heat that simmered in his eyes every now and then when he thought she wasn't watching.

She pondered what it meant. In playing the role of his mistress, she had given him another excuse to demand the use of her body, and yet he did not. She wondered what held him back and thought that perhaps it wasn't desire she saw in his eyes but anger that she had forced him to bring her along.

She finished the bowl of goulash and lay down in her night rail to await his return, but by the time he arrived, she had fallen asleep. She let him in when he knocked, then turned her face to the wall while he undressed and prepared himself for bed, trying not to remember the hard-muscled lines of his body.

In the middle of the night she awakened. A bad dream she could only vaguely recall. She rose up on an elbow, sweeping back the pale hair that had tumbled into her eyes, then searched the shabby room for the pallet where Adrian slept. He lay on his back, an arm thrown haphazardly across his eyes, his thick, muscular chest exposed above the thin woolen blanket that had settled low around his hips.

She watched the rise and fall of his breathing, let her eyes wander over the curly dark hair across his chest, arrowing out of sight below the blanket. His stomach was flat, and small ridges of muscle formed a ladder above it. His hips were narrow, and she could see the round indentation of his navel.

Her heartbeat quickened and her mouth felt dry. She wanted to lift the blanket and examine the rest of that hard male body, to touch him as she once had, to kiss the corner of his mouth and breathe in his masculine scent. She wanted to feel those strong, powerful hands skimming over her flesh, lifting her to sheathe himself inside her. She could almost feel the movement of his hips as he surged into her body, the hot, sweet pleasure that he could arouse.

She knew she should look away, that it was an invasion of his privacy to stare at him so boldly, but she couldn't seem to stop herself.

"I hope you like what you see."

Oh, dear God! He had caught her out and there was no way to deny it. She prayed it was too dark to see the hot color burning in her cheeks. "I—I'm sorry. I was having trouble sleeping."

"Look at me that way much longer, angel, and I'll come over and make certain you are able to sleep."

She flushed to the roots of her hair to think he had read her thoughts. "No, I don't want . . ." Even as she said the words, she felt guilty for the lie. If it hadn't been for his betrayal with Lady Kainz, she knew without doubt she would have welcomed him into her bed. "Good night, Colonel."

He didn't answer. The night sounds crept in: rough male laughter from the tavern downstairs, the neighing of horses in the stable behind the inn. She heard his restless movements and knew it took a long time for him to fall asleep.

They traveled the next day, farther into the Waldviertel, the forest district, passing gently rolling hills covered by oaks and stands of tall pine trees. Small farms and a few tiny villages marked their way, providing them with food and drink.

Late in the afternoon, they passed through the town of

Ottenstein, and Elissa admired the majestic medieval castle at the outskirts of the village, its massive central tower a stone-walled guardian of the occupants within. Other castle ruins, crumbling remnants of the past, imprinted the landscape along the way.

At the end of the day, they reached their destination, the small market town of Zwettl, surrounded by rolling hills, the village itself a walled city guarded by six stone towers.

"Until we find the exact location of the army," Adrian said, stepping down from his big black stallion, "we'll stay here in Zwettl. If Ravenscroft's information is correct, Charlie and his men should be somewhere close by or on their way."

They took two rooms again, in a pleasant inn near a big stone Romanesque church. Once they were settled, Adrian left her in the hope of discovering information, and Elissa was thankful that at least for a time, their journey was at an end.

At least so she thought until Adrian returned from his scavenging about the village.

"We're in luck." He stood in the hall outside the door to her room, his sensuous mouth curved with excitement. "According to local gossip, the archduke and his men are camped near the town of Weitra, about a day's ride west of here. Charlie has commandeered the castle as his headquarters, perhaps for the next several days while his men are resting for the march to Vienna."

"Oh, Adrian, that's wonderful news." She would see Peter on the morrow, at last be assured he was safe.

"Are you hungry?"

"Starved."

He chuckled as he took her arm, resting it lightly on the sleeve of his coat, then he led her downstairs to the comfortable dining room at the back of the inn, and they sat down at a heavy wooden table in the corner. The innkeeper, a whiskered blond man with his hair tied back in a queue, brought them a supper of roast pork and bread dumplings, which they both attacked with fervor after a long, weary day.

From beneath her lashes, Elissa studied Adrian as he ate.

His jacket was unbuttoned partway down, the dark skin at his throat visible through the opening. She watched the strong pulse beating there and wished she could press her lips against it. When he reached across the table to set a tankard of beer in front of her, his coat pulled tight across the breadth of his wide shoulders, and she recalled how beautiful his body had looked stretched out on the floor of their room.

"With any luck," he said, drawing her mind from the dangerous path it had taken, "tomorrow we'll find your brother. And of course there is Becker."

Elissa swallowed the bite of dumpling she had been chewing. "I've been thinking, Adrian. What about Steigler? He is bound to be suspicious when he sees us. He's certain to wonder why a countess is following an army of soldiers, even if I am with you."

Adrian took a long drink from his tankard. "Steigler was assigned to Hiller and his forces. They turned south from Landshut and are heading for Vienna by a different route. For a while, at least, Steigler shouldn't be a problem."

She relaxed a bit at that. They finished their supper with little conversation, both of them weary, and that night slept once more in separate rooms. It was strange, she supposed, but in truth she preferred the raucous tavern and the small, shabby room they had shared the evening before, with Adrian asleep on the floor.

The sun formed a hot yellow ball in the west as they crested the rise outside a sloping field at the outskirts of Weitra. Elissa's eyes widened at the great sea of humanity stretched like a colorful carpet on the landscape below her.

"Dear Lord, how many are there?"

"The archduke split his forces, so probably seventy or eighty thousand. It's hard to tell from here."

"Eighty thousand," she whispered, awed by the sight of so many soldiers, horses, tents, and an endless array of equipment. Supply wagons, cannon and caisson, regimental flags snapping in the breeze, soldiers' knapsacks and muskets, and even musical instruments strewn about.

Battle-weary men, many of them swathed in bloody bandages, clustered in small informal groups around cooking fires, tended their horses and equipment, or squatted over wooden boxes, tin cups of coffee in hand, playing games of chance to pass the time.

As she rode down off the ridge, any thought that Adrian's scarlet tunic would stand out among the Austrian soldiers flew right out of Elissa's head. The men were uniformed in dark green, gray, white, light and dark blue, their coats trimmed with heavy gold braid and faced with red, gold, blue, or green. The only thing that made Adrian's red coat stand out was simply that it was so clean.

Following close behind his big black stallion, Elissa's little dappled mare picked its way through the clutter of saddles and bridles, sabers and muskets, tents and wooden canteens. Everywhere they rode, the air smelled of sweat and horses, freshly oiled weapons, and a residue of gunpowder.

She had never seen men who looked more weary and her heart went out to them. Haggard faces roughened by unkempt beards watched them pass, staring through hollow, sunken eyes, their uniforms dirty and ragged, the trim hanging loose, the fabric darkened with old, dried blood. She wished she could help them, yet the vast numbers alone were daunting. The deep lines of battle etched in their faces made worry for her brother surface again.

They stopped once in a circle of tents while Adrian asked directions to one of the areas set aside for the women, a place he hoped to find some of them working to take care of their men. A few minutes later, he reined up amidst a small cluster of cooking fires where a number of them scurried about carrying firewood and water, getting ready to prepare the evening meal.

"I've got to leave you for a while. I need to report to the archduke and discuss our plans for Becker."

"Will you tell him our suspicions?"

He nodded. "By now he knows there is a traitor. I'm hoping he'll be glad for any help we might be able to give him." He glanced around at the gaggle of women. "You'll be safe here until I get back, but don't go wandering off. I don't want you getting into trouble.''

A hint of irritation trickled through her. Didn't he know trouble was the last thing she wanted? He said something else, but she didn't really hear him, awed instead by the jumble of strange sights and sounds. She focused on the women, some of them garishly made up, their cheeks rouged, their lips painted, all of them obviously bone weary.

''I'll be back as soon as I can,'' she heard him say as he reined his stallion away and began to pick a path back toward the perimeter of the camp, heading toward the castle in the distance where the archduke had taken refuge.

Elissa watered the little gray mare while he was away, then spoke to several of the women, who merely grunted a reply and continued to ignore her. She began to fidget, bored with nothing to do, more anxious by the minute to find her brother. She tried to imagine where he might be, if indeed he was even in the camp, then thought that if he was, he would be grouped with the Chevauxlegers.

She stopped one of the women, a matron in her forties with a wrinkled face and tired blue eyes. A soiled mobcap covered most of her dirty brown hair.

''Excuse me. I'm sorry to bother you, but I'm looking for one of the soldiers. I was hoping perhaps you could help me.''

''Lookin' for one of the soldiers?'' she replied with irritation. ''Do ya think I know every man jack in the camp?'' Her bony shoulders hunched forward. ''I'll admit I've tumbled my share, but it wouldn't make a dent in this sludge pot of an army.'' She started to walk away, but Elissa caught her arm.

''He's with the Fourth Chevauxlegers. I saw some dark green uniforms in the distance when we rode in. I wondered if that might be them.''

She nodded. ''Dark green sounds right for the Fourth.''

''Unfortunately, there's so many men, I don't exactly remember where I saw them.''

The older woman harrumphed some sort of answer, then

pointed through the sea of tents toward a cluster of men camped to the south and west. "Some of the Chevauxlegers are there. Other groups are scattered about. Ya'll have to ask one of them." The woman grabbed a basket full of just-washed laundry, rested it on a bony hip, and walked away.

Elissa glanced off in the distance, wondering if she dared to leave the spot where Adrian had left her. It wasn't really that far. Surely he couldn't get back from the castle before she had time to ask the soldiers about her brother and return. Still, just to be safe, she walked to a broad-hipped woman stirring a huge iron pot that hung over a small cooking fire.

"I'm sorry to bother you. I wonder if you might do me a favor?"

The woman eyed her with suspicion. "You're the woman who just rode in with the handsome Brit."

She smiled. "Colonel Kingsland. Yes, I came here with him. I was hoping—if he happens to return before I get back, would you tell him I went to the camp of the Chevauxlegers? That group over there." She pointed in that direction. "Tell him I won't be gone long."

The woman dipped a big wooden spoon into the bubbling iron cauldron over the fire, then tapped it against the rim of the pot to drain off the excess liquid. "I will tell him." She grinned, a wide gap yawning between her two front teeth. "You had better stay close to that one. The women—they will all be fighting to get him into their beds."

Elissa felt a sharp sting in the area around her heart. Even here she was reminded how easily Adrian could make a conquest. She thought of Cecily Kainz and what must have been dozens of others, though she wasn't really worried about the ragtag group of women she had seen thus far.

"Thank you for the warning. And thank you for telling him if he comes." Elissa turned to leave and began making her way through the endless sea of soldiers, careful to mark her path so she could find her way back to the small group of women.

As she walked farther away, she began to hurry her pace, beginning to grow uneasy, noticing the soldiers in a way she hadn't before. Until now she had merely seen their suffering, their weariness, and the pain they carried of their grim defeat. Now she saw that they were a motley crew of misfits and drunkards, men like the ones who had stared at her in the taproom. There were Turks and Hungarians, Croatians, Slovenians, and Germans, all from the lowest rungs of society.

Anxiety began to gnaw like a rat in her stomach. Perhaps she should have done as Adrian said and stayed where he had left her. But the other women had seemed impervious to the men's lascivious stares. Stiffening her spine, she walked on, spying a cluster of dark green uniforms ahead, certain once she reached them, she would be safe.

She almost made it. Might have if she hadn't stumbled over a tent stake and nearly fallen. The bearded soldier who caught her, saving her from a painful landing, grinned down at her through rotten yellow teeth.

"She's a pretty un', eh, Zoltan? Ripe enough to satisfy even *your* lusty appetite."

A second man, a big, boisterous Turk, roared with laughter and swaggered forward, blocking the way to her destination.

"You must be new," he said in his broken, guttural imitation of German, shoving a big blunt finger beneath her chin and forcing her head up. "From Zwettl you came, no? Or maybe as far away as Ottenstein."

"Let me go." She jerked her head away and tried to free herself from the yellow-toothed soldier's painful grip on her shoulders. "I'm not a doxy. I'm here with a British colonel. You had better let me go or I promise you won't like the consequences."

The Turk's bold black brow shot up, obviously taken aback by the educated, upper-class tone of her words. Then he laughed.

"So . . . you are a colonel's whore instead. What do I care?" The big Turk shoved the smaller man away and dragged her against his chest, pinning her arms at her sides so she couldn't move. "Another man will not matter. You can service me as well as you service him."

She started to scream, but he clamped a meaty hand over

her mouth and it came out as a choked sound of protest. Fear shot through her. Biting down hard on his dirty callused palm, she kicked backward, sinking the heel of her riding boot into his shin. He merely laughed and tightened his hold, squeezing her so hard she had to fight to drag in a breath of air.

Her heart was pounding, slamming against her chest like a battering ram. His crushing hold had her breathing in short, sharp gasps, and blackness swirling at the corners of her vision. Ignoring her struggles, he lifted her off the ground with appalling ease, dragging her backward through the space between a pair of tents toward a flat spot behind them.

Her limbs shook with fear and true panic set in. Dear Lord, wouldn't somebody help her? Why in the name of God hadn't she listened to Adrian and stayed were she was told? She tore at his hands and kicked him again, glancing frantically about for help.

It came bearing down full tilt. Above the top of the tents, she saw a mounted rider racing forward. As she recognized the scarlet tunic and big, angry man on the huge black horse, her heart leapt with hope.

Adrian swooped down like a hawk over a rabbit, vaulting off the stallion, tackling the beefy Turk, and in the process, knocking all three of them to the ground. The Turk's hold on her vanished, and Elissa rolled away, hauling herself unsteadily to her feet and dragging in great breaths of air. Adrian made a single swift move—grabbing the powerful Turk by the front of his coat, raising him up, then crashing his big ugly head several times against an equipment box sitting at the back of a tent.

He stood over the huge man's prone body, feet splayed, hands balled into fists. Sprawled in the dirt, greasy black hair falling forward, the Turk let out a keening moan but he didn't try to get up, just cradled his bleeding, aching head between his hands and looked at Adrian as if he wanted to murder him.

"From now on," Adrian warned with undisguised fury, "I'd advise you to keep your hands off another man's woman. Especially *my* woman. That is, if you wish to live another day.'' He tossed a glance at the second man, who had scampered to safety at the first sign of trouble and now stood peering at the scene from around a corner of the tent.

''That goes for you, too,'' he said to the thin, bearded soldier. With a last backward glance at the Turk, Adrian strode toward Elissa, his chest heaving in and out, his uniform covered with dry grass and dirt. Fury darkened his eyes and etched every line of his face.

Elissa watched him and a shot of apprehension trickled through her. She had never seen him quite this angry—at least not at her. He didn't say a word and neither did she, but she could feel the tension in his muscles as he lifted her roughly up on the stallion, setting her sideways in front of him then swinging himself up behind.

She started to ask him to take her on to the camp of the Chevauxlegers, but the rigid set of his shoulders and the fierce way he gripped the reins warned her it wasn't the time.

He reached an open space at the perimeter of the camp, and drew the stallion to a halt, swinging a long leg over the saddle to dismount. Strong hands clamped around her waist and he jerked her down, setting her firmly on her feet.

''I told you to stay where I left you.'' His face was red and his eyes blazed like hot green fires as he towered above her, glaring as fiercely at her as he had at the Turk.

Elissa swallowed hard. ''I—I wasn't going far. There was a group of cavalrymen just a short distance away. I only wanted to ask about my brother.''

''But you never got there, did you? As a matter of fact, you are lucky you got as far as you did.''

''But I—''

''You don't understand, do you? These men are fresh from battle. Their blood is running high and any woman in their way is fair game. Especially those in the camp who go about unprotected. They hardly expect to cross paths with a countess.''

''I—I'm not a real countess.''

His eyes blazed anew. ''No, you are not, and even if you were—among these men it wouldn't matter.''

She glanced down at the toes of her riding boots, misery washing through her in waves. "I know now that you are right. I'm sorry. 'Tis just that I am new to all this. I didn't realize the sort of men these were."

For a moment his hard look softened. "Dammit, you scared the bloody life out of me. If your washerwoman friend hadn't told me where you'd gone, God knows what would have happened." He gripped her shoulders. "I ought to put you over my knee."

Elissa said nothing. She was too grateful he had come when he did.

He looked down at the bruises on her arms, at the dirt and leaves in her hair, and the muscles in his jaw went tight once more. "This is my world, Elissa. Here you have no one to depend on but me. If you are to survive, you have do exactly what I tell you. You must trust me to know what is best."

Elissa looked up at him and nodded. "As I said, I'm new at this, but I am not a stupid woman. I won't make the same mistake again."

"You said you would obey me. You gave me your word."

"I didn't mean to break it. I just didn't see the danger. From now on I'll do as you say."

He relaxed at that, the tension in his jaw ebbing away. "You aren't hurt, are you?"

"Only my pride." She tossed him the hint of a smile. "At least you arrived in time to save the remnants of it."

A corner of his mouth curved up. "Perhaps a lesson learned so early will save you from even greater danger later on."

Her stomach tightened and a shiver slid down her spine. She wasn't sure exactly what he meant, but she knew he was right—this was his world and in the days ahead she must bow to his authority. It rankled a little, but if they meant to catch the Falcon, it was the only choice she had.

He lifted her back up on the horse, a little more gently this time.

"Did you speak to the archduke?" she asked, then glanced

off in the direction he was taking her. ''Where are we going?''

''I spoke to him, yes. He has heard about the traitor. He was not pleased to think the spy might be among his own men, but he was grateful for the information I brought and thankful for any help we might be able to give him. As to where we are going, after we gather your mare, we're going to join a regiment of cuirassiers that just happen to be under the command of General Klammer.'' He grinned. ''I've conveniently been assigned to assist him and his aide, Major Becker, in whatever way I can.''

Excitement slithered through her. Her heartbeat quickened again. ''Thank God the archduke was amenable to our plans.''

''We'll be supplied with an officer's tent and whatever equipment we might need, and a lieutenant named Helm has been ordered to act as my aide.''

Elissa glanced wistfully back toward the cluster of dark green uniforms she could no longer see. ''What about my brother?''

''As soon as we're settled, I'll take you to him.'' A dry smile touched his lips. ''You wouldn't have found him among the cavalrymen you sought. He is stationed on the north side of the camp.''

Something warm unfurled. He had cared enough to ask about Peter. She flashed him a radiant smile. ''Thank you, my lord Colonel.''

Adrian pulled the black to a halt next to her gray. ''Trust me to take care of you, Elissa. I promise you won't be sorry.''

He was looking at her with such sincerity she wanted to reach out and touch him, to ease the concern she read in his face. It was a foolish, idiotic sentiment, but she couldn't make the feeling go away.

''I trust you,'' she said softly, turning away. *I trust you with my life, Adrian, but I dare not trust you with my heart.* A wave of sadness stole away the excitement she had been feeling only moments before.

Chapter *E*ighteen

Adrian helped Elissa unpack and get them settled in the tent they would be sharing. As he watched her work, he tried not to think of the worry he had felt when he had discovered her gone from the place he had left her—the consummate rage that swept through him when he'd seen her manhandled by the Turk.

There were good men among the soldiers serving in the ranks, but most were men down on their luck, petty criminals, and drunkards, the very worst lot in society. Their only interest in enlisting was fear of being tossed into prison or need for the meager bounty paid to them for joining.

He should have warned her, explained things more carefully. As she had said, she wasn't a stupid woman. Headstrong and willful, but not the least bit stupid. He would remember that in future and try to act accordingly.

In the meantime he would take her to the camp of the 4th Chevauxlegers and hope she would be able to find her brother—and that Peter hadn't been injured or perhaps even killed. Afterward he would report to General Klammer and get his first look at Becker. In time, he would introduce them to Elissa . . . or perhaps he would let her seek Becker out on her own.

Across the tent, Elissa leaned against the broom she had borrowed. "I've made it as comfortable as I possible can."

She had finished sweeping away the stones and loose dirt on the earthen floor. "Now can we go and find Peter?"

He smiled, enjoying the excitement on her face that made her cheeks turn rosy. Against his will, his pulse began to quicken and thoughts of bedding her rose like a storm in his blood. He forced the notion away.

Surveying the interior of the tent, he noticed she had unpacked and hung their scant clothing from a line strung at the rear and neatly placed his boots and a pair of sturdy brown shoes beneath them. Then his glance fell on the two narrow cots placed well apart, and a shot of annoyance filtered through him. Reaching down, he dragged the beds together so it appeared they would be sleeping side by side.

"You're supposed to be my woman, remember?"

She eyed the cots with a look of trepidation, but she didn't complain. "Now can we go?"

"In a minute." Crossing to the front of the tent where the flaps had been tied open to catch the breeze, he turned to face her. "Come here."

There was something in his voice that must have made her wary. With a look of hesitation, she finally obeyed, stopping in front of him in the opening.

"What . . . what is it?"

Though the tent sat a bit off by itself, there were at least a dozen men milling about within sight of where they stood. Reaching for Elissa, he dragged her into his arms and took her mouth in a searing kiss. For a moment she stiffened, her slender body rigid, her palms pressing hard against his chest. Then she made a soft little sound in her throat, slid her arms around his neck, and kissed him back.

It was more than he'd bargained for. His fiery kiss was meant to protect her, to show his possession, lay claim to her in front of the men and let them know without doubt she was his. Now as her soft lips trembled and her breath came in shallow little gasps, Adrian's blood began to pool low in his groin. His shaft went rock hard, and he wondered if the men would think it was she who possessed him.

And bloody hell, they would be right.

With an effort, he ended the kiss, wishing instead he could drag her back in the tent, tear off her simple garments, and make passionate love to her. Instead, he lifted his head and eased her away, trying not to notice the bloom of desire in her cheeks and her bewildered expression.

"We'll finish this later," he said gruffly, turning her in the direction they were headed, giving her a smart, proprietary slap on the bottom.

He didn't miss the sparks of blue that shot from her eyes or the stiff set to her shoulders. She opened her mouth to rail at him, but he dragged her back into his arms and silenced her with another quick, hard kiss.

"This was your idea, sweeting," he whispered in her ear. "Try to remember your part."

She straightened away from him and forced herself to smile, then relaxed into the role she had come to play, giving him a wink and a saucy grin. "Whatever you say, my lord Colonel."

Her posture had subtly changed and even her speech sounded different, less refined. He thought that perhaps her mother's thinking was correct, that she could have been a talented actress after all.

"Come on," he said. "We've better things to do than stand about wasting time."

Her eyes narrowed and for a moment she looked as though she wanted to hit him. Instead she smiled the same smile she had used to charm Pettigru and the rest of her admirers.

"I'll remember that, my lord. And later," she purred, "when we are alone"—her gaze ran over his body—"I'll find a way to make you pay."

They left the men staring after them, and as they passed among the soldiers on the way to the Chevauxlegers' camp, Adrian kept a proprietary hand at her waist. Word traveled fast among a group like this: the story of the colonel and his woman, newly arrived in camp; the beating he had given the big Turk for trying to harm her.

Just thinking of her attacker made the hair rise at the back of his neck. If the man had been under his command, he would have had him flogged. As it was, he didn't want to draw more attention to them than necessary.

Perhaps in one way it was good that it had happened. The warning he had delivered wouldn't insure her complete protection—there was no real way to do that—but as long as she was careful and he kept a watchful eye, she should be safe.

It took a while to reach the area near the perimeter where the Austrian light cavalry—the Chevauxlegers—had pitched their tents. By the time they arrived, dusk formed a purple haze on the horizon. Campfires blazed across the landscape and the sound of a distant harmonica drifted on the air.

Adrian urged Elissa straight to the commanding officer's tent, his attention focused on the sandy-haired soldier drinking from a tin mug of coffee out in front.

"Good evening, Major," he said. "Colonel Kingsland, British Third Dragoons."

The lanky soldier straightened his bearing into a military stance. "Major Berg, Fourth Regiment, Kinsky's Chevauxlegers." Since Adrian wore no hat, the major didn't salute. Instead he smiled. "British, eh? I don't suppose there are a few thousand more of you around?"

Adrian smiled. "Sorry, I'm the only one. And I'm strictly here as an advisor."

The major wasn't surprised, though his disappointment was clear. After the Austrians' series of defeats, the army needed all the help it could get. "What can I do for you, Colonel?"

"I'm looking for a lieutenant named Tauber. Do you happen to know where I might find him?"

The major flashed Elissa an appreciative glance, and nodded. "The lieutenant walked over to the infirmary to have his bandages changed. He should be back any minute."

"B-bandages?" Elissa's face went pale. She looked as though she weren't sure whether to be thankful her brother was alive, or worried that he had been injured. "Peter has been wounded?"

"A saber cut to the shoulder," the major said. "He took

a blow to the head as well, but it doesn't appear to be serious and he seems to be healing quite well."

"Thank God."

Adrian felt her slender body trembling against him with relief. "Mind if we wait?" he asked.

"Of course not. Make yourself at home, Colonel. As I said, he should be back—" He broke off as his gaze snagged on a tall, blond soldier in a dark green uniform walking briskly across the camp. He moved a little stiffly and a wide white bandage encircled his forehead. "As a matter of fact, there he is now."

Adrian smiled. "Thank you, Major." He didn't have to urge Elissa forward. She was already grabbing up her skirts, racing across the camp toward her brother.

"Peter! Peter, wait!"

He turned at the sound of her voice and his whole face lit up. "Elissa! Good God, is it really you?"

"It's really me!" She flung herself into his arms, laughing and crying, a tide of happy tears cascading down her cheeks.

Peter held her away from him to look at her, then pulled her back into his arms. "I can't believe it. What on earth are you doing here?"

"It's a long story," Adrian put in before she had time to answer. "Is there somewhere we can be private?"

Peter's gaze took in the epaulettes on Adrian's shoulders. "Of course, Colonel. Right this way." With an arm wrapped tightly around his sister, who fussed over his bandaged head and asked if he was in pain, Peter grabbed a lantern and led the way to a small, dusty clearing where they could be alone.

A young man no more than twenty, Peter Tauber was as blond and fair as Elissa, but his eyes were hazel instead of blue. He was lean and broad shouldered. Handsome, with his elegant cheekbones and fine blond brows, but there was a toughness about him, his youthful features already stamped with the weary look of battle.

Peter set the lamp on a fallen log at the edge of the clearing, and once they were safe from prying eyes, Elissa reached for her brother's hand.

"Peter, this is Colonel Kingsland. He brought me here to see you."

The younger man eyed him from top to bottom, taking his measure, it seemed. "Lieutenant Peter Tauber, Colonel. Kinsky's Fourth Chevauxlegers."

Adrian extended a hand and the lieutenant shook it. "A pleasure, Lieutenant. Elissa has spoken of you often." He could see the speculation in Peter Tauber's eyes, then the subtle stiffening of his shoulders at the rising suspicion that Elissa was more to Adrian than a friend.

"Your sister is here for a number of reasons," Adrian told him. "Why don't I give the two of you time alone so that she can explain what is going on." He pinned the young man with a look of warning. "I caution you, Lieutenant, whatever you learn here this eve is strictly confidential and a matter of the highest importance."

"Yes, sir. You may rest assured your confidences will remain with me."

Adrian nodded, certain Peter Tauber had already heard a good deal of the story from his older brother, Karl, or perhaps in letters from his mother. "I'll leave you, then. Elissa, I'll be back in an hour. If you have questions, Lieutenant, you can ask them of me then."

"You're leaving?" A look of surprise flashed in her eyes, and if he hadn't known better, perhaps a hint of disappointment.

"I thought you would rather be with Peter alone."

Her features softened; her pretty blue eyes tilted up. A smile of such tenderness broke over her lips something tightened in his chest. "Stay . . . please. I was hoping the two of you would have a chance to get acquainted."

An odd warmth crept into his stomach. She wanted him to stay. She was inviting him to join them as if he were part of the family. He tried not to feel pleased but he couldn't seem to help himself. "All right. I'd like that, too."

Peter's stance became less rigid. He left for a moment to fetch a blanket, spread it on the ground, and they made themselves as comfortable as they could. Elissa asked again after

Peter's health, unbuttoning his shirt to inspect the fresh bandage he wore around one shoulder. Satisfied he was all right, she launched into her tale, refreshing Peter's memory of the letters she and her mother had sent him after Karl's death, reminding him of their belief the man responsible was a spy who called himself the Falcon.

"I remember only too well," Peter said soberly. "But I still don't understand why you are involved, Elissa. Catching a spy is hardly a job for a woman."

Adrian felt the pull of a smile. "That's what I told her. She has been, however, extremely good at getting close to these men. We're hoping she'll be able to get to Becker."

"Becker . . . yes. I remember Mother said he was one of the men Karl suspected. Becker is among the men here?"

"That's right."

Peter squeezed his sister's hand. "I don't like this, Lissa. You might wind up injured or perhaps even killed." He turned a hard look in Adrian's direction. "I realize you are my superior, Colonel Kingsland, but I must in all conscience protest your use of my sister in such a dangerous fashion."

Adrian wasn't about to argue, since he felt the very same way, but perhaps he might be able to reassure him. He started to speak, but before he could open his mouth, Elissa jumped in to defend him, rounding on her brother like a she-wolf protecting a pup.

"This is hardly Colonel Kingsland's fault," she said with a determined tilt of her chin. "He's done everything in his power to dissuade me. But the fact is, I might be able to help. Finding this spy was what Karl wanted above all things and I would see his wishes fulfilled."

"Karl didn't mean for you to—"

"I know that. He wouldn't have wanted me to do anything that might put me in danger. But in the beginning, there was no one else. Now that I've gone this far, I'm not going to quit until we catch him."

Peter flushed and held up his hands in surrender. "All right, I know when I'm beaten." He turned a sheepish look on Adrian. "I suppose this is what you put up with?"

"Exactly so."

"I guess I had forgotten."

Adrian chuckled softly. "I don't like having her here any more than you do. I can promise you, however, she is in good hands with me. I'll do everything in my power to keep her safe."

"Thank you, Colonel."

Elissa smiled, apparently satisfied with the way things were turning out, and she and Peter began to speak of other matters. Adrian watched them in the light of the lantern, noticing the radiance in her features, enjoying the sweet sound of her laughter. She was happy as he had never seen her, basking in the love she shared with her brother. Adrian had never known that sort of affection, doubted that he ever would.

A stab of envy caught him off guard, opening the old wounds, the pain he had buried years ago. He felt a squeezing in his chest and suddenly wished he had left them alone. Draping an arm around his knee, he leaned back to watch them, hearing their easy laughter, the sparkle of amusement in their eyes at some tale of mischief remembered from their past. There was a time he had yearned for that sort of love from his brother, for just a glimmer of that same warmth from his mother and father. It had taken years to burn out the final flames of hope, but he had finally learned his lesson.

He watched Elissa smile into Peter's youthful face, watched the affectionate way she touched him. She had missed him, he could see. And she loved him. It was obvious as well that Peter loved her.

Old memories rose up, of Richard, eight years old, a single year older than he, yet more distant than any stranger.

"Papa says I don't have to play with you if I don't want to. He says these are *my* toys. Papa said he bought them just for me." Richard was taller then, a gangly boy with reddish brown hair, sloping shoulders, and a cruel, taunting smile. The image of their father. "Can't you see?" Richard shouted. "No one wants you here! No one likes you. Why don't you just go away?"

He could still feel the cold chill in his heart when Richard spoke to him that way, or when his father punished him for deeds they both knew Richard had done. The icy emptiness stayed with him during the months after his twice-yearly sojourn into the hellish bosom of his family, living inside him during his distant, isolated years at Mr. Pembrook's very strict boarding school.

If it hadn't been for the friendship he found with Jamie, he wasn't sure what would have happened to him.

"Adrian?" Her soft intonation broke into his ugly thoughts. He wondered why they had surfaced, wondered how he could have let them after all of these years.

"What is it, love?" He used the endearment without thinking, saying it in a way that made it more than an affectionate address. Stupid. He could see Peter Tauber bristle, see Elissa's fingers dig into her brother's arm.

"We ... we are playing a role, Peter." She smiled but a slight tint of color infused her cheeks. "We've explained that. You must try to understand."

The young lieutenant relaxed. "I'm sorry. I should have known you would never do anything ... anything the least bit dishonorable." The color in her face bled away, giving a pale cast to her complexion.

Adrian rose swiftly to his feet. "The hour grows late. 'Tis past time for us to leave." He smiled at Elissa. "You'll be able to visit your brother again before we break camp."

She gave him a brief smile of gratitude then turned and hugged her brother. "Remember, Peter, you mustn't tell anyone who I am. Here I am simply Elissa, a friend, perhaps, of someone you once knew."

"I'll remember," Peter said, not looking as though he liked it one bit. "Good night, Lissa. Take care of yourself."

"As I would have you do, little brother." Crossing the short distance between them, she accepted the arm Adrian offered and they started back toward their tent.

"He seems like a nice-enough lad. I'm glad he came through the fighting all right."

Elissa smiled. "Thank you for bringing me here, Adrian.

No matter what happens, it will have been worth it only for this.''

Adrian returned the smile, trying not to feel envy for the brief warm glance she cast back over her shoulder to the blond man walking away.

His tent was spacious. And the lantern on his desk cast a pleasant yellow glow. He lifted the lid of his compact oak traveling desk, uncorked the inkwell, picked up his quill pen and dipped it in. As he started to write, he smiled, feeling the satisfaction, the thrill of the game, planning his next move, working out exactly the right strategy. It was more than just feeding the French information. It was the power, the control, the part he was playing in winning such a major campaign.

Lifting out a sheet of foolscap, he laid it carefully in front of him, settled the pen between his fingers, and began to scroll the letters.

Archduke pressing hard for Vienna. Seventy-four thousand men. Hiller and balance of forces providing rear guard, likely to cross Danube at Krems. Convergence of forces most likely at Brunn.

He wanted to add a few words of advice but thought better of it. He would wait until he had a bit more information, then perhaps he would suggest a plan. The little corporal would undoubtedly chafe at his temerity, but the man knew sound advice when it was given. Hadn't Bonaparte done as he had advised and split the archduke's forces at Ratisbon? It would be gratifying if the upcoming French victory could also be insured by the Falcon's hand.

He finished the message, inked the emblem on his ring, and pressed it to the paper, then folded the letter and sealed it with wax. Tomorrow he would order it delivered to the man who would carry it west, a man who waited as usual at a tavern somewhere along their route. It was more difficult with the army on the move, but the heightened danger only made the challenge more interesting.

He smiled to think of the next great victory that he would help to win.

The sun was well up, Adrian long gone, as Elissa tidied up the tent and pulled the cots back together in case anyone should happen to look inside. As soon as they'd arrived home last eve and the flaps of the tent had been lowered, Adrian had pulled them a distance apart then turned his back, silently undressed, and lain down on his narrow bunk to sleep.

Elissa smoothed the folds of his bedroll, her hand lingering over the blankets that still carried the scent of him, of brandy, starch, and wool, and the subtle fragrance of man. Earlier she had watched him shave, the thin, sharp blade of his razor skimming with precision over the long, smooth muscles of his throat. His skin was dark against the creamy soap, and his mouth curved faintly as the blade ran over the hard angle of his jaw.

As she watched the graceful movements of his hands, her face grew warm and her stomach fluttered. She recalled times those clever hands had touched her, made love to her in their practiced, skillful way.

Elissa shook her head, clearing the images, forcing the unwanted thoughts away. She had more to think about than Adrian and things that could never be. Today she would finally meet Josef Becker. Even now Adrian was in conference with General Klammer. He would meet Becker and decide the best way for her to approach him. In the meantime she would spend time with Peter, then perhaps do some washing. They would be on the move again soon. There wouldn't be time for it then.

Peter was as glad to see her as he had been the night before. They shared a meal of dried beef and biscuits and she was happy to discover, as Major Berg had said, his wounds were healing nicely. Peter told her he had been asking after Becker, but hadn't learned anything that might be of help.

"I wish I could stay with you longer," she told him, "but

I doubt your commanding officer would approve and I have chores to do.''

Peter laughed. "It's hard to imagine Lady Elissa Tauber working as a camp follower. Papa would turn over in his grave.''

"Papa would be the first one here trying to discover Karl's murderer.''

Peter sobered. "That is beyond the truth. I only wish I could be the one to do it.''

"You are doing what you can, as all of us are." She hugged him fiercely then left him to his duties and returned to her own camp.

Earlier she had learned each group of soldiers had an area set aside for the women who traveled with them. A central cooking area, a place to wash and mend. Elissa headed there now, a basket of dirty clothes propped on her hip.

Aside from the mélange of gaudy, unkempt women who usually surrounded the cooking fires, she was surprised to see a girl, perhaps a year or two younger than she, washing clothes next to two young children who played in the dirt nearby. The girl had big dark eyes and olive skin, slender hips and high, full breasts. Her hair was as black and shiny as obsidian, but was cropped even shorter than her own and fell perfectly straight against her head, giving her a boyish, pixie appearance.

Oddly, instead of making her look less feminine, it gave her an exotic, sensual appeal few men would be able to resist.

"Hello," the girl said, surprising her with a warm, welcoming smile. Her voice was deep and husky. Elissa wondered if she might be a Gypsy. "I am Nina Petralo. This is my little brother, Tibor, and my sister, Vada. I have not seen you before. You must be new in the camp." She spoke German, but with a thick Hungarian accent.

Elissa smiled, liking her straightforward approach. "My name is Elissa. It's nice to meet you. I'm a . . . a friend of Colonel Kingsland's. We just arrived last night."

"Ah, yes. I heard the story of your colonel and the Turk."

She laughed, a rich, throaty sound. "I don't suppose you have to worry about being bothered by the soldiers with that one around."

She thought of Adrian and tried not to feel a glimmer of warmth. "The colonel is very protective." That he was. A sense of duty was something Adrian had never lacked. She wished it was something far more. "What about you?" Elissa asked. "Is your . . . husband one of the soldiers?" Surely a woman as beautiful as Nina Petralo would have a man to protect her.

Nina shook her head. "My father was a friend of General Klammer's. He was killed in the fighting at Ratisbon."

"I'm sorry." She said a silent prayer of thanks that her brother had been spared. "And your mother?"

"She died some years back. We have relatives in Vienna who will take us in. We are traveling there with the army under the general's protection."

The little girl tugged at her sister's skirt. Nina bent down so the child could whisper in her ear, then Vada raced off to catch up with her younger brother. The children were as dark as Nina, with the same black hair and big dark eyes. Pretty children, now orphaned by the war.

"The colonel and I will also be traveling with the army," Elissa said.

Nina smiled. "Then we will be traveling together." She glanced toward the children. "I suppose I must go. They will get into trouble if I do not watch them closely."

"Perhaps I'll see you later," Elissa said hopefully, liking the girl already.

"I will look for you," Nina said in her forthright way.

Elissa watched her leave, glad to have met someone near her own age who might become a friend in the days ahead. Nina disappeared and Elissa set to work, filling a bucket with water from a nearby stream, then scrubbing their dirty clothes against a cluster of rocks the women used for that purpose. When she had finished, she loaded the clothes into the basket and started back to the tent.

She paused at the perimeter of the camp, spying Adrian's

tall frame ducking out of the general's tent. She watched him cross the camp, striding with his usual purposeful grace, heading perhaps to check on their horses. Another man stepped out of the tent behind him.

He was only a hint above average in height, clean shaven, as all of the officers were, a man of medium build with dark brown hair streaked with gray at the temples. He was wearing the uniform of a major, and Elissa knew immediately the man was Josef Becker.

Her pulse picked up speed as he walked in her direction, his head down, his brow furrowed, his mind obviously on something besides where he was headed. It was the chance she had been seeking, the perfect opportunity to meet him. Catching a quick, deep breath, she stepped into his path and they collided head-on, the basket toppling sideways, the major catching both her and the basket as she teetered precariously off balance.

She took a solid grip on his arm and righted herself. "I'm sorry," she said. "I didn't see you coming."

"The fault was mine entirely." He released his hold and stepped back. "I should have been paying attention."

Her mouth curved up in a full, inviting smile. "I suppose we were both to blame. At any rate, your quick thinking has saved me from having to rewash all of these clothes. Thank you . . . Major . . . ?"

"Becker. I'm General Klammer's aide-de-camp." The major took the basket from her hands. "Here, let me carry this for you. It's the least I can do."

She flashed another winsome smile. "Why, thank you, Major. I appreciate your help." She walked beside him back to her tent, her hips swaying, forcing him to slow his pace to keep up with her, giving him time to assess him.

With his casual manner and plain appearance, he seemed so nondescript, so completely average, she couldn't help a twinge of disappointment. Then again, what had she expected? A brutal man like Steigler? Or perhaps one of obvious cunning, with narrow, beady eyes and thin, deceitful lips?

Not this man. He was simply a soldier, not particularly handsome, not repulsive, either. And yet as they walked along, there was something odd about him. Something she couldn't put a name to. On the surface it didn't seem sinister, yet it was there in the remoteness of his smile, in the impersonal look he gave her when she thanked him and bade him farewell.

She wondered if Adrian had sensed it, too, and set out to find him as soon as the major was gone.

"Over here," he called out to her, lifting an arm in greeting. He was standing next to Minotaur, brushing the stallion's glossy coat with the same capable hands she had admired earlier that morning.

"I met Becker," she told him with no little excitement. "We just happened to cross paths while I was returning with the laundry."

A dark, knowing brow arched up. "You just happened to cross paths."

She flushed a little. How did he manage to read her so easily? "Well, I might have helped things along a bit. You met him, too, I gather. What did you think of him?"

The brush paused midway down the stallion's muscled neck. "I'm not sure." He shook his head. "He's different from what I imagined. Milder, somehow. He is not unlikable, yet there is something odd about him."

"Yes, I noticed that, too."

"He'll be in camp tonight. If our luck holds, you'll have another chance to talk to him then." Clearly, it wasn't something he was happy about. He was frowning, the brush stroking a little too fast and hard down the stallion's neck. Minotaur snorted and flung his beautiful head. "Sorry, boy."

"We need to get into his tent."

He nodded. "We'll be breaking camp in the morning, moving on toward Vienna. Things will be more chaotic. It should be easier then."

"We'll be leaving here tomorrow?"

He paused in his grooming. "The archduke's spared all the

time he dares. He has to get his army into position for the next assault.''

''Then we mustn't waste a moment. I'll seek out Becker tonight.''

Adrian said nothing. Just went back to grooming his horse. Still, as she walked away, she could have sworn she felt his eyes on her all the way back to the tent.

Chapter Nineteen

Elissa dressed with care for the last night in camp before the long march on to Vienna. In the center of the circle of tents not far from theirs, a campfire blazed and a gathering of soldiers stood around it. Adrian was among them, she knew, and so was Josef Becker.

Earlier, she had prepared a simple meal of bread and boiled sausages from the supplies they had purchased in Zwettl. She had washed their plates and cooking utensils then returned to the tent, trying to determine her strategy for the evening ahead. Now she changed into a clean cotton skirt and white peasant blouse, adding a red linen bodice that laced up the front, pushing her breasts into soft hills above the neckline.

She wore nothing beneath the skirt. When she walked, the firelight would outline the shape of her legs and hips, and she intended that Becker would see them.

And so would Adrian. She couldn't help a perverse need to remind him what it had been like when they had made love. For whatever reason, he no longer wanted her in that way, and though she knew she shouldn't want him, couldn't afford to want a man incapable of the least amount of fidelity, the fact was she did.

She desired him. Beyond that she was in love with him. Unreasonably, irrationally, regretfully in love with him, and she seemed powerless to do anything about it.

The sound of men's voices drifted up. The scent of tobacco and leather hung in the air. The faint echo of singing rose from a campfire in the distance. Elissa ran her fingers through her curly blond hair, longer now than when she'd first come to Vienna, fluffing it out around her face in a manner she hoped looked softly enticing. Pasting on her most sensuous smile, she lifted the flap and stepped out of the tent.

The night air felt cool against her skin. A gentle breeze lifted the hair from the nape of her neck and molded her skirt against her legs. Darkness surrounded them, an endless sea of black brightened by campfires like intermittent diamonds. She spotted the major almost instantly, speaking quietly to one of the men. Adrian had been talking to him earlier, she knew, but now the colonel stood a few feet away—speaking to dark-haired, dark-eyed, sensuous Nina Petralo.

Elissa's stomach did a queer little twist, and a tremor ran through the hand that rested against her hip. Nina was laughing at something Adrian had said and he was laughing with her. Elissa hadn't heard that easy note in his voice for as long as she could remember.

Her stomach knotted and her mouth felt cotton-dry. She wished she could see his eyes, know what he was thinking, then suddenly was glad she could not.

Was he looking at Nina the way he used to look at her, his eyes hot and hungry, burning straight into her heart? Was his fierce gaze promising fiery kisses and a touch that could set her blood on fire?

Elissa's palms went damp and an icy chill tingled down her spine. If he went to Nina as he had done with Cecily Kainz—dear God, she didn't think she could bear it. Tears pricked the backs of her eyes and she panicked to think they might actually begin to fall.

Not now! Dear Lord, not here!

She sucked in a shuddery breath and forced herself to calm. She didn't realize she had paused, that she was staring in Adrian's direction until his eyes swung to hers and he smiled. It was a warm, soft smile, and the hot look in his eyes wasn't directed at Nina—it was directed at her.

Sweet God in heaven, surely she was wrong. The dark-haired girl raised an arm and beckoned her over, and Elissa nearly swooned in relief. She forced her legs to move, forced herself to cross the camp with an air of nonchalance she didn't feel. When she reached Adrian's side, she summoned a halfhearted smile. When she spoke, she was amazed her voice could sound so normal.

"Good evening, Colonel. I see you've met Nina."

He nodded. "Apparently the two of you got acquainted earlier in the day."

Elissa glanced at Nina, saw nothing of seduction in her eyes, just a simple look of friendship. "That's right. I also met her little brother, Tibor, and her sister, Vada. They're adorable children. It'll be nice to have company on the march ahead." They talked for a while, Nina as forthright and unpretentious as she had been before.

"Your colonel was telling me how you managed to convince him to bring you along."

Elissa's brow arched up. "Was he? And exactly how was that?"

"He said you seduced him. He said you promised to cook for him and he is a terrible cook."

She laughed at that and relaxed a little more. "I promised to cook and clean. I must have been crazy."

Nina laughed. "I do not think so. I would be happy to cook for such a man if he looked at me the way your colonel looks at you."

Elissa tried to smile, but she thought that it came out a little wobbly. True, he looked at her as if he cared, as if he still desired her, but he didn't. He hadn't come near her in weeks.

Adrian said nothing. His interest had wandered and his forehead was lined with a frown. He was staring at her thin cotton skirt, she saw, and it occurred to her that standing as she was with her back to the fire, he could see right through it. Satisfaction jolted through her. He was a man, after all, and a man had needs. It felt good to know she could still affect him.

Hopefully, she could also affect Josef Becker.

"I see you dressed for the occasion," Adrian said with a dry, mocking half-smile.

"You could say that." She glanced toward Becker. She didn't want to leave. For certain, she didn't want to leave Adrian with Nina, but she had work to do and only a short time to finish.

She tilted her head toward Becker, and Adrian clamped his jaw. "If the two of you will excuse me," she said, "I'd like to thank Major Becker for his chivalry earlier in the day."

Adrian's mouth curved thinly. "By all means." Nina watched the exchange with interest, then excused herself to see to the children, making Elissa's departure a little less painful. Walking around the campfire, she crossed to where Becker stood smoking a pipe of tobacco.

"Good evening, Major."

His head came up. Until that moment, he had appeared lost in thought. "Good evening . . . Elissa."

She smiled. "I just wanted to thank you . . . for your gallantry this morning, I mean."

"My pleasure," he said absently.

"You don't . . . you don't have a woman in the camp to take care of you, Major?"

"After fifteen years in the army, I've learned to take care of myself."

"Not married?"

"No."

Elissa studied him a moment, wishing he was easier to read. She ran a finger down the front of his uniform coat. "You're a very attractive man, Major. I imagine you could have just about any woman you wanted."

He glanced toward where Adrian had been standing and Elissa's eyes followed. Fortunately, Adrian was gone. "For the present, I'm content as I am." He eased her hand away. "Besides, I don't think Colonel Kingsland would approve."

Elissa shrugged her shoulders. "We have an understanding. He does as he pleases and I do the same."

"That isn't the story I've heard."

Another offhand shrug. "The colonel is a gentleman. He doesn't like to see a woman hurt. Besides, he knows I'm not interested in selling myself to a common soldier. I enjoy men of power and position. Men like yourself, Major Becker."

"And the colonel?"

"Adrian has any number of women. I am only one of them."

He smiled at her indulgently, but there wasn't the least spark of interest. "As I said, Elissa. I'm happy taking care of myself."

Elissa eyed him with speculation. The approach she had chosen was obviously the wrong one. "Then perhaps, Major Becker, we could simply be friends. I would enjoy that, I think, having a man for a friend."

He smiled then, more relaxed than he was before. "I believe I would like that, too."

"The colonel says we'll be moving in the morning."

"That's correct. Have you followed an army before?"

"No. I am rather looking forward to it. Do you know where we are headed?"

"Somewhere in the general direction of Vienna. That is all I know."

"Napoleon will be following on our heels, will he not?"

"Yes."

"Will the archduke—"

"I'm afraid I'm not privy to the archduke's plans. Perhaps Colonel Kingsland will have a better answer."

"You are aide to a general. I thought perhaps you might have heard something of interest."

"Nothing I'm free to discuss."

She glanced away, pretending a look of chagrin. "I hadn't thought of that. I suppose I shouldn't have asked."

"It's all right. You're new to all of this."

"So I am." She tossed him a last warm smile. "But I will always be curious. Surely there is nothing wrong with that."

He smiled. "Perhaps not, but it has been said, curiosity killed the cat."

An uneasy tremor moved through her. "So I've heard."

She glanced toward the tent she shared with Adrian, suddenly wishing she were there. "It's getting late. I suppose I had better be going before the colonel begins to wonder where I am. Good night, Major Becker."

"Good night, Elissa."

He watched her as she walked away, and she wondered what he was thinking. Not the best encounter, but at least she knew where she stood. Perhaps Becker had a woman somewhere, one he cared about enough to remain faithful. Unlike Adrian, there actually were such men. Her brothers were like that. Her father.

She lifted the tent flap, ducked her head and walked in, wishing she could have fallen in love with a man more like them. In the light of the single candle burning on an upended ammunition box, she saw Adrian, his jacket unbuttoned, his eyes hard and fixed on her face.

"How did it go?" he asked.

Elissa sighed. "Not the way I had hoped. He isn't interested in me, not as a woman. Perhaps he'll accept me as a friend."

"Don't be a fool," Adrian snapped, surprising her. "There isn't a man in this camp who isn't interested in you 'as a woman.' Becker might not show it, but it's there just the same. There isn't a soldier here who isn't jealous of what they imagine I'm doing to you in here right now."

He couldn't have said anything worse. Her eyes burned with the unexpected sting of tears. She thought of him laughing with Nina and blinked to force them away.

"But you aren't doing anything to me—are you, Adrian? You aren't kissing me. You aren't touching me." She glanced down, saw the cots had been carefully pulled apart, leaving a modest distance between them. "You have no more interest in me than Becker."

She turned away from him then, unable to stop the tears she had been holding back for so long. Her heart ached, felt like a crushing weight inside her chest. Rejection tasted bitter on her tongue.

"My God, you're crying," Adrian said, gently resting his

hands on her shoulders, turning her slowly to face him. "Why are you crying?"

She only shook her head.

"Tell me, Elissa. I want to know."

She looked up at him and a hint of her old bravado returned. "You tell me, Colonel—explain why it is that you don't want me anymore."

His fingers tightened on her shoulders. "What are you talking about?"

"You know what I'm talking about. I'm talking about touching me, making love to me. There was a time when you wanted me, but not anymore."

His features hardened. The muscles across his cheeks seemed etched in stone. "That is what you believe? That I do not want you?" He took her hand, roughly slid it down his body to the front of his breeches. He was hard and pulsing. She could feel the heat of his desire through the tight material of his breeches, and the blood began to thunder in her ears.

"I want you," he said in a voice thick and rough. "I've never stopped wanting you. Every time I look at you, I get so hard I ache. I can't sleep at night for remembering what it was like to be inside you, to kiss your beautiful breasts, to taste that soft, delicious mouth. I want you, Elissa. I can't remember ever wanting a woman so badly."

A little thrill shot through her, a heady, womanly feeling of power she hadn't known in weeks. "Then why—"

"Because I promised myself I would not touch you. I forced you into my bed before. I blackmailed you into giving me your body. I swore I wouldn't do it again—not unless it was your idea. Not unless you wanted me as badly as I wanted you."

Her heart was beating so incredibly hard. She felt light-headed and her hands were shaking. He wanted her. He had wanted her all along.

A finger ran down her cheek. "Is that what you want, angel? For me to make love to you? Because it's damned well what I want."

Her heart squeezed tight, stole the breath from her lungs. *Of course it's what I want,* she silently screamed. *I love you. I love you so much.* She wanted him to kiss her, hold her. She wanted him to love her. But he didn't even care enough to stay out of another woman's bed.

The giddy feeling began to slide away. Her throat clogged with a fresh lump of tears and her chest felt suddenly leaden. "It doesn't matter what I want. There are other things to consider."

He sighed. "Yes, there are. Your family. Your reputation. You were an innocent, the daughter of a nobleman. You deserve better than to wind up some man's mistress."

She only shook her head. "None of that matters to me."

He frowned. "What, then?"

Her eyes searched his face. "I know . . . I know about you and Lady Kainz."

"Lady Kainz? Of course you know about Cecily. You were sleeping in her bed the first time I saw you, the night I came into your room at Blauenhaus. You're certainly smart enough to realize we'd been having an affair."

She glanced away, misery washing over her, making it hard to speak. "I know about the other times . . . after we made love. The times you went to see her in Vienna."

"What! What are you talking about? Who told you I went to see her?"

"She did. She said she saw you at a dinner at the Belevedere Palace. She said you took her home. She said she knew how to make you happy, how to please you . . . that the two of you had been *friends* far longer than we had."

Fury blazed in his eyes. His hands balled into fists. "That conniving, lying little baggage. I took her home, all right. I escorted her to the front door of her town house and I left her there. I saw her a few times after that at social functions, but I was never alone with her—and I never touched her. I haven't been with another woman since the night I came into your bedchamber at Blauenhaus. I haven't wanted any woman but you."

Elissa stood there staring. Sweet God, could it possibly be

true? Could the viscountess really have been lying? She studied his face, tried to read the truth there.

Adrian caught her chin with his hand. "I have never lied to you, Elissa."

His jaw was set, sincerity etched in his features. He was telling the truth, she could see it in the depths of his beautiful eyes. He had never been unfaithful. He wanted her and she wanted him. Dear Lord, how badly she wanted him.

Tears blurred her vision. "Adrian . . ." She took a single step and he crushed her against him. His heartbeat thundered against her breast, nearly as loud as her own, and Elissa slid her arms around his neck. "I've missed you," she whispered. "I've missed you so much."

His hand slid into the loose curls of her hair, and he cradled her head against his shoulder. "I need you, angel. God, I need you so damned much." He kissed her then, a hot, fierce, passionate kiss, yet so achingly tender her heart seemed to melt inside her. He needed her. He had only been trying to protect her from himself.

Adrian kissed her again, a deep, drugging, mind-numbing kiss that sent her head spinning, made her legs feel as if they were made of India rubber. Reaching behind him, he snuffed out the candle, but light from the fires outside the tent bled through the canvas, giving the room an exotic glow. The kiss continued, deeper now, softly probing, his tongue sweeping in, radiating heat out through her limbs.

She kissed him back, slid her fingers into his dark, silky hair. His lips moved along her jaw, trailing small, moist kisses down her throat and across her shoulders. He pulled the string at the neckline of her blouse, slid it down to bare her breasts, and his mouth settled there, his tongue flicking over the stiff bud of her nipple, making it ache and distend. He moved to her other breast, tending it with equal care, his lips and teeth closing over the end, nipping gently, then parting to take the fullness inside. She whimpered at the sensual tugging, at the heat licking over her skin.

"I want to feel you," she whispered. "I have to touch you."

His eyes found hers, dark with heat and wanting, need burning like fire in their depths. He stripped off his jacket, let her help him peel off his shirt. Muscles bunched and moved beneath the dark thatch of hair across his chest. She wanted to touch him, to skim her fingers over those dense, smooth muscles, but Adrian's plundering kiss had her clinging to him instead.

He pulled the laces at the front of her red linen bodice and tossed it away, then drew her blouse up over her head, leaving both of them naked to the waist.

"I've wanted you for so long," he said, nipping the side of her neck. "I tried not to. I told myself it was wrong. But now that we are here like this, it doesn't seem wrong at all." He kissed her deeply, his lips hot and insistent over hers. Taking her hand, he guided her fingers to his hardness. "See what you do to me? It's all I can do not to tear off your clothes and bury myself inside you."

"Yes . . ." she whispered. "That's what I want, too."

He only shook his head. "Not this time. This time I won't hurry. I want all of you. I want to see you, touch you all over. I want to kiss you until neither of us can stand it a moment more. Then I'll come inside you."

She was shaking as he reached for the buttons on her skirt, unfastened them, and pooled the material around her ankles. Adrian smiled at the sight of her in nothing but her garters and stockings and a pair of sturdy brown shoes.

"Those have to go." He kissed her as he pulled her down beside him on the single cot, bent and untied each one, set them carefully away, then dispensed with her garters and stockings. He removed the rest of his clothes, setting his boots beside her shoes then stripping off his breeches. Elissa watched each of his movements, marveling at his long, powerfully muscled flanks, at his narrow waist and rounded buttocks.

Tentatively, she reached out to touch him, allowing her fingers to glide through the hair on his chest, over his flat stomach, and down the ridges of muscle that tightened beneath her hand. His shaft was big and hard, straining upward against his belly. She reached for it, let her fingers wrap around it, felt the hot, slick surface, and heard Adrian groan.

"Easy, love. It's been far too long and I've only got so much control."

She cupped his face between his palms and kissed him. "Adrian . . ." Then she was lying beneath him on the narrow cot, feeling his hands on her body, his mouth against the hollow at the base of her throat, his fingers probing, stroking, working their skillful magic.

"Please, Adrian," she whispered, clutching his thick neck, her body arching against him. "I need you. I can't . . . I can't stand any more."

"Soon," he promised in a voice gone rough. "Soon, sweet angel, but not yet." Lowering his head, he began to kiss his way down her body.

Elissa nearly swooned at the erotic sensations, bit down on her lip against the heat roaring through her body. He kissed her breasts and belly, kissed the insides of her thighs, then he was looming above her, sliding his hard length inside, filling her nearly to bursting.

His loins flexed. Bands of muscle rippled across his chest as he began to move in and out, and waves of pleasure rolled through her. Her nails dug into his back. She reached down to cup his buttocks, felt them tighten as he drove into her again and again. A second climax hit her, so sweet it made her dizzy. She felt his body go rigid, felt the dampness of his seed spilling inside her, and knew he had followed her to release.

She stroked his back and whispered that she loved him, knowing he couldn't hear, knowing she dared not say the words aloud for fear he would withdraw from her again. Instead she held him tightly against her, kissing the side of his neck, praying what they shared this night would be a new beginning.

*   *   *

They broke camp at dawn. Elissa hurriedly packed the few sparse items they had brought with them, then paced the earthen floor of the tent, waiting for Adrian to return from his meeting with General Klammer.

She smiled as she glanced down at the two narrow cots, positioned side by side now, as Adrian had placed them during the night, once they had finished making love. Of course it hadn't really stopped with just that one time. Twice more before dawn, he had reached for her, taken her as if he couldn't get enough. Perhaps she was a fool, but it had changed the way she felt about him, made her begin to look at him in an entirely different way.

Where before she had been holding herself back from him, trying to protect herself from the heartbreak she was certain she risked in loving a man like him, now she thought of Adrian and wondered what *he* might be feeling. Perhaps he cared for her more than he was willing to admit.

Perhaps he even loved her.

Major St. Giles had told her a little about him. He had never known love as a boy. Perhaps he had never known love as a man. It was something she could give him if he would only let her.

He ducked into the tent just then, his strides long and elegant, pausing a few feet in front of her. The scowl was back on his face. She hoped last night was not the cause.

"Are we ready to leave?" she asked.

"Soon. Lieutenant Helm will be here shortly to disassemble the tent and take care of the cots. In the meantime, there is something I need to say."

A thread of unease trickled through her. "Do not tell me you regret last night—if that is so, I refuse to hear it."

His hard look softened. A hand came out to cup her cheek. "I do not regret it. I am far too selfish for that. But I . . . last night I should have been more careful. The times before when we made love, I did my best to protect you. Last night I did nothing. I wanted you and I took you. It was a stupid, reckless thing to do. I fear for you, Elissa. If we continue as we did last night, sooner or later, I am bound to get you with child. Neither of us wants that.''

Elissa smiled to think how wrong he was. ''I would love to have your child, Adrian.''

His head jerked as if she had fired a shot. Something flickered in the depths of his eyes, then it was gone. He drew himself a little away. ''A child of mine is the last thing you should want. I wouldn't marry you, Elissa, and even if I did, I would leave you at home and return to my life in the army. I'm a soldier. I'm not cut out to be a husband. I never will be.''

She only shook her head. ''I don't care.''

''You do care. I don't want you hurt—even if it means I have to give you up.''

''There were others before me . . . you didn't worry about those things with them.''

His jaw tightened beneath his scowl. ''The other women I've known knew how to protect themselves.''

Elissa's chin went up. ''Then I shall learn. There are women in the camp who know the ways. I'll get one of them to teach me.''

''But you shouldn't have to—''

''You aren't the only one with a say in this, Colonel. If you don't want children, there are ways to prevent them from occurring. If by chance I should conceive, the problem will be mine.''

He gripped her arms and dragged her solidly against him. ''I didn't mean I would ignore my obligations. I would see to your welfare, and that of the child. 'Tis just that you deserve so much more.''

She relaxed a little, reached up and cupped his face. Raising up on the tips of her toes, she gently kissed him. ''You're enough for me, Adrian. You're all I want. I'll speak to the women—but I will not give you up again.''

For a moment he said nothing, as if he couldn't quite believe the words. ''You're sure this is what you want?''

''I have never been more certain.''

The tension drained from his body and a smile broke over his face. For the first time in weeks, she saw his dimples. "I'm a lucky man, angel. A very lucky man."

Elissa only smiled and went into his arms. If there was any way she could arrange it, she would make him feel like the luckiest man in the world.

Chapter Twenty

They pressed hard for the next several days, traveling up to twenty miles across the rugged landscape. Each night the army set up a makeshift camp, the officers mostly in tents while the enlisted men slept on the ground. The weather continued to hold and there was no sign of rain.

During the journey, Adrian spoke to the men in the general's command, discreetly asking questions, hoping to turn up something that would implicate Becker or point to someone else. So far nothing seemed the least bit promising. With the archduke's assistance, he was, however, able to track down Karl Tauber's commanding officer, Colonel Shultz of the 6th Regimental Infantry, a blond, stern-faced man with wide-set eyes deeply weathered at the corners.

Adrian found him on the far side of camp just as dusk began to fall. Introductions were made and the subject of Karl Tauber introduced.

"I'm a friend of the family," Adrian said. "I offered to look into Captain Tauber's murder while I was here . . . presuming that's what it was."

"Tauber was murdered, all right. Shot in the head at close range. His body was discovered outside a tavern called Reiss's in Vienna."

"Reiss's?" Adrian arched a brow as he remembered the Falcon's courier's death in that same place. Why hadn't Ravenscroft known? Then again, with the archduke on the move, communications were spotty at best.

"You've heard of it?" the colonel asked.

"I've been there once. Not the sort of place I would expect an officer like Tauber to be spending his time."

"Those were my thoughts, as well. It's a seedy establishment, and Karl was never one to overindulge in gaming or drink."

"Do you know why he might have gone there?"

"I wish I did. I saw him earlier that evening and he seemed a little edgy. I asked him if something was wrong and he seemed uncertain how to answer. He said he wasn't sure, but he might know something later on. That was the last time anyone saw him alive."

"Did he ever mention a major named Becker? It might not have seemed important at the time."

The colonel frowned. "Becker? Why, yes, as a matter of fact, he did. He said he had heard rumors, something unpleasant about Becker, but as yet he wasn't at liberty to discuss what he had heard."

"Anything else?"

"Only that he hoped to know more in the very near future."

Adrian pondered that. Unfortunately Karl Tauber hadn't had a future. "After the shooting, did you ever speak to Becker?"

"Yes, I did. Since Tauber had mentioned him so shortly before his death, I thought it might be a lead. The major was visiting a friend the night of the murder. He had a solid alibi for his whereabouts and I had no reason to suspect him further."

Adrian nodded, his questions answered for now. "Thank you, Colonel Schultz, I appreciate your cooperation."

"My pleasure, Colonel. Please pass my condolences on to the family. Karl Tauber was a fine young soldier and a good and decent man. Let me know if there is anything else I can do."

Adrian left the colonel, intrigued yet frustrated by what he had learned. If Tauber was killed at Reiss's tavern, the same place the Falcon's courier had been murdered, there had to be some connection. But what did Becker have to do with it? According to Schultz, Becker hadn't been anywhere near the tavern that night.

Whatever the major's involvement, Adrian didn't like it, nor the fact that Elissa continued to spend time with him, working to establish a friendship. As she had rightly guessed, it was the only sort of relationship Becker seemed the least bit interested in. Adrian would have seen that himself if he hadn't been so damned jealous.

Becker was a strange, enigmatic man, and more and more Adrian wondered what lay beneath the surface of his almost-maddening calm. He called few men friends, yet he always did his job in what appeared to be a conscientious manner.

Still, several times during the march, the major had ridden off by himself late in the afternoon, returning to camp just before nightfall. Adrian had followed him, watching from the shadows as Becker entered an out-of-the-way tavern along the route the army followed. But there had been no sign of an illicit meeting. Becker had simply sat in the taproom by himself, sipping a tankard of beer, staring off into the shadows.

Adrian thought of him again as he stooped to enter the much smaller traveling tent he now shared with Elissa. She wasn't there when he arrived and in a way he was glad.

Things had changed between them since the night she had welcomed him into her bed, and as much as it pleased him, it worried him as well. He was growing far too fond of her, letting her get too close. He had always been careful not to let that happen.

He sighed to think of it. Perhaps if he were younger . . . perhaps if he were a different man . . .

There was a time it might have worked between them, a time he had wanted a woman to love. Once he had craved a home and family of his own, the chance to build something for the future. He'd been little more than a boy back then, a naïve, callow lad who still believed in foolish dreams.

He was only nineteen when he met Miriam Springer, Lord Oliver's beautiful daughter. At last, he'd believed, he had found what he had been seeking for so long. He had courted her, then asked her to marry him. He thought he loved her and believed she might love him.

Adrian scoffed at the notion. She had played him for a fool and he had let her. It wasn't until his wedding day that he had finally discovered the bitter truth—that she cared not one whit about him. She had crushed his heart beneath her dainty velvet slipper and he wasn't about to risk that pain again.

"Adrian!" Elissa flashed a sunny smile as she ducked into the tiny makeshift tent, too small for either of them to stand fully upright. "I've been looking for you all afternoon. Where have you been?"

"I went to see Colonel Shultz, Karl's commanding officer."

Pain flickered briefly in the blue of her eyes. "What did he say?"

In the low-ceilinged tent, he sat down on the bedroll they shared, and pulled Elissa down beside him. Briefly, he told her what Schultz had said about her brother, including what a fine man he had been, and mentioned the connection to Reiss's tavern.

She discreetly brushed away a tear. "What do you think it means?"

"I don't know. The murders took place months apart. I presume your brother must have found out the tavern was frequented by the courier. Someone must have discovered Karl's interest and killed him. Why the courier was murdered all those months later, I don't know, unless someone worried he was becoming too conspicuous. If your brother had discovered the man's involvement, so could someone else."

"Perhaps there is no connection. Perhaps the tavernkeeper was right and the courier was murdered simply for cheating at cards."

Adrian mulled that over. It was a definite possibility, though he rarely believed in such coincidences. He drew her against his side, looped a strand of her hair behind an ear. "I also followed Becker again."

"You did?"

He nodded. "He did exactly as he did before—made his way to a nearby tavern, then simply sat in the taproom sipping a tankard of beer."

"Perhaps he is waiting for someone and the man has yet to appear."

"That was my thinking as well. Unfortunately, there is no way to prove it unless we catch them together."

"Perhaps you will discover something tonight."

He arched a brow. "Tonight?"

Her mouth curled up at the corners. "I've challenged the major to a game of chess. Apparently he finds the notion of playing against a woman amusing. I'm sure he thinks I shan't have the slightest chance against him."

"Perhaps he'll be in for a surprise."

She grinned. "No doubt about it. My father was an excellent player and a very good teacher. I shall try not to best him too soon."

Adrian laughed. "I'll remember that. If you are that good an opponent, I believe I should enjoy a game myself."

She brushed a quick kiss on his cheek. "I'll hold you to it, Colonel. In the meantime, I'll be certain to set the board up where Becker won't be able to see his tent, and in the darkness perhaps you can slip inside."

He smiled, enjoying the excitement he could clearly read on her face. "All right. Perhaps we'll get lucky. We are certainly overdue."

But once more they came up empty. Becker's tent was spartan to say the least, with only a change of uniform and his personal cavalry gear. His portable writing desk contained a single stack of letters and those came from his mother. It seemed a dreary existence, even to a man accustomed to the austere life of a soldier.

Adrian wondered if a man who seemed disinterested in even the most basic comforts might indeed be one who gleaned his excitement from intrigue.

*   *   *

The hot May sunshine beat down on the long column of soldiers trudging forward in the heat. A blistering wind rolled in off the plains, stirring the dust beneath the horses' hooves, choking off the air engulfing the weary riders.

Leading her dappled gray mare, Elissa walked next to one of the supply wagons at the rear of the column, perspiration soaking the hair at the nape of her neck. Nina walked beside her, looking nearly as bedraggled as she. Riding atop the mare, five-year-old Tibor sat in front of his six-year-old sister, the hot spring wind ruffling the dark hair around his face.

The children were tired and dusty, the day's march long and grueling. Usually they traveled in the back of one of the supply wagons, but they had grown fussy, bouncing over the rough terrain, and Nina had let them walk for part of the way.

"Thank you for letting them ride," she said with a soft smile at her siblings. "They love horses. At home they had a pony of their own. He was beautiful, as white as the snow on the mountains. Vada named him Sali."

"What happened to him?" Elissa asked.

The olive skin tightened over her finely carved cheekbones. "Killed in the fighting at Ratisbon. A cannonball hit the building where he was stabled." Her big dark eyes stared off toward a stand of pine trees at the edge of the road. "They miss Sali, just as they miss our father. Riding your mare has pleased them. For a while at least, it helps them to forget."

Elissa's heart went out to them. She knew only too well the pain of losing a loved one. "What about you, Nina? Sometimes you look so sad. Will you ever be able to forget?"

The dark-haired girl ran a hand through her short-cropped hair, shoving the heavy locks back as if they were her unpleasant memories. "I will never forget. Sometimes late at night, I can still hear the screams of the wounded. The walls of the city were old, no match for Bonaparte's cannon. The French swarmed in and there was no way to stop them. When things began to look bad, my father sent us ahead, north across the Danube with some of the soldiers. He was afraid of what might happen to us if the town should fall to the French. He never made it out of the city."

Elissa reached out and took her friend's hand. "It's too late for your father, but maybe there is hope for victory yet. Perhaps the archduke will stop Napoleon before he reaches Vienna."

"Perhaps. He must gather his forces, regroup his army before he can attack. There may not be time to save the city."

Elissa said nothing. Only the archduke knew what lay ahead. She prayed whomever he trusted would not let the information fall into the hands of the Falcon.

She was exhausted by the time they made camp in the dusty yellow rays before dark. As soon as the evening meal was finished and she had washed their cooking utensils, she made her way wearily back to the tent. Adrian was waiting. One look at the fatigue etched into her face and he pulled her down on the pallet he had fashioned on the floor and began to gently strip away her clothes.

"You're exhausted," he said gruffly. Pulling her cotton night rail from her traveling satchel, he raised her arms, tugged the gown gently on over her head, then eased her down on the pallet. "Dammit, you shouldn't have walked so far."

"The other women walk. It doesn't seem to hurt them. And the children loved riding the mare."

"The children should have stayed in the wagon, and as for you— You have to take better care of yourself or you'll wind up getting sick. Dammit, I told you this would be hard."

"I'm not complaining."

He pulled off his boots, shrugged out of his shirt, and stripped away his breeches. "You rarely complain. I am the one who is complaining." He lay down beside her on the pallet and curled her against his chest, fitting them together and enfolding her in his arms. "Now go to sleep. We've another long day in the morning."

She told herself that was what she wanted, just blessed sleep and oblivion from the aches and pains of the march. But as Adrian snuggled against her, the muscles moving across his chest with each of his softly indrawn breaths, she knew there was something she wanted more. She wriggled against him, pressing her bottom into his groin, and heard his soft-muttered curse.

"Lie still, dammit. I'm trying to behave like a gentleman. You need to get some sleep."

She smiled at his hardening arousal. "What if I'm not ready to sleep? What if I am not yet tired?"

His breath caught on an inward sweep of air, then she thought that perhaps he smiled. The arm he draped around her began to caress her breasts, cupping them gently, plucking at the ends.

He bit the side of her neck. "There is a limit to my chivalry, madam, and as usual you have managed to surpass it."

She laughed softly, felt his warm breath beside her ear. Then he was lifting her gown, running his hands up and down her thighs, stroking insistently between the folds of her sex. She gasped as he parted her legs and slid himself inside her, fitting them perfectly together.

"Perhaps you are right," he whispered, slowly beginning to move. "We shall both sleep better after this."

Elissa smiled and gave herself up to the delicious sensations.

His loving left her sated, but even then she couldn't fall asleep. And neither, it seemed, could he.

"Adrian?"

"Yes, love?" A big hand sifted through the loose curls around her face. Adrian came up on an elbow and she eased onto her back so that she could see his face.

"I want to know something about you. Please—won't you tell me just a little? I know your body nearly as well as I know my own, but you never let me see inside your mind."

"What makes you think there is anything to see?" he teased.

"I know there is. I can read it in your eyes. Tell me what you were like as a boy. Major St. Giles said your parents sent you away to school when you were only five. I don't think you were happy.''

"Were you happy?'' he asked.

Elissa smiled. "Oh, yes. I was the luckiest of children. My parents loved each other. My family loved me. I had two handsome brothers who worshiped me—not that we didn't fight on occasion.''

He chuckled into the darkness. "Nothing is ever perfect, I suppose.''

"What about you?''

He sighed, his breath feathering out against her ear. "I was an unwanted addition to a family that knew little or nothing of love. They sent me away to school because they couldn't bear the sight of me. They never cared about me and I learned to care nothing for them.''

An ache of sympathy rose in her chest and her heart went out to him. "How could that be? You were only a little boy. You must have been a beautiful child, with your big green eyes and finely carved dimples—how could they help but love you?''

He shook his head. She could feel the tension that tightened the muscles across his shoulders. "My father hated me. Every time he looked at me he was reminded of my mother's infidelity. I was a continual rub between them, a constant source of irritation. Even my mother wanted me out of her sight.''

Her breathing caught, stayed suspended for a moment then resumed. "Your father . . . your father wasn't the man who sired you?''

Adrian lay back on the pallet, a long sigh whispering past his lips. "I never understood what I had done wrong, why they cared nothing about me when they obviously cared so much for my brother—not until years later. I had just turned sixteen the day my mother died. She called me to her deathbed and finally told me the truth. Sixteen years earlier, she'd had a brief affair, no more than several weeks, but the man she had slept with had gotten her with child. Her husband—

the man I thought of as my father—had guessed the truth—that the child she carried wasn't his.''

Her heart twisted. She wanted to touch him, to take away the pain she could hear in his voice, but she was afraid the spell would be broken and he would close himself off to her again. ''Does your real father . . . does he know about you?''

Adrian shook his head. ''No, and he never will.''

''But you *do* know who he is.''

For a long while he said nothing. ''My father is the Duke of Sheffield.''

Elissa sucked in a breath, barely able to believe her ears. ''Sweet God, the Duke of Sheffield is your father?''

''I shouldn't have told you. I don't know why I did. Even Jamie doesn't know.''

She still couldn't get over it. Sheffield was one of the most powerful men in England. ''His Grace was a friend of my father's. I have known him since I was a girl.''

Adrian came up over her. In the light bleeding into the tent, she could read his displeasure in the tautness of his expression. ''I want your word you'll say nothing of this.''

''You look like him—do you know that? I never would have thought of it, but now that I know the truth, I can see it in every line of your face. The same strong jaw, the same straight nose. You even have the duke's green eyes.''

''Your word, Elissa.''

''His son died, you know. He was killed two years ago in a carriage accident.'' She reached out and clasped his hand. ''You must tell him, Adrian. You're his only living child. You must tell him the truth.''

''You're mad. The Duke of Sheffield would hardly appreciate having an illegitimate son foisted off on him at this late date in his life.''

''You're not illegitimate. Your mother was married at the time you were born.''

''True, but that is hardly the point. Legitimate or not, I'm a grown man now. I'm a baron and a man of considerable wealth. I don't need a father anymore, and he most assuredly wouldn't want a son he never knew existed.''

"Have you ever met him?"

"I've seen him once or twice."

"And did you not notice the resemblance?"

"Perhaps I did. I thought it more likely the resemblance was merely in my head."

Elissa shook her head. "No, 'tis there, all right. I can see it in each of your strides, the powerful way you move, even in the gestures you make. The duke's son, William, took after his mother. You are the very image of your father."

"It doesn't matter," he said doggedly. "Perhaps it would have once, but not anymore."

Elissa didn't argue. Adrian was as stubborn as the duke, as well, and odds were he wouldn't change his mind. Leaning forward, she pressed a soft kiss on his mouth. "Thank you for telling me, for trusting me with your secret."

Adrian said nothing, just lay back on his bedroll and closed his eyes. Even after he had fallen into a troubled sleep, Elissa watched over him, her heart aching for the lonely child he had been and the father he never knew, wishing she could find a way to ease the pain still lingering inside him.

Chapter Twenty-one

The next day's march was grueling, miles of rocky, uneven terrain under a broiling sun, the horizon hazy with waves of dust and heat. Elissa walked behind one of the supply wagons, her muscles aching with every step, her face damp with perspiration. Beside her, Nina led the mare, her brother and sister perched on the saddle.

Elissa studied little Tibor, whose cheeks were flushed with heat, his thick black hair stuck to his forehead. Vada looked little better, her face damp beneath an old straw bonnet three sizes too big that Nina had borrowed from one of the women.

Elissa took another weary step, unwilling to ride while her friend and the other women walked. As tired as she was, when Adrian's big black stallion came into view, wending its way in her direction, the sight of his tall figure riding toward her with such purpose made her heart leap with excitement. Adrian rode up in a sweep of dust, looking nearly as hot and weary as she, but a smile softened his features and his eyes danced with what looked suspiciously like mischief.

"Give me your hand," he commanded, reining the big horse up beside her. Elissa smiled as Adrian reached down and clasped her wrist, swung her effortlessly up behind him. "There is something I would show you."

Her excitement grew, making her stomach flutter. "Where are we going?"

His mouth curved roguishly. "You will have to wait and see." Reining away from the endless line of soldiers, he urged the stallion into an easy gallop, cutting a path across the open fields toward the line of trees that marked a dense, shady pine forest on the side of a sloping hill. Elissa clung to his waist, her cheek against his back, enjoying the solid feel of him, the closeness she had begun to feel since he had spoken to her of his past.

He slowed the stallion as they entered the forest, allowing the animal to pick its way deeper into the woods. Pine boughs formed a canopy above their heads. A thick carpet of needles padded the horse's steps as they rode along. The sound of water gushing over rocks alerted her to the presence of a stream and seconds later, the horse burst upon it.

"Oh, Adrian—I can hardly believe it!"

He grinned, exposing his beautiful dimples. "I thought her ladyship might enjoy a bath."

Elissa laughed with pure delight. "Sweet Jesu, there is nothing that would please me more."

He turned the horse and followed along the muddy bank. "There's a pool off to the left up ahead. I think it will serve our purpose." In minutes they had reached it, a gently swirling eddy hidden behind a thicket of boulders and sheltered beneath the pines. Pulling the stallion to a halt, he threw a leg over the horse's neck and slid to the ground, then reached up and lifted her down, setting her firmly on her feet.

"Lieutenant Helm told me about this place. He used to live on a farm near here."

Elissa surveyed the frothy little waterfall tumbling into the gently circling pool, the thick vines of clematis draping over the edge of the water, the mossy banks sheltered by sweet green grasses.

"It's lovely, Adrian. Perfect." Hurrying ahead of him, she raced to the bank and began to strip off her clothes, her fingers fumbling in her excitement as she pulled off her blouse and unfastened the buttons on her simple brown skirt. She tossed them over a nearby shrub, then sat down to pull off her shoes.

"We won't have much time," Adrian said, coming up behind her, already shirtless, his boots resting on a flat gray stone. "We don't want to get too far behind."

She grinned and reached for the buttons at the front of his breeches. "Then we had better hurry."

Adrian laughed, the excitement contagious. Tugging his breeches down over his long, powerfully muscled legs, he added them to the pile of clothes strung over the bushes. He was grinning when he scooped her up, both of them naked, carefree for the first time in weeks.

"It's freezing!" she cried, goose bumps replacing the hot, moist skin of only moments ago. Laughing, she splashed icy mountain water all over his chest. "And it feels delicious!"

"*You* feel delicious," he teased, his hands coming up to cradle her breasts. He cupped them gently, the ends already hard from the freezing water, then he kissed her, quick and hard. He was grinning when he pulled away. With a single, quick movement, he knocked her legs out from beneath her and she plunged beneath the surface of the water. She came up sputtering, gasping for breath, and laughing for the sheer joy of it.

"That wasn't fair! You were kissing me. I thought we were going to make love."

Adrian grinned. "Count on it, angel, but I rather thought a bath was in order first."

She made a sound of outrage and leapt in his direction, bringing him down like a landed fish in the water beside her. He came up spitting and grinning, water streaming off his dark hair and running in rivulets through the curly hair on his chest. "Did I call you angel? I meant hellion. A beautiful little hellion, but a hellion just the same."

Elissa laughed and darted away from him, diving under the water then surging back to the surface. Adrian followed, the two of them playing like otters in the cold water of the pond. She couldn't remember being so happy. And she thought that Adrian looked happy, too.

They made love there in the pool, Elissa wrapping her legs around his waist, enjoying the firm, flat muscles there as he lifted her astride him. Their mating was fierce, a tangling of tongues and a surging of bodies that later turned slow and languid, matching the pace of the hot afternoon. Afterward they stretched out on a rock to dry, their eyes shaded by a pine bough arching protectively over their heads.

Elissa ran a finger along the muscles across his shoulders, tracing the sinews and valleys. "Adrian . . . ?"

He grunted a fuzzy response, half asleep in the afternoon heat.

"Have you ever been . . . in love?"

His eyelids drifted open. She thought that he would not answer, then he lazily smiled and propped himself up on an elbow. "I thought I was once . . . a long time ago. I was a fool back then."

"What happened?"

"Her name was Miriam . . . Miriam Springer. I was twenty and she was nineteen, the daughter of a nobleman my father had dealt with in business. She was beautiful. Slender, dark auburn hair, and the palest, smoothest skin. She was the kind of girl I'd always dreamed of, laughing and happy, always reaching out to take my hand. I thought she would make the perfect wife, the perfect mother for my children."

A pang of envy rippled through her. It hurt to think he had loved a woman so much. "Why didn't you marry her?"

A soft sigh whispered past his lips. "I wanted to. I asked her and she said yes. A wedding was planned for the fall and I could hardly wait for the time to arrive. I actually believed that from that day forward, everything would change, that my life would finally be the way I'd always imagined." His voice faded off and she realized he was drifting into the past, seeing that day as if he were there once more.

"I was nervous," he said. "So terrified I was sick to my stomach. I wanted everything to be perfect for her. *I* wanted to be perfect for her. I stood at the altar, my heart pounding so hard I could barely hear the organ in the background, my neck cloth so tight I couldn't breathe. I can still remember my new shoes pinching my feet." A sigh slid out. "In front of five hundred people, I stared up the aisle, looking like the veriest fool, waiting for my bride to come through those big church doors. But Miriam never appeared.''

Elissa's stomach tightened. ''What happened?'' She stared into his face, saw the lines of sadness there, saw that his expression looked distant, turned inward to somewhere in the past.

''She ran away,'' he said. ''It wasn't too difficult to discover what had occurred. You see, my brother Richard was also missing. The next day I learned they had eloped to Gretna Green.''

Elissa's heart squeezed as if a heavy weight sat on her chest. Her throat closed up, aching for him, clogged with unshed tears. ''Oh, Adrian . . .'' Dear God, how could the woman have done it? How could she have abandoned him just like his father and mother, just like everyone else he had ever loved? More pain, more suffering. His life had been so full of heartache, so full of loneliness. Curled against him on the rock, Elissa felt a tremor run through his body, and an ache tore through her own.

She blinked to hold back tears, determined to discover the rest of the story. ''Miriam . . . did she love Richard?''

Adrian scoffed. ''My brother was heir to my father's estate, a far better catch than I, merely a second son. As it turned out, Richard didn't give a whit about her. He married her because I wanted her—it was as simple as that.'' Bitterness formed lines across his forehead, turning his features icy and hard. ''In the end, my brother lost everything my father left him in the first two years. He died just a few years later. It was God's little jest when through a distant cousin, the Wolvermont title and fortune came to me. God's little joke on us all.''

''Adrian, sweet God . . .'' She turned to him, her heart aching, pulled his head down to her breast and stroked her fingers through his hair. ''I can't bear to think of it . . . the way you must have suffered year after year. I don't know if I could have survived it.'' Tears collected, spilled down her cheeks, and a crushing ache for him rose in her chest. ''Life can be so unfair.''

Sweet God, she hurt for him. She hurt for him so much.

Adrian released a pent-up breath and slowly sat up, drawing himself away. He stared off into the distance. "It isn't important anymore, and in truth it was probably for the best. She was unfaithful to Richard, as she would have been to me. I would have made a terrible husband and—"

"That's not true! You are kind and you are considerate. You are brave and you are strong. You would have made a wonderful husband."

"Yes . . . well, be that as it may, it is hardly important now. I enlisted in the army the following week, and over the years, I've made a life for myself. I am content. I am also older and wiser—and I'm not fool enough to believe in love."

The lump in her throat ached harder. He didn't believe in love—how could he after all that he'd been through?

"You're wrong, Adrian." She leaned over and kissed his cheek, her heart breaking for him. "There *is* such a thing as love. Some people just never find it."

She wanted to say more, to tell him that Miriam might not have loved him but she did—madly, passionately, more than life itself. She wanted to say that she was nothing like Miriam Springer, that if he would trust her, love her half as much as she loved him, she could give him the dream he had always wanted.

But she didn't say the words. The cold look on his face held her back, and she was afraid he wouldn't believe her. If he did, it might be worse. He might pull away, and she would be certain to lose him. She had to give him time, pray his feelings for her would grow, as lately they had seemed to.

He snuggled her against him, hugged her briefly, saw the tears on her cheeks. "Bloody hell—you're crying."

She released a shaky breath, tried to smile and faltered. "I'm sorry. It's just that what they did to you was so wrong."

He bent and pressed a soft kiss on her lips. "I told you, it isn't important. All that is in the past."

She nodded, tried to be brave. "Are you . . . are you still in love with her?" She hadn't meant to ask him, couldn't believe she had actually spoken the words.

Adrian shook his head. "In truth, I don't think I ever really loved her. She was simply part of a dream, a fantasy that wasn't real—could never be real—at least not for me.''

Elissa said nothing. A swell of emotion rose inside her. She swallowed past the lump in her throat and forced herself to smile. ''She didn't deserve you. Miriam was the fool, my love, not you.''

His gaze swung to hers. Something shifted across his features, then it was gone. He came to his feet with brusque purpose and began to pull on his clothes. ''It's time we started back. We should have left before this.''

Elissa glanced toward his tall black stallion, munching grass a few feet away. ''Minotaur will catch up to them in no time, and the trip was well worth it.'' She smiled, her heart overflowing with love for him. ''Thank you, Adrian. I shall never forget this day. I shall cherish the memory always.''

Adrian nodded, but there was something different in the look he gave her, as if he had already begun to pull away. It seemed as though each time he let his guard down, he did his best to distance himself again.

He finished dressing then waited while she dressed and pulled on her shoes. Gathering Minotaur's reins, he led the great horse through the cool pine forest to the open country where they would pick up the army's trail.

From beneath her lashes, Elissa watched him, wondering if she should have told him the truth of how she felt. Perhaps she was wrong to keep silent when he needed her love so badly. Still, it was risky, better perhaps to wait.

In the distance ahead, something flashed in the sunlight, drawing her attention in that direction. She squinted against the brightness trying to make it out. The long, glinting barrel of a musket on the top of a boulder came into view, and she blinked, unable to believe her eyes.

A jolt of terror ripped through her—the musket pointed straight at Adrian's heart.

''Adrian!'' There wasn't time to think. Hurling herself in front of him, her arms outstretched to protect him, she heard the crack of the musket the same instant Adrian spotted the gun, but it was already too late. A blinding pain crashed into her head and Elissa cried out, slumping forward, sliding the length of Adrian's tall frame, barely hearing his deep voice shouting her name. Adrian shoved her to the ground, shielding her with his body, carrying her, inch by inch, behind a covering of boulders. The blue sky above was the last thing she saw as she slipped into darkness.

Adrian forgot to breathe. Elissa lay motionless in the grass beneath him and his hands were shaking so badly he was afraid to touch her. His heart was thundering, trying to pound its way through his ribs, and his stomach was knotted in fear.

"Elissa . . . angel." His throat closed up. He eased himself away from her, saw the blood oozing from the side of her head, beginning to mat her golden curls. He wanted to call back the seconds, change the course of events, but he knew that he could not. "Elissa—love, it's Adrian, can you hear me?" She didn't answer.

Adrian searched the distance, trying to locate the man who had fired the shot, dimly aware they were both still in danger. He saw no one, and the barrel of the musket had disappeared.

Stay calm, he told himself. *You've seen thousands of men injured in battle. Get hold of yourself. You've got to make yourself think!* But he had never felt like this when he had been in battle, never felt this gut-churning, all-consuming terror for one of his men.

He dragged in a deep breath of air and once more scanned their surroundings for any sort of danger. The distant thunder of hoofbeats told him their assailant was leaving, but he couldn't be sure. With hands that shook, he pulled a handkerchief from his pocket and pressed it against the gash at the side of Elissa's head to staunch the flow of blood. She continued to breathe, he saw with relief, her breasts rising and falling softly. He checked the pulse at the base of her throat and thankfully found it steady.

"Easy, love. Just take it easy." He hauled in a shaky breath and fought for control, scarcely able to believe a seasoned soldier like him could be so badly shaken.

He studied Elissa's face, saw the streak of crimson that trickled down her cheek and dripped onto her cotton blouse. She was as white as alabaster, so pale he could see the blue veins running beneath her skin.

He squeezed his eyes closed against the fear for her still pulsing through him. She'd be all right, he told himself. She had to be. Head wounds always bled like the bloody devil. All he had to do was get her back to the army and into the hands of a surgeon. He studied the horizon. In the meantime, he had to be sure it was safe.

Tying the handkerchief snugly around her head, he rested her gently among the grasses, bent and kissed her forehead. "Rest easy, love. I'll be back in a minute." God, he didn't want to leave her. She had risked her life to save him. He couldn't bear the thought that she had been hurt because of him.

With a last check to be sure she was all right, he headed into the forest, circling off through the woods to the spot where the man had fired the shot. As he had guessed, their attacker was already gone. Adrian tracked the man to where his horse had been standing, saw that the animal had been shod with standard army-issue shoes, then hurriedly returned to the place he had left Elissa.

She was moaning softly as he knelt beside her. He eased her head into his lap and smoothed back her hair. "It's all right, love. I'm going to get you back so the surgeon can take care of you."

She moaned again and her eyes fluttered open. "Adrian?"

Relief trickled through him, but worry swiftly replaced the emotion. "I'm right here, angel."

"My head hurts." She touched his makeshift bandage. "I'm think . . . I think I'm bleeding."

His stomach twisted, tightened into a knot. "Someone shot you. Or more likely they were shooting at me. You stepped in front of a musket ball and it grazed the side of your head. We need to get you back so a surgeon can take care of you."

Elissa reached for his hand, alarm in her pretty blue eyes. "The man with the gun . . . is he . . . is he still out there?"

He shook his head. "The coward is long gone."

"Did . . . did you see who it was?"

"No, but I intend to find out." He didn't tell her the man was a soldier, that he could be any one of the men they were living among each day. He didn't want her to worry—he just wanted her to be all right. "Put your arms around my neck. I'm going to lift you up and set you in front of me on the saddle."

Elissa nodded weakly, and her slim arms locked around his neck. When he lifted her against his chest, tiny tremors ran through her, and the knot in his stomach tightened with painful force.

Speaking quietly to Minotaur, who had shied a few steps at the sound of the gun, Adrian carried her to the animal's side, placed her gently up on the saddle, then swung himself up behind her. Settling her against his chest, he wrapped his arm tightly around her waist, then nudged the big horse forward.

At the pace they were forced to travel, it took longer than he imagined to catch up with the archduke's army. By the time they drew even with the long column of marching men, Elissa was asleep in his arms. His chest ached at the sight of the blood on her face, the streaks of scarlet in her pretty blond hair. It was his fault she had been hurt. His fault for bringing her along. The thought made him sick to his stomach.

Adrian swore beneath his breath. God's blood, he had known how dangerous this was. He should have forbidden her to come, should never have let her leave Vienna. He looked down at the dark blond lashes resting against her pale cheeks. He was supposed to protect her and he had failed. She could have died out there today and he would have been the one to blame.

His stomach rolled at the image of his beautiful angel lying dead and lifeless in the hot Austrian sun. His body shook to think of it and a cold sweat broke out on his forehead.

For the first time he realized how much he had come to care for her, how much she had come to mean. When had it happened? How had she slipped past his defenses? How had she broken through the wall he had built to protect himself and burrowed her way into his heart?

The breeze lifted her fine pale hair against his cheek, and he wanted to awaken her, assure himself that she was all right. He heard her gentle breathing and he wanted to put his hand over her heart to be certain the beat was strong, that she would not die and leave him.

It came to him like a blow out of nowhere—bloody hell, he was in love with her!

God's breath—it couldn't be true. He couldn't have been that stupid, couldn't possibly have allowed it to happen. It *wasn't* true, he told himself. He cared for her, yes. Too damned bloody much. But love? Love was for fools and dreamers, and he had long ago stopped being one of them.

She awakened just then, stirring a little, relaxing when she realized she rode in his arms. "Are we there yet?"

He tried for a smile but only a faint curve touched his lips. "I can see the end of the column just ahead."

"I'm feeling a little bit better. My head doesn't hurt so much."

He pressed a soft kiss on her forehead. "I'm going to find you a surgeon. It's nearly the end of the day. Soon they'll be stopping to set up camp and you'll be able to rest."

Elissa nodded faintly, closed her eyes, and burrowed into his shoulder. So innocent. So trusting. Adrian mulled over what had happened to her this day, the gut-tightening, mind-numbing loss of control that had gripped him—and what he meant to do about it.

It occurred to him the last person she should ever have trusted was him.

Inside their makeshift tent, Elissa awoke with a start. Her head was banging, hammering away at her temple. She gingerly reached up to touch it, felt a swath of cotton tied next to her ear. She shifted on the pallet, her fingers reaching out, searching for Adrian, but he wasn't there. Outside the tent, the army was up and moving about; she could hear the neighing of horses and the jangle of harness.

Still, it took a moment to get her bearings, to remember the shooting that had occurred yesterday afternoon. She recalled Adrian's care of her, so tender, so concerned, seeing to her every need. As he had promised, he had carried her directly to a surgeon, waited for the man to assure him she would be all right, that the wound was only superficial, then he had left her alone.

Elissa thought back to those last, final moments. There was something in his face, a distance that hadn't been there before. She had forced herself to ignore it, told herself it was only worry, concern about the injury she had suffered. But in her heart she was afraid that something had changed in the hours since the shooting, and a coil of fear clutched at her insides.

She didn't want to lose him. Not when he had begun to care, perhaps begun to accept her into his life. Worry churned in her stomach. Fear for the future, terror that she might lose him. She wished she knew what he was thinking. As soon as she had the chance, she would ask him, she decided, find out the truth.

But part of her was afraid of the answer. And part of her suspected she should be.

Adrian ducked his head through the opening of General Klammer's tent. He straightened to receive a salute from Major Becker, then turned and saluted the general.

"You sent for me, sir?"

Klammer nodded. He was a stout, graying man, barrel-chested and hard-edged, fit, and stamped with the look of a seasoned soldier. "Word just arrived this morning, Colonel. More bad news, I'm afraid." His gaze shifted down to the paperwork on his desk. "As you know, our retreat has been covered by General Hiller's Third Corps. His objective was to buy time, allow us to reassemble, and give Vienna a chance to muster its defenses. Unfortunately, just north of the river Traun, the French converged on Hiller's army. Both Lannes and Masséna attacked. The bridge, the castle, and the village at Ebersberg were completely overrun."

"Casualties?" Adrian asked, feeling the chill of another defeat run through his blood.

"Perhaps three thousand, as many as four thousand captured."

"And Hiller?"

"Headed north to Enns, then most likely on to Krems for a Danube crossing."

"Which leaves Vienna directly in Bonaparte's path."

"The city will be summoning its defenses and the army will soon be regrouping."

But would it be enough? "Is there anything I can do?" Adrian asked.

"Perhaps there will be, Colonel, once Hiller has arrived. Your regiment is stationed just east of Vienna, is that not correct?"

"The last I heard."

"Any word on the coalition?"

"Still nothing official. But rest assured, General Klammer, England stands solidly behind the archduke and his men. If there is any way we can be of service—"

"The best service you British could provide would be to send us some forty or fifty thousand men. Since that is not likely, there's another task I would have you do."

"Which is?"

"I believe you have met my wards, the Petralo children."

"Yes, sir, I have. They seem like a very nice family."

"I want you to take them to Vienna. At present, the capital is the safest place for them. Can I trust you to see it done?"

Adrian nodded. "Of course, General Klammer." He didn't want to leave, not after the shooting, not when he was closing in on the Falcon, but it seemed he had no choice. And it was definitely the excuse he needed to return Elissa to safety.

His attention strayed across the tent to where Major Becker stood beside the tent flap, his spine erect, his expression, as usual, inscrutable. Adrian wished he could voice his suspicions to Klammer, but until he had some sort of proof, the effort would be futile. And the fact remained, only the archduke and his closest advisors knew Adrian was there to find the traitor. Until the identity of the Falcon was known for sure, every person was suspect, even the general. Adrian didn't dare take the risk.

"I'll expect you to leave first thing in the morning," Klammer said. "Ivan Petralo was once a soldier in my command. He was an old and trusted friend. I'll expect you to keep his family safe."

"Yes, sir."

"That will be all, Colonel."

Adrian managed a smart salute, turned on his heel, and strode outside. Making his way across the encampment, he found Elissa dressed and sitting on a blanket outside their small tent, a clean white bandage wrapped around her forehead. A few feet away, his aide, Lieutenant Helm, was in the process of pulling up stakes and seeing to their meager amount of gear.

"How are you feeling?" Adrian asked, coming down on a knee beside her. "I've arranged for you to ride in the back of one of the wagons. I want you to rest as much as you can."

"I'm much better today. Nearly back to normal. 'Twas only a graze, after all. Even the doctor said the wound was superficial."

Guilt whispered through him. She shouldn't have been there at all. "Even so, you will rest in the wagon." He thought that she might argue but she only pursed her lips.

"Lieutenant Helm said you had gone to see Klammer." She accepted his hand, let him help her to her feet and pull her out of the way of the soldiers working around them. "Is there news?"

"Nothing good, I'm afraid. Another big battle, this one at Ebersberg. Hiller lost to Lannes and Masséna. Napoleon is bearing down on us and it won't be long before he reaches Vienna."

"Charlie will stop him. He'll do whatever it takes to protect the capital."

"That's right. Which means that is the safest place for you, Elissa."

"What!"

"General Klammer has ordered me to take the Petralo family on to Vienna. I'm taking you there with them."

"But that's insane! I can't possibly leave here now. We have to stay with the army. We have to find the Falcon."

"We've done all we can."

Elissa's chin went up. "What about the shooting? Becker must have been behind it. Surely that means we are getting close. It is only a matter of time until you catch him passing secrets."

"I pray that is so. In the meantime, I want you safe." She started to argue but Adrian cut her off. "Yesterday someone tried to kill us. If you won't think of yourself, think of your brother. Should the Falcon discover the connection between Karl and you and Peter, you could be putting Peter's life in danger."

Elissa chewed her bottom lip, studying him beneath her thick dark-gold lashes, and Adrian glanced away, hoping to avoid the question in her eyes.

"What about you?" she asked softly. "Will you be staying with me in Vienna?"

His stomach tightened. He wasn't going to stay, at least not for long. "I'm a soldier, Elissa. I go where I am sent." He reached out and took her hand, gently kissed her fingers. "Please . . . you must trust me to do what is best. I'll get Becker for you—or whoever this traitor is. I give you my word."

Her eyes searched his. She looked as though she wanted to protest, but in the end she did not. He thought that perhaps her head was hurting more than she let on, and her face still looked a little pale.

"When do we leave?" she asked.

"Tomorrow morning. You can spend the evening with your brother. We'll get a good night's sleep and be on our way at dawn."

Elissa merely nodded, but tension tightened her features and her face looked taut and strained. He wondered what she was thinking.

Chapter *Twenty-two*

Nina Petralo worked the muscles in her neck and shoulders, trying to get comfortable in the back of the weathered old hay wagon Colonel Kingsland had commandeered for their journey back to Vienna. The horses jogged effortlessly behind, Elissa's dappled mare and the colonel's big black stallion. Little Tibor and Vada faced them, their short legs dangling over the tailgate as they bounced along the rutted road.

At the front of the wagon, Elissa sat on the worn wooden seat beside the colonel, disappointment at their leaving obvious in the set of her shoulders. Beside her, the colonel sat perfectly erect, his bearing as straight as if he sat his big black horse. Elissa's posture was equally rigid, both of them watching the road ahead, speaking only when necessary, always in politely formal tones.

It hurt just to look at them, Nina thought, to read the worry in her friend's pretty face, the tension that ebbed from the colonel's powerful body. It seemed to increase with every mile closer to Vienna.

Though the archduke's army continued to march due east toward an undisclosed rendezvous point with General Hiller's forces, by turning to the south, it was only a single day's ride to the capital. Nina would be grateful to get there, to leave her difficult days with the army for the comfort of a roof over her head and the care of family, no matter that the Krasnos were distant cousins she had never met and knew almost nothing about. At least they would have a place to stay, food to eat, and the children would have the chance for a new home.

Nina glanced toward the front of the wagon, studying her newfound friends, wishing the solution to their problems were as simple as her own. It wasn't possible, she knew. Not when Elissa was so desperately in love with the handsome colonel, and the colonel equally desperate to guard his heart. Though he shrouded his feelings in aloofness, hid his love for the woman beside him even from himself, Nina could see it as clearly as if he stood on a mountaintop and shouted it to the world.

Her friend did not see it. If she did, she was afraid to believe it. Or perhaps she knew that even if he loved her, in the end he would leave her.

Nina sighed, her heart going out to them. She had come to admire the colonel. He was loyal, and as brave as any Hungarian tribal warrior. He was capable and strong, yet he was a man who could be gentle. The love he felt for his lady was deep and abiding, yet Nina thought that Elissa's fears were well-founded. The colonel's dark countenance held a wealth of suffering and dark, painful secrets. They were there in his eyes whenever his expression went unguarded.

Nina knew Elissa had seen them, and that she ached for the hurt he carried inside.

"We'll rest the horses up ahead," the colonel called over one wide shoulder. "At the rate we're going, we won't reach Vienna until nightfall. Once we've arrived, you and the children can spend the night in my town house. You'll be able to rest and refresh yourselves, get a good night's sleep. In the morning I'll see you safely to your new home."

"What about me?" Elissa asked.

His eyes found hers, intense yet oddly shuttered. "I thought you could stay there as well," he said a bit gruffly, "since we'll be so late in getting in. You'll want to bathe and change before returning to the duchess's palace."

There was something in the way he said it, a slight roughness in his voice, that hinted at the grief he felt at her leaving. He said nothing more and neither did Elissa, but Nina thought that her friend had heard it, too.

Dust rose from the wheels, leaving a hazy trail in their wake as Nina leaned back against the side of the wagon, hurting for the two of them, wishing she knew how to help them. She wondered what it must feel like to love someone so much. There should be joy, she thought, not sorrow, happiness instead of pain.

Perhaps one day she would find a man to love her as the colonel loved Elissa.

She prayed, if she did, that she would never lose him.

The lights of Vienna sparkled like jewels in the emperor's crown, the spires and towers reaching skyward into the starry blackness of the warm May night. Winding its way through the crowded streets of the Innerstadt, the wagon rumbled over the cobblestones toward Adrian's town house on Naglerstrasse.

By the time the creaking conveyance pulled up in front, Elissa was exhausted, and grateful for Adrian's thoughtfulness in suggesting she stay the night before returning to the palace. With Nina and the children acting as chaperones, there was no fear of gossip, though surely it meant she would be spending the night in her bed alone.

Adrian helped them down from the wagon, then shepherded his weary brood into the foyer, little Tibor asleep in his arms. Vada clutched one of his legs, her eyes half closed, the starving puppy she had rescued at the last stop on their journey trotting along at her side.

Elissa smiled to think of it, remembering the sight of the little girl hugging the dog to her chest.

"Please, Colonel," the child had begged. "Please, could we keep him? He is hungry and there is no one to take care of him. We cannot leave him here." The scruffy little mutt had followed the wagon to the well where they watered the horses, begging for a drink and a scrap of food. He was a scraggly black-and-white mongrel, his thin bones protruding indecently through his dull, shaggy coat.

"He is starving," Vada repeated, lifting the puppy into her short, chubby arms. "Someone must have left him." She petted the animal's dirty fur and the puppy wriggled against her, its pink tongue darting out to lick her cheek.

Vada hugged the puppy and started to cry, turning her sad face up to Adrian as if he were the only man in the world she could turn to for help. "He will die if we do not take him. He will die just like Sali . . . just like my papa."

Adrian looked into those pleading dark eyes and he was lost. He grumbled something about children and dogs, then gave a sigh of resignation. "I'll find out if the little beast belongs to anyone. If he doesn't—and your sister agrees— you may take him along."

A quick look at Nina, who smiled and nodded. Vada grinned at Adrian as if he had just hung the moon. "Thank you, Colonel. Thank you so very much." She reached an arm up to hug him, the puppy still clutched to her chest, and Adrian bent down and enveloped her in his arms.

Watching them, Elissa felt a thick lump rise in her throat. She blinked and glanced away, trying not to wish the child he held was their own.

"Adrian!" A surprised Major St. Giles striding into the foyer of the town house drew Elissa's attention from the past. "Damn and blast, man—it's good to see you."

The men shook hands and warmly clasped each other's shoulders. "You, too, my friend," Adrian said.

The major made a slight bow to Elissa. "Lady von Langen." His greeting rang oddly, since she hadn't thought of herself that way since she had left Vienna. Beside her, Nina tossed her a sideways glance.

"It's a long story," Elissa said softly before turning to smile at the major. "It's good to see you, Jamison."

"And this lovely lady is Nina Petralo," Adrian said. "She and her family are friends of General Klammer's."

"A pleasure, Miss Petralo." The major bowed formally over her hand and Nina's full lips curved into a pretty smile.

"I am pleased to meet a friend of the colonel's, though I hope you will call me Nina. I am no longer used to such formality."

"All right . . . Nina. If you will call me Jamison."

"Jam-i-son," she repeated in her deeply accented Hungarian. "I have not heard this name before. Jam-i-son. Do I say it correctly?"

He smiled in a way Elissa had never seen, warmer somehow, with a hint of building interest. "Not precisely. Perhaps you had better call me Jamie, the way the colonel does."

Nina smiled, white teeth flashing against her olive complexion. "Jamie. Yes, I like that much better." She turned to the children. "And this is my sister, Vada, and my brother, Tibor."

The interest in the major's eyes grew more acute. Not children of her own but merely siblings, that look said. Apparently she didn't have a husband. His eyes ran over her face, taking in the high, exotic cheekbones and thick-lashed dark eyes, briefly sliding down to the curve of her breast. They made a striking pair, Elissa suddenly thought, both of them slender and black-haired, Nina fitting nicely beneath the major's chin.

"Miss Petralo lost her father at Ratisbon," Adrian explained, motioning for the housekeeper to take the children—and the puppy—up to the room they would share with their sister. "She's come in search of the Krasnos family, cousins who live here in Vienna."

The housekeeper stepped forward. Nina bent and whispered something to Vada, and the little girl clasped her brother's hand. The two siblings followed the older woman up the stairs.

The major eyed Nina with concern. "I'm sorry for your loss," he said. "Already so many have died in the fighting. Unfortunately, in coming to Vienna, your timing may not be the best."

Adrian frowned. "What's happened?"

"Then you haven't yet heard. Bonaparte is said to be less than a day's ride west of the city. After Hiller's retreat, his movements went unchecked. His progress has been faster than anyone suspected. People are afraid. As soon as news of the defeat at Ebersberg arrived, they began leaving the city in droves. Nina's family may be among those who have already fled.''

Adrian's look grew more intense. "I noticed as we entered the outskirts that the roads seemed more heavily traveled than usual. If I hadn't been so damned tired, I probably would have guessed the reason."

"No one knows when Napoleon will attack. Probably not until his troops are rested and ready for battle. In the meantime, the city's defenses have been strengthened and hopefully the archduke's army will be arriving any day.''

"Yes, well, I still don't like it. I wouldn't have brought the women if I had thought they might be in danger."

"The danger to them was far greater traveling with the army. A battlefield is hardly the place for a lady.''

Adrian didn't look convinced. "That was my thinking at the time."

"As for Elissa," Jamison continued, "the duchess has returned to her summer house at Baden—strictly as a precautionary measure, but it is probably a good idea. Elissa's lady's maid has gone with her. The duchess left word, should the countess return to Vienna, she was to join her at Blauenhaus with all haste."

Some of the tension in Adrian's stance seemed to ease. "That's a relief." He smiled. "The old girl always seems to stay a jump ahead. If we can't find Nina's family, she and the children can accompany Elissa to Baden. They'll be safe there, even should Bonaparte overrun the city."

Elissa said nothing. She was trying to digest all she had learned and decide which course she should take. Adrian might think he was still in command of her life, but now that they were back in Vienna, those decisions were once again hers. "What will you do, Adrian?"

He tried to smile, but there was a tightness around his mouth and a bleakness in his eyes that frightened her more than the upcoming battle.

''In the morning I'll report to General Ravenscroft. After that, unless my orders are changed, I'll be returning to the army.'' He tipped her chin with his hand. ''If you recall, my lady, there is still the matter of the Falcon—and I have a promise to keep.''

His eyes ran over her face almost as if they touched her, and Elissa felt a tightening in her chest. Something was wrong. She had sensed it the moment she had seen him standing at her bedside in the surgeon's quarters, his expression remote, his gaze so painfully distant it was hard to believe he was the same man who had tended her with such gentle care just hours before.

Her stomach clenched with worry. Something had changed between them, something dark and elusive that could well destroy them both. She had to fight it, but she hadn't a clue what it was.

''We had better be getting to bed,'' Adrian said. ''We've a long day on the morrow, and we could all use a good night's sleep.''

The housekeeper returned to guide the women upstairs. At her brisk instruction, Nina and Elissa followed her up to their rooms. A small bathing tub filled with scented water sat waiting in the corner of Elissa's bedchamber, steam rising up in a welcoming mist. Grateful for Adrian's thoughtfulness, she stripped out of her dusty peasant clothes and stepped into the small copper tub, drawing her legs up to her chest as she tried to make herself comfortable, the heat of the water beginning to ease a little of her fatigue.

Reluctantly she admitted it felt good to be there, safe and protected from the dangers they had faced traveling with the army. The bedchamber was the same one she had slept in before; several forgotten items of clothing her maid had brought still hung in the armoire.

She tried not to imagine Adrian in his room down the hall, tried not to wish that she were there beside him. She fought to block him from her thoughts, but her mind refused to cooperate. If she closed her eyes, she saw him as if he stood there, his tall frame perfectly correct, a tender smile softening the hard line of his jaw. She forced the image away, but her mind remained a jumble of confusion, of uncertainty, loneliness, and fear.

Sweet God, she wished she could see into the future, discover what fate held in store for them, or at least find a clue as to what she should do. With a weary breath, she stood and stepped out of the tub, dried herself on a white linen towel, then wandered over to the window.

The lights of the city brightened the darkness outside, but obscured the stars overhead. She prayed again for an answer to her troubles, but no answer came.

Finally, exhaustion won out. Hanging the towel on a small brass hook beside the dresser, Elissa picked up her night rail, intending to pull it on, then rebelled at the notion of wearing the restricting garment and tossed it aside instead. Naked, she lay down on the bed, gazing up at the canopy but not really seeing it. Surely she was tired enough to sleep.

Blowing out the lamp on the nightstand beside the bed, she closed her eyes, but sleep remained elusive. The distant toll of church bells was her only solace as the minutes ticked past and the house slowly lapsed into silence.

Stuffing the tail of a clean lawn shirt into the top of his breeches, his hair still damp from his bath, Adrian stood at the door of his bedchamber, thinking of Elissa, calling himself ten kinds of a fool—trying to dissuade himself from the destructive course he had set. A single lamp burned beside the bed, throwing his outline into shadow, a grotesque, overblown image of the villain he was about to become.

A wave of self-loathing slid through him. He knew he should leave her alone, that their parting on the morrow would be difficult enough without the intimacies of a last shared night together. He hated himself for what he was about to do, yet try as he might, he could not seem to stop himself. Only a merciful God could do that, and He appeared unwilling to intercede.

It wasn't fair, he knew. Not to Elissa. Not to himself. And yet he had to see her, touch her one last time.

Ignoring the voice that tried to call him back, he snuffed out the lamp on the dresser, crossed to the door by the light of the moon slanting in through the windows, and strode down the hall to her bedchamber.

The latch lifted quietly as he let himself in and stood in the darkness, content for the moment just to look at her. Moonlight filtered across the embroidered sheet covering a portion of her slender frame. The material had slipped below her waist, leaving her lovely breasts exposed, the tips like perfect pink roses against the paleness of her skin.

He wasn't sure how long he stood there, only minutes perhaps. Perhaps it was more. Time seemed unimportant, now that there was no time. Precious as they were, he meant to savor these few moments that remained.

He moved closer to the bed, stared down at the slight rise and fall of her breasts. He studied the arch of her neck, the delicate curve of her cheek, aching to reach out and touch her. When his gaze came to rest on her face, he found that her eyes were open, that she had been watching him, just as he had been watching her.

"You should be sleeping," he said softly.

She simply looked at him and slowly drew back the covers, inviting him to join her. "I was waiting for you."

He didn't hesitate. Only a bigger fool than he would do that. Instead he sat down on the edge of the bed and pulled off his boots, unfastened the buttons on his shirt, unbuttoned and slid out of his breeches.

He joined her on the bed, a hand coming up to cradle her cheek. Bending his head, he brushed his lips over hers in a faint caress then settled his mouth more deeply over the soft, delicate curves. He kissed her thoroughly yet gently, drawing her into himself, absorbing the taste of her, the feel, inhaling the soft scent of roses drifting up from her hair. Her arms went around his neck as his tongue slid in, claiming her more fully, seeking the dark, sweet cavern of her mouth. He filled his hands with her breasts, felt the tiny buds at the ends go hard and lowered his head to take one between his teeth.

He felt her hands in his hair, cradling his head against her as if she wanted what he offered, as if she needed it as desperately as he. Her skin was smooth and damp from the patterns he traced with his tongue. He trailed soft kisses across her belly, ringed her navel, then claimed the hot, wet sweetness at her core.

With his mouth and his hands, he gave to her, told her how much he had come to love her. *Love.* His mind rebelled at the thought, yet his heart could no longer deny it. He loved her, but still he would leave her.

This night was all he would allow himself. This night and no more. He would take from her all that she was willing to give and pray it was enough to last him a lifetime without her. He probed her more deeply, claiming more of her, demanding she give to him as she never had before. Her body arched in climax, and his heart swelled at the knowledge he had pleased her, given her something in return for all that she had given to him.

Coming up over her, he claimed her mouth in a ravishing kiss, stroking deeply with his tongue, possessing her, branding her in the hope that she would always remember this time they had together.

Her slender body trembled beneath him, her fingers digging into his shoulders, urging him to take more of her. He kissed her deeply, thoroughly. Parting her legs with his knee, he buried himself inside her, sinking into her, filling her womb, forcing her to take all of him. Her body tightened around him, owning him, claiming his battered soul. He started to move and a soft little cry broke from her lips. Again and again, he surged into her, possessing her, absorbing her into his very skin. Pleasure deep and raw tore through him, sweet and nearly unbearable.

He felt her body tighten, heard her restless moan, felt the tiny ripples of her climax spasm around him. Heat enveloped him. Hunger caught him in its thrall. His hands gripped her hips and he buried himself more fully, giving in to his devouring need and spilling his seed inside her.

Words of love caught in his throat. He wanted to say them, to let them spill forth like water from a pent-up dam. He clamped his jaw against the urge, bit down on the foolish impulse that could only destroy him. Love was impossible for a man like him. He didn't even know what loving really was.

Fighting back a surge of emotion, he eased himself from inside her and lay down at her side, curling her against him. There were hours yet till dawn and he knew that he would take her again, try to satisfy his ravenous hunger.

For this night she was his and his alone. His to hold, his to cherish, his to love. With the dawn, whatever they had shared would end. He wondered how he would endure his loneliness once she was gone.

Chapter *T*wenty-three

Elissa awoke with a start, troubled by a vague, unpleasant dream she could only distantly recall. She reached for Adrian, felt the indentation left by his body in the feather mattress, but Adrian had already gone. A pang of loneliness slid through her, his absence even more poignant after the hours they had spent making love.

He has only gone to see Ravenscroft, she told herself, recalling his words of last night, yet her hand trembled as it ran over the pillow where he had slept, and worry formed a cold knot in her stomach. He had never made love to her the way he had last night, with so much passion, so much undisguised longing. Each touch betrayed his feelings for her, his fathomless need of her. He had never caressed her with such aching tenderness, never taken her with such undeniable hunger. It was as if he wished to consume her, make her a part of his very soul.

It made her heart ache to think of it, for she sensed that last night's loving, the culmination of all that had passed between them, might be the end and not the beginning she so fervently prayed it was.

Dear God, what if he had merely been telling her goodbye?

Anxiety sat heavy on her chest, but she forced herself to ignore it. Heedless of the tender aches in her sweetly sated body and the dampness of Adrian's seed between her legs,

Elissa struggled out from beneath the covers and made her way to the dresser to begin her morning ablutions. She finished quickly then dressed in a yellow muslin day dress she found in the armoire. After a last glance in the mirror that betrayed her passionate night, she made her way downstairs.

Nina was waiting in the dining room, a smile of welcome lighting her face. Elissa sat across from her and a servant poured them steaming cups of coffee. A plate of sausage and strudel appeared on the table in front of her, but she merely slid the morsels around on her plate. It was difficult to eat with so much on her mind. Even the thought of food made her slightly sick to her stomach.

"The children are still sleeping?" she finally asked, breaking into the silence.

Nina nodded. "A rare occasion. They were exhausted after traveling all day." She smiled. "Your colonel will forever be a hero to Vada. It was kind of him to allow her to keep the puppy."

Elissa smiled faintly. "Adrian likes children, though I don't think he cares to admit it." She took a sip of her coffee. "Has Major St. Giles left, as well?"

A spark of warmth appeared in Nina's dark eyes. "He and the colonel left at first light. I heard them riding out before the sun had crested the horizon."

"I wish I knew what was going to happen." She sighed. "I know it's silly but I miss Adrian already. Perhaps General Ravenscroft will order him to stay."

Nina's dark gaze shifted away. "Perhaps he will." But it was obvious she didn't believe it, and neither did Elissa.

Misery washed over her. Fear of what she thought must lie ahead. She tried to smile, to make some effort at polite conversation, but her lips began to tremble and her eyes glazed with tears. Bending forward, she covered her face with her hands and started to weep. "I don't know if I can stand this. God, I love him so much."

Nina was out of her chair in an instant, rounding the table, urging her up and into her comforting arms.

Elissa cried on her shoulder. "I love him, Nina. I tried not to, but God help me, I do."

Nina patted her gently on the back. "I know you do."

"He came to me last night," Elissa said tearfully. "What we did . . . it was beautiful . . . so beautiful. And so incredibly sad."

Nina nodded sagely. "He does not wish to leave you."

Elissa dragged in a shaky breath and drew herself away, brushing the tears from her cheeks. "I wish I could believe that."

Dark eyes centered on her face, knowing eyes, filled with wisdom beyond her years. "I know little of the love between a man and a woman, yet I believe that the colonel loves you. If you love him, too, then you must tell him."

Elissa sighed and glanced away. "I've wanted to. The time just never seemed right. And last night . . . last night I was afraid to."

"You are afraid that if you tell him the way you feel, you will lose him."

She nodded. "Yes . . ."

Nina reached for her hand, gave it a gentle squeeze. "If you want him, you must fight for him. Tell him before he leaves. Let him know the way you feel."

Nina was right, she knew, yet her stomach twisted to think of it. What if she opened her heart and all he felt in return was pity? What if desire for her was all he had ever felt?

By the time Adrian returned late that morning, her stomach was a bundle of nerves and her heart hammered with fear.

Dear God, she loved him so much.

He strode into the house as he always did, his movements forged with purpose, yet his expression held none of the tenderness she had seen in his face last night.

"Things are progressing as we planned," he said brusquely, approaching where she waited in the drawing room. "Ravenscroft has ordered my immediate return to the archduke's army. Jamie is to see Nina settled and you returned safely to Baden."

Her eyes squeezed shut for a heartbeat. "I thought . . . I

thought you would be staying at least for a couple of days.''

He only shook his head. "Time is of the essence now. I have to be on my way. With Bonaparte so close, I'll have to head east out of the city then cut north until I find the archduke's forces.'' He glanced toward the door as if he couldn't wait to leave. "I'm already packed. Jamie will be along within the hour.'' His smile looked distant and remote, as though the man she had known last night was already gone. "Minotaur waits out in front. Why don't you walk me to the door?''

"Yes . . . yes, of course.'' Dear God, she couldn't think, couldn't believe this was happening so quickly. Adrian's big hand settled at her waist, urging her across the room and out into the foyer, then the butler opened the door.

In seconds they were standing outside the town house, Adrian standing at the bottom of the steps, checking his saddle and equipment, turning to smile at her like the stranger he had become.

Don't go! she wanted to say. *There are things I have to tell you, things I need to say!* Perhaps that was the reason he was leaving in such a hurry. Perhaps he didn't want to hear them.

"Time to go, angel,'' he said lightly. "Take care of yourself. I'll send word of the Falcon as soon as there is news. Jamie will see you get the message.'' He started to turn away, to swing himself up on his horse, but her softly spoken words held him in place.

"Aren't you going to kiss me goodbye?''

He stared at her and the mask he wore began to crumble. Stark pain twisted his features, despair unlike anything she had ever seen. "Of course,'' he said gruffly, taking a step in her direction.

She was in his arms before he had started up the stairs, clinging to his neck, pressing her cheek to his, unmindful of her tears.

"Don't cry, angel,'' he whispered. "I can't bear it if you cry.''

She captured his face between her hands, dragged his

mouth down to hers for a fierce, aching kiss. Adrian's arms tightened painfully around her. He deepened the kiss, claiming her as if he tried to reach into her soul. She could feel him trembling, hear his sharp, raw intakes of breath.

"I have to go," he whispered, but he didn't release his hold, just stood there on the steps, his arms wrapped tightly around her. His hands smoothed over her hair. "I have to leave."

Fresh tears rolled down her cheeks. "Please, Adrian, hold me just a few moments more."

His eyes slid closed as if he were in pain. He pressed his face into the curve of her neck and she could feel the tremors running through his big, hard body. It was time to say the words, time to speak the thoughts crowding her heart. It should have been easy—she loved him so much. And yet she was afraid.

She steadied her nerves. Held him even tighter against her. "Before you go," she whispered, "there is something I would tell you."

His big hand cradled her head, but he didn't let her go.

"I love you," she said. "Adrian, I love you so much."

His whole body went rigid. For a moment he didn't even breathe.

"I wanted to tell you," she stumbled on. "I tried, but I was afraid."

His hold on her eased and she felt him begin to draw away. She wanted to call back the words, wanted desperately to pull him back into her arms.

"You don't love me," he said gently, looking into her tear-stained face. "You may think so now, but in the end you'll see it was only an illusion."

The ache in her throat began to swell, making it difficult to speak. "You're wrong, Adrian. I'm not like the women in your past. I'm nothing like Miriam Springer. I'm not the sort of woman who gives her love at a whim and then takes it away." She reached out and cupped his cheek. "I love you— deeply and without reservation. No matter what you do, no matter where you go, that will not change. I'll always love you, Adrian. I'll love you forever.''

Adrian stared at her, his eyes full of regret and darkened with pain. She looked into his dear, beloved face, read the despair, saw the heartache and need that surpassed even her own, and knew in that moment that he loved her, too.

Dear God, he loved her—as she had prayed that he would—and yet it did not matter. The tension in his body, the harsh rise and fall of his chest, made it clear that he still meant to leave her.

She closed her eyes, felt the wetness sliding down her cheeks. ''You won't be back,'' she said softly, aching at the words she knew were true. ''This isn't just goodbye until your return, this is goodbye forever . . . isn't it, Adrian?''

He glanced away, his grief so tangible she thought that if she reached out she could touch it. ''My regiment is here,'' he said softly. ''I'll have to return sooner or later.''

Her chest ached, felt as if the air were being sucked from her lungs. ''But you won't be returning to me. Today is the last time you will ever kiss me, the last time you'll ever hold me. It's over between us—isn't it, Adrian? Last night you were telling me goodbye. Last night when we made love, that was the last night we'll ever be together.''

He didn't answer, made no move to speak, but the agony in his features, the torment etched in his eyes, confirmed what his words did not. Pain tore through her, fierce and numbing, making it hard to think.

''I have to go,'' he said. ''In time, you'll forget all about me. You'll find someone else. A man who will love you as you deserve.''

She only shook her head. ''I don't want someone else. It's you I love, Adrian. You're the only man I'll ever love.''

Regret darkened his features. ''I'm sorry,'' he said. ''I never meant to hurt you.''

She swallowed past the tightness in her throat. ''I know.''

Adrian looked one last time into her face then turned away, starting back down the steps toward his horse. She watched him go, her heart squeezing painfully, her eyes glazed with tears. *If you love him, you must fight for him.* Nina's words hovered at the edge of her mind. *If you love him . . . if you love him . . .* The litany washed over her, broke through the sorrow numbing her senses. *If you love him, you must fight.* Strength poured through her. The words gave her the courage she needed, the will to take the biggest risk of her life.

She drew herself up and called out to him, halting him at the bottom of the steps. When he turned, she looked into his pain-etched features and knew the next few moments would determine the course of her life.

"I know what you are thinking, Colonel. You believe you are simply leaving, finishing what we once shared. That is what you *want* to believe, but it isn't the truth. The truth is you're running away."

Adrian's gaze turned fierce. She lifted her chin and forced herself to meet those hot green eyes that had suddenly turned so hard. "You know what I think, Colonel? I think you're in love with me. I think that perhaps you love me almost as much as I love you. But the fact is you're afraid. All your life you've searched for love and each time you failed to find it. You believe if you try again, you'll only fail again—and this time you might not survive it."

She straightened her shoulders, her chest aching, her gaze locked with his, willing him to look inside his heart. "Until this moment, I admired you, my lord Colonel. You are strong and you are smart. You are kind and you are gentle. But today I discovered something about you that I did not know. Until this morning, I thought you were the bravest man I had ever met. But the truth is, Colonel Kingsland, you're a coward. And because you're afraid, both of us will suffer for the rest of our lives."

Adrian's face went from pale to a deep shade of rose, anger replacing the despair she had seen just moments ago.

"If a man said those words to me, I would kill him. In your case, my lady, I am simply grateful to know your true opinion of me. It shall make our parting far easier, I assure you." Turning away from her, his shoulders rigid, he swung himself up in the saddle and snatched up the reins. "Farewell, *Countess*. Have a safe trip back to England."

Digging his heels into the stallion's ribs, he urged the big black out into the crowded street, riding away from her without a single glance back. Elissa watched his tall frame disappear among the throng of people leaving Vienna and thought her heart must surely be breaking in two.

Dear God, what have I done? She sank down on the steps, staring at the place Adrian had been, wishing she could take back her taunting words. Perhaps if she hadn't spoken, they might have at least parted friends. Instead he was gone for good. Her cruel words had driven him away.

Elissa swallowed past the ache in her throat. She should have known he would react the way he did. He had wanted an excuse to leave her and she had given him one. She pressed her knuckles against her mouth and wept for him, wept for what they might have had if only she could have reached him. Instead she had driven a wedge between them no words could ever repair.

"Come into the house." Nina's deep, commanding voice cut into her misery, the no-nonsense tone pulling her from her despair. "There is no point in sitting out here, making yourself sick with grief. Come inside and I will make you a cup of tea."

Nina was right, as she usually was, but still her legs felt leaden. Sucking in a shaky breath, she pushed herself to her feet. Crying would do her no good. Weeping wouldn't change the fact that he was gone. "I've lost him, Nina. I did everything wrong. I drove him away."

Nina wrapped an arm around her shoulders, leading her back inside the house. "You did the best you could. That is all any woman can do. You have told him the way you feel. It is up to the colonel to decide what he must do."

But Elissa believed he had already chosen. She had seen it in the grim set of his shoulders as he had ridden away. He wouldn't be back—at least not to her. She would have to find a way to live without him.

* * *

The morning dragged past. Though her heart felt leaden, Elissa was determined to put her life back into some kind of order, to fight the cold, numbing pain of Adrian's loss. Driven by a desperate need to forget him, she waited for the major's return with a renewed sense of purpose. She had to keep busy. There were things she needed to do, things she hoped would help erase him from her thoughts.

Jamison arrived at the town house just before noon, his saddle horse tied to the back of a carriage. A groom led the animal to the stables at the rear of the house while the major climbed the front porch stairs two at a time and surged into the entry.

"The Krasnos family is still in Vienna," he said without preamble when he found them in the drawing room. "I spoke to them this morning. They were saddened by the loss of Nina's father but assured me they would welcome her and the children into their home."

Nina breathed a sigh of relief but there was a tightness around her mouth that said much of her worry remained. For the past half hour, she had been pacing the floor, waiting for Jamison's return, uncertain of the welcome she would receive in her cousin's home.

Elissa wondered that same thing. What are they like? she wanted to ask, knowing it was the question that darkened her friend's exotic features.

Instead Elissa forced herself to smile. "That's wonderful news, isn't it, Nina?"

"Yes, it is very good news, indeed." She flicked a glance upward as if she could see into the rooms on the second floor. "The children are playing with the puppy. Our clothes are already packed. I will tell them you are ready to leave."

Jamison nodded. "The carriage awaits out in front. I should like to get you and the children settled as quickly as possible. It's a three-hour journey on to Baden and I'd like to see the countess safely to Blauenhaus before it gets dark."

This time Nina didn't let the reference pass. "You are a

countess?'' she asked, a sleek black brow arching with curiosity.

"Not really, though I arrived here pretending that I was. I came to Vienna to investigate my brother's murder. That is what the colonel and I were doing together, the reason we were traveling with the army.''

"Ah, yes, now I see.'' Nina said no more, merely turned and left to collect the children and their meager possessions. Nina wasn't one to press for information. Her friendship was offered simply, with no strings attached. When Elissa was ready to explain the rest, Nina would be ready to listen.

As soon as she was gone, Elissa turned to the major. "You needn't worry about taking me to Baden. I don't intend to go there.''

Jamison's blue eyes widened in surprise, then his brows pulled into a frown. "My orders are to take you to Baden. That is exactly what I mean to do.''

Elissa eyed him boldly. "Need I remind you, Major, that I am a civilian? Colonel Kingsland has the right to command your actions—he hasn't the least right to order me about.''

He clamped his jaw in a gesture that reminded her of Adrian. "Don't be a fool, Elissa. Napoleon will be marching on the city any day. You'll be safer if you are in Baden.''

"Two hundred thousand people live in Vienna. Even should Bonaparte capture the city, the danger to me would be no greater than it would to anyone else.''

"Why is it you wish to stay? What do you plan to gain by being stubborn?''

"I'm not sure. Perhaps I could learn something of what happened at Reiss's Tavern. My brother's commanding officer said that is where Karl was murdered, just like the Falcon's courier.''

His mouth went thin. "Even if there is a connection, you can scarcely go into a place like that. You're a woman. You wouldn't find out a bloody thing.''

"Then I'll find someone who can. In the meantime, I'm sure the duchess will not mind if I impose on her friendship a little while longer and stay in the palace while she is away.''

The major swore softly beneath his breath. "This is insane. You have to go to Baden."

"I don't have to do a damnable thing I don't want to. And I am not going to Baden."

He blew out a frustrated breath, anger warring with the fact he knew she was right. "Is there nothing I can say to dissuade you? Adrian will be sorely displeased to learn you have disobeyed him again."

Her chin shot up. "I am no longer concerned with what does or does not please the colonel—as I am sure he is no longer concerned with what pleases me. As for you, Major St. Giles, with or without your approval, I intend to stay in Vienna."

Jamison ground his teeth. "Hell and damnation but you are a vexing woman."

Elissa found herself smiling for the first time that day. "I assume that means you will escort me to the duchess's palace."

A hard look came into his light blue eyes while a corner of his mouth curved up. "On the contrary, my lady. If you are determined to remain in the city, you will stay here in the town house where I can personally see to your safety."

"But I couldn't possibly—"

"I'll be happy to send for your lady's maid, if that will make you feel better. But one way or another, you will stay or I promise you, Elissa, I will truss you up like a Christmas goose and cart you all the way to Baden—which is doubtless exactly what I should do."

Amused laughter filtered through the doorway. Nina stood there smiling, enjoying their battle of wills. "I warn you, Jamie. I have witnessed this lady's determination. The task might prove more difficult than you believe."

The edge of a smile touched the major's well-formed lips. It slid away as he turned to Elissa, a scowl rising in its place. "Which is it to be, my lady?"

From the hard look he gave her, it was clear that Nina's warning had fallen on deaf ears. And Elissa liked him far too much to challenge him that way. Besides, she couldn't deny there was a certain amount of comfort in remaining here in the town house, in company with a soldier who would do everything in his power to protect her.

Elissa smiled. "All right, Major—you win. At least for the present. In the meantime, I'm sure Nina is eager to reach her new home and see the children properly settled."

But Nina didn't look eager at all. In fact, as the dark-haired girl stared at the major, it seemed she almost hated to leave.

"Are you ready?" Jamison asked softly. He appeared reluctant as well.

Nina gave him a nod of agreement. "The butler has seen our satchels loaded into the carriage . . . what little we were able to bring. Most of our belongings were left in Ratisbon."

"Possessions aren't important," the major said gently. "What matters is that you arrived here safely and that soon you'll have a new family."

"Yes . . ." Nina agreed, but uncertainty clouded her big, dark eyes. The Krasnos were unknown to her. What would she discover when she got there? Elissa prayed she would find acceptance for the children as well as for herself.

"Goodbye, Nina." Elissa reached out and hugged her. "You've been a wonderful friend."

Nina returned the embrace. "I hope we will see each other often."

Elissa hugged each of the children. "Take care of your sister, will you? She gets lonely sometimes, just like you."

They stared up at her as if the thought had never occurred to them. Nina was so strong. It didn't seem possible she could have such a weakness.

Little Tibor reached out and took his sister's hand. "I will take care of you. I will look out for you, just like Papa used to do."

Elissa's throat closed up. Her emotions had been close to the surface all morning. She couldn't help thinking of the children she and Adrian might have had.

"Thank you, Tibor," Nina said solemnly. She squeezed his hand and smiled. "Now we had better be on our way.

I'm sure the major has more important things to do than worry about a ragged bunch like us.''

Jamison started to protest, but the children rushed past just then, racing for the door and nearly bowling him over. He chuckled as he turned to Nina, his features softening as his eyes came to rest on her face. ''I was wondering, Miss Petralo . . . Nina . . . if it might be possible . . . if you would mind if I called on you, once you are settled in your new home?''

Nina's innocently sensual expression betrayed the pleasure she felt at his words. ''I would like that very much . . . Jamie.''

The major smiled in that warm way Elissa had only begun to see. ''Shall we?'' He offered Nina his arm and led her out the door, down the front steps, to the carriage.

Elissa watched him help her climb in and lift each of the children inside, then the vehicle rolled off down the cobbled streets. Elissa watched them leave, suddenly tired and unbearably lonely. She couldn't give in to the feeling, she knew. If she did, the grief she had buried inside would surface and overwhelm her.

Stiffening her spine, she turned away from the window in the entry and climbed the stairs up to her room. She needed to think, to plan what she should do. But even in the solitude of her bedchamber, it was difficult to concentrate. Her heart ached with bitterness and loss, and her mind was clouded with sadness. She tried not to glance at the bed. It reminded her of the beautiful night she had spent with Adrian, the last night they would ever have together.

Elissa sighed. Tomorrow she would feel better. Tomorrow she would start to forget.

But in her heart she knew Adrian Kingsland was the one man she would never be able to forget.

Chapter *Twenty-four*

Napoleon didn't wait to rest and re-form his army as everyone believed. Instead he moved forward, taking command of Prater Island in the center of the Danube, and on May the tenth began to bombard Vienna. Panic ensued. People streamed in droves out of the city. Major St. Giles and his regiment of British cavalry worked from dawn to dusk, assisting the evacuation of diplomats and higher government officials, helping remove antiquities and valuable archives that might be in danger should Napoleon conquer the archduke's defenses.

"All bloody hell has broken loose out there," Jamison told Elissa late that afternoon. "I want you to stay indoors where it is safe." She was sitting in the dining room, trying to force herself to eat when he appeared in the open doorway. "I've only got a moment. I just stopped by to make certain that you were all right."

"I'm fine," she said as he began striding toward her, though her nerves were taut and had been since word of the attack reached the town house.

"I want you to keep the doors locked and the curtains drawn. Don't let anyone in you don't know."

"I—I was hoping to see Nina this afternoon. I want to make certain that she and the children are safe."

The major shook his head. He was far less tractable than

she had originally believed. He was stronger and more protective. She had found these were not bad qualities to discover in a man. "I want you here," he repeated. "If I'm ordered to leave, I'm taking you with me."

Elissa hid her surprise, but a trickle of relief slid through her. In truth, she should have gone to Baden as Adrian insisted. "What about Nina?" she asked. "What about the Krasnos family?"

"I checked on them early this morning. They're thinking of leaving the city, but so far Ivar Krasnos hasn't made a decision."

"What is he like? Does he seem a decent sort of man?"

Jamison sighed. "I can't say I've a liking for him." He hesitated, started to say more than stopped himself.

Elissa rested a hand on his forearm. "Please, Major. Nina is my friend. I've been worried about her. I'd like to know the truth."

A muscle tightened in his jaw as if the words were too painful to speak. "Ivar Krasnos is loud and overbearing. His wife cowers at his every glance. The children are terrified of him. Thank God they have Nina to intercede in their behalf. She isn't afraid of him at all."

"Or if she is, she wouldn't let him know it."

"Frankly, I'm worried about her. I think the family resents the intrusion and they're taking it out on Nina and the children."

Pity for her friend welled up. She wished there was something she could do. "It's a difficult transition. In time, perhaps it will all work out."

"Perhaps." But the tautness of his features said he wasn't so sure.

"Will you be seeing her again?"

Jamison's hard look softened. "I plan to stop by this evening. I won't be able to stay very long, but at least I can check to see if she's all right."

"She's a lovely girl," Elissa said.

"She's beautiful." A note of reverence roughened his

voice. "She's intelligent and strong. I've never met a woman like her."

Elissa smiled softly. "I'm glad she has you to look out for her. She's lucky to have made such a friend."

Jamison seemed a little embarrassed. "Yes, well . . . I only wish I could do something to help." He glanced toward the door. "I've got to get going. I shouldn't have stopped at all, but I was worried about you."

"How goes the fighting?" Elissa asked.

Jamison shook his head. "Not good, I'm afraid. Perhaps you should pack some things, just in case we have to leave in a hurry."

A little shiver ran through her. "All right." He turned and started walking away and Elissa followed him out to the foyer. "Take care of yourself, Jamison."

He smiled. "You may be certain I will." He left her there, instructing the butler to lock the door. It was well after midnight when she heard his footfalls on the stairs. By the time she awakened in the morning, he was already up and gone.

Jamison rode through the melee of people fleeing the city, heading for the Krasnos apartment in Kurrentgasse. Smoke clogged his throat and a thick black-powder haze hung over the city. Screaming horses, the distant thunder of cannon, angry shouts, and hysterical weeping filled the heavy night air. Wagons overloaded with household possessions, furniture, carpets, boxes of goods and tools, all pressed together in the narrow cobbled streets, heading toward the Franzensbrucke leading over the flooding Danube out of Vienna.

As chaotic as the city had become, Jamison's worry centered not on the bitter clash with Napoleon, but the war Nina Petralo fought with her distant cousin. It seemed to worsen with each passing day. Last night when he had stopped by, he had found her face to face with the stout, barrel-chested man, her slender legs splayed and her fists clenched as she stood between him and little Tibor, who had broken a crock of butter.

"Fetch my belt!" Ivar had shouted to his wife. "The boy

needs a lesson in the value of goods. I'll see he gets one he won't soon forget!''

Nina shoved Tibor farther behind her back. "He didn't do it on purpose." Jamison could see the boy trembling. It was all he could do not to jerk the man off his feet and send a fist crashing into his face. He forced himself to hold his ground. He didn't want to cause Nina any more trouble. She would have to live in her cousin's house long after he was gone.

"I've a few coins left from our travels," she said. "I will pay you for the butter."

He grumbled something beneath his breath, clearly not happy that she had defied him. "See that you do," he said. He spotted Jamison just then, standing in the doorway, and a tight smile curled his thick lips.

"Come in, Major. I am sorry you had to see that. But surely you agree children must be disciplined. My own are grown and married. They learned to obey their elders, and in time these children will, too."

Jamison said nothing. He knew if he said one word, his temper would explode and he couldn't afford to have that happen. "Miss Petralo?" he said instead. "I'd like a word with you if you don't mind."

She smiled at him, some of the tension easing from her slight yet sturdy frame. "Of course." She glanced down at little Tibor. "Go find your sister. Get ready for bed and I will be there in a few minutes to tell you a story and tuck you in."

Tibor had glanced shyly in Jamison's direction, flashed him an uncertain smile, then turned and raced away.

Tonight, Jamison's mind was on Nina once more. Ignoring the high-pitched scream of a cannonball soaring overhead, the bits of dust and plaster that rained down when the ball crashed into the side of a building down the block, he urged his horse a little faster toward his destination.

The Austrians were losing, he knew. To everyone's surprise, the archduke had declined to bring up reinforcements. It seemed Charlie had decided to wait, to regroup his forces and make a stand somewhere north of the Danube. The arch-duke had suffered too many losses. He meant to win the next battle, even if it meant he must sacrifice his beloved Vienna.

Jamison reined up in front of a tall brick building in Kur-rentgasse that housed the Krasnoses' second-floor apartment, the place a little too cluttered for his taste and smelling of rancid sausage grease. At the top of the stairs, he could hear a man's deep voice shouting from inside, and a hard knot twisted inside him.

Good Christ, don't let it be Nina again. But his mouth had gone dry and his chest felt tight. His sharp, impatient rap on the door ended the shouting. He heard the sound of footfalls and Yana Krasnos pulled it open.

"Major St. Giles," she whispered with a worried glance over her shoulder. She was a short, pudgy woman nearing forty, with dark, graying hair and a haunted look in her eyes.

Jamison followed her uncertain gaze through the door to the parlor, a lump of worry balling in his chest. Standing next to the empty hearth, Ivar Krasnos glared at Nina, his hairy hands balled into fists. She stood just a few feet away, facing him with defiance, a trace of blood on her lip and a purple bruise darkening her cheek.

Her eyes found his and a glaze of tears welled up. "Ja-mie . . ." she whispered, a deep rasp in her throat, her olive cheeks flushed with humiliation.

Jamison strode toward her, anger nearly choking him. When he reached her side, he pulled her against him and cradled her head on his shoulder. "Get your things," he said softly, feeling her slender body tremble. "You and the children are coming with me."

Ivar Krasnos swore a Hungarian curse. "The girl goes no-where. She is family. She has no one else but us and you will not take her."

"She has me. If you wanted her to stay, you shouldn't have beat her."

"She interferes with the children. They must learn to obey, just as she will learn."

Jamison didn't answer. Turning Nina toward the door, he

gave her a gentle push in that direction. "Do as I say. Trust me, Nina. Everything is going to be all right."

She hesitated only a moment, then walked out of the parlor in search of Vada and Tibor.

"The city is about to fall," Jamison said harshly. "If you wish to leave, I'll see you get safely out of Vienna. After that, you'll be on your own."

His wife looked hopeful, but Ivar merely grunted. "What does it matter who governs the country? My life will not change." He spat into the ashes of the hearth. "Take the girl and good riddance."

Jamison turned and found Nina waiting in the hall, her face still pale, her lip beginning to swell. A fresh wave of anger tore through him.

"We're leaving the city," he told her. "You and the children can ride my horse as far as the town house. There's a wagon in the stable. We can take it on from there."

She rested a hand on his arm, her touch gentle, yet as always he sensed her strength. "You are certain of this, Jamie?"

He looked at her, saw the trust and gratitude in her lovely dark eyes, and his heart tightened painfully inside him. "More certain by the minute. Are you ready?"

A smile broke over her face, its radiance hiding the darkening bruise. "I have never been more ready in my life."

Jamison led his small brood out of the apartment, wondering at the step he had just taken. Nina and the children were his responsibility now. What happened to them would rest squarely on his shoulders. The thought should have been frightening. Instead he felt only a sense of relief that they were going with him.

Chapter Twenty-five

Elissa rode next to the children in the back of the wagon Jamison drove out of the city. It was midnight, May 12, when they crossed the river over the pontoon bridge Franzesbrucke. The Danube was in flood stage, a formidable barrier the Austrian rear guard used to its advantage. The soldiers destroyed the bridge as they fled, leaving Bonaparte's conquering forces unable to ford, trapping them on the south side of the Danube.

By the following day, the cannon fire had ceased and Napoleon marched triumphantly into Vienna, setting up his headquarters in the fleeing emperor's palatial Schönbrunn Palace. All the while, the wagon continued its journey, following the British regiment, who marched with the Austrians toward a rendezvous with the archduke's main body of men in the Marchfeld plain southeast of Vienna.

Making camp at the end of a grueling day, Elissa couldn't help a feeling of despair. She was following the army as she had done before. Nina and the children were there and even Vada's scruffy little puppy. Only Adrian was missing. Only Adrian—and the pieces torn from her broken heart.

"You are quiet today," Nina said. They worked well together as they had before, and now stood stirring a steaming cauldron of goulash that they had made for supper.

Elissa flicked Nina a glance. "I guess I haven't felt much like talking." She smiled faintly. "Then again, neither, it seems, have you. Perhaps you were thinking of the major."

Nina sighed. "We have spoken very little since we left my cousin's apartment. I am a burden to him. It was not fair of me to push my troubles onto him. I am happy to be rid of my cousin, but still I should not have gone with him."

Elissa wiped her hands on the apron she wore tied over her skirt. "He wouldn't have insisted if he didn't want to help you."

"At the time, yes, perhaps he did. He felt sorry for me. I should not have taken advantage of his generous nature."

Elissa inwardly smiled. "The major has a lot of good qualities, it seems."

A slight flush tinted Nina's cheeks. "He is a very special man."

"Handsome, too," Elissa added with a knowing smile.

Nina's lips curved up at the corners. "Yes, he is very handsome."

"Things will work out, Nina. You have to believe that."

Her friend began a vigorous stirring of the stew and Elissa said nothing else. She knew Nina was worried, but Elissa believed Jamison had acted out of more than just pity. She could see it in his eyes whenever he looked in the dark-haired girl's direction. But Nina wouldn't believe it. It was up to Jamison to convince her, and he had been so busy they had rarely seen him.

His duties kept him away again that evening. It was long after they had eaten and put the children to bed that he arrived in camp, stepping out of the darkness into the circle of light cast by the low-burning fire. His high black boots were dusty and he smelled of leather and horses, yet his light blue eyes and tall, leanly muscled frame would still turn any woman's head.

"Sorry I missed supper. General Ravenscroft held a staff meeting and it ran longer than we expected." He took a deep whiff of the goulash they had kept warm for him. "I hope there is some of that left."

Nina smiled, the shadowy light making her dark eyes look

even bigger than they were, her lips curving softly. "Of course," she said. "I will get you some."

She heaped a tin plate with the delicious stew and brought him a steaming cup of coffee, then she and Elissa sat across from him while he ate.

"What news, Jamison?" Elissa asked, once he was settled and well into his meal. He looked tired but alert, worried about what was to come, yet ready in some soldierly fashion for the fighting to begin.

"Charles is re-forming his army. The battle isn't long away, perhaps as early as the end of the week. On a more cheerful note, I found your brother. His regiment is camped about a mile away. Perhaps tomorrow I can take you to see him."

Peter! Gratitude trickled through her. She had been so worried about him. "Thank you." She wanted to ask about Adrian, but she didn't dare. She had to forget him. As he was determined to forget her.

When the major finished his meal, Nina cleared his plate, and Elissa noticed the way he watched her, his assessing glance following her every move. He crossed to the place where she washed his plate in a pan of soapy water.

"I know it's late," he said, "but I was hoping we might speak. I'm sure Elissa won't mind keeping an eye on the children."

Elissa smiled. "Not at all."

Nina flicked her a nervous glance but a hint of color rose beneath her olive-skinned cheeks. Accepting the major's outstretched hand, she let him lead her away. Elissa prayed St. Giles's intentions were more honorable than the thoughts she read in the lines of his handsome face.

Nina felt the major's strong hand at her waist as he guided her unerringly through the sea of soldiers, equipment, and tents out to a copse of trees at the perimeter of the encampment. It was dark, but a thin slice of moon lit the way and stars flickered through a scattering of clouds.

He paused beneath the branches of a pine and Nina turned

to face him, uncertain what he might say, worried he would send her away.

Knowing she should insist upon leaving, making her own way without him.

Jamie cleared his throat, as nervous, it seemed, as she. "I've been meaning to talk to you sooner. With the army on the move and Napoleon breathing down our necks . . . well, tonight was the first chance I've had." He studied the toes of his dusty black boots. "And in truth, I wasn't sure exactly what to say. I mean, I promised I would help you, but . . . well, at the time, it didn't seem quite so complicated."

Her heart sank. He was going to send her away. She rested a hand on his forearm, felt the lean muscles bunch beneath her fingers. "It is all right, Jamie, you need not worry for me. You have helped me escape my cousin. I will always be grateful for that. I am a very hard worker. The children and I will be fine on our own. We will find a way."

He took her hand and lifted it to his lips, pressed a soft kiss on her palm that sent little shivers running through her. "You don't understand. I'm not trying to abandon you—I'm trying to ask you to marry me. I'm just not doing a very good job."

Her heart skipped, began a slow, steady thrumming in her ears. His face looked so intense, his eyes so very blue. "You are asking me to wed you?"

He cleared his throat again. "I know we haven't known each other very long, but sometimes people can sense things about one another. From the start, I've admired you. I've seen your strength and your courage. I've watched the way you care for the children. Aside from that, I've developed certain . . . feelings for you, Nina. If you think that someday . . . in the future, I mean . . . you might share some of those same feelings, then I hope that you will say yes."

Nina said nothing. Her throat had closed up, choking off her words. A mist of tears blurred her vision.

Jamison glanced away, his face closing up, his expression suddenly remote. "I didn't do this right, did I? I've said it all wrong and now you won't have me."

Her heart clenched, gently turned over. She reached out and cupped his cheek, her hand trembling as she turned his head, forcing him to look at her. "You do not do this out of pity?"

"Pity?" A look of disbelief flashed in his eyes. "Good God, no. You're beautiful, Nina. You're generous and giving, intelligent and brave. You're everything a man could want in a wife. If you say yes, I'll feel like the luckiest man on earth."

Nina blinked and a tear slid down her cheek. "What about the children? I cannot leave them. They have no one but me."

"They'll have both of us, if you agree."

Nina's heart squeezed. She smiled through her tears. "Then I would be honored to marry you, Jam-i-son." She was in his arms before she knew exactly what had happened, and it felt so good, so incredibly right.

"I have feelings for you, too," she whispered. "I hoped—prayed—that you might care for me just a little."

"Nina . . . sweetheart." He bent his head and she saw that he meant to kiss her. She closed her eyes and his lips settled gently over hers, fitting them perfectly together. It was a soft, tender kiss yet beneath it she sensed his desire for her and it made her feel womanly and warm.

When he coaxed her to part her lips for him, she did so eagerly, allowing him to deepen the kiss, then felt the wildest, sweetest sensations. She kissed him back with all the joy she felt in that moment, all the happiness bursting in her heart.

Jamie groaned. It was he who broke away. Still, he held her against him, wrapped tightly in his arms.

"I've been wanting to do that since the moment I first saw you." Another sweet, hot kiss had her clinging to his neck, her body arching toward the long, hard length of him.

Jamie smiled down at her, his eyes a darker blue than they were before. "You've so much passion—so much life—and soon it will all belong to me." He pressed his cheek to hers and she felt the roughness along his jaw. "You're not like any other woman," he said, "and I am grateful for it. We'll be married as soon as I can arrange it. My enlistment will be up in less than a month—'' He frowned and drew a little away. "You won't mind living in England?"

She shook her head, making her short black hair swirl around her face. "I would love to see England. I have heard it is very beautiful. And even if it is ugly, as long as you are there, it will not matter."

Jamie laughed then, a carefree sound she hadn't heard from him before. "I'm not as rich as the colonel, but neither am I poor. I've a small estate not far from Wolvermont Castle—that's where Adrian lives whenever he is home. I think the children will like it. I hope you will like it as well."

Fresh tears burned her eyes. "I know I will. And I will make you proud of me. I will grow my hair." She ran her fingers through the short, inky strands. "It was long before we left Ratisbon. I cut it to travel with the army."

"You don't have to change a single thing," Jamie said. "I'm proud of you just the way you are."

She smiled up at him. "You have made me very happy, Jamie St. Giles. I promise I will make you happy, too."

Jamie kissed her, then hugged her tightly against him. For the first time Nina understood what it felt like to be in love.

Adrian stood at the crest of a rise overlooking the camp below. For the last three days he had come here, each time swearing he wouldn't return. Yet against his will, he found himself riding to the spot again. It was torture, but he could not seem to stop himself.

He looked down at the maze of tents, horses, and dusty, faded uniforms that should have made it impossible for him to find her, but his eyes picked her out in less than a heartbeat, her gleaming cap of hair shimmering like the tip of a flame against the colorful background.

Though he was still assigned to General Klammer's regiment and camped some distance away, Jamie had sought him out and told him of their arrival. At first he had cursed her, stubborn little fool that she was, for not going to Baden as he had commanded. Then he realized he no longer had the power to demand anything of her. He had given up that right the day he had left her in Vienna.

He watched her working below, bent over a washboard scrubbing clothes, though it was hard to make out her movements so far away. He was worried about her, fearful of what might happen once the army went into battle. It was torture to see her and yet he could not make himself walk away. He wanted to go to her. He wanted to hold her, touch her. He wanted to make love to her for hours on end.

Days ago, his anger at their parting had faded. Perhaps he was never really angry at all. He had wanted to leave her, and she had given him cause. But even as he'd ridden away, he couldn't block the sight of her tears or shake her taunting words.

You're a coward, Colonel Kingsland. You think you're simply leaving but in truth you're running away.

The words had filtered through his mind a dozen times, stabbing into his heart, gnawing at his insides. In truth he *was* a coward. He couldn't lie to himself any longer. He was in love with Elissa Tauber and he had never been more frightened in his life. He knew the sort of pain loving someone could bring. He had worked his whole life to insulate himself from that kind of emotion. And yet here he was, standing on a hill like a lovesick fool, aching for a glimpse of her.

A noise behind him pulled him from his thoughts. Jamie threw a long leg over his tall black gelding and dismounted.

"There you are—I've been looking all over. One of the men said he saw you riding in this direction." Jamie strode toward him, a smile on his face. It faded as he glanced down at the scene below and realized why Adrian had come up to the knoll.

He shook his head. "Sweet Christ, man, if you care for the woman so damned much, why don't you do something about it?"

Adrian scoffed. "I am doing something. I'm staying away from her. That is the only thing I can do."

"It isn't the only thing. Don't you see? You have a choice here, Adrian. You can leave the army and make a life for yourself. You can have a home, a family—the things you've always wanted.''

"That isn't what I want—not anymore."

Jamie looked down to the distant spot where Elissa worked over a pile of laundry. "She's in love with you, you know. You hurt her very badly."

Adrian's hand shook where it rested against his thigh. "She'll get over it. In time she'll find someone else."

"What about you, Ace? How fast will you get over it?"

He grunted. "Fast enough. As soon as I get the chance, I'll find another woman. I'll plant myself between her legs and ride her till I forget Elissa Tauber ever existed."

Jamie said nothing, just stared at him with a trace of pity. It angered him to see that look on his best friend's face.

"I presume there was something you wanted."

Jamie straightened, drawing himself up so that he was nearly as tall as Adrian. "I came up here to tell you I'm getting married."

"Married!" The word fell between them like a tree toppling to earth. "Who the hell are you going to marry?"

"I'm marrying Nina Petralo. She and the children need me." His shoulders went even straighter. "And the truth is, I need her."

Adrian could scarcely believe his ears. "You're leaving the army? You've devoted your life to the service. I thought you were happy."

"I was for a while. In the last few years, I've felt as if something were missing. Now I know what it was."

Adrian didn't reply. The words hit too close to home.

Jamie's eyes locked with his. "We both have choices, Adrian. I've made mine and I'm damned glad I did. I'm marrying Nina Petralo. I just hope I live to see it done."

Adrian knew what he meant. Ravenscroft's regiment wouldn't officially be ordered into battle. They were there in a support position, but there wasn't a doubt in any man's mind they'd get more than their share of the fighting. The battle would be long and fierce and anything could happen.

"Nina is a lovely girl," Adrian finally said, clamping a

hand on Jamie's shoulder. "Congratulations, my friend. I wish you both the greatest happiness."

Jamie smiled. "Thank you. In the meantime, if anything should happen—"

"It won't." Adrian cut off the words he didn't want to hear. "But if by some remote chance it did, your lady would be safe in my care."

Jamie nodded. "As yours would be in mine."

Neither said anything more and the silence grew between them.

"Any progress on the Falcon?" Jamie asked, thankfully changing the subject.

Adrian sighed. "He seems to have gone to ground. The archduke's put a tight lid on communications. Perhaps the man has nothing new to report. Or simply being on the move has cut into his effectiveness."

"Any idea who was behind the shooting?"

"Not the foggiest. I've been prowling about asking a number of questions. No doubt the man was shooting at me, but I'm still damned glad Elissa is with you and for the most part out of danger."

Jamie stared off toward the camp, at the hustle and bustle of more than a hundred thousand men, their horses, wagons, and supplies. "You think he'll try it again?"

Adrian followed his gaze, wishing he could see through the throng to the man who had nearly killed Elissa. A shiver passed through him at the image of her, pale and still in the grass, a scarlet stain spreading from her temple.

"I don't think he'll chance it—not until the fighting starts. Then he'll have the perfect opportunity. A stray bullet would go unremarked, even if it happened to kill a British colonel."

"The army's gearing up. Hiller's arrived. It won't be long before we're heading into battle."

"No, and with Hiller here, that means Steigler has also arrived. The man could still pose a threat to Elissa. Fortunately, he's camped some distance away. Odds are, he'll be too damned busy to think of anything besides the war."

Jamie nodded, glanced across the rolling Marchfeld plain

stretching toward the Danube. "Perhaps we should move the women and children to a safer position."

A muscle bunched in Adrian's jaw. He had been thinking that same thing. "The trouble is, we aren't exactly sure where *safe* really is. We can't send them back to Vienna. We can't get them to Baden, and there is no one to look after them anywhere else."

"Best then just to move them when the time comes."

Adrian nodded. "I suppose that is all we can do."

Jamie clapped him on the back. "In the meantime, I'll keep an eye on them. Take care of yourself, Ace."

Adrian watched his best friend walk back to camp. First Elissa. Now Jamie. Even in boarding school, he had never felt more alone.

Elissa sat at a small writing desk Jamison had provided, penning the letter she was determined to send. A British courier was being dispatched to London and Jamison had secured a place in the pouch for a letter to her mother as well as the correspondence she now scripted—a message to the Duke of Sheffield.

Elissa had pondered long and hard over the decision to write him. Adrian had entrusted her with his secret and she didn't take that responsibility lightly. On the other hand, she loved Adrian Kingsland, whatever his feelings for her. She wanted to give him the one thing she knew he desired above all else—the love of family he had never had. Elissa believed she might have the power to give it to him.

She glanced down at the words she had written on the paper.

Your Grace,

I realize it has been some time since last we occasioned to meet. I impose upon your friendship with my father in writing this letter and trust that you will read it in the spirit it was written, the hope that good will come for both of the parties involved.

Though I realize this may come as a shock, I have reason

*to believe that you have fathered a child of which you are
unaware. You will, I believe, recall your brief association
with the child's mother, Madeline Kingsland, a little over
thirty years ago. The result of that liaison was a son—Adrian
Kingsland, the current Baron Wolvermont.*

*Your son is a colonel in His Majesty's Army, a war hero
of some renown, one of the bravest, finest men I have ever
known. If you have met Adrian in the past, perhaps you will
recall a certain similarity in your features. In fact, your son
is gifted with your same dark hair and magnificent green
eyes. He stands even taller than you, and is of your same
broad-shouldered build.*

*Adrian is unaware that I write this letter and should you
decide you do not wish to pursue your relationship with him,
I pray that you will not embarrass him by mentioning this
correspondence. The colonel does not believe you would wish
to learn of his existence. His mother and her husband treated
him with little care, and Adrian is not convinced that a father
would harbor any special feelings for a son of his own blood.*

*I send you this letter with the highest hopes that you will
wish to meet your son. I pray you will forgive my interference
in such a private matter and please rest assured that should
I receive no reply, no word of this matter will ever surface
again.*

*I close with the hope that this letter finds you in good
health and that it will bring you a measure of joy as it was
intended.*

> *Most sincere regards,*
> *Lady Elissa Tauber*

Elissa reread the letter, dusted the sand shaker over it, then
folded it, and carefully sealed it with several drops of wax.
A few minutes later, Jamison picked it up, along with the
missive to her mother, and the letter was on its way to England.

She prayed she had done the right thing. It was hard to
know for sure, but the future was so nebulous, life itself so

precious and uncertain, she felt she'd had no other choice.

Taking a steadying breath, she set the lap desk aside and stood up. As soon as Jamison returned he would take her to see her brother. Worry for Peter, Adrian, and Jamison in the upcoming battle hovered at the edge of her mind. She thought of Sheffield one last time, praying he would get the letter. She wondered, when he read it, what look she might see on his face.

Chapter Twenty-six

The fighting erupted on the morning of May 20. Napoleon crossed to Lobau Island, four miles southeast of the city, improvised a pontoon bridge the following day, crossed the river, and fanned out over the Marchfeld, attacking the archduke's advance guard and capturing the two small villages of Aspern and Essling.

Jamison had moved Elissa, Nina, and the children to safety behind the lines, but as the morning wore on and news of the terrible casualties began pouring in, she and Nina left the children with one of the older women and made their way back to the hospital tent.

Cannon fire rumbled in the distance. Musket shots rose and fell in frightening crescendos, and a pall of black smoke hung over the late morning sky. As she crested a rise above the grassy field set aside for the wounded, Elissa paused, unable for a moment to comprehend the grisly scene spread out before her. Wounded men, their once-bright uniforms bathed in blood, stretched as far as the eye could see. The sobs of the injured mingled with the cries of agony erupting from the surgeons' tent. Stacked outside against the canvas, a pile of severed limbs climbed nearly as high as the tent post. Flies had begun to gather, and the smell of putrid flesh rose on the wind.

"Dear sweet God." Staring at the sea of injured men, the

bile rose up in Elissa's throat. Her chest squeezed so hard she could hardly breathe. Nina reached out and gripped her hand, and Elissa could feel her trembling.

"I hoped never to see such a sight again. I do not understand why there must be such a thing as war."

"There must be hundreds of them . . . thousands. Dear God, it looks like a scene from hell."

"For those poor men, it is."

Elissa took a steadying breath and slowly released it, forcing her nausea down, fighting the light-headedness that threatened to make her swoon.

"We have to help them," she said, but now her fear had begun to grow. Was Adrian among those lying in the field? Were Jamison or Peter injured or dying out there?

As she started toward the row of tents on unsteady legs, she couldn't help thinking of the battle the men had been fighting, couldn't help wondering if the Falcon had played some part in it. For days she had pushed thoughts of Becker away, buried them behind her worry about the war and her grief for Adrian. Though her failure to catch the traitor gnawed at her conscience, she knew Adrian had not given up, and if anyone could stop him, she believed that her colonel could.

Elissa glanced down at the men she passed, heard their pitiful moans, and the inside of her mouth went dry. The voices of the surgeons reached her from inside the tent. She heard the rasp of saws tearing through flesh and bone, heard a terrible piercing scream, and another wave of nausea ripped through her.

"I—I don't know if I can do this."

Nina stopped and turned. In the harsh sunlight, her smooth, dark features looked taut and grim. A thin line hardened the soft curve of her lips. "The men must fight. We must help them. There is no other choice."

Elissa looked at the men lying helpless on the ground. Some of them were old, some young, some dark-skinned and some fair. All of them were in pain and in desperate need of care. She sucked in a deep breath and nodded. "You're right, of course. Let's go."

Fortunately, just outside the tent, one of the orderlies, a thin young man with hollow cheeks and a tired expression, stopped them before they could enter.

"Thank you for coming," he said. "We need all the help we can get. But perhaps it would be best if you worked out here. Can you help dress the wounded?"

Elissa felt a wave of relief. Anything but the surgery tent. "Yes, of course."

From that moment on, the hours ran together. The orderly set them to work cleansing wounds and applying dressings. They carried water and bandages, administered laudanum to help ease the pain, bathed foreheads to try and control the fever, all the while doing their best to lift the spirits of the injured men.

It was a grueling, endless task. By the time dusk had fallen, Elissa's skirts were stained with blood, her hair and clothes damp with perspiration, her back aching with fatigue. Her arms were so tired she could barely lift them, yet the endless string of casualties continued rolling in.

Jamison arrived just before midnight, his scarlet tunic dirty and torn, the hilt of his sword darkened with dense dried blood.

Standing at her side, Nina saw him, turned, and ran in his direction. Jamison enveloped her in his arms, holding her tightly while she tried not to cry. She had hidden her worry all day, just as Elissa had. Now it spilled over into droplets on her cheeks.

"It's all right, love," Jamison said softly. "I'm fine. I heard that you were here. I came to see how you fared." He glanced at Elissa, saw the fatigue that no amount of effort could disguise. "The doctors say the two of you have been here since this morning. You need to get some sleep. You won't do anyone any good if you're too tired to stay on your feet. I'll take you back and—"

"Not yet." Elissa surveyed the endless sea of men. "We can't leave yet."

"No, we must stay," Nina agreed. "There are so many men, and all of them are hurting. We will sleep for a few hours here."

He read their determined expressions and a look of resignation settled into his battle-weary features. "All right, but try to get at least a couple of hours of rest." He leaned over and brushed a kiss on Nina's lips. "I'm proud of you." He smiled at Elissa. "Both of you."

Elissa reached out and caught his arm. "What of Adrian, Major? We heard the British had been engaged. Is Adrian all right?"

"We went in this afternoon with Liechtenstein's cavalry. The fighting was heavy but our casualties were light. Adrian is fine. I saw him less than an hour ago." His eyes came to rest on her face. They were filled with sympathy and concern. "He asked about you. He wasn't too happy to discover you are here, working in the infirmary. He worries you are too close to the action. If something were to go wrong—"

"He has to fight. I must do whatever I can to help."

He studied her for several long moments, then nodded. "I'll tell him. I think he'll understand." Jamison turned once more to Nina, and Elissa left the two of them alone.

She only wished Adrian had come, wished she could see him one more time. She would tell him she was sorry for the harsh words she had spoken in Vienna, that she hoped at least they could be friends. She would tell him again that she loved him.

But Adrian hadn't come and there were wounded men to attend. Working the kinks from her aching neck and shoulders, her legs shaking with each exhausted step, Elissa prayed that he would be safe and went back to her grueling work.

A cannonball screamed overhead and plowed into the earth behind him, raining dirt into the air, pelting him with splinters and sharp bits of gravel. Smoke burned his eyes, nearly blinding him, yet Adrian pressed on, riding at the head of his men, grim-faced, his shoulders set with determination. Minotaur pounded the earth next to Jamie's tall black gelding, the British regiment having formed with the Austrians into two massive blocks of four thousand horsemen.

Saber drawn, Adrian leaned over Minotaur's neck, urging the stallion faster, carrying him farther into the wall of charging soldiers. Musketfire crackled and a shot tore through his sleeve, leaving a small round hole but missing flesh and bone.

Adrian barely noticed. A calm had settled in as it always did in battle; his mind sharply focused, burning with single-minded purpose—to achieve his objective and defeat the enemy. He had known this same calm at least a hundred times, yet this time it felt somehow different, the numbness more intense and vaguely disturbing.

The thunder of hoofbeats grew stronger. A Frenchman appeared on his left and Adrian brought his saber arching down, taking the man in the chest, the soldier's pistol sailing into the air, dropping to the ground a few feet away, burying itself in the dusty earth thrown up by the blast of a cannon. Adrian watched it happen as if from afar, seeing himself in the fray, yet feeling as if the man in scarlet wielding the heavy sword was really someone else.

It was dangerous, he knew, this distancing of himself. An instant of carelessness, a single moment of allowing his thoughts to wander and he would be dead.

"Behind you!" Jamie shouted.

Adrian whirled the stallion, pulled his pistol and fired with the same precision he had used a thousand times. The Frenchman fell beneath a dozen trampling hooves, and Adrian continued his savage attack, wielding his bloody saber with deadly force.

For two grisly hours, the battle raged unchecked, men on each side falling like trees blown down in a storm. Then the tide began to turn. The French line began to fall back, and little by little, the Austrians began to gain the advantage.

Adrian's unit was ordered to regroup and he pulled back with his men, reining Minotaur to a halt at the top of a low, sloping hill. At seven o'clock that morning, the French had attacked, led by Marshal Bessières, advancing in dense battalion columns. The Austrians had fought with every ounce of their will and as Adrian looked out on the bloody field, it appeared they might prevail.

But the cost of victory was immense. In the past two days, twenty thousand Austrian soldiers had been killed or wounded, matched by nearly twenty thousand French.

Staring out at the ground littered with bloody corpses, Adrian clamped his jaw, a weariness washing through him that had nothing to do with the fighting. By the time he had left the blood-soaked killing field and ridden to the ridge above the infirmary, he knew something inside him had changed—that he'd had his fill of war and of fighting, that he was sick unto death of blood and gore, of good men maimed and dying.

He was tired of a life of austerity and loneliness. He had served his country long and well, and now he simply wanted to go home.

It was a surprising discovery and yet somehow it was not. Deep inside, perhaps it was the thing he had yearned for all along. Perhaps it was what Elissa had seen in his eyes that he himself could not discern.

He thought of her now and an ache rose up. He was in love with her, and now he wanted to tell her, as he should have done before. He wanted to return with her to Wolvermont, to make it the home it had never really been. He wanted to fill it with children. He wanted to hear them call him Papa, wanted to share his life with a woman who loved him, perhaps one tenth as much as he loved her.

He looked down the hill to where his lovely blond angel bent over an injured soldier, talking to him softly, reaching out to hold his hand. He saw the way the light fell onto her golden hair, the way the slight breeze lifted it away from her cheeks, and his chest went tight with longing. He thought that he had never seen a more beautiful sight than her dirty, powder-smudged face, her weary smile, and tired, heavy-lidded eyes.

For long moments, he simply watched her, trying to work up his courage, knowing he had wronged her, groping for just the right words. He wanted to tell her she'd been right about him, that he *had* been a coward, but he wasn't a coward anymore.

He was no longer afraid of loving. Sometime during the past two days, he had found the courage he needed to face a far greater enemy than the one he had encountered on the field of battle. He only feared that he might have waited too long, that he might not be able to convince her, that she might not forgive him for hurting her so badly.

He nudged the big horse forward, his heart hammering harder than it ever had during the fighting. What would she say? What could he possibly say to her to make up for all the pain he had caused?

The sound of a voice shouting from behind drew his hand up short on the rein.

"Colonel Kingsland!" Lieutenant Beasley, an officer of his regiment, rode forward. "I'm sorry, sir, but General Ravenscroft sent me to find you. He says it is urgent."

Adrian glanced wistfully over his shoulder to the woman still working over the injured man. Damned, but it seemed something always came between them. He gave up a weary sigh, regret forming a hard knot in his belly. "All right, Lieutenant. Lead the way."

News filtered back to the infirmary. The tiny villages of Aspern and Essling alongside the Danube were taken and retaken ten times during the bitter fighting. But by the evening of May 22, it was clear the Austrians had won. Through it all, Elissa worked ceaselessly, determined to do what little she could to help them.

Pressing a damp cloth against a wounded soldier's forehead, she shoved back a strand of her unkempt, perspiration-damp hair, and drew in a ragged, weary breath. Every bone in her body ached, every muscle, every joint, and still the injured kept coming. She glanced down at the feverish man she tended, saw that his eyes had opened and he was watching her. There was a strange look on his face.

"Am I . . . am I dead?"

She gave him a halfhearted smile. "No, you're not dead."

"Then you aren't an angel?" ·

Hardly that, Elissa thought. She shook her head. "Just a woman who is trying to help. You've been wounded in the shoulder, but the ball passed all the way through. You've a fever, but chances are very good you'll be all right."

His dry lips curved into a weak, grateful smile. "Thank you."

She wrung out the cloth and pressed it against his forehead. "Rest now. I'll be back to check on you later." The soldier's eyes slid closed and he drifted once more into sleep. A few feet away, a moan rose up, drawing her attention to a man in the group of wounded that had just been brought in. She saw that he was lifting a hand in her direction, his fingers shaking as he reached out, begging her to help him.

Elissa hauled herself upright, forced her weary legs to move in his direction. When she reached his side, she saw that he was wounded in the chest, blood spreading over his coat. Reaching down, she caught his groping hand.

"It's all right. We're going to help you." He was a young man, blond and fair, who somehow reminded her of Peter. She said a small prayer that God would keep her brother safe and tried to force a smile to her face. "I know that you are hurting. I'll get one of the orderlies here as quickly as I can." She turned to leave, but he wouldn't let go of her hand, his hold tightening almost painfully.

"No . . . please . . . you must . . . listen. You must . . . help me."

She glanced down at the wound in his chest, saw that it had started to bleed again, and began to unbutton his uniform jacket. Again he stayed her hand.

"No . . . time," he whispered, coughing until his face went pale. When the coughing fit subsided, he reached a shaky hand into the pocket of his coat. "You must take this . . . see that it gets to where it should go."

"But I don't—" He pressed a bloodstained scrap of paper into her hand, a wax-sealed message, she saw, and noticed the seal had been broken. She unfolded the paper, skimmed the words, and a sliver of ice ran down her spine. In the lower right-hand corner of the page was the blue-inked image of a bird. The etched seal of the Falcon.

The soldier tugged her closer. "There is a man . . . near the granary . . . at Essling. I was ordered to deliver the message . . . to him."

Anger jolted through her. More lives lost. More treachery. "Who gave you this? Who ordered you to carry this letter?"

The man dragged in a raspy, pain-filled breath of air. "Major . . . Becker. Tenth . . . Cuirassiers. They are camped . . . not far from here. The major said it was . . . urgent."

Her blood pumped faster, forcing the anger into her limbs. *Urgent.* Elissa didn't doubt it. The French were losing. The Falcon would do anything in his power to prevent that from happening. Turning away from the soldier, she scanned the message once more.

Hold your position—do not pull back. Hiller's hands are tied. Has been ordered not to pursue. Now is the time to attack.

Dear sweet God. Elissa knew little of battle, but it was obvious this was crucial information. The tide could yet be turned if the note fell into enemy hands.

"Do you know what is in this message?" she asked.

He shook his head. "But it must be . . . very important."

She brushed back the young soldier's hair. "I'll see this gets to where it will do the most good," she promised, believing the man had been duped, just like everyone else.

He nodded and his grip on her hand relaxed. Elissa motioned for an orderly, instructing him to do everything in his power to keep the man alive. At last they had a witness. Combined with the note, it was the proof they had needed so badly.

Her breathing came fast. Elissa's eyes searched the camp, looking for someone who might help her. *God's blood, if only Adrian were here!* But he wasn't, of course. According to Jamison, he was commanding his regiment and she had no idea where they were. Orderlies and surgeons would do her no good. Night had begun to fall, blanketing the field in dark hues of gray and blue. Time was of the essence.

Elissa started walking, her objective suddenly clear. General Klammer was Becker's commanding officer. With the note in her hand and the wounded soldier to confirm her accusations, Klammer would have to listen. The general could have Becker arrested and held until she could get to Adrian or even the archduke himself.

"What is wrong?" Nina strode up beside her, her hair mussed, her clothes dirty, as ragged and unkempt as she. "Where do you go in such a hurry?"

"I have to find General Klammer. I've finally got proof that Becker is the traitor we've been looking for."

"If that is so, you must tell the colonel."

Elissa sighed. "I only wish he were here." She stopped and turned, gripping Nina's shoulder. "If Jamison stops by, ask him to find Adrian. Tell him we were right about Becker. Tell him I've taken the proof to Klammer. He'll know what to do from there."

Nina nodded, a worried look on her face. Elissa waved a quick goodbye and hurried away, her blood pumping with determination. She stopped only long enough to ask directions to Klammer's campsite, which wasn't that far, the soldiers said. The general was headquartered in a farmhouse he had commandeered just over the rise and down the hill.

In the glowing light of the campfires springing up across the field, Elissa made her way toward the small stone building in the distance. All the way there, her gaze searched for Becker, but she didn't see him. She hoped he hadn't decided it was time to run and gone over to the enemy camp.

Finally, she reached the farmhouse. Pausing at the heavy oak-planked door, she spoke hastily to one of the soldiers standing guard out front, and a few minutes later, he ushered her into the thick-walled interior.

General Klammer sat behind a makeshift desk fashioned of upended ammunition boxes, his gray hair gleaming in the light of the fire in the small stone hearth. He wasn't that tall, but he was imposing, with an iron jaw and hard dark blue eyes.

"What can I do for you, young woman?" he asked, leaning toward her over the desk. "Corporal Deitrich says you need to see me. Apparently you have convinced him the matter is urgent."

She walked toward him, the paper outstretched in her hand. "It is, General Klammer. It's a matter of national security."

The general turned to the soldier. "Leave us," he commanded. Corporal Deitrich backed through the door, closing it securely behind him. "Go on," the general said.

"I'm not certain how much you've been told, General Klammer, but for nearly a year—perhaps longer—a man has been passing secrets to the enemy. A few weeks back, I traveled with the army accompanied by a British colonel named Kingsland. I believe you know him."

His jaw seemed to harden. He nodded. "The colonel was assigned to me in an observatory position. He only just recently returned to his regiment."

"That is correct, but his assignment was actually far more important. In truth, he was here to unmask a traitor—a man who calls himself the Falcon." She handed him the crumpled, bloodstained message. "We believed it was an officer in your command, your personal aide in fact—Major Josef Becker."

His mouth curved faintly. "And now you believe you have proof." He looked down at the message on his desk.

"That note came from Becker. It proves he is the man we've been seeking."

"Does it?" A gray brow arched. "I find that quite astonishing." He turned and shouted toward the door. "Corporal Deitrich!"

The door swung instantly open. "Yes, sir?"

"Place this woman under arrest. Take her to the storeroom and see she is securely locked in."

"What!"

The corporal stepped forward and an instant later a pistol pressed into her ribs. A second armed soldier appeared in the doorway.

"This woman has been carrying secrets to the enemy," Klammer said. "I want her guarded round the clock. At dawn tomorrow, she will be executed for treason."

Elissa's heart slammed hard, began to thunder in her ears. "Are you insane! I'm no traitor! Becker is the traitor!"

"Take her away."

"But this is ridiculous! I haven't done anything wrong!"

The pistol pressed harder. "You will please come with me." The corporal's voice burned with accusation. After two bloody days of fighting, there was little sympathy for a woman believed to be an enemy spy.

She stared hard at the general, beginning to comprehend. "It's both of you, isn't it? You're in this together. God, I should have known."

The general merely smiled and the corporal shoved her toward the door. Elissa stumbled through the opening and out into the night. They marched her the short distance to a small stone storehouse, opened the door and pushed her in. In the darkness, her foot connected with a heavy sack of grain and she fell, sprawling on the hard-packed floor.

Her breath came harshly, burning inside her chest. Her heart thumped a ragged tattoo. Still dazed by the turn of events, she glanced around the storeroom, trying to get her bearings. One wall was lined with harness, the other with sacks of grain. There were no windows. The only light in the room filtered in through the gaps between the thick rock walls and the heavy wooden roof, barely enough to see.

Sweet God, of all the scenarios she might have imagined this was not one of them. Klammer *and* Becker. Both of them traitors. Why hadn't she been able to see? Then again, she thought, sitting down on a sack of grain, the archduke himself had been taken in. He had been certain that Klammer was one of his most loyal officers. It was only at Adrian's insistence that the man had been kept unaware of their mission.

Or perhaps he hadn't been. Perhaps Klammer had ordered the attempt on Adrian's life. A cold chill slid through her. Undoubtedly that was so. And she had left word for Adrian to follow. Even now he might be on his way. He wouldn't be prepared. He would be as unsuspecting as she. Dear Lord, he might be killed!

Elissa stood up in the small, confining room, her fists clenched, her stomach tied in knots. She wished she could see through the walls, wished there was some way to warn Adrian. Perhaps he wouldn't come. Perhaps he wouldn't get the message.

If he didn't, she was certain to die in the morning.

Perhaps he would bring help, she thought wildly. Yes . . . she had to hope for that. It was the only chance either of them had to escape the fate Klammer had in store for them. Elissa knelt on the earthen floor and began to pray.

Adrian swung up on Minotaur's back and reined the animal away from the infirmary. He had come to find Elissa, to tell her that he loved her and beg her to forgive him. He had come to ask her to marry him. Instead he'd found Nina and now icy fear pumped through his veins.

She had gone after Becker. Good Christ, surely she wouldn't confront the man on her own! Surely she would go to Klammer or one of his top-ranking officers. But even that might be dangerous. There was no way to be certain exactly who was involved.

Adrian rode hard toward Klammer's headquarters, then swung down in a shower of dust. Pausing for a moment to speak to one of the guards, he followed the man inside the farmhouse. He spotted Klammer behind his makeshift desk, sorting through a stack of papers. The man rose to his feet with a smug smile on his face—and Josef Becker stood beside him.

A warning bell went off, but his concern for Elissa over-rode it. "I'm looking for a woman. Her name is Elissa Tauber. Where is she?" A stirring erupted behind him. He sensed the tall, lean corporal's presence then the sound of something solid cut the air. With a savage oath, he turned to block the blow, but he was an instant too late. A sharp pain burst inside his head, driving him to his knees, making the room spin crazily. Fearing for Elissa, cursing himself for a fool, he pitched forward onto the floor.

He was beginning to stir by the time they dragged him into the storeroom, though his mind was still fuzzy and his head pounded against his skull with brutal force. They released his arms and shoved him inside, then backed out and slammed the door, sliding a thick length of wood through the heavy iron latch to secure it.

He groaned as he swayed to his feet.

"Adrian . . . !" Across the storeroom, Elissa stood not far away, her feet splayed, a length of rotten wood gripped in her white-knuckled hands. It dropped limply from her fingers as she started toward him, worry lines carved into her face. She had almost reached him, when suddenly she paused, a strained tension rising between them. "Are you . . . are you all right?"

For days he had watched her, thought of her even in the midst of battle, ached to speak his heart to her. Now that she stood in front of him, his mind had gone completely blank.

"You're bleeding," she whispered, reaching toward the streak of blood at the side of his face that she could see in a slice of moonlight. "You're injured."

Still he did not answer. Instead he drank in the sight of her, standing so close he could lift his hand and touch her, wanting to, more than he had ever wanted anything in his life.

"Adrian?"

"I've missed you," he said, blurting the words out like a fool, unable to stop himself from saying them, praying she would know how much he meant them. "I've missed you so damned much."

She was in his arms in a heartbeat, clinging to his neck, pressing her cheek against his shoulder, her slender body shaking. "I love you," she whispered. "It doesn't matter if I can't be with you. It doesn't matter what happens. I love you. I love you so much it hurts."

Something burned at the back of his eyes. Adrian blinked and slid his hands into her hair, cradling her against his chest.

"I came to the infirmary to find you. I wanted to tell you how sorry I was that I hurt you. I wanted to say that you were right—I *was* a coward. But I'm not afraid anymore. I love you, Elissa. I think I have for a very long time."

She looked up at him and tears rolled down her cheeks. "Adrian . . ."

His eyes slid closed. Emotion rippled through him. "Elissa . . . love." Bending his head, he kissed her with all the feelings he had buried for so long. Enfolding her in his arms, he held her as he had wanted to do since the instant he had left her in Vienna. For sweetly tender moments, he just stood there, watching the moonlight slanting down on her golden hair, feeling the warmth of her body pressed to his.

He kissed the top of her head, wishing they were somewhere else, somewhere safe and warm where he could make love to her as he had dreamed each night since she had been gone. Instead they were imprisoned, their future as grim as the one he had faced without her.

Several more moments ticked past. Elissa shifted in his arms, tilting her head back to look into his face. "I was afraid you would come. I was just as afraid you wouldn't."

"I played right into Klammer's hands. I was just so worried I couldn't seem to think."

Elissa rested her head on his chest. "They're going to kill us," she said softly.

Adrian glanced around their stone-walled prison, measuring how impregnable it was. A curse rumbled up from his throat. "All the time it was Klammer. God, I was such a bloody fool."

Elissa reached up and cupped his cheek. "We were both of us fools. We should have known. Somehow we should have suspected Becker wasn't in it alone. If he hadn't behaved so strangely, sneaking off all the time the way he did—"

"He wasn't passing secrets—that much I finally discovered. He was hoping to meet someone of his similar . . . persuasion."

Elissa frowned. "Persuasion? I don't know what you mean."

Adrian sighed, his hand coming up to test the lump at the side of his head. He winced and drew his fingers away, noting a faint trace of blood. "Becker is one of those men who enjoys the favors of other men. He is very discreet about it. That was why he kept riding off on his own."

A flush stole into Elissa's cheeks as she realized what he was saying. "You are telling me that Karl was mistaken, that Becker is not involved?"

Adrian sighed. "Klammer is certainly the Falcon, but—"

"But the note I found was sent by Becker, which means both of them must be involved."

"Apparently so."

"What are we going to do?"

Nothing for the moment, he thought. There was little they could do until someone opened the storeroom door. Even then, they wouldn't stand much of a chance. He searched the room, nonetheless, found nothing but the rotten length of wood Elissa had been holding, the sacks of grain, and a brittle leather harness.

"Nina is bound to tell Jamison," Elissa said as he searched. "When neither of us returns to camp—"

"Jamie's with Ravenscroft. Odds are he'll be busy until at least tomorrow afternoon."

In the moonlight streaming in, he saw her chin go up. "Surely they can't just shoot us!"

He didn't want to tell her the truth—that there was every likelihood that was exactly what Klammer would do. That forty thousand men had been killed in the past two days— two more casualties would hardly make a difference. In war, errors were made, men mistakenly killed. He and Elissa could easily be listed among them.

"It's nearly midnight," he said instead. "You've labored for days—you must be exhausted." He pulled down a couple of sacks of grain to use as cushions, eased her down beside him and turned her head into his shoulder. "There is nothing we can do for the present. Why don't you get some sleep?"

"I don't want to sleep."

"But you need to rest. You've been working night and day."

She looked at him a moment, surprised, it seemed, to discover he had been following her movements. "I'm not a fool, Adrian. I know the odds aren't good we'll get out of this alive. If I've only one night left on earth, I don't want to spend it sleeping. I want to be with you."

His chest went tight. His hand shook as he brushed back fine gold hair from her temple. Damned but he wished there was something he could do! "We mustn't give up. Anything could happen between now and dawn."

Elissa faintly nodded, both of them recognizing the lie, each of them determined to believe it. "Would you kiss me, Adrian? I've imagined it so many times."

His heart twisted, seemed to come apart. Cupping her face in his hands, he settled his mouth over hers, absorbing the taste of her, the warm, sweet softness of her lips. He felt her fingers on the buttons of his tunic. The fabric parted, and her slim hands slipped inside. She pulled his shirttail from his breeches, slid her fingers over his bare skin, and Adrian heard himself groan.

"Make love to me—please?"

"Elissa . . . love . . . there is nothing I want more, but taking you here—"

"I need you, Adrian. I want to feel you inside me one last time."

An ache swelled in his throat. Surely this wouldn't be the last. Surely God wouldn't be so cruel as to finally give him a woman to love and then take her from him.

But perhaps that was the final irony. He had found what he had been seeking all these years, and now it was too late.

"Adrian?"

"I love you," he whispered, taking her mouth again, his hands seeking her breasts, baring them, his fingers stroking the diamond-hard tips. He worked the buttons on his breeches then began to shove up her skirts. Her skin felt sleek and smooth. He stroked her gently, found her moist and ready for him. He lifted her astride him, easing her onto his hardness, letting her slender body adjust to his heavy size and shape. Holding her firmly in place, he began to move inside her, long deep thrusts that made his blood run hot and fire scorch through his veins. He heard her soft whimpers, felt her body begin to spasm around him, felt his own driving need, but held himself back.

For long, sweet moments, he remained locked inside her, desperate to make her his in these last, final hours as he had never been able to before.

"You're mine," he whispered. "You always have been. No matter what happens, you always will be."

"I love you," she whispered and the words, and the soft way she said them, sent him into a towering climax. Minutes later she still clung to him as he clung to her. In those moments he vowed that somehow he would save her. His own life didn't matter. Elissa was all-important. Only Elissa. Only the woman he loved.

Chapter *T*wenty-seven

Elissa awakened to the sound of voices. Nestled in Adrian's arms, she felt his body go rigid as he heard them, too. Quickly he came to his feet, drawing her up with him. His gaze scanned the thick stone walls, prowling the meager contents of the storeroom, searching as he had done several times last night for anything that might serve as a weapon. His final effort had uncovered a worn ax handle, the blade long missing, half buried in the hard-packed earthen floor.

The voices grew louder.

"Get behind me," he commanded, pulling her protectively out of the way.

Her heart slammed hard. Fear jabbed icy needles into her stomach. Adrian gripped the heavy length of wood worn smooth by years of use and braced his feet apart, the muscles in his forearms straining with tension. The moment the door swung open, he slammed his makeshift weapon into the ribs of the corporal who had dragged him into the storeroom. The soldier screamed in pain and doubled over, gasping for air and clutching his ribs.

A second man appeared and Elissa sucked in a breath as Adrian shoved the long handle deep in the man's flat belly, then brought it crashing upward, into the soldier's chin. The corporal tumbled backward over a sack of grain.

"Let's go!" Adrian grabbed Elissa's hand and jerked her

forward, out the door and into the early predawn light.

"Very good, Colonel Kingsland. I should have known you wouldn't go down without a fight."

Adrian stopped dead still and Elissa froze at the sight of the dozen uniformed soldiers surrounding them, bayonets fixed, muskets cocked and ready to fire. General Klammer stood beside them.

"Drop your weapon, Colonel," the general commanded. "Unless you wish the lady's life to end even earlier than I had planned."

The ax handle shook with the fury burning in Adrian's eyes. "Let the woman go. You have the letter. She no longer has proof of who you are. Even if she were to speak out, no one would believe her."

The general laughed, a cruel, self-satisfied sound. "The woman is a spy, just as you are, Colonel Kingsland. Spies are dealt with swiftly in the midst of war. You are fortunate to have lived out the night. Now drop your weapon—such as it is—before I am forced to shoot you both right here."

The muscles quivered in Adrian's arms. Clenching his jaw, he let the ax handle fall from his hands.

Elissa spun to face the group of soldiers surrounding them. "We are not spies! General Klammer is the spy! For months, he has been passing secrets to the French. That is why the colonel and I came here in the first place. The English general, Ravenscroft, will tell you. If you will just—"

Klammer's hand came down hard across her cheek, knocking her into the dirt. Adrian surged forward, but the barrel of a musket shoved into his chest stopped him before he could reach her.

"Turn around," Klammer demanded. For several long moments, Adrian just stared at him, his chest heaving in and out with rage. "I said turn around."

With a sigh of defeat, Adrian grudgingly complied. Two men held him while another man roughly bound his wrists, and Elissa's were bound as well. "Line them up against the wall," Klammer commanded.

Stumbling as a soldier shoved her forward, her heart beating frantically, her mouth as dry as the dust at her feet, Elissa walked beside Adrian. The regret and sorrow she read on his face made the tears rush into her eyes. A dirty-haired soldier prodded them viciously with the end of his bayonet till they came up against the rough stone wall of the farmhouse. Twenty feet away, soldiers formed a solid line in front of them.

"Well, Colonel Kingsland, the time has finally arrived. Do either of you wish for a blindfold?"

Elissa looked at Adrian, swallowed back her fear, and shook her head, barely able to see for the wetness blurring her vision.

"No," Adrian said with a slight shake of his head. He edged closer, until their shoulders touched, turned and looked into her eyes. "I'm sorry, love. It seems all I've ever brought you is pain."

Elissa smiled through her tears. "This isn't your fault and I am not sorry. I am happy for the little time we've had."

His gaze held a world of grief. "I wanted us to marry. Would you have said yes?"

Elissa's throat closed up. The beating of her heart seemed to suspend. "You know I would. You were the husband of my heart from the first time we made love."

"Ready!" Klammer shouted to the line of men. The rattle of muskets falling into position made the hairs stand up at the nape of her neck.

"Aim!"

She squeezed her eyes closed, turned her head into Adrian's shoulder, counting out the seconds, all that remained of her life.

"Hold your fire!" The shouted words rose above the thunder of galloping hooves. Elissa's eyes snapped open. Her heart raced with hope as three mounted riders slid to a halt just a few feet away. Joseph Becker swung down from his horse in a cloud of dust. She saw Jamison's tall figure hurriedly dismount and the third man, General Ravenscroft, slid down from his horse as well.

"Lower your weapons, men!" Major Becker strode forward. "There has been a terrible mistake."

"What do you think you're doing?" Klammer demanded, his face puffing up in outrage.

"Righting a wrong I've unwittingly been part of for almost a year."

Klammer turned to the line of men. "Fire! That is an order!" But the soldiers looked suddenly uneasy and the muzzles of their muskets began nosing down.

Ravenscroft spoke up. "Listen to me, you men. Major Becker has come to me for assistance, and I thank God he did." He stared hard at Klammer. "Your general is correct—there is a traitor in your midst, but the traitor is a man you all believed in, trusted with your very lives. For at least the past year, General Klammer has been passing secrets to the French."

Elissa sagged against Adrian, the hope that burned in her heart bursting into a full-fledged flame.

"I order you to arrest him," Ravenscroft commanded. "The bloody bastard is a spy!"

With a glance at Becker, who nodded, the line of soldiers turned their guns in Klammer's direction and his face went from angry to pale.

"Thank God," Elissa said.

A smile broke over Adrian's lips. "It wasn't Becker at all. Last night when I arrived, the major must have realized what was in those notes he'd been passing and that Klammer had used him. He must have guessed that finding the traitor was the reason I'd been assigned to his regiment. Apparently he went to Ravenscroft for help."

Jamison hurried toward them, a worried expression on his face. "Damned but that was cutting it close."

"Far too close," Adrian agreed as his friend sliced through the ropes that bound their wrists.

Ravenscroft moved forward, stopped in front of where the general stood. "You're under arrest, General Klammer. For treason against your country and the murder of Captain Karl Tauber."

Tears burned Elissa's eyes. "It's over," she whispered. "It is finally over and we can go home."

"*Home,*" Adrian repeated with soft reverence, hauling her into his arms. "I've never heard a word that sounded quite so good."

Epilogue

ENGLAND

THREE MONTHS LATER

Elissa smoothed the skirt of her pale blue silk gown, then reached up to straighten the spray of white roses she wore in her hair.

"Your hands are shaking," Nina said. "Let me do it."

They were standing in an anteroom off the small, ivy-covered chapel in the pretty little village next to Wolvermont Castle. A week ago, Adrian had finally come home. There were times Elissa had wondered if he would change his mind, forget the promise he had made to wed her, and remain instead in the army. But the moment she opened the door and saw the love in his magnificent green eyes, she knew that nothing had changed between them.

"I missed you every moment," he said, sweeping her into his arms. "I should have married you before you left Austria. I never should have let you leave."

But the fighting was not yet ended and she had wanted him to have the time he needed to be sure. The war for the Austrians had been costly. They had won at Aspern-Essling, but the price of victory had been high. The French had lost their beloved Marshal Lannes and three of their top commanders. General Steigler and Captain Holdorf had also been killed in the fighting. Elissa thought that perhaps in their case God's vengeance had played a part.

General Klammer was dead, hanged for the traitor he was,

along with the men who had aided him in his cause. Adrian had left the country as soon as the Fifth Coalition was officially forged. The war had gone on, but a decisive battle had been lost to the French at Wagram the first week of July, and the emperor had been forced to surrender. Wily as he was, Francis had managed to wed his daughter, Louise, to Napoleon, insuring his country's future as well as his own.

In the meantime, Adrian had arrived on Elissa's doorstep, his uniform gone but looking even more handsome in his dusty traveling clothes. Jamison and Nina were already back in England, married and living happily with the children at the major's small estate not far from the castle, both of them terribly in love.

Elissa glanced toward the door leading into the chapel. Her mother was there, seated next to Peter, who'd been granted leave to attend the wedding, a grateful archduke's gift for the service Elissa and Adrian had performed in helping to unmask the Falcon.

Nina's voice cut into her thoughts. "It is time for you to go in. You do not wish for your colonel to worry."

Elissa smiled. The last time he was supposed to marry, the foolish woman had left him standing at the altar. "No," she agreed, knowing how nervous he was. "We wouldn't want him to worry."

Nina opened the door to the anteroom and Elissa stepped out into the hall. General Ravenscroft was waiting, acting in the stead of her father. He smiled as she accepted his arm.

"You look lovely, my dear. Shall we join your future husband? I believe if we tarry a moment longer, we may have to scoop him off the floor."

She laughed, a carefree, joyous sound. She had never been quite so happy. Everyone took their places and the organ started to play. It was an intimate wedding, with only their dearest friends. She smiled at her mother on the way down the aisle, thankful to see the bloom back in her cheeks, then flashed a happy smile at her brother, who looked incredibly handsome in his dark green uniform.

Several close friends of Adrian's sat in the pew ahead:

Matthew Seaton, the Earl of Strickland; his lovely wife, Jessica, and their two towheaded children; Adam Harcourt, Viscount St. Cere, and his fiery, dark-haired wife, Gwendolyn. Then her gaze swung toward the front of the church and her breath suspended in her chest.

Dressed in spotless white breeches and a silver-trimmed dark blue tailcoat, Adrian stood rigid, his eyes fixed on her as if she were the only one in the room. His gaze held so much love, so much joy and happiness, a painful ache swelled in her throat. He lifted her fingers and pressed a soft kiss into her palm, and she noticed a tremor in his touch.

The ceremony began, but Elissa barely heard the vicar's words. Her gaze remained on Adrian. She listened to him speak the vows in a deep voice filled with pride and love, and she repeated them as well, meaning every word. A few moments later, the ceremony ended. Sliding an arm around her waist, Adrian kissed her, a fierce, possessive kiss that had soft laughter coming from their friends and made the color rush into her cheeks.

"You're mine," he whispered. "I love you, angel. I love you so much it hurts."

Elissa smiled, blinking to hold back tears. They walked toward the rear of the church and had almost passed through the portal when a tall, dark-haired man stood up at the back of the chapel. Stepping into the aisle, he blocked their way, his green eyes turbulent with emotion.

Adrian stared at him, his jaw clamping down, but he made no effort to speak.

The Duke of Sheffield met his hard look squarely. "I know you are surprised to see me. Perhaps I shouldn't have come, but your wife was kind enough to invite me and I have wasted too much time already."

A muscle jerked in Adrian's cheek. "What do you want?"

The duke smiled softly. "I wanted to be here when my son got married. I wanted him to know how pleased I was and that I wished him every happiness in the years ahead."

Adrian's fierce gaze swung to Elissa. "You gave me your word."

A thread of worry slid through her. She prayed that she had done the right thing. "I never promised. I only said your secret was safe with me. I do not believe your father poses any sort of threat." She turned to the tall, handsome duke who looked so much like his son. "Is that not so, Your Grace?"

"I never knew about you, Adrian," his father said. "If I had guessed . . . if I had believed for an instant that you were my son, I never would have left you in that miserable household."

Adrian said nothing, just continued to stare at the duke, his jaw flexing, his eyes a very dark green.

"I don't suppose you will ever forgive me," the duke went on. "If you do not, I will certainly understand. But I would have you know that I am proud to discover that you are my son. I have learned a great deal about you these past few months. I know the kind of man you are and I am proud that my blood runs through your veins."

Something flickered in Adrian's eyes, something desperate, yet uncertain.

"It is my fondest wish," the duke said, "that one day you might find a place in your heart for the man who is your father." His mouth curved into a sad, wistful smile. "From the moment I saw your face, from the instant I realized you were truly my own, I have loved you as a son."

Adrian's throat constricted. He glanced away, but not before Elissa caught the fine sheen of tears. He turned back to the tall, dark-haired man who looked so much like him. When he spoke his voice sounded deep and rusty.

"Until I met Elissa, I didn't believe I would ever find love. I've never had a family. I've never had a father. Perhaps, now that my wife has shown me the way, I can learn to accept those things, too."

The duke's own eyes glistened. His hand came to rest on his son's broad shoulder. "Thank you."

Adrian simply nodded. When he turned to Elissa, the darkness in his eyes was gone. The green depths shone with love and joy and hope for the future.

"I believe they are preparing a wedding celebration at the castle," he said. " 'Tis past time for us to go home."

Elissa smiled. *Home.* She would make it so, she vowed. She would care for him and give him children. She would help him accept his father and make the duke a part of their family. She would love him with every ounce of her heart, and he would never be lonely again.

Adrian seemed to know what she was thinking, for his green gaze turned suddenly fierce. "You'll never regret marrying me, angel—not for a single moment. I promise you that, my love."

Elissa did not doubt it. Her beloved colonel always kept his word.

Author's Note

The Austro-British Alliance endured on and off throughout the Napoleonic Wars. Aspern-Essling was Bonaparte's first true defeat in battle, and references to it and other battles I mentioned are correct, as was England's determination to forge a Fifth Coalition. However, though the British often sent envoys to Austria in observatory capacities, no record surfaced of British troops actually engaged in the action I described.

However, in August of that same year in an effort to assist the Austrian cause, 40,000 British soldiers landed on the island of Walcheren, part of Zeeland in Holland. Unfortunately, the ravages of "Walcheren Fever," a form of malaria, soon began to decimate the British forces. By the time they left Holland, 4,000 soldiers had died of disease.

Thankfully, by then Adrian was safely returned to his home and happily married to Elissa.

I also took liberties with Austrian military titles. *Generalissimus* is the highest command, *Fieldmarschall, Fieldzeugmeister, General de Cavallierie, Fieldmarschall Lieutenant,* and *General Major* followed. I altered them for the sake of simplicity.

Originally I intended to write this story around a battle that occurred at Austerlitz during the final months of 1805. As it turned out, at the time Adrian was in England, attending the funeral of Admiral Lord Nelson. He was busily engaged in rescuing the lovely wife of his good friend the Earl of Strickland in a previous book, *Innocence Undone*. Oddly, during my research of the period, I discovered a French spy actually existed during that year, perhaps costing the Austrians to lose that great battle.

It was fun writing Adrian and Elissa's story. I hope you enjoyed reading it and that you will watch for my next book, *Wicked Promise*. Happy reading!

Warmest wishes,
Kat

Bestselling, award-winning author

SHIRL HENKE

takes readers on magnificent journeys with her
spectacular stories that weave history with timeless
emotion, breathtaking passion, and unforgettable
characters . . .

BRIDE OF FORTUNE

When mercenary Nicholas Fortune, amidst the flames of
war, assumes another man's identity, he also takes that
man's wife . . .

_____ 95857-9 $5.99 U.S./$6.99 Can.

DEEP AS THE RIVERS

Colonel Samuel Shelby is eager to embark on his mission to
make peace with the

Osage Indians. The dangerous wilderness is a welcome
refuge from his troubled past -M- until he meets beautiful,
headstrong Olivia St. Etienne . . .

_____ 96011-5 $6.50 U.S./$8.50 Can.

KAT MARTIN

Award-winning author of *Creole Fires*

GYPSY LORD
_____ 92878-5 $6.50 U.S./$8.50 Can.

SWEET VENGEANCE
_____ 95095-0 $6.50 U.S./$8.50 Can.

BOLD ANGEL
_____ 95303-8 $5.99 U.S./$6.99 Can.

DEVIL'S PRIZE
_____ 95478-6 $5.99 U.S./$6.99 Can.

MIDNIGHT RIDER
_____ 95774-2 $5.99 U.S./$6.99 Can.